A Good American

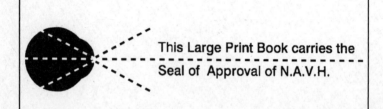
This Large Print Book carries the
Seal of Approval of N.A.V.H.

Current Check-Outs summary for Butcher, Athalia D.
Wed Apr 30 18:23:19 CDT 2014

Barcode   Title   Due Date
31139005083174 A good American / by Alex George. May 21 2014

A GOOD AMERICAN

ALEX GEORGE

THORNDIKE PRESS
A part of Gale, Cengage Learning

GALE
CENGAGE Learning®

Detroit • New York • San Francisco • New Haven, Conn • Waterville, Maine • London

Thorndike Press® Large Print Basic.

The text of this Large Print edition is unabridged.

Other aspects of the book may vary from the original edition.

Set in 16 pt. Plantin.

LIBRARY OF CONGRESS CATALOGING-IN-PUBLICATION DATA

George, Alex.
    A good American / by Alex George. — Large print ed.
      p. cm. — (Thorndike Press large print basic)
    ISBN-13: 978-1-4104-4628-2 (hardcover)
    ISBN-10: 1-4104-4628-X (hardcover)
    1. Brother and sister — Fiction. 2. New Orleans (La.) — Emigration and immigration — Fiction. 3. Large type books.
    I. Title.
PR6107.E53G56 2012
823'.92—dc23

                                       2011045150

Published in 2012 by arrangement with Amy Einhorn, an imprint of G. P. Putnam's Sons, a member of Penguin Group (USA) Inc.

Printed in the United States of America
1 2 3 4 5 6 7 15 14 13 12 11

For Catherine

ONE

Always, there was music.

It was music — Puccini, to be precise — that first drew my grandparents into each other's orbit, more than a hundred years ago. It was an unusually warm afternoon in early spring, in the grandest municipal garden in Hanover, the Grosse Garten. My grandmother, Henriette Furst, was taking her usual Sunday stroll among the regimented flower beds and manicured lawns so beloved of city-dwelling Prussians. At twenty-five, she was a fine example of Teutonic rude health: Jette, as she was known by everyone, was six feet tall, and robustly built. She walked through the park with none of the feminine grace that was expected from ladies of her class. Rather than making her way by trippingly petite steps on the arm of an admirer, Jette clomped briskly along the graveled paths alone, too busy enjoying the day to worry about the unladylike spectacle

7

she presented to others. Rather than squeezing her considerable frame into the bustles and corsets that constrained the grim-faced ladies she so effortlessly outflanked, Jette preferred voluminous dresses that draped her outsized form like colorful tents. She swept along in a dramatic, free-flowing swirl, leaving all those rigidly contoured women hobbling in her wake.

And then, as she passed a sculpted wall of privet, a song drifted out from behind the topiary. The singer was male: his voice, as clear and as pure as a freshly struck bell, fell on Jette like a shower of jasmine. She stopped, stilled by the tune's simple beauty. Jette could hear hope and enchantment in every syllable, even though she could not understand a word of Italian. Unable to pull herself away, alone by the privet hedge, her act of listening felt shockingly intimate. The invisible singer seemed to be whispering in her ear, performing for her alone.

The voice that had halted Jette's afternoon walk belonged to my grandfather, Frederick Meisenheimer. In fact, her intuition had been exactly right: he *was* singing just for her. Frederick had been waiting for Jette as she made her way around the path. When she passed in front of the hedge he was hiding behind, he crossed his fingers and began to sing.

This was no impromptu performance. Frederick had been watching Jette walk through the Grosse Garten for several consecutive Sundays, enchanted by her unusual size. He had spent his time between those delicious weekly sightings wondering how best to attract her attention. In the end he had chosen to ambush her with an aria, "Che gelida manina," from Puccini's opera, *La Bohème*. The opening lines translate as "Your tiny hand is frozen" — not especially appropriate, given that Jette's hands were not, even by the most charitable standards, tiny; they were also rather clammy, due to the unseasonably warm weather. Still, Frederick knew what he was doing. When he had finished his song, he stepped out from behind the hedge and thrust a concoction of lupins, dahlias, and pansies into Jette's (big, sweaty) hands. By then, caught squarely in the crosshairs of Puccini's gorgeous melody, she was helpless.

Frederick did not look like the sort of man who could pull off a stunt like this. If you are picturing a suave, attractive suitor, think again. Physically, he and Jette were a good match, insofar as neither of them quite met the prevailing expected standards, and neither of them especially cared. He, too,

9

was huge, in every sense: taller than Jette by an inch or two, he possessed a quivering gut of heroic dimensions that he made no attempt to hide. Waves of thick red hair washed across his head. Instead of the prim mustache favored by most Hanover men, he wore a magnificent ginger beard that sprouted from his cheeks in chaotic exuberance.

For the next few weeks, Frederick and Jette met each Sunday afternoon by the same privet hedge. They walked side by side through the park, past the fountains and waterfalls. Every so often Frederick would step away from Jette and break into song. He serenaded her with Mascagni, Verdi, Donizetti, and Giordano. He was a terrible ham, acting out every lyric as if his life depended on it. He changed from lovelorn Sicilian peasant to fiery French revolutionary with barely a breath in between. His histrionics earned baleful looks from other passersby, their quiet Sunday strolls disturbed by this barrelful of song, but he ignored them all. Jette soon learned to do the same. With Frederick by her side, the rest of the world retreated into bland anonymity.

Before long, the young couple began to live for their Sunday walks, the long days in between a gray sea of tedium. In each other these two oversized misfits found refuge from the choppy, unforgiving sea in which both had been unhappily drifting. Frederick was enraptured by all of Jette's big-boned loveliness. He was simply grateful that there was so much of her for him to worship. And Jette loved him right back. She adored the lines he had first sung through the privet hedge:

Per sogni a per chimere
e per castelli in aria,
l'anima ho milionaria.

When it comes to dreams and fancies
and castles in the air,
I have the soul of a millionaire!

It was Frederick's capacity to dream that dazzled Jette the most. When she was with him, anything was possible.

Two

At least, *almost* anything was possible. For not even Frederick's considerable, if unorthodox, charms were enough to win over Jette's mother.

Snobbery ran uncut through Brigitte Furst's veins, and she regarded her daughter's marital prospects as the means by which her family might elevate itself into the more rarefied strata of Hanover society.

Brigitte had chosen her own husband carefully. Elias Furst did not possess the dashing looks or charm of some of her other suitors, but that was what she liked about him. She knew that a man overburdened with qualities of his own might be more trouble than he was worth. Elias was a rich, hardworking lawyer, and that was good enough. Soon after their wedding, at Brigitte's insistence, Elias quit his law practice and became a judge. He developed a knack for handing down politically astute judgments from the bench, and from time to time he accepted small bribes to let it be known that he was a reasonable man. He was swiftly promoted. All in all, he had proved most satisfactory.

Brigitte had not been so lucky with her daughter. Soon after Jette's eighteenth birthday, Brigitte had begun to make discreet inquiries about potential suitors for her, but my grandmother refused to sit and flutter her eyelashes at the young men who called. Instead she either teased them or ignored them, depending on her mood. It didn't take long for word of her rude behavior to spread. The young men of Hanover were a feeble lot. Nobody wanted to risk their dignity at the hands of a precocious young girl, especially one who did not conform to the usual ideas of feminine beauty. Men wanted their wives thin-boned and frail. Women needed only the strength to lift china cups to their delicate lips, but Jette looked capable of romping over the Alps with a sheep slung over her shoulders. Gentlemen soon stopped calling.

Brigitte had never forgiven Jette for sabotaging her plans. She had retreated behind the haughty frostiness of the Prussian upper classes to which she so ardently aspired, grimly hoping that the right match for her stubborn, galumphing daughter would one day present himself.

It had been a long wait. By the time Frederick serenaded Jette through the privet hedge, Brigitte had given up hope of marrying her off at all, but she still had standards. It was clear from her solitary interview with Frederick that he failed to meet them. Rather than being the wealthy scion of one of the local grand families, he was an orphan. He worked as a junior clerk in a small bank. He had no money, no family, and no future.

Appalled both by Frederick's lack of breeding and his affable fecklessness, Brigitte briskly informed Jette that she was forbidden from seeing him again — which suggests that she did not know her daughter very well. If anything, it made Jette determined to love Frederick even more.

The young couple continued to meet, away from Brigitte's bitter gaze. The streets and parks of the city became the backdrop to their love affair. They took long walks, lingered in cafés, and visited every museum in the city many times over. Jette would return home, chilled by the cold northern wind but glowing at the memory of Frederick's touch, his whispered endearments still warm in her ear.

Denied the ability to conduct a conventional affair, Frederick and Jette had little reason to conform to the social orthodoxy that would have governed a more traditional courtship. As the months passed, their passion for each other outgrew the public arena in which it had flourished. Frederick lived in an all-male lodging house, and the sour-faced superintendent who patrolled the stairway up to the tenants' rooms would have died before allowing a woman into his domain. Jette's house was obviously out of the question. And so Frederick persuaded his best friend Andreas to lend them his apartment.

Andreas lived above a pharmacy. A never-ending tattoo of hacking coughs drifted upward from the shop floor as customers queued for their medicine, a diabolical hymn of the unwell. It was in that small room that Frederick and Jette first fumbled clumsily with each other's clothes, their fingers numb with excitement and fear. It was there that those two large bodies first rolled together in joyous abandon, a heavenly excess of flesh, while the small bed teetered on the brink of collapse beneath them. In that room they learned each other anew, and, delighted by their discoveries, drowned in long afternoons of private bliss. And it was there, one afternoon in the fall of 1903, that Jette fell pregnant.

Frederick greeted the news with jubilation. Not only was he overjoyed at the prospect of becoming a father, he was sure that the pregnancy would persuade Jette's mother to relent and agree to the marriage that they both longed for. Jette, though, knew better. There was no telling what manner of maternal wrath might be visited upon them when Brigitte discovered that her daughter was carrying the bastard child of a man she despised. She persuaded Frederick that they should wait before announcing the news — although she had no idea what it was they were waiting for. At least time was on their side; Jette's size and her preference for loose-fitting clothes meant that she would be able to hide her condition for months without arousing suspicion.

And so they watched and waited, paralyzed by the inevitability of the baby's arrival. There was nothing to be done; and so they did nothing. They knew that those months were a last, peaceful coda before the unwelcome attentions of the outside world crashed in on their private bliss.

In the end, unsurprisingly, it was Jette's mother who brought matters to a head.

Frederick had a fine singing voice, and performed whenever he could in the city's beer halls. One evening in the early summer of 1904, Frederick was giving a recital at a hostelry in the Nordstadt district. Most of the people in the room were, as usual, doing their best to ignore the fat man standing next to the piano, singing his heart out. He was halfway through a sprightly Rossini aria when Jette walked in. She carried a small suitcase and wore a shawl over her shoulders. The men at the bar stared at her. The only unaccompanied women who frequented the beer halls were whores or alcoholics, and Jette was clearly neither. She was seven months pregnant, and the baby had lent her some additional heft, thickening her ankles and infusing her cheeks with a flush of health. She could not have looked more different from the pale, sharp-faced women who trawled the city's taverns looking for work, or a drink, or both.

Frederick stopped singing at once when he saw her. There was an ironic cheer from the back of the room. He hurried over to where she stood.

"Jette? What is it? Why are you here? What's wrong?"

"She knows," said Jette.

Frederick stared at her. "Your *mother?*"

"She came to speak to me in my bedroom, and walked in without knocking. I was undressed. I couldn't turn away in time."

"And?"

"I've never seen such anger," said Jette, her voice flat. "Such hate."

"She'll come around. She's your mother. She loves you."

Jette shook her head sadly. "You don't understand, my darling. You don't know what I've done to her. She told me I might as well have plunged a knife through her heart. She said she's going to die of shame."

"But this is her *grandchild*," protested Frederick.

"No. This isn't new life, not for her." Jette rubbed her stomach. "As far as she's concerned, this is the end of everything. The family name is ruined, don't you see? She'll never forgive me."

Frederick put an arm around her shoulder. "When she sees the baby, she'll change her mind."

"She won't ever see the baby," said Jette quietly.

"Don't say that."

"Frederick, my love, you didn't hear the words that came out of her mouth." Jette shuddered. "Such vile words." Her eyes filled up with tears but she blinked them away before they could fall. "Our life here is over."

"Over? What do you mean?"

"We have to leave, Frederick."

"Leave? Why?"

Jette sighed. "My mother will never leave us in peace. She'll persecute you and terrorize me. Heaven knows what she's capable of. She'll make our lives a misery, I can promise you that."

Frederick looked at her. "Well, suppose you're right. What are you proposing? Where would we go?"

Jette was silent for a moment before she spoke. "I thought perhaps America."

For the first time that either of them could remember, Frederick was lost for words.

"There's a ship that leaves from Bremen tomorrow," said Jette.

Finally Frederick managed to speak. "America," he croaked.

"The land of the free."

Frederick pushed a worried hand through his hair. "Do we have to go so *far?*"

"If my mother doesn't want to see me again, she can have her wish."

They were both silent for a moment.

"And what about all this?" Frederick gestured around him.

"Your beer halls?"

"Not just that. Hanover is the only place I've ever known. I've never lived anywhere else."

Jette looked around, her face a mask of regret. "Neither have I," she said. "But it's time for a fresh start. For us and the baby."

"How are we going to *pay* for all this, Jette? I don't have much —"

Jette bent down and reached into the suitcase between her feet. She held a golden disk between her fingers.

"Is that a *medal?*" said Frederick.

Jette nodded. "The Kaiser awarded it to my grandfather. The Kaiser pinned it on my grandfather's chest himself."

"What for?"

"He was an infantry commander during the war against the French."

"You never told me that."

"I don't like to talk about him. He wasn't a good man. He ordered the massacre of hundreds of French troops at Spicheren. They were trying to surrender at the time. Of course, nobody cares about that anymore. He won, that was all that mattered." Jette paused. "Later in the war he began using a hot-air balloon during battles. It was tethered to the ground. From the air he could follow the fighting better. He would bellow instructions down to the command post below him."

"Clever," said Frederick.

"Not really. One day the rope got loose, but nobody noticed. Unfortunately for my grandfather, the wind was blowing the wrong way. The balloon drifted into enemy territory. The French followed it. They knew who was in it. They hadn't forgotten what he had done."

Frederick turned the medal over thoughtfully. It was surprisingly heavy. An eagle was emblazoned on one side. On the other was the Kaiser's profile, and a date: 1870 — the year of the slaughter at Spicheren. Even without its monstrous provenance, it was a disgusting thing, gaudily imperial, cast heavy in military pride. "How did you get this?"

"It was in my parents' safe," said Jette. "I stole it."

Frederick looked at her, aghast.

"I took all the money that was in there as well," she continued. "We have enough for the journey. But I wanted the medal, too, in case of emergencies." She looked grim. "Besides, now my mother will at least be sorry when I'm gone. She'll miss the medal, even if she won't miss me."

"Jette, what have you done? Your father's a judge. He knows the chief of police. The minute they find out what you've done, we'll be arrested."

She shook her head. "Not their own daughter."

"Well, that's the thing. Of course they won't blame *you*. They'll say that I put you up to it."

Jette looked affronted. "But it was *my* idea."

"My love, you're seven months pregnant. They'll say it all just shows how thoroughly I've bamboozled you. I've seduced you, shamed you, and now I've made you steal from your own parents. Don't you see what a scoundrel I am?"

"I won't put it back," said Jette, defiant.

"In that case, I don't think we have much choice." Frederick sighed. "America it is."

THREE

As quickly as they could, Frederick and Jette made their way to Andreas's apartment above the pharmacy. It was the only safe place in the city they could think of. They did not dare return to Frederick's room — for all they knew the theft had already been discovered and the police were there, waiting for him. Jette lay back on the small bed, exhausted. Frederick looked at her and his heart ballooned. "America," he whispered, this time in wonderment.

They made a plan. Andreas would leave early the next morning and find a carriage to take them to Bremen, seventy miles to the north. Frederick and Jette would remain hidden until it was time to leave. There would be no time for good-byes.

Jette had packed a few things before she fled her parents' home, but Frederick had nothing. When he performed he always wore a dark green velvet suit. It was not the best outfit in which to flit unnoticed from the country. As it was, he had no choice but to venture forth on the greatest adventure of his life dressed for another bravura performance.

At first light, Andreas slipped out of the apartment clutching some of Jette's stolen money. Frederick and Jette watched dawn break over the Hanover rooftops for the last time.

Andreas arranged for a carriage to meet them in a nearby market square. At the appointed time, they cautiously made their way through the busy stalls, avoiding eye contact with strangers. Vendors called out encouragement to the shuffling lines of shoppers. A flock of pigeons congregated at one corner of the square, squabbling with each other. Frederick would remember these details for the rest of his life.

The carriage was waiting for them. Jette hugged Andreas warmly and climbed inside without a backward glance. Frederick wrapped his friend in a giant hug and clung on to him. Finally Andreas wriggled free.

"You have to go," he said.

"I like it here," said Frederick sadly. "This is my home."

"And you'll be back one day," said Andreas. "But go now. Off with you both."

Frederick nodded, and climbed up into the carriage. Jette's solitary suitcase sat between them. They looked out the window in silence as they passed through Hanover's northern districts, and wondered if they would ever see the city again.

They arrived at the docks in Bremen late in the afternoon. In front of the quay, families stood by small mountains of luggage, hugging each other, smiling through tears, joining the hymn of a thousand farewells. By the edge of the dock sat pallets of tarpaulin-covered cargo. An army of laborers heaved sacks up a gangplank. Beyond this seething mass of activity, a ship waited, huge and serene, its vast chimney stack coughing thick smoke into the air.

Frederick approached the ticket booth clutching a fistful of notes. He pointed to the waiting ship. "Are there still tickets available for that ship?" he asked.

The clerk nodded. "We have some for the third-class cabin."

"And it's headed for New York?"

"The *Copernicus*? No sir. It's going south. New Orleans, Louisiana."

Frederick frowned. "That's in America? The United States?"

"Of course," answered the clerk.

Frederick was doubtful. "I've never heard of it."

Jette squeezed his arm. "New York, New Orleans, what's the difference? They're both New. That's good enough."

And just like that, our family's destiny took an abrupt turn.

Clutching their tickets, Frederick and Jette joined a line for physical examination and vaccination. They waited silently with the other chattering passengers, a quiet island of regret in that cheerful sea of hope. The rest of the day was spent in the cold shadow of the ship, a slow procession of interviews and inspections. Papers were scrutinized, questions asked, precious stamps administered. Finally they were allowed to climb up the embarkation walkway onto the *Copernicus*. The rails that ran the length of the ship were decorated with colorful bunting that snapped against the cold wind tearing in off the North Sea. As Frederick turned to look at the crowd that remained on the quay, he felt the faintest rolling beneath his feet.

The third-class cabin was deep in the belly of the ship. It was a huge windowless dormitory, with no beds or walls. At the door a steward handed them two blankets and told them to find a place to sleep. Around them children wailed, mothers comforted and

26

admonished, men argued with each other, staking out territory for the two-week voyage ahead. They found a spot at the far end of the room. Frederick fashioned a makeshift bed out of the blankets and they lay down and held each other close. Neither of them spoke. It was too late for words.

The rumble of the steam turbines reverberated through the floor, and a low blast from the ship's horn echoed through the vessel. Outside, the crowds began to cheer as the *Copernicus* made its way out of Bremen harbor. Frederick closed his eyes. He would not go up for a final farewell. He did not want to say good-bye.

An hour later, however, Frederick was standing on the deck, his hands gripping the ship's rail. He struggled to marshal his heaving insides as he watched the shoreline recede. A squadron of seagulls swooped and dived in the ship's wake, chorusing good-bye, good-bye, good-bye. He turned his face into the wind and felt the tang of sea salt in his nostrils.

Night was closing in. As they pushed out into the open sea, a heavy fog descended. The *Copernicus* slowed to a crawl, and then stopped completely. Somewhere high above him, the ship's horn began to echo long, mournful honks into the darkness. The fog assumed a ghostly luminescence as it lingered off the bows, just out of reach.

Frederick stared out into the nothingness. When a large swell rose underneath the hull, he vomited noisily onto his shoes.

By the time the fog had lifted, the last lights of the shoreline had disappeared. His home had quietly faded out of sight, without fanfare. The *Copernicus* shuddered as its engines cranked into life again.

My grandparents' journey finally began, full steam ahead.

That evening Frederick lay awake, listening to the low thrum of the ship's turbines as Jette slept. The night was punctuated by the bruising sounds of heavy machinery, a ceaseless chorus of clanks and bangs. From time to time a child's cry echoed through the huge room, followed by a mother's anxious hushing. Every small movement of the ship caused a fresh noxious spill in Frederick's stomach. Waves of unhappiness crashed over him, his insides a riot of nausea and regret.

Jette, in contrast, slept peacefully. The following morning she left Frederick shivering beneath his blanket and went to look for the dining room. There she ate a hearty breakfast of barley soup, herring, and brown bread. The rhythmic swells that were causing Frederick such distress soothed the baby inside her like a giant rocking hand. She spent much of the day walking from one end of the ship to the other, gazing out at the water. After so many months of hiding her condition from the world, the child inside her was no longer a guilty secret. She began to speak with the other passengers. Everyone had a story to tell. Some were following friends and family across the ocean. Others had been promised jobs. A few were following a dream. But they all had the name of a strange-sounding town on their lips, and Jette envied them the luxury of a final destination to whisper like a prayer. She longed to know where her own journey would end.

Frederick remained in the cabin and battled his seasickness. By the morning of the second day, his condition had improved enough for him to stagger out onto the deck. The first thing he saw were huge cliffs to the north, dazzling white, rising out of the sea: The *Copernicus* was near Dover. Frederick gazed longingly at the land in the distance, wishing for solid ground beneath his feet.

"We've missed you," said Jette with a smile, patting her belly.

"I realized something while I was downstairs," said Frederick. "We're *free*, Jette."

She smiled. "Free as birds."

"So let's get married."

"Well, of course," she laughed. "Once we get to America and find —"

"No." Frederick took her hands in his. "I've wanted to marry you since the moment I first saw you," he said. "And I don't want to wait anymore."

Jette put her arms around him and kissed him softly on the cheek.

That evening, Frederick and Jette were ushered into the plush quarters of the ship's captain, Herbert P. Farrelly, the first American either of them had ever met. The room was thickly carpeted and elegantly furnished. Polished brass fittings shone warmly in the muted gaslight. The captain had just returned from his evening meal, and his breath smelled faintly of wine. He looked benignly at the young couple as the chief purser explained their request. Jette and Frederick held hands and smiled anxiously at him, not understanding a word.

The captain took an old Bible out of a drawer and began reading from a card that had been inserted at the back of the book. Prompted by the purser, each of them hesitantly said, "I do." The first words of English that either had ever spoken would bind them together for the rest of their lives.

In five minutes, it was over. The captain

sat down at his desk and filled out a form with his heavy fountain pen. Frederick and Jette signed at the bottom, followed by the captain and the purser. Herbert P. Farrelly handed the certificate to Frederick, and shook his hand. He bowed deeply toward Jette and kissed her hand.

They walked silently back to the cabin and lay side by side beneath their blankets.

"I'm sorry, Jette," whispered Frederick.

"What for?"

"This probably isn't the wedding night you dreamed of."

She poked him in the chest. "What makes you think I ever dreamed of my wedding night?"

"Didn't you?"

"Never. I always told myself I would never get married." She paused. "But then I met you."

"All the same. We've got no cake, no guests, no fancy band." Frederick plucked at his blanket. "Not even a proper bed."

Jette looked at the man she adored, unable to speak. There was a dark stain on the lapel of his suit where he had spilled his soup at lunch. The collar of his shirt was grubby with days of sweat and worry.

"Oh, Frederick," she whispered.

For the rest of that night, my grandparents

clung to each other fiercely, still dressed in the clothes they had been married in. After so much sacrifice, neither was willing to let go of what they had left.

When they awoke the next morning, the newlyweds were ravenously hungry. After breakfast they stood alone at the rail of the ship and gazed at the sea. By now the *Copernicus* was forging into the Atlantic, striking out toward the limitless horizon. There was nothing to interrupt the vastness of the ocean, save for the occasional ship that would appear for an hour or so on the horizon before slipping out of sight again, off the edge of the world.

Jette introduced Frederick to the acquaintances she had met. They held hands and said "my husband," and "my wife," over and over again, wide-eyed with wonder at the sound of the words.

Finally, they began to talk of America. One man had a large map of the country, and after much badgering Frederick persuaded him to sell it. At every opportunity he would bend low over the creased paper, murmuring the strange names of the towns beneath his fingers. He learned to recognize each state. He relished the chaotic topography of the eastern provinces, and saw hopeful poetry in the vast asymmetries to the west, a draftsman's pen taming the wild country by sharp-edged constructs.

After the fourth day most of the passengers had found their sea legs, and a variety of entertainments were put on in the dining room after supper. Jette usually returned to her makeshift bed to rest, exhausted by the baby's kicking, but Frederick remained with his fellow passengers. There was an old piano, and it was often pushed into service. Frederick sang whenever he could. Another passenger, a young man from Potsdam, was sailing to America to seek his fortune as an opera singer. Together they breezed through arias and songs, always concluding their performance with a duet from *The Pearl Fishers* that brought down the house. The evenings usually ended with the whole room joined in a chorus of German folk songs. Frederick often led the singing, conducting the swaying crowd with one hand and waving his tankard aloft with the other. They sang rousing marches, maudlin songs of love, and sentimental ballads about the land they had left behind. The words rose up to the ceiling, joyful and elegiac.

Frederick quizzed people about their travel plans, seeking advice. He was gripped by anxiety every time he gazed at his beloved map. America was simply too huge to be contemplated in the abstract. He needed a destination, something to unshackle him from all that limitless hope. One evening he fell into conversation with a man who was traveling with his wife and four daughters. He was heading west to join his brother, who had left Westphalia five years earlier and now owned an orange grove in California, near the Mexican border.

"My brother has struggled a great deal," said the man, shaking his head. "The soil is not like in Germany. Too dry." He rubbed his fingers together and watched an imaginary clump of mud disappear into thin air. "Do you farm?"

Frederick shook his head. "But I'll try anything."

"I've heard there is a state with wonderful, rich soil. You can grow anything on it. There are many prosperous farmers there. Also they make excellent wine."

Frederick laughed. "I like it already. Where is this?"

The man leaned back in his chair. "It's called Missouri," he said. Within moments Frederick's map was spread out on the table, and they peered at the oddly contoured state. Three of its boundaries were arrow-straight, but the eastern edge was prescribed by the meandering course of the Mississippi River, defiantly uneven in contrast to the man-made order imposed to the north, south, and west. In the southeast corner, a blocky promontory of land extended into Arkansas and Tennessee. It looked like the heel of a boot that had been dug stubbornly into the ground.

Another man approached and peered at the map. "There are many Germans in Missouri," he said.

"Oh?" said Frederick.

The man nodded. "My mother's great-uncle moved there in 1837. Now the family owns a fleet of steamboats. They haul iron ore and pine lumber down the Missouri River from the Ozark forests. My cousin runs the business now."

"You're going there to join him?"

The man shook his head. "I'm headed for Georgia. But they say Missouri is a fine place. My cousin is always looking for good workers for the boats. He likes Germans. Says Americans are lazy."

Soon afterward my grandfather lay down next to Jette, clutching a scrap of paper on which he had scrawled the name and address of the stranger's cousin — the man who owned the boating operation and who liked hardworking Germans. He was too excited to sleep.

Frederick finally had the plan he had longed for.

Over breakfast he explained his idea to Jette. When they arrived in New Orleans, they would take a train north. The shipping business was in Rocheport, a town halfway between Kansas City and St. Louis. It did not appear on Frederick's map, but he was able to guess within the width of a thumbprint where it might be. When they arrived, Frederick would present himself for employment. They would settle down. The baby would come. Then they would see.

Now Frederick and Jette were impatient to arrive, their imaginations racing toward the future. Boredom became their greatest enemy. There was little to fill the changeless days as the ship crawled westward across the ocean.

The first-class passengers kept to themselves, never venturing outside the refined splendor of the upper decks. Jette and Frederick sometimes crept up the stairs and stood at the engraved-glass doors of the first-class dining room. The aroma of linseed oil and brass polish mingled with delicious smells coming from the kitchen. Jette gazed through the doors at the glittering spectacle within. Ornate chandeliers cast clusters of light across the room. The table settings were exquisite, glimmering arrangements of silver and crystal. Frederick, meanwhile, read that day's menu, his stomach rumbling in wistful appreciation. He spent every meal swearing that he would never eat herring again.

Halfway through the morning of the thirteenth day, a cheer went up at the stern of the boat. A gull had been spotted, the first sign that landfall was close. Frederick gazed up at the solitary bird as it swooped and dived overhead, and the tedium of the journey was instantly forgotten. That evening, a pencil of shadow appeared on the horizon. People gathered at the rail and stared at the distant shoreline in silence. America, at last.

By the following morning, the land had disappeared. Frederick and Jette stared in disbelief at the empty sea. Later they learned that the land they had seen the previous evening was the east coast of Florida; during the course of the night the *Copernicus* had circumvented the panhandle and was now steaming northwest across the Gulf of Mexico toward the southern coast of Louisiana.

The two days that followed were an agony. After that brief glimpse of land, passengers now anxiously scanned the horizon. When, early one morning, a thin line of trees finally appeared, Jette did not take her eyes off it, in case it disappeared again. The ship continued to track the coastline, but still America kept its distance, shimmering in the haze of the southern sun. Finally three pilot boats appeared, and the great bow of the *Copernicus* turned north and began its final journey into dock at New Orleans. As the ship approached the port, it was hailed on all sides by a chorus of bells and horns from the fishing boats that dotted the bay. To Frederick and Jette, it was the most beautiful music in the world.

It was the sound of their future.

FOUR

The ship's arrival at the dock prompted a flurry of activity. Frederick and Jette stood on the deck and gazed down at the troop of men who ran to and fro, securing ropes and erecting gangplanks, shouting to each other in a strange language. Jette's fingers curled around her husband's arm.

"Look at them," she whispered.

The Negroes' dark muscles gleamed in the afternoon sun. Some laughed and joked as they hauled cargo along the gangplank and onto the quay. Others whistled and sang. Frederick thought of the grim-faced men at Bremen who had silently loaded the same cargo two weeks earlier. His heart ballooned. What sort of country can this be, he wondered, when even the hardest jobs are performed with such joy?

When Frederick and Jette arrived onshore, there was a fresh battery of inspections and interviews. Frederick entered his name and occupation in a large ledger and signed his name with an exuberant flourish.

A few years ago, on a trip to New Orleans, I went to the Louisiana Historical Society and found the book my grandfather signed. Its heavy covers were sheathed in decades-old dust, its spine a mosaic of fragmented leather. The paper was ocher-stiff beneath my fingers, and pungent with the smell of creeping decay. And there it was: FREDERICK MEISENHEIMER, ANGESTELLTE. Clerk. Next to it, the date: June 5, 1904. Page upon page of faded signatures preceded this entry, and page upon page followed. Our story was just a single line in this vast narrative of hope. Every family had begun their journey here before spreading out in waves across the country, on the crest of their immigrant dreams.

Frederick's signature was utterly unreadable, a defiant, optimistic scrawl. I traced a finger across the faded ink.

As part of the price of their tickets, the steamer company had booked each passenger one night's stay in a hotel immediately opposite the docks. That evening Frederick and Jette ate at the hotel restaurant. In the middle of the room stood a table groaning with food. There were hams dotted with cloves; thick, dark slabs of Creole pork; vast platters of fried chicken; piles of shrimp the size of a child's fist and coated in fiery red sauce; and ribs, more ribs than you could imagine, glistening sweet and brown. There were huge ears of corn, shining with butter; potatoes, fried and boiled; buckets of green beans; and, at the center of the table, a huge, bubbling pot of jambalaya. There was a hill of white rolls, so fresh that they spilled steam, and plates of fresh fruit — oranges, bananas, mangoes, thickly sliced pineapples, plums. Jette and Frederick piled their plates high and then went back for more. They were silent as they ate, every mouthful a new eruption of strange flavors. Their lips tingled with the kiss of spice.

When the meal was over, Jette let out a small moan, equal parts distress and satisfaction. "I've never eaten so much in my life," she said. "I need to lie down."

Frederick looked around him. Some passengers were still eating, blinking in astonishment as they chewed. His first night in America! He sat at the bar and drank a glass of cold beer and thought about the new world waiting for him outside the hotel. His fellow passengers had begun to sing again, but this time he did not join in. He pushed his empty glass across the counter and stepped out onto the street.

It was murderously humid, even though the sun had long since gone down. Frederick stood for a moment on the street corner. He caught the sharp aroma of fresh tar from the nearby docks, then the sweet scent of bougainvillea, drifting by on a languid breeze. He planted his hat firmly on his head and set off down the street, away from the water: into America.

Frederick must have been quite a sight. He had not shaved for two weeks, and his ginger beard was even wilder than usual. He still wore his velvet suit, which by now was filthy and crumpled. Trams shuttled past him, bells clanking loudly as they sailed up the wide street, clouds of gravel dust floating in their wake. On the sides of the tall brick buildings were paintings of giant bars of chocolate and bottles of milk. Beneath the pale glow of the streetlamps, the sidewalks teemed with life. Couples walked past arm in arm, their heads close together. Sharply dressed men prowled, their hats pulled down over their eyes. Packs of thin-limbed Negro children scuttled by in the shadows. Frederick felt their hungry eyes upon him. As he walked on, the cobbled streets narrowed. The windows of upstairs apartments were flung open to the night and the warm air was punctuated by raucous laughter and angry shouts. Women leaned out of their kitchen windows and gossiped to their neighbors across the street. He listened to snatches of their crackling, high-pitched conversations, not understanding a word.

After an hour or so, Frederick sat down on a bench and rested. He was thirsty, and hot. He wiped his brow and thought about returning to the hotel. Just then, the sound of a cornet floated through the air. This was not the sort of dry fugue that echoed through Hanover concert halls. The instrument had been unshackled: it spiraled upward, a whirlwind of graceful elision and complex melody. The music streaked into the night, every note dripping with joy. He stood up and followed the sound.

Halfway down a nearby side street stood a building lit up like a beacon, bathing the sidewalk in its warm glow. A sign hung over the door: CHEZ BENNY'S. The music spilled out of open windows. As he approached, Frederick could hear other instruments — clarinets, a trombone, a banjo. He peered inside and saw a large room crammed with people, some at small tables, some standing, others dancing. At the far end of the room, six musicians stood on a stage. The cornet player was at their center, his eyes tightly closed as he blew his horn. Staccato flurries

43

of notes ripped into the night, ragging the up-tempo tune. Behind him the other men were swinging in a sweet, scorching counterpoint of rhythm and harmony. The cornet player bent his knees like a boxer as he delivered each new blistering line of attack. Hot glissandos shimmered in the air, tearing up the joint.

After a moment, Frederick became aware that a tall black man was watching him from the front door of the club. He took a step toward Frederick and said something. Frederick shook his head in apology.

"No English," he mumbled.

The Negro said something else — which, to his astonishment, Frederick understood. It took him a moment to register why: the man was speaking French.

"We're full," he said, his accent fragrant with the echo of elsewhere.

"Who is that?" asked Frederick in French, pointing through the window.

"You can't come in. We're full."

"But I just want —"

"Are you blind?" said the man angrily. "This club is for blacks."

Frederick blinked in surprise. He turned and looked again at the audience.

"You can't come in," said the man again.

"I've never heard such music before," said

Frederick. He looked back at the stage. One of the clarinet players was soloing now, a wailing chorus of glee. "Who is that cornet player?"

The Negro slowly extended his index finger, pushed the rim of his hat upward, and then pointed through the window. The cornet player stood at the side of the stage, his instrument tucked under his arm. He was clapping his hands and stamping his foot in time to the music. "That," said the man, "is Buddy Bolden."

Some time later, Frederick retraced his steps to the hotel, the sound of the strange music still echoing through his head. It was like nothing he had ever heard before — chaotic and loud, but full of hope and life. A perfect new music for his new country.

Jette did not stir as he climbed into bed beside her. The fresh linen felt cool on his skin, the bed wonderfully wide and soft. Frederick stared into the darkness, listening to his wife's calm breathing. Any lingering homesickness had been eradicated by his first excursion onto the streets of America. Everything he'd seen had been unimaginably different from the dry, dour streets of Hanover, and to his surprise he was not sorry in the slightest. He was smitten by the beguiling otherness of it all.

And so began my grandfather's rapturous love affair with America — an affair that would continue until the day he died.

The following morning, after another gargantuan meal in the hotel dining room, Frederick made inquiries about trains heading north. The station was not far away. They set off up Canal Street, their single suitcase beneath Frederick's arm.

A crowd of people was milling about outside the station entrance. Jette waited while Frederick went inside to buy tickets. As he strode across the concourse, he realized that something was wrong. People were moving too slowly. There was none of the suppressed delirium of time-tabled existence. His pace slowed as he noticed that there were no trains waiting at any of the platforms.

"Hey!"

He turned in the direction of the shout, and saw the tall man from outside Chez Benny's striding toward him. His hat had been replaced by a cap in turquoise and red livery. He looked more friendly in the daylight. Indeed, he was smiling.

"I remember you!" he said, his French muddied by his curious accent. "You're the Buddy Bolden fan, *non*?"

Frederick nodded. "Buddy Bolden, yes."

He gestured around him. "Where are all the trains?" he asked.

"There *are* no trains. There's been flooding upriver. The Mississippi burst its banks near Greenville."

"But we can't wait," said Frederick. "My wife and I have to get to St. Louis as soon as possible." He turned and pointed to where Jette stood. Her swollen stomach was unmistakable.

The man nodded slowly. "Can you wait here?" He sauntered back the way he had come and disappeared behind a door. Moments later he reappeared, a newspaper tucked beneath his arm. He unfolded it as he approached, his eyes scanning an inside page. Finally he gave a grunt. His long finger rested on an advertisement.

**SAINT LOUIS AND NEW ORLEANS
PACKET COMPANY**
Leaves on Monday, 6th Inst. at 5 P.M.
FOR ST. LOUIS, CAIRO, MEMPHIS and all
Intermediate Points
the Fine Passenger Steamer
GREAT REPUBLIC,
W. B. Donaldson, master,
Will leave as above.
For freight or passage. Apply on board,
or to C. G. RUMBLE, agent, 87 Natchez Street

Frederick scanned the page. "I'm sorry," he said. "My English —"

"This is for a journey upriver, all the way to St. Louis."

"Upriver? You're talking about a *ship?*"

The man nodded. "It leaves this afternoon."

Frederick's shoulders slumped. "There's no other way of getting to St. Louis?"

"You could hire a carriage. But it would cost more and take longer."

There was a long pause.

"What is your name?" said Frederick.

"Everyone calls me Lomax."

"Well, Monsieur Lomax, come and meet my wife."

With no trains to deal with, Lomax took them to the booking agent on Natchez Street. There he spoke to the man behind the desk while Frederick and Jette stood nearby and watched the clerk's face twitch with suspicion. Lomax kept pointing in their direction. Finally, he returned to where Frederick was standing and jerked a thumb over his shoulder. "He wants to speak to you himself," he said.

"But why?" asked Frederick. "I won't be able to —"

"He won't sell a white person's ticket to a

black man." Lomax saw the astonishment on Frederick's face. "You really have just arrived, haven't you?" he said.

A while later, tickets finally purchased, the three of them walked down to the wharf. The sickly sweet smell of rotting bananas mingled with the aroma of fresh bread from a nearby bakery. They stood on the edge of the quay, looking up at the ship. After the oceangoing bulk of the *Copernicus,* the *Great Republic* seemed like a toy. Its exterior gleamed with fresh paint, and the ironwork was embellished with delicate filigree. Two thin chimneys rose into the sky, each topped by a dark corona of iron oak leaves. At the stern sat a huge wheel, the lower portion of which was submerged in the water.

"Fine vessel," said Lomax.

"Thank you for all your help," said Frederick.

Lomax shrugged. "I didn't have anything better to do. Besides," he added, "you liked Buddy Bolden."

The two men smiled at each other.

"Good luck to you," said Lomax.

"Good luck to *you*," said Frederick.

Lomax shook Frederick's hand and tipped his cap to Jette. "Thank you," he replied, "but I think you're going to need it more."

Then he stuck his hands deep in his pockets and strolled away down the quay, whistling as he went.

FIVE

The *Great Republic* left New Orleans at exactly five o'clock, as advertised, and began its journey up the Mississippi. Black smoke billowed out of the ship's chimneys as it edged past velvet swamps and headed for the famous waterway that would take them north. Downriver from the flood that had cut off the railroads, the Mississippi was a seething, roiling mass of fury. Dark water roared past the ship. The river is so vast that it follows no set course, especially in times of flood. There is no single current or velocity. Its waters move in layers and whorls, unpredictable in the chaotic rush to the sea. As the *Great Republic* crawled against the current, it stayed close to the western bank of the river, protected by the Louisiana shoreline.

Compared to the grim austerity of the *Copernicus,* the new ship was a swoon of luxury. The upper level was dominated by a long saloon that ran almost the length of the vessel, flanked on each side by a series of staterooms. The ceiling was as high as a church's and decorated with a lattice of elegantly carved mahogany. At one end of the saloon, the Ladies' Cabin was a women-only domain where passengers read, performed needlework, or engaged in uplifting Christian song. Iced tea was served all day. The sun flooded through the large windows, warming the polished pine. Separated from the women by a sea of dining tables, and usually half-hidden behind a wall of cigar smoke, there was a well-stocked bar. Behind a counter of burnished oak stood a glittering wall of inverted bottles, a rainbow of liquor. Here the male passengers chased away the tedium of the journey with drink. It would take five days to reach St. Louis.

At dinner that evening, Jette was unable to eat more than a few mouthfuls. All day she had felt a constant pain in her abdomen. Now as she sat miserably fingering her knife and fork, she began to feel the hot creep of fever. They returned to their cabin and she gratefully climbed into the lower of the two bunk beds. Frederick kissed her head and held her hand until she fell asleep. He did not want to disturb her rest. He thought about the saloon upstairs and felt a glow of conviviality and warmth toward his fellow passengers. He stood up and quietly closed the door behind him.

Several hours later, Frederick stumbled back to the cabin. All of his attempts to strike up a conversation in German or French had been rejected, usually with a look of suspicion or distaste, sometimes with a salvo of angry words that he could not understand. The flamboyantly mustachioed bartender was faultlessly polite, but not even he was prepared to converse with him. Frederick watched as other men came into the bar and easily began to talk with their fellow travelers. As the evening wore on, he descended into a pit of morose introspection. Embarrassment was not an emotion that Frederick Meisenheimer was well acquainted with, and his instinct was to flee from it, right to the bottom of the nearest bottle. He pushed his glass toward the taciturn bartender, and the bartender filled it up.

The next day, neither Frederick nor Jette felt well enough to face breakfast. Jette's face was chalk-white beneath the blankets that she had heaped upon herself. She lay on her bunk, shivering in the grip of fever. Frederick, meanwhile, was suffering from a monstrous hangover. He thought blackly about the previous evening. This was a new form of torture for him, to be surrounded by men he couldn't talk to. As his head throbbed in reproach, he resolved to learn English at once.

Later that morning, he staggered to his feet and went out onto the deck for some fresh air. The ship passed a procession of soupy bayous, lazy crucibles of iridescent green, fringed by small forests of cypress and hanging moss. Across the vast expanse of water, Frederick could just make out tiny trees on the far shore. The Mississippi was still running high. Water rippled and broke into silver flashes as the *Great Republic* plowed its way upriver.

Frederick considered his position. He had to find someone to teach him English, but it seemed unlikely that any of the ship's passengers would be willing to help. Then, through the fog of his hangover, he had an idea. He walked toward the saloon. Inside, waiters were beginning to lay tables for lunch. At the far end of the room, the bartender was at his post, holding a glass up to the light. He watched Frederick approach with an inscrutable look in his eye.

It took several minutes for Frederick to establish, by means of zesty pantomime, that he wanted language lessons, not a drink. Finally, the bartender understood. He said that his name was Thomas. It was agreed that, for the duration of the journey, Thomas would provide such instruction in English as was possible, subject to his professional obligations. There followed a brief negotiation as to fees. At its conclusion, Frederick marveled at exactly how much *could* be communicated simply by gesticulation and facial expression. Even before the first lesson had begun, the two men understood each other perfectly.

Jette was too ill to leave the cabin. The ship's doctor examined her and prescribed bed rest and plenty of liquids. While she did as instructed, Frederick roamed the ship, watching the country unfurl before him. The *Great Republic* made several stops on its journey north, tying up alongside crowded levees to off-load cargo and passengers. Frederick watched, hungry for clues about his new country. He stared at the dark-skinned roustabouts as they skipped along the narrow gangplanks that perched precariously between the ship's hold and the shore, backs bent double beneath their loads. They worked quickly, stacking up cargo on the quay under the watchful eye of the ship's clerk, a short, corpulent man in a bowler hat. A small fortification of merchandise would soon appear on the side of the wharf: sacks of cottonseed meal and rice, barrels of oil, sugar, and molasses. The clerk strutted between the waiting merchants, completing paperwork, while the workers regained their breath in the ship's cool shade. Then the process was reversed, with new crates and sacks and barrels carried back onto the ship for delivery to destinations farther upriver.

Frederick also had his lessons with the barman to occupy him. For an hour in the middle of the morning and for longer in the afternoons, he perched on a tall stool in front of the bar and began to learn English. Given that teacher and pupil did not share one word of common language, the process was necessarily a slow one. Every day Frederick arrived with a list of new words he wanted to learn, and the first hour or so was spent establishing the correct translation for each one. Without access to a dictionary, Frederick had to identify the words in other ways. Objects were easy enough — a rudimentary drawing would usually do. Abstract concepts such as love, or hope, or lies, were more difficult. Adverbs and adjectives were murder. They must have presented a peculiar spectacle, Frederick gravely performing his charades to his unblinking audience of one. The final part of each lesson was spent on establishing a basic idiomatic repertoire. Since he was the only one with a grasp of the local vernacular, Thomas was responsible for deciding exactly which phrases would be most useful. It is possible that the bartender was not entirely honest in communicating with his pupil the exact substance of what it was he was being taught. Soon Frederick's lexicon of expressions included:

Let me give you a large tip.
I like big mustaches.
My wife is a witch, you know.
I am a German idiot.
God bless the United States of America!

Frederick was an eager student. At Thomas's insistence, he spent his evenings in the cabin, going over that day's work rather than practicing on the other passengers. The strange words felt heavy on his tongue, as new and different as the spicy food of their first night in New Orleans. He hardly recognized his voice as the alien sounds emerged cautiously from his mouth. His head was filled with foreign words and syntax, a bewildering storm of meaning. Still, Thomas would applaud every morning as Frederick showed him what he had learned.

The ship continued its steady progress north. Jette finally emerged from the cabin at Cape Girardeau. She watched the off-loading of cargo and passengers in silence, her eyes dull in the bright afternoon sun. The worst of her fever had passed, but she had barely eaten anything in days.

When they docked at St. Louis the following afternoon, Jette wept, unwilling to quit the cocoon of their cabin. Frederick waited patiently for Jette's tears to stop, and then they walked down the gangplank and stood on Missouri soil for the first time.

Frederick had planned to travel the last leg of their journey, from St. Louis to Rocheport, by carriage. He had explained all this to Thomas by way of tortuous mime, and so was equipped with the necessary phrase, which he repeated and repeated in his head: *I need to hire a carriage for a long journey.*

As they walked away from the crowded dockside, there were signs to a hundred different destinations. Frederick understood none of them. Crowds streamed past them. This constant velocity! Did nobody in America remain still? Clouds were massing overhead, dark with the threat of rain. Next to him, Jette shivered.

They made their way onto the street that ran alongside the wharf. Gas lamps cast pale yellow light onto the cobbles. A policeman was standing on the other side of the street.

"I'll ask this man," Frederick said to Jette.

"He'll help."

The policeman watched him approach without expression. Frederick took off his hat. "I need to hire a carriage for a long journey," he said.

The policeman ignored him.

Frederick tried again. "Please. I need to hire a carriage."

This time the policeman responded, his tone sharp. Frederick did not understand a word. "I need to hire a carriage for a long journey," he said again. He turned and pointed to Jette. "My wife is a witch, you know."

The policeman unleashed another torrent of words, his fingers tightening around the long, black nightstick that hung from his belt. Frederick smiled politely and retreated back to where Jette was watching.

"What did he say?" she asked.

"I have no idea," admitted Frederick. All his hard work with Thomas had been of no use at all. For the next hour he approached a succession of people, bowing politely before carefully announcing, *I need to hire a carriage for a long journey.* He was shouted at and ignored in equal measures. Jette was looking paler by the minute, and when an elderly couple shook their heads in a display of harmonious distaste,

Frederick lost his patience. He stood in the middle of the sidewalk and raised his hands above his head.

"I need to hire a carriage for a long journey!" he shouted. His words rose into the air, unheeded. The only discernible effect of the outburst was to create an island in the ebb and flow of traffic as people shifted direction to avoid him. Frederick clenched his fists into fat knots of distress and shook them at the sky.

"Excuse me." A man in an immaculate three-piece suit was standing in front of him. He looked about sixty years old. He had spoken in perfect German.

Frederick dropped his arms to his sides in surprise. "Yes?"

"Can I help you?"

Frederick took a deep breath. "I need to hire a carriage for a long journey," he said in English.

"A carriage, yes, I see," replied the man, again in German.

Frederick gave up. "*Meine Frau ist ziemlich krank*." My wife is ill. The familiar sound of the words made him want to weep.

"Ill?" said the man.

"She is expecting a baby. She has a fever."

The man took off his glasses. "I am a doctor. May I see her?"

"Of course. If it's not too much trouble."

"Not at all." He put out his hand toward Frederick. "My name is Joseph Wall."

Frederick shook his hand. "How could you tell I was German?"

"I studied there for a while. In Königsberg. I recognized your accent."

"I've only just begun to learn your language," Frederick said. "It's difficult."

Joseph Wall nodded. "It certainly is."

"You're the first person who has offered to help," said Frederick, unable to hide his bitterness.

"Well, what do you expect?"

Frederick frowned. "What do you mean?"

"You do know where you are, I presume?"

"Of course. This is St. Louis, Missouri. The United States of America."

"That's right. So why were you standing in the middle of the street shouting in Polish?"

Soon the extent of the bartender's cruel hoax became clear. Frederick had wanted to return to the ship and confront him, but Joseph Wall gently persuaded him that Jette's health was a more pressing concern.

The doctor's offices were nearby. There, inspection and diagnosis were swiftly conducted. The baby was nearly engaged, he reported. The safest course of action was complete rest until the birth.

Frederick explained that it was impossible for them to remain in St. Louis. Joseph Wall listened without comment as Frederick told him of their plans to reach Rocheport as soon as possible. When he had finished, the doctor said, "You understand that undertaking such a journey at this juncture would not be without risk?"

"Of course."

"If I arrange for a carriage for you, will you at least promise me one thing?"

"Certainly."

"You need a proper night's rest before you begin your journey. Much better to start in the morning."

"Very well," said Frederick. "Can you recommend a cheap hotel?"

Joseph Wall smiled. "I believe I can do better than that," he said.

That evening Frederick and Jette sat down and ate supper with Joseph Wall and his wife. Reina Wall was a short, neat woman, a contained bustle of domestic efficiency. Her brown hair was twisted into a bun on the back of her head. She and her husband spoke softly to each other in a cocktail of English, Polish, and Yiddish, before Joseph would turn to their guests and address them in perfect German while Reina sat next to him and smiled.

The food was simple, wholesome, and good. Thick white soup, coils of pink sausage, slabs of heavy black bread. For the first time in days, Jette ate.

During the meal, Joseph Wall told their story. He and his wife had arrived in America from Poland thirty years earlier. Their first act as new immigrants was to undertake a bureaucratic metamorphosis, shrinking their name from Walinowski to Wall with a single stroke of a pen. Those last three syllables were lost forever, ghosts from their old life. Joseph and Reina had faced the future with their new name — simple, unforeign, monumental.

"That was the biggest mistake I ever made." The doctor sighed and looked at Frederick. "If I may give you some advice. Learn the language, but don't ever change your name. This is a land of immigrants. I don't just mean you and me. I mean *everyone*. We all came here from somewhere. But who am I now? Who are my sons? *Wall*." He shook his head. "It's a good name, but it's not ours."

Frederick nodded, and just like that, we were doomed to our own polysyllabic heft of German nomenclature.

The following morning, the doctor watched as Jette climbed into the carriage that he had procured. Two horses waited patiently in their harness, eating sugar lumps out of the driver's hand.

"How much is this going to cost?" asked Frederick anxiously. "Two horses is more than I can really —"

Joseph held up a hand. "I've borrowed them from a friend of mine. I explained the situation. He says you're welcome to them. He won't miss them for a few days."

"But you don't know us," protested Frederick. "How do you know we'll send them back?"

Joseph pointed at the driver. "*He'll* come back, and he'll bring the horses with him. Besides," he said, "I do know you. I *was* you, once."

The two men looked at each other for a moment, and then shook hands.

"I don't know how to thank you," said Frederick.

"Live your life," answered Joseph Wall. "Look after your wife and your new baby. Cherish your family. That will be thanks enough."

"God bless the United States of America," said Frederick solemnly, in Polish.

The doctor laughed. "Go," he said. "Go

to your new home, Frederick Meisenheimer. Go and be a good American."

"A good American. Yes. That is what I shall be." Frederick smiled at him. "I shall never forget you, I promise you that."

"All right, then. Good. Don't forget us." The doctor's hand landed in the middle of Frederick's back. "But, go, please, before your wife has her baby right here on the street."

With a final wave, Frederick climbed into the carriage. The driver shook the reins and the horses moved away.

Frederick turned to his wife. Jette lay limply against the cushions. She smiled weakly at him, her face cast into shadow by exhaustion. "I can feel every cobblestone we go over," she said.

He held her hand. "Don't worry," he said. "With two horses, we'll be in Rocheport before you know it."

By then, of course, Frederick was getting used to making mistakes.

Six

The carriage clattered westward, mile after mile. Frederick stared out the window at the fields of crops that stretched away to the horizon. Occasionally he saw men in the distance, solitary workers toiling beneath the sun. The land went on forever. Jette lay with her face turned to the wall. Every bump in the road, every uneven bounce of the wheel, made her wince. Frederick wished there was something he could do. He wanted the driver, a sour-faced man called Childs, to hurry the horses on to Rocheport, but he didn't want Jette to suffer the discomfort that a speedier journey would cause. As it was, their progress was steady and unspectacular. At midday they stopped to rest the horses and eat the lunch that Reina Wall had packed for them. Childs preferred his own company, standing near the horses as he ate. My grandparents stared silently at Jette's stomach, wondering how long they had.

That night they stayed in a small inn. Childs had declined Frederick's invitation to join them for supper with a terse shake of his head. Frederick had seen him later in the tavern, alone at a table, staring silently into a glass of beer.

The next day they set off at dawn. As they traveled west, the quality of the roads deteriorated. The carriage shuddered as it jumped crevices and hurdled ridges. By the middle of the morning, Jette's face was shining with perspiration. She lay with her eyes tightly shut, her belly cradled in her hands. Frederick stroked her forehead, promising that it would soon be over.

Halfway through the afternoon they felt the carriage slow to a standstill. Childs clambered down from his seat. His face appeared at the window, and he motioned that the horses needed water. Frederick opened the carriage door and looked out. They had stopped in a small town. Single-story buildings lined both sides of the street, a wooden sign hanging outside each one. Dirty-faced boys in torn shirts ran back and forth across the road. In front of one shop, boxes of fruits and vegetables were displayed on a long trestle table. Frederick watched a woman with a basket on her arm bend over and inspect some pears. The sign above the shop read

LEBENSMITTEL.

"Jette," he whispered. "The grocer's sign is in German." When she did not reply, Frederick looked around. Swamped by the sudden bliss of stillness, she had fallen asleep. Frederick climbed down from the carriage. At that moment a man walked by, singing softly to himself in German.

It is hard to imagine the effect on my grandfather of hearing the familiar cadences of his native tongue at that particular moment. For the last two days he had been brooding about being hoodwinked by the Polish barman. Not even Joseph Wall's kindness had been able to soften the sting of his humiliation, and with that humiliation came a new, unfamiliar suspicion of those around him — now he saw a rapacious glint in the eye of every native, an unscrupulous trick lurking up every foreign sleeve. So when he stepped out onto that street, he was vulnerable to the faintest echo of home. He hurried after the man. "Excuse me," he called out in German.

The man stopped and turned to look at him.

"Forgive me for interrupting you," began Frederick. "My name is Frederick Meisenheimer. My wife and I have just arrived in this country."

The man studied Frederick. He was well over six and a half feet tall. A scar ran across his right cheek, casting his face in a shadow of violence. The bruised ribbons of torn tissue had grafted themselves back together in an uneven crest of ugliness, a scabbed exclamation mark. His hands were calloused slabs of leathered flesh. Long, thick fingers were interrupted by knuckles the size of walnuts.

"Where are you from?" asked the man, also in German.

"Hanover."

"And what brings you here?"

"We're just passing through," said Frederick. He pointed behind him. "The horses need water."

The man nodded. "Where are you headed?"

Before Frederick could answer, there was a loud scream from inside the carriage.

Hours later, Frederick was pacing up and down a corridor, listening to Jette's labor from behind a closed door. The man Frederick had spoken to earlier that day sat nearby, calmly smoking a cigarette. His name was Johann Kliever. They were in his house.

"I don't like this," said Frederick, for the seventh time.

Kliever stretched his long legs out in front of him and studied his boots, which were caked in yellow dust. "He's a good doctor," he said simply.

After their conversation on the street had been interrupted, Frederick and Kliever had carried Jette from the carriage to the bed where she now lay. Childs had refused to help, complaining instead about the mess caused by Jette's broken waters. The doctor had appeared at the house a few minutes later. Since then, the bedroom door had remained shut.

Another howl of agony echoed through the house. Soon afterward the doctor, Mathias Becker, appeared in the corridor. He was a short, rotund man with an anxious manner about him. His shirtsleeves were rolled up, and his face was red.

"Herr Meisenheimer?" he said in German, wiping his hands on a towel as he spoke.

Frederick stepped forward. "Yes?"

"Your wife's labor is progressing, but slowly. The baby seems determined to take its time."

"Can I see her?" asked Frederick eagerly.

"You will have to do more than that." The doctor looked at his watch. "I must go home, at least for a while. A tired physician is of no use to your wife, I can assure you. I will return in the morning. If anything happens in the meantime, Kliever knows where to find me. I can be here in five minutes."

"I see," said Frederick.

"Don't worry," said the doctor. "I doubt much will happen for a while yet. She may even sleep a little. Encourage her to do so. She will need all her strength tomorrow." He shook Frederick's hand. "I will see you in the morning, and then we will meet this new baby of yours." With a brief nod he turned and went down the stairs.

Frederick opened the bedroom door. The curtains had been drawn against the night that was closing in. Jette lay on a narrow bed in the middle of the room. Her eyes were closed. The only other furniture was a wooden chest of drawers, on top of which sat a large terra-cotta angel.

"Jette?"

On hearing his voice, Jette's eyes opened. Frederick squatted down beside her. He could see the exhaustion and fright in her face.

"Where have you been?" she whispered.

Frederick reached for her hand. "I was outside all along."

"If you leave me again, I'll kill you," she told him.

"But there was nothing I could —"

Frederick's reply froze in his throat as Jette's face contorted into a mask of pain. A low sob escaped her. The scream that followed knocked the world off its axis, obliterating reason. Shocked beyond words, Frederick watched the contraction pass.

"I won't ever leave you," he said.

They clung to each other then, not saying a word.

As the night drew on, Jette's contractions became worse. They had a terrible rhythm all of their own, a ghastly pulse of agony.

In the calm between contractions, Frederick and Jette tried to sleep. At about three o'clock in the morning, Frederick was drifting in and out of exhausted slumber when Jette's hand landed on his shoulder. He struggled to his feet. Jette's mouth was stretched open in a silent scream. When the pain subsided, her eyes met his. "The baby's coming," she whispered.

"But it's not — The doctor said — He's not —"

Jette grunted, a noise whose quiet ferocity was more unnerving than the howls that had gone before. Her eyes narrowed, then closed. Another grunt. Then a whole series of them, short, harsh, utterly terrifying.

"Wake Kliever," she gasped. "Tell him to fetch —"

She got no further, silenced by another wave of pain. A minute later, Frederick was back by her side. Down the corridor, Kliever was pulling on his trousers. Jette's chest rose and fell violently, breath rasping in and out of her. The noise filled the room. Frederick suddenly understood that there would be no time to wait for the doctor. He went to the end of the bed and peered nervously between Jette's open legs.

"Frederick," moaned Jette. "Stop staring and come here."

Abashed, Frederick scuttled around to her side. It occurred to him that he had never seen her so determined, so afraid, or so beautiful.

"What is it?" she hissed through clenched teeth. "What's wrong?"

He bent down toward her. "I was just thinking how beautiful you looked."

The punch was impressive, both accurate and strong. Jette's fist caught her husband squarely on the jaw. It was an absolute peach of a shot, and it propelled him backward into the chest of drawers. The impact sent the terra-cotta angel crashing to the ground. Frederick lay sprawled across the floor, his jaw stinging. Before he had the chance to wonder what he had done to deserve such a mighty wallop, Jette let out a last cry, filled with a world of agony and hope, and her body went limp. Then the room filled with a high-pitched mewl.

It was the first note of millions that my father would sing.

Dr. Becker arrived a few minutes after the birth. He had gently taken the child out of Frederick's trembling hands and cut his umbilical cord. After a brief inspection he declared him healthy, if a little on the small side. After the sun had risen and the first day of my father's life had begun in earnest, Jette lay propped up in her bed, the new baby in her arms. Kliever and his wife gathered around to inspect the child. Frederick stood next to Jette, gazing in awe at the tiny sleeping bundle of creased flesh. One hand rested on his wife's shoulder. The other gingerly rubbed his chin. The terra-cotta angel was lying forgotten on the bedroom floor. One of its wings had broken off when it hit the ground. It lay a few inches away from the rest of the body, alone and dislocated, a misshapen heart.

"A beautiful baby boy," Anna Kliever said, smiling.

Kliever nodded approvingly. "What will you call him?"

Jette thought about Joseph and Reina Wall, and wondered what would have happened without their kind and timely intervention.

She reached up and felt for Frederick's hand. Her fingers closed around his. "We'll call him Joseph," she said.

Just then there was a knock on the bedroom door. Dr. Becker and Childs stood side by side in the corridor. Becker beckoned Frederick out of the bedroom.

"Herr Meisenheimer," began the doctor. "How is your new family?"

Frederick blinked through his exhaustion. "Tired," he said.

"Splendid," said Becker. He looked at his shoes for a moment. "Mr. Childs here has been asking when you will be able to continue your journey. He tells me that he is required to return to St. Louis in two days."

"I see."

"Your son is very small and weak, Herr Meisenheimer. He must be properly looked after." The doctor paused. "If I could insist upon it, I would have you all stay here, for several days at least. Your wife needs to recover from her labor, and your son is too young for the rigors of a long journey."

Frederick nodded. "Yes. I understand."

"If you do as I suggest, Mr. Childs can return to St. Louis today."

The driver's small, bloodshot eyes shifted between the men as he listened to them speak in German, a sullen scowl of incomprehension on his thin lips. Frederick sighed. "Well, then, I suppose we should wish him a safe journey home."

Dr. Becker nodded, and turned and spoke to Childs in English. The driver listened in silence, and then walked away without giving them another glance.

The two men stood alone in the corridor for a moment.

"Doctor?" said Frederick.

"Yes, Herr Meisenheimer?"

"Where are we?"

"How do you mean?"

"I mean, what is the name of this town?"

A smile spread across the doctor's face. "Didn't you know? You're in Beatrice, Missouri."

SEVEN

That evening, when both mother and child were asleep, Johann Kliever and Frederick walked through the streets of Beatrice to the Nick-Nack Inn, the town's only tavern. Sawdust covered the floor, belching small tornadoes of beige dust with every footfall. Men hunkered down over tables pockmarked with angry craters. Chairs rocked on uneven legs. A haze of smoke hung low in the air. Kliever strode through the room, nodding at people as he went. As they sat down at an empty table, an old man approached. He was wearing a long black apron tied at the waist and carried a battered metal tray under his arm. In the dim light of the saloon his skin was gray, tissue-thin, and deathlike. His small, pale eyes were sunk deep within the craggy lines of his face.

"This is Polk," said Kliever.

The barman gazed at the floor, saying nothing. Kliever slapped the top of the table with his enormous hand. "Give us two beers and two shots. This man is the proud father of a new baby boy, Polk. We're here to celebrate."

Without a word, Polk turned and wobbled toward the bar at the back of the room. Frederick watched him go. "Is that man all right?" he asked.

"Polk? He's so drunk he doesn't know his own name. But that's when he's at his best. He never forgets an order, never gives wrong change. And he won't say a word to anyone. He's a machine."

Moments later the barman returned and deposited four glasses on the table in front of them without spilling a drop, and then staggered wordlessly back to his post. Kliever raised his glass.

"To fatherhood," he said.

"Heaven help me," said Frederick, and threw back his drink. He felt the heat of the liquor inside him. "Do you have children?"

"One son. A baby, too. He's just a few months old. Stefan."

"So you know all about it."

"Not really. You would have to ask my wife."

"Women's work?"

"Perhaps." Kliever shrugged.

The two men drank.

"Have you lived here long?" asked Frederick.

"Most of my life." Kliever spoke in a low, gruff voice. His German was perfect, without a trace of an accent. He wiped his mouth on his sleeve and settled his huge frame back in his chair. "My grandfather was from Bavaria. He settled in the Mississippi Delta in 1856. My father and my uncles ran a farm for one of the big cotton families down there. They were good farmers, but they spent most of their time fighting with each other. In the end my father couldn't stand it anymore, and moved away. I was still young when we left." Kliever paused. "He died ten years ago. I work the farm he left me."

"So you've never been to Germany?"

Kliever shook his head. "I'm an American, born and bred."

"But your German is excellent."

"That was all we spoke growing up. I only learned English when I got to school."

"I suppose I shall need to go back to school myself, then," mused Frederick, looking around him. In the far corner of the room he noticed a piano covered by a cobwebbed tarpaulin. "Your town seems a fine place."

Kliever nodded. "The land is good. Rich soil. And the river does its bit."

"The river?"

"The Missouri River. The longest river in America. Runs right through the town. I'll show you on the way home."

Before Frederick could reply, there was a loud crash from the far end of the room. Kliever got to his feet and beckoned Frederick to follow him. A crowd of people were peering over the bar. Polk's prostrate body lay across the floor behind the counter, quite still. His eyes were open, staring sightlessly up at the ceiling. A small halo of shattered glass was sprinkled around his head. Frederick looked down in shock at the barman's crumpled, empty face.

"He does this every night," said Kliever. "He'll be fine by tomorrow. Help me with him, will you?"

They carried the old man through the back door of the tavern and left him on a mattress behind the building. "He'll wake up in a few hours and make his way home," said Kliever as they went back inside. "Won't remember a thing about it."

"What happens now?" asked Frederick.

"Someone usually volunteers," said Kliever. He looked at Frederick and scratched his nose.

Frederick spent the rest of the evening behind the bar. It was a night he would never forget. Men greeted him warmly in German, and soon he was drowning happily in one long conversation. His worries about reaching Rocheport gradually dissipated in the warmth of the Nick-Nack's friendly welcome.

Hours later, Kliever and Frederick staggered back to Kliever's house. Frederick sang arias as they weaved through the empty streets. He gazed up at the sky, so different from home. In Europe the stars hunkered down low across the night, dull and pendulous. Here, though, the heavens were filled with a million dazzling celestial bodies, each one casually brushing up to infinity.

"I could get to like this place," he said.

"It's home," said Kliever.

"Beatrice is a strange name for a town, though."

Kliever clapped him on the shoulder. "Come with me," he said. After a short walk they arrived in the town's main square, which was dominated by a large redbrick building, hulking and sinister in the shadows cast by the moonlight. It dwarfed the tidy, single-story shop fronts that surrounded it.

"Church?" guessed Frederick.

Kliever shook his head. "That's the Caitlin County Courthouse," he said. "Beatrice is the county seat. Here. Come and see this." On the sidewalk in front of the courthouse there was a bronze statue of a middle-aged woman. She had a long nose and a grim expression on her face. The two men gazed up at her. Frederick leaned forward and read the plaque at the foot of the statue. It read BEATRICE EITZEN.

"Beatrice," he said softly.

"Her husband, Nathaniel Eitzen, founded this place," said Kliever. "They were from South Carolina originally, but Eitzen had an itch he needed to scratch. He came west to seek his fortune. And he brought his wife with him."

"Doesn't look as if she was too happy about it."

"Oh, she wasn't. She missed the sunshine. In fact when they reached southern Indiana, she refused to go another step. She'd had enough. Told her husband to go on without her."

"And?"

"And so he did. He hopped on his horse and drove out of town. Left her in the middle of nowhere. She had no choice but to wait for him to come back." Kliever yawned. "Anyway, after a week or so, Eitzen started to feel guilty about what he'd done. So he wrote her a letter, asking her to come and join him." He pointed up at the statue. "But she was as stubborn as he was, and refused.

This went on for a couple of months — he'd beg her to come, she'd say no. Every day, of course, he was moving farther west, until he arrived here, when he decided that he'd gone far enough. So he established a township, and pretty soon there was a fair-sized group who joined him here."

"But not his wife," guessed Frederick.

"Not his wife," agreed Kliever. "That's when Eitzen had the bright idea to name the town after her, to see if that might tempt her to come."

"Did it work?"

Kliever nodded. "Not even she could resist having a town named after her. Eitzen put on a big parade to welcome her, and had this statue made in her honor. So the carriage pulled into the town, and stopped right about here. Everyone had turned out to welcome her. There was a hush from the crowd as she climbed down from the carriage and looked around. She slowly took it all in. Then she looked up at the statue, went very still, and climbed back into the carriage without another word. The horses started to move off. 'Wait, wait,' cried Eitzen. 'Where are you going?' 'Home,' she shouted out of the window. 'But why?' he yelled. And just as the carriage rolled out of the square, his wife shrieked, 'My nose is too big!' Last words he ever heard from her. Still, he kept the town's name, in case she ever came back. But she never did. A minute and a half in this place was enough for her." Kliever yawned again. "We both need some sleep. Come on. I'll show you the river. It's on the way home."

A few minutes later, the two men stood at the end of the municipal pier, a perilous edifice of old wood that stretched out into the river. Frederick listened to the water as it coursed beneath his feet, a smooth, strong pulse in the darkness. "This is beautiful," he said.

"Tell you what, though," said Kliever. "The sound of running water always has the same effect on me." He began to unbutton his flies.

Frederick felt his own bladder bulge, and did the same thing. As he emptied himself into the Missouri River, Frederick experienced an epiphany of sorts. After a lifetime spent in the city, this alfresco piss was his first true communion with nature. It felt exhilarating.

"I like it here," he said when he had finished.

"It's as good a place as any," agreed Kliever.

"It looks as if we'll have to stay for a while," said Frederick. "Doctor's orders."

"You'll stay with us," said Kliever.

The two men looked out across the dark water for a moment.

"Thank you," said Frederick.

And so, as they stood side by side, making their own modest contributions to the longest river in America, did Frederick Meisenheimer and Johann Kliever become friends.

That night Frederick slept on the floor next to his wife and son. When he awoke the next morning, Jette was propped up in the bed with Joseph on her chest. The baby's eyes were tightly shut as he sucked hungrily at her breast, oblivious to everything else. Frederick got to his feet and stroked his son's tiny head. It felt hot to his touch, full of life.

"A late night," observed Jette dryly.

"Yes, well," said Frederick, abashed.

Jette smiled. "I suppose a celebration was in order."

"The doctor says that we must stay here for a while. He wants to be sure the baby is healthy before we go any further."

"If that's what he says, then that's what we'll do."

"The driver went back to St. Louis yesterday. We're on our own now."

Jette nodded at this news with a faraway look in her eye. The baby was not the only one being nourished, Frederick saw. His wife was tranquil, replete with new discoveries. "We'll manage, when the time comes," she said, hugging Joseph to her.

After the unhappy chaos of the previous few weeks, Frederick wondered whether some measure of calm might finally be returning to their lives. He was not a superstitious man, far less a religious one, but he couldn't ignore the serendipity of it all: the driver's decision to stop to refresh the horses, Jette's waters breaking just then, Kliever strolling by. They were less than a day's ride away from Rocheport, but at that moment the final miles of their journey seemed as daunting as a return voyage back across the Atlantic.

Rocheport had only been the vaguest of destinations. Nobody was expecting them there.

That evening, Frederick and Johann Kliever returned to the Nick-Nack. Frederick became increasingly preoccupied as the evening drew on.

"You seem quiet tonight," remarked Kliever.

"Sorry." Frederick tapped the side of his head. "I've been thinking. I'm wondering if perhaps we should stay here."

"Perhaps you should," said Kliever.

86

"If Jette agrees, of course. And if I can find a job."

"There are always jobs for hard workers."

"You know I'm not a farmer."

"There are other things in this world apart from farming," said Kliever. "Besides, it's backbreaking work. Terrible hours. And you're a slave to the damned weather. If you have a drought — *poof.*" Kliever's large hands collided over the table with a heavy, cataclysmic thud. Polk tottered up, his tray laden with fresh drinks, and silently unloaded the glasses onto the table. "I've just had an idea," Kliever said. He stood up. "Back in a moment." He turned without another word and strode out of the bar.

When Kliever returned a few minutes later, Frederick was surprised to see Dr. Becker following him. As the two men sat down, Polk materialized and put a glass of beer down in front of the doctor.

"Good evening," said Becker, after a lengthy contemplation of the tabletop. "Kliever tells me you're thinking of staying with us."

"We've had such a warm welcome."

"You would need to find suitable employment."

"That, and to convince my wife."

Becker nodded and looked over his shoulder toward the bar. "You've met Polk," he said.

"A phenomenon."

"Yes, well. His crashing into unconsciousness at the end of the evening is getting tiresome."

"Tiresome?"

The doctor drained his glass of beer in one long swallow. "The thing is," he said, "the Nick-Nack belongs to me."

"To you?" said Frederick.

"Perhaps you think it inappropriate that a member of the medical profession should own a tavern."

"Not at all," replied Frederick.

"Well, there are enough people who *do*," said the doctor bitterly. "Anyway. No matter. We were speaking of Polk. Frankly, I prefer drunks on the *other* side of the bar." The doctor turned and watched Polk wobble precariously between the tables. "After he collapses I never know who's in charge. Volunteers are all very well, and they're all good men, but I'd like to know there's someone here I can trust to protect my investment. A manager, in other words." Becker laced his fingers together. "You seem like a reliable man. And from what I hear, you have a natural talent for bar work. If you want it, the job's yours."

"I want it," said Frederick at once.

"You'll have to learn English, of course," continued Dr. Becker. "Not everyone here speaks German."

"I understand," said Frederick.

"And since you'll be staying, you're going to need somewhere to live. As it happens, I have a house you can rent. You could move in straightaway. It's a little run-down, but nothing that a lick of paint wouldn't fix. And I wouldn't ask much."

Frederick beamed at him. "I'm sure it will be perfect."

Just then there was a crash from the back of the room. The men turned and saw customers leaning over the bar. The doctor sighed. "Well," he said, "now I can watch you in action myself."

The following morning, Frederick went back to the Nick-Nack with Becker. The doctor introduced him to Polk and explained to the barman that Frederick would be working with him from now on. Polk listened silently to the news. Frederick could smell stale alcohol seeping through the old man's skin. He remembered that first night on board the *Great Republic,* the only time he had ever drunk alone. The same sodden misery that had haunted him then lingered in every line of Polk's gray face.

That evening, Frederick stood proudly behind the bar of the Nick-Nack, a pristine white apron around his considerable girth, and informed customers of recent developments. The drinkers of Beatrice approved of the new addition to the Nick-Nack's staff. For all his robotic efficiency and entertaining collapses, Polk provided little of the warmth that people expected when they went to a tavern. Frederick, in contrast, was always ready with a cheerful welcome and a sympathetic ear. Together they made a fine team, at least until the old man crashed to the floor, at which point Frederick worked alone until the end of the evening.

Exactly a week after Joseph's birth, Frederick and Jette moved into the house that Dr. Becker had promised them. The small wooden bungalow was nestled in the cold shadow of the tree-blanketed bluff that marked the northern perimeter of the town. The house had not been lived in for several years, and the slow creep of decay and disrepair had gone unchecked. Doors hung off their hinges. Untended window frames had splintered beneath the frost and fire of countless Missouri seasons. The panes were so thickly smeared in grime that only a few pallid rays of sunlight fell through the glass. Cobwebs crisscrossed the rafters in such delicate profusion that the ghostly filigree appeared to be holding the house together.

The rooms were empty cocoons of shadows. Spiders scuttled into corners at the first footfall. There was a large fireplace in the living room, ancient ash lying in its grate. An old stove leaned against the wall by the back door. In the yard was a wooden outhouse, half hidden by overgrown grass. Beyond it a solitary sugar maple tree stood silent sentry to the forest behind.

Frederick and Jette stood on the Klievers' porch as they prepared to walk the four blocks to their new home, the final leg of the journey that had started in the street outside Andreas's apartment. As Frederick picked up Jette's suitcase, Kliever stepped forward. "Here," he said to Jette. "This is for you." He was holding the terra-cotta angel's wing that Frederick had broken as he had staggered backward under the force of Jette's punch, just as Joseph was being born.

Jette took the wing and put it in her pocket.

That evening, while Joseph slept, Frederick fashioned a hook out of a short piece of wire. He hung the broken angel's wing high up on the wall of the living room, directly over the fireplace. They gazed up at the bright patch

91

of color, their new home's only decoration. The terra-cotta heart glowed warmly in the light of the flames below.

Finally, they had stopped moving.

EIGHT

In the weeks that followed, Frederick watched Polk closely and learned as much as he could about running the Nick-Nack. Once the old barman realized that he was going to keep his job, and that Frederick intended to ignore his furtive nips from the whiskey flagon, his icy detachment thawed, but only a little. Nothing would entice Polk to interact with his fellow men with the same enthusiasm that he communed with a bottle. Every afternoon he began the same, slow process of getting stupendously pickled.

Like Polk, the tavern had a certain run-down charm about it. The sawdust that covered the floor hid a legion of cracks and holes. The wall of beveled glass behind the bar had acquired its own misty patina, the fog of age creeping slowly inward from its perimeter. Sometimes Frederick would eye the piano hidden beneath the tarpaulin in the corner of the room.

Johann Kliever often spent evenings propping up the bar at the Nick-Nack until it was closing time. Sometimes he would pester Frederick for a song as the two of them made their way home. Every night they would walk to the end of the pier and urinate beneath the stars. Frederick's deposits into the Missouri River became a sort of spiritual investment, an act of primeval connection with this new land. The unchecked force of nature that surrounded him could not have been more different from the prim streets of Hanover. Those visits to the pier were a constant reminder that this was, above all, somewhere new.

By tacit agreement, neither man burdened the other with his innermost thoughts. Frederick often found himself reflecting how little he knew about his new friend. Sometimes Kliever would vanish for several days at a time, and then reappear without comment or explanation. After these mysterious absences he often moved gingerly, the ghost of a painful grimace haunting his face.

When he was not at the Nick-Nack, Frederick began work on his new home. He painted the house a brilliant white, both inside and out, and scoured the windows until they relinquished all those years of dirt. He sang while he worked; the rooms were filled with sunlight and music. Frederick repaired the rotten window frames and built a bed. He was not a natural handyman. His only assets were a cast-iron will and a newly acquired phlegmatic streak that saved him from being crushed by disappointment when his efforts failed. Ladders toppled, pipes burst, wood splintered, glass broke, but Frederick gritted his teeth and plowed on. He relished the small satisfactions of a newly daubed wall or a freshly chopped pile of wood. Little by little, he turned their small house into a home.

In what little spare time he had, Frederick began to study English. He borrowed books from Dr. Becker and read for an hour each morning. Every week he bought the town's newspaper, the *Beatrice Optimist,* and slowly worked his way through it, dictionary by his side. He listened closely to conversations at the tavern, eager to grasp the language's strange vernacular. Frederick was an assiduous student. A year after their arrival in America, he had amassed a fair vocabulary and was rarely caught out by the army of irregular verbs that lurked in ambush. But for all his hard work, Frederick had no gift for English. After the dour rigidity of his native tongue, its anarchy unnerved him. There was always a glimmer of apprehension in his eye when he spoke, as if every sentence were a high wire from which he was liable to topple at any moment. His unease made him retreat from the perils of idiom. He adopted a cautious, formal mode of speech, although this wasn't just because of his fear of opaque colloquialisms: English was the language of his family's future. It deserved to be spoken with respect, not sullied with lazy elisions and cheap slang. As he listened to the alien words form themselves in his mouth, his heart would swell with pride.

Because Frederick loved America. He loved its big open spaces, the sunsets that drenched the evening sky in blistering color. He loved the warmth of the people. Above all, he loved the smell of promise that hung in the air. Europe, he could see now, was slowly suffocating under the weight of its own history. In America the future was the only thing that mattered. Frederick turned his back on everything that had gone before, and looked ahead into the bright lights of the young century. Here, a man could re-invent himself. His determination to learn a new language was his own path toward such reincarnation. German became just an echo of his past. Frederick addressed everyone in his newly starched English, his words muddied by the thick accent that he would never lose, every tortured syllable pronounced with relish.

Jette was not so lucky. Joseph's birth, rather than directing her eyes toward the future, instead turned her gaze back toward the home she had left behind. Motherhood changed everything that she thought she knew. Everything was now refracted through the prism of a new mother's love. She stared down at Joseph as he slept, and knew that she would be destroyed if he ever left her. Suddenly, remorse flooded through her as she thought about her parents, alone now on the other side of the world.

She hid her dismay behind a faultless mask of contentment. She sewed curtains and embroidered cushions, and persuaded Anna Kliever to teach her how to knit. But no matter how assiduously she busied herself in domestic industry, she found herself missing Hanover terribly. It had been her idea to come to America, but now she began to wish that they had never left. As she watched Frederick eagerly immerse himself in his new country, she kept her homesickness a guilty secret.

Unlike her husband, Jette learned scarcely a word of English. Almost everyone in the town still spoke German, and she found her old language a welcome comfort in the face of the strange parade of foreign customs outside her front door. Jette's quiet yearning for home manifested itself in other ways, too. She cooked only traditional German fare — bland, hefty dishes, fortified by mountains of starch. Possessing no cookbooks, she picked her way back to distant memories. By dogged experiment she extracted the tastes and textures of her childhood from deep within her. Over time she constructed a gastronomic mosaic, each dish a quiet elegy to all she had left behind. Spareribs with sauerkraut, steamed ham, caraway meatballs with *spaetzle,* fried apple slices, barley porridge with buttermilk — these concoctions came freighted with memories. A mouthful of *streuselkuchen,* laced with golden almonds, took her back to long summer afternoons spent in the garden of her childhood home. The heavy rye of *roggenbrot* brought the chill northern evenings closing in. Jette's kitchen became a shrine, turning out culinary museum pieces. Every day she baked mountains of white bread, laced with milk and sugar. And there were *lebkuchen,* Joseph's favorite — crumbling fortifications of molasses, spices, raisins, and lard.

While Frederick was at work, Jette secretly began to write letters home. She filled page after page with detailed reports on their new lives, the lines smudged by her tears. In between these reports she begged her parents for forgiveness.

She never received a reply.

One Friday morning, a few months after Joseph's first birthday, Frederick was sweeping the floor of the Nick-Nack when there was a knock on the door. "We are closed!" cried Frederick in his awkward English. "You must wait until lunch!" He carried on with his work. After a brief pause, the knock came again.

Frederick put down his broom with a sigh. He went to the front door of the tavern, pulled back the bolt, and opened the door. Leaning against the door frame in an elegant slouch was a black man no more than five feet tall. He was dressed in a light gray suit and black patent leather shoes. The brim of his hat was pulled down over his eyes. A gold fob chain hung on his vest, glimmering in the morning sun. Frederick tried to hide his astonishment. Since he had arrived in Beatrice he hadn't seen a single Negro.

"I am sorry," said Frederick, "we are closed."

"Don't want no drink," said the man.

"Well then, how is it that I can help you?" asked Frederick politely.

The man pushed himself away from the

door frame. "Heard you got a piano."

Frederick nodded. "Yes, that is correct. We have a piano."

The man scratched the side of his neck. His fingers were long and thin. "I can play."

"No thank you," said Frederick.

"Folks like to hear me play."

"No thank you," said Frederick again, stepping back inside. As he closed the door, the gleaming tip of the man's shoe appeared, blocking its progress.

"But you ain't heard me play yet," he said through the crack. He spoke without rancor.

When it came to matters of race in America, Frederick was hopelessly out of his depth. Here his innate warmth toward his fellow man was outflanked by history. Only a few decades earlier, Missouri had been ripped apart by the Civil War. Fathomless atrocities had been committed on its soil, a slave state at the frontier of Confederate territory. Thousands of soldiers had perished, innocents were slaughtered, women were raped and beaten to death. Children were taken from their beds, never to be seen again. A cloud of terror had hung over the land. All this in the name of freedom. The tragedy of it all was that the Union's eventual victory did not erase the shadow of slavery. People's thinking would not be altered by a peace accord and new laws that they did not want.

Frederick, unsullied by the blood of local history, was perplexed by the unreflective racism that he had witnessed in many of his customers. He struggled to reconcile the casual bigotry he heard at the bar with what he knew of the men who said such things.

It was his customers who caused him to hesitate now. He had never seen a black face inside the Nick-Nack, and he supposed that there must be a good reason for that. He gazed down at the man's shoe, and thought fast. After the generous welcome he had received in this town, the least he could do was to offer the same to another, now that he was in a position to do so. He glanced over at the piano in the far corner of the room. It had remained beneath its blanket since the day he had arrived.

Nobody would complain about a little music.

Frederick looked down and saw the man's toe twitch. He opened the door.

The Negro stepped into the room and looked around him, apparently untroubled by the silent standoff that had just ended. "Let's see this piano, then," he said cheerfully.

The two men rolled the piano into the middle of the room. Frederick removed the tarpaulin. The instrument's panels were decorated with elegant marquetry. The ivory keys had yellowed with age. The stranger extended his right index finger and pressed down on a key. The note echoed through the room.

The man took off his hat and drew up a chair from the table behind him. His feet could barely touch the pedals. "Name's William Henry Harris," he said. "Pleased to make your acquaintance."

Before Frederick could respond, the man began to play.

For the next hour Frederick listened, the broom forgotten in his hands. William Henry Harris played that piano as if his life depended on it. Without a note of music in front of him, he delivered languid anthems, shimmering with funereal grace; stately marches, their formal pomp subverted by sharp syncopation; and breezy romps, melodic lines prancing onward, as light as air. Frederick watched as the man's fingers danced across the keys. His right hand spun each melody out of the air and simultaneously constructed around it a gorgeous confection of harmony. His left hand steamed up and down, pounding out a rumbling bass counterpoint. The piano, unplayed for so long, emitted the odd sour note of protest, but nothing could dilute the beauty of the music. Even the faster numbers were shrouded in mournful dignity — what some were already calling the blues. A cracked holler of remorse lingered in the echo of each note.

Frederick didn't know it then, but this was his first encounter with ragtime, Missouri's greatest gift to American music (although there are some who might argue that Charlie Parker, flying the coop of Kansas City and touching down on New York's Fifty-seventh Street to ignite bebop's flame, had a stronger claim). Scott Joplin was in Sedalia, Missouri, flush with the success of "Maple Leaf Rag," and playing like a man possessed. William "Blind" Boone had cut his chops in the whorehouses of the tenderloin district in St. Louis, and now was pulling in large crowds across the state, stomping and wailing long into the night. Everyone was crazy for that syncopated style! The pebble had been dropped in Missouri, and the music, bright-eyed and restless, was slowly rippling outward toward the flame-bearers on the coasts, who would take that new rhythm and make it *swing*. Frederick stood mesmerized as William Henry Harris redrew his musical map. He had not moved when Polk came in through the back door of the tavern. The old barman came and stood silently next to Frederick as Harris continued to play.

Finally Polk spoke. "Who's the nigger?" he asked.

Frederick frowned. "This gentleman, Polk, is tonight's entertainment."

Polk did his best to make Frederick change his mind. Men wouldn't want to be disturbed by a piano-playing midget, he protested. Frederick refused to listen. The music had put him beyond reason. He was determined to see William Henry Harris play. They agreed on a modest fee, and with a tip of his hat, the Negro disappeared, promising to return that evening.

That afternoon, Polk anxiously drank himself into oblivion in record time. He was already sleeping peacefully on the mattress behind the building before the bar was even half full with the regular evening crowd. Frederick manned the bar alone. The piano was back in its old position in the corner of the room, but the tarpaulin had been removed and the wood polished. Frederick had decided to keep William Henry Harris hidden in the stockroom until the last possible moment. As a further precaution, he charged half price on all drinks in the hope of securing a sympathetic audience. Rather than descending into a benign haze of ine-briated fellowship, though, the Nick-Nack was soon crackling with alcohol-fueled tension. Already one pair of rowdy drinkers had been shepherded outside to finish their argument in the street.

When it was time for the show to begin, Frederick went to the stockroom where William Henry Harris was waiting patiently. The pianist straightened his tie and put on his hat. Frederick pushed open the door and led him into the crowded tavern. As they made their way toward the piano, the room fell silent. The only sound was William Henry Harris humming softly as he trotted along behind Frederick. He put his hat on top of the piano and settled himself on the stool. Frederick stood next to him, meeting every glare. When Harris had stopped fidgeting, Frederick looked down at him. "Play," he hissed.

Harris looked affronted. "You ain't gonna announce me?" he whispered. "You know, give me a buildup, tell a few jokes, get them warmed up a little?"

"*Play,*" growled Frederick.

William Henry Harris flexed his fingers, and tore into a blistering rag, a double-timed, jazzed fugue of cascading sixteenth notes. For the next hour a continuous stream of music flowed from the Nick-Nack's old piano. The customers watched him play, stunned that he should be in this place, doing this thing, but not one of them moved to object. They were too busy listening.

Finally William Henry Harris removed his fingers from the keys and placed them quietly in his lap, his head bowed — man and music exhausted. Frederick looked around the room. Men stared quietly into the bottoms of their glasses. The silence grew more menacing with every passing second. It suddenly occurred to Frederick that William Henry Harris might not get out of the tavern alive.

And then from somewhere came the slow, dry slap of skin on skin. After a few seconds — the longest few seconds of his life, Frederick would later call them — the lone hand clap was joined by another, from deep in the shadows. A moment later, another. It was just enough. The small eddy of approval slowly pulled others into its orbit. One by one, others joined in. Soon the room was filled with applause.

From the piano stool William Henry Harris looked up at Frederick. His face was shining with perspiration. There was the smallest glimmer of triumph in his eye. He said: "I *told* you folks like to hear me play."

■ ■ ■ ■

After he had unblinkingly renegotiated his fee, Harris agreed to come back to the Nick-Nack on a regular basis, and those evenings of ragtime became hugely popular. Word soon spread about the tiny Negro who could conjure such mesmerizing music out of the old piano, and a little judicious publicity on Frederick's part ensured that the tavern was full every time Harris arrived in town. Regular customers found themselves having to fight for tables.

On those subsequent nights, Frederick no longer felt the need to stand guard over the piano, but he remained cautious. Harris always stayed in the stockroom until it was time to begin, and left immediately after his performance. Where he came from or disappeared to, Frederick never discovered. He arrived promptly, immaculately dressed, and played for precisely the agreed-upon length of time.

Over the years that the pianist came to the tavern, he and Frederick never became friends. Despite, or perhaps because of, the precarious nature of their joint endeavor, there was a necessary caution between them, a tacit understanding that no matter what boundaries they might breach on the floor of the Nick-Nack, others remained impregnable. Frederick's reticence was also due, in part, to lingering guilt. In his memory, the tip of William Henry Harris's polished shoe remained firmly wedged in the crack of the door, a reminder of all that still separated the two men.

Frederick could not forget that he had been reluctant to let him in.

Encouraged by the success of the ragtime evenings, my grandfather began to plan other musical events at the tavern. He placed an advertisement in the *Optimist* announcing auditions. Soon the Nick-Nack was hosting marching bands, creaky violin trios, and pennywhistle recitals. Musicians came from neighboring towns to play. On weekends, bands performed during the afternoon, and the room was filled with families who had come to listen. Before long, music filled the place most nights of the week.

Johann Kliever had always enjoyed Frederick's singing as they meandered back home at the end of another night at the Nick-Nack. It was he who suggested an evening of opera. Frederick was thrilled by the idea. His natural affinity for the limelight had been muted since his arrival in Beatrice, but now it returned, stronger than ever. He persuaded the town's best pianist, Riva Bloomberg, to accompany him. They rehearsed in the Nick-Nack during the afternoons, Frau Bloomberg's nose a perpetual wrinkle of disapproval at the lingering odor of alcohol and tobacco. Riva Bloomberg was a farmer's wife who rose at five every morning to strangle a chicken for her family's dinner with those delicate pianist's fingers of hers. It is fair to say that she and Frederick were not natural collaborators. During their performances Frederick pounded his chest and leaped about, while Frau Bloomberg sat motionless at the piano, not raising her eyes from the music except to glare at the audience. Still, the opera evenings were a great success. On those nights Jette and Joseph were always at the back of the darkened room, listening to the songs that had swept Jette off her feet back in Hanover. Ambushed by old memories, my grandmother wept as Frederick performed his repertoire of the lovestruck and the lovelorn, the blessed and the doomed.

Joseph lay in his mother's arms, listening, taking it all in. The music ran into his blood.

Frederick's belief in the greatness of America never faltered, not even for an instant.

He had never forgotten Joseph Wall's parting advice, to be a good American.

One clear April afternoon in 1907, Frederick and Jette went to the courthouse to swear the Pledge of Allegiance. Frederick had not needed the small card on which the words were printed. He had long since committed them to memory, that spell that would grant him what he longed for most. As he recited the oath he stared in wonder at the American flag that hung behind the judge's bench. Next to him, Jette held her own card up to her face to hide her tears.

To mark the occasion Dr. Becker arranged for a photograph to be taken after the ceremony. It sits now on my mantelpiece, its faded sepia tones a quiet hymn to its century-long life. Frederick and Jette are standing on the steps of the courthouse. Frederick is beaming at the camera from beneath the brim of a brand-new homburg, purchased for the occasion. His hand rests on his young son's shoulder. Joseph's gaze has drifted away from the camera, his attention caught by some drama unfolding behind the photographer. Trapped in his tieless white shirt, the overstarched collar pinching his young neck, this newly minted American seems anxious to escape. Jette's

face is shrouded in shadows of sadness.
She is wearing a pretty floral print dress,
and stands a little apart from her husband
and son. Her hands are resting protectively
over her belly, which swells out in front of
her.

NINE

Two months after that photograph was taken, Rosa was born. My grandparents' joy at the arrival of their daughter — the first true American of the Meisenheimer brood, both conceived and delivered on this soil — was tempered by the baby's manifest irritation at being sprung from the sanctuary of Jette's womb.

From her first breath my aunt drew on a seemingly limitless well of dissatisfaction. The slightest disappointment provoked screams of staggering ferocity. Her fury quickly acquired its own devastating momentum, and there was nothing her parents could do but wait for her to yell herself to a standstill. Her stamina was extraordinary. She often cried through the night, falling into a deep sleep just as the sun was rising. The rest of the family was left to stumble through the morning in frazzled exhaustion. Frederick, who was already keeping peculiar hours at the Nick-Nack, sometimes went for days without sleep. Before long Rosa's tactics had crushed all opposition in the house. Her whims were cravenly indulged; all domestic decisions were based solely on whether or not she would approve. Joseph's good-natured calm was no match for his sister's spiky irascibility. Although it was his angel wing that hung in pride of place above the fireplace, Joseph soon became a furtive presence in his own home. His sister's endless demands for attention slowly eclipsed him from view.

In fact, Joseph did not especially mind Rosa's tyrannical domination. He spent most of his time playing with the Klievers' son, Stefan. The two boys roamed through the neighborhood together, lost in imaginary worlds. Stefan was usually the architect of their adventures, and in Joseph he had a willing accomplice. The people and creatures they encountered became characters in the drama unfolding in their heads. Old ladies morphed into evil witches. Cats became ferocious tigers. Men lurched along streets, evil in their hearts and violence burning in their eyes. All were dispatched with devastating blows from the boys' arsenal of invisible weapons. They left a trail of bloody carnage in their wake.

Their favorite place to play was Tillman's Wood, a windswept copse at the top of the hill that overshadowed the town to the north. Separated from the surrounding forest by a ragged corona of scrubland, it was perched on the crest of the river bluff, edging up to a drop of several hundred feet down to the Missouri River. At the heart of Tillman's Wood there was a tall oak tree, and the boys loved to swarm over its weathered limbs. In early summer, when the tree was wreathed in young leaf, they would be cocooned by verdant camouflage, invisible from the ground. They spent many blissful hours there, sometimes playing, sometimes lulled into stillness by torrents of sweet birdsong. There, far away from the adult world below them, Joseph and Stefan were kings.

When Joseph was seven, Frederick asked Riva Bloomberg whether she would be willing to give his son singing lessons. Riva cautiously agreed. The apple, she knew, never fell far from the tree, and she was unsure whether she really wanted to be responsible for ushering another musical show-off into the world. Joseph himself was no more enthusiastic about the idea. He was terrified of the lady behind the piano who scowled her way through his father's recitals at the Nick-

Nack. Frederick held Joseph's hand as they walked to his first lesson. The Bloombergs lived in a large farmhouse half a mile out of town. All the way there, Frederick promised him everything would be wonderful. Joseph said nothing, but his young eyes were clouded by doubt.

In fact, Frederick was right.

The first time Joseph stood in Riva Bloomberg's living room and sang back the patterns of notes that she picked out on the piano, his untutored voice brought her fingers to a standstill. As she listened, Riva Bloomberg felt as if she were hearing music for the first time. Each note Joseph sang was a small starburst of beauty, too perfect for the world into which it emerged.

Joseph had no idea of the effect he was having on his teacher. He mistook Riva Bloomberg's misty-eyed rapture for the same disapproval she showed while Frederick cavorted about during his performances. But not even that disquiet could dampen the euphoria that swept through him when he sang. The music filled him up, and made him whole. As the notes flew from his throat, the rest of the world receded. All that was left was beauty.

Melody and rhythm came to him as naturally as breathing. Riva Bloomberg only had to play a tune once for it to be deposited, note for note, in his faultless musical memory, and then he could reproduce it perfectly on demand. After a few months, Joseph had worked his way through every piece of music Riva Bloomberg had for solo treble. She asked Frederick what they should try next.

"Oh, there is plenty of music out there," Frederick said cheerfully. "Just not for boys."

So it was that Joseph and Frau Bloomberg began to explore some of the great soprano opera roles. Every week my father underwent a peculiar metamorphosis, changing from a shy young boy into one of a gallery of unhinged women. He played scheming maids, a suicidal Japanese concubine, a collection of flaky consumptives, an oversexed gypsy, several aristocratic *grandes dames,* and at least one witch. He did not possess Frederick's flair for melodrama, but the music, distilled in a voice like his, needed no histrionics. This was just as well, because most of the time Joseph had no idea what he was singing about. Riva Bloomberg did not approve of most of opera's greatest female characters, who were (in her opinion) either hysterical hotheads or dissolute fornicators. She was determined to protect Joseph from all that depravity. Whenever he asked the meaning of a particular foreign word, Frau

116

Bloomberg said the first thing that came into her head. As a result, when Joseph wistfully sang about the imminent return of a long-lost lover from overseas, he believed that he was telling a touching story about penguins. His innocence breathed new life into those arias. In that parallel universe of meaning, unshackled from messy human context, the music existed simply for itself and acquired a new, luminous beauty. Joseph's voice was high and lovely, impossibly pure. The notes chased each other through Frau Bloomberg's living room, a shimmering tail of melody.

Ever since my grandparents' arrival in Beatrice, Anna Kliever had been Jette's closest friend. The two women recognized in each other the perfect confidante. The town was small; everyone lived their lives in front of a silent, watchful chorus of their fellow citizens. Wary of this unwanted audience, Anna Kliever had learned to bury her feelings deep within herself. But Jette's guileless friendship opened her up like a flower feeling the first warm touch of summer sun.

As for Jette, the patina of breezy good humor that she maintained for the benefit of her husband and the outside world could not survive the intimacy she shared with Anna.

When they were alone she was unable to halt the choked litany of regret that stewed inside her. It was Anna who listened to Jette's frustration at Frederick's inability to concede, even for a moment, that their new life was anything but perfect.

Jette's quiet confessions to Anna gave her the strength to return to her family with her mask of contentment still in place. Her decision to hide her unhappiness from Frederick was not the result of any cooling in their marriage. Quite the opposite: it was her devotion to her husband and children that made her want to protect them from her sadness. Her silence was the greatest gift she could give them.

It was certainly true that Frederick was happier than he had ever been. As the Nick-Nack's musical reputation grew, business boomed. Frederick built a rudimentary stage in the corner of the room where the piano had lain silent for so long.

There was one problem, however. Dr. Becker was happy to shower Frederick with compliments, but he was reluctant to give him a raise in salary. Frederick was not a greedy man, but he thought it only fair that he should benefit a little from all his hard work. His sense of injustice began to erode the pleasure he took in his job. Finally he confessed his disenchantment to Kliever.

"You need to stop complaining and do something about it," said Kliever.

"Yes, but what?"

"Do it the American way. Buy the place off him."

Frederick lay awake for most of that night, staring at the ceiling. Buy the place! The thought had never occurred to him. *But this is America,* he kept telling himself. Such things were possible here. By the time the early-morning sun crept across the bedroom window, his head was filled with plans. It was that night, with no ceremony or certificate required, that my grandfather finally became a true American.

He began to save every cent he could. Rather than joining his customers in convivial drinks, he pocketed his tips. Here and there he denied himself small pleasures. The pain of forbearance was sweetened by the thought that one day, the Nick-Nack would be his. Money accumulated in a small jar that he hid beneath a floorboard in the bedroom. But too slowly.

"It's hopeless," he complained to Kliever one evening as they stood at the end of the pier. "I'll never save enough money."

"Of course you won't," agreed Kliever. "You'll be dead long before, the amount

Becker pays you."

Frederick stared out across the Missouri River. "What am I going to do?"

"Have you still got that medal?" asked Kliever after a moment. "The one that belonged to Jette's grandfather?"

"Of course."

"Can you get off work this weekend?"

"Why do you ask?"

Kliever buttoned up his fly. "Come by the house first thing on Saturday morning," he said. "And bring that medal with you."

At sunrise the following Saturday, Frederick kissed Jette good-bye as she lay sleepily in their bed and walked to the Klievers' house. The medal was hidden in his pocket. The previous evening he had quietly removed it from the back of the chest of drawers where Jette kept it. He was sure that whatever Johann Kliever had in mind, she would not approve.

Outside the Klievers' house, a horse stood waiting, attached to a small buggy. Johann was loading bags into the back. He waved as Frederick approached.

"Got the medal?" he asked.

Frederick nodded. "Where are we going?"

"You'll see," said Kliever. "Come on." He climbed up onto the buggy and took the reins. Moments later the horse was trotting through the town's empty streets.

As they drove south, the sun rose high in the sky, and a haze of heat shimmered on the road ahead of them. Frederick looked out at the passing countryside. Since their arrival in Beatrice, he had rarely left the town. The journey from Hanover had extinguished any appetite he might have had for travel. Now he felt the first stirrings of excitement at the prospect of discovering new places.

By mid-morning, the buggy was bouncing over the bridge that spanned the river at Jefferson City. The capitol building sat in imperial splendor on a bluff overlooking the banks of the Missouri. Kliever drove through the town and brought the horse to a stop in front of a row of shops. "That medal won't do you any good sitting in a sock underneath your bed," he said as he tethered the horse to a pole. "You need to make it work for you." Without another word he turned and pushed open the nearest door and went inside.

Frederick lingered on the sidewalk for a moment, wondering whether he should follow. A wooden screen had been erected in the shop window, obscuring the interior from curious eyes. The door opened and Kliever's head reappeared. "Come *on*," he said, blinking with impatience, and then vanished again. Frederick stepped inside.

The shop was long and narrow. Knotted floorboards ran the length of the room. Two gas lamps glowed dimly from the ceiling. There was a row of glass-fronted cabinets along one wall, each secured by a heavy padlock. Their shelves were crammed with a bewildering assortment of articles. A violin was propped up next to a crystal decanter. An oil painting depicting a hunting scene was flanked by a coiled necklace of tiny emeralds and a gold carriage clock, its hands long since stopped. And there were guns, more guns than Frederick had ever seen in his life.

Frederick made his way past the display cases. Kliever stood at the far end of the room. Behind a counter stood a tall, thin man in a dirty apron.

"So," said the man, his voice high and sharp, "this is the gentleman with the, ah, famous medal." His eyes bulged from his long, gaunt face.

"This is him," agreed Kliever. "Frederick, show this man your medal."

"Well, you know, it's not actually mine," began Frederick.

The man in the apron waved his long, bony hands in front of his face as if to shoo the words away. "I'm no attorney or nothing, but I always live by the principle that possession is nine-tenths of the law. Let's see what you have."

Hesitantly Frederick reached into his pocket and laid the medal on the countertop. The shopkeeper bent down to examine it. "And this was awarded by the Kaiser himself?"

Frederick nodded. "My wife's grandfather was a general, during the war with France."

The man looked skeptical. "Can you prove it?"

Kliever reached across the countertop and snatched the medal back. "Plenty of other places we can try," he said.

"All right, all right." The man wiped his fingers anxiously on his apron. "You can't blame a man for wanting to establish due provenance. May I see the item again?"

Kliever placed the medal back on the countertop. As the shopkeeper reached for it, Kliever grabbed his fingers. "Offer a fair price," he said, "or I'll break every bone in your rotten body." Before the man could reply, Kliever twisted his hand sharply downward. The shopkeeper fell to his knees with a cry. "How much will you give for it?"

From behind the counter came a muffled moan, half swallowed by fear. The man named a figure so high that Frederick thought he must have misheard.

Kliever's giant knuckles paled as he tightened his grip. There was a terrified sob. "Please," said the shopkeeper. "I don't want no trouble. Take what you —"

"We don't want to rob you," said Kliever irritably. "We just want a fair price." He gave another squeeze of encouragement, which drew another yelp of pain. The man gasped another figure, twice as much as his first offer. Kliever looked at Frederick. "Well?" he said.

The amount and the method that had been employed to arrive at it left Frederick speechless. He gave a helpless shrug. Kliever grunted. "All right, then." He released his grip. The shopkeeper's hand slithered off the counter, out of sight. "Get the money," growled Kliever.

Without saying another word the man retreated into a back room. Moments later he returned with a fistful of notes. As Frederick watched the shopkeeper deal the money onto the countertop, his shock was mutely shuffled away to some distant corner of his consciousness.

He understood what this was.

It was his chance.

Soon afterward Frederick and Kliever

climbed back onto the buggy. Rather than returning across the bridge, however, Kliever pointed the horse west.

"We're not going home?" said Frederick.

Kliever looked at him. "Do you think I'd drive all this way just to pawn your medal?"

"I have no idea," admitted Frederick.

"Where we're going, you need capital to invest," explained Kliever. "Now you have it."

"Where are we going, then?"

"You'll see."

Frederick sat back and tried not to think about what Jette would say. The banknotes in his pocket crinkled with possibility, but with each whisper of promise came an echo of apprehension.

They headed toward the Ozark Mountains. By late afternoon Kliever had still given no explanation as to where they were going. Finally he pulled the horse off the main road onto a gravel path that they followed for several miles. Despite the remoteness of the location, they suddenly found themselves surrounded by people. Men, ill-shaven and dressed in clothes dirtied by the day's labor, were engaged in animated debate, all headed in the same direction. Kliever pulled his hat down over his eyes and directed the horse past the ambling crowds.

They arrived in a clearing in which a mass of people had already assembled. The focus of activity was centered beneath the boughs of an enormous oak tree, where two squares had been marked out by rope and wooden stakes, one inside the other. Men were exchanging fistfuls of money for hastily scribbled notes. Most of the crowd were laborers, but Frederick also saw the uniforms of professional men. There were women there, too, and he had lived long enough in a big city to recognize what sort of women they were. He looked at Kliever. "What sort of event brings whores and lawyers out into the middle of the countryside?"

"The manly art," answered Kliever. He put up his fists and threw a mock punch.

"A *prize fight?*"

"With excellent odds."

"Yes, but —"

"Don't worry. I know the right man. Come on."

Frederick followed Kliever through the crowd. Perched high up in the branches of nearby trees, men gazed down at the ring, waiting for the fight to begin.

"They'll have the best view," said Frederick, pointing up.

"They're not up there to watch the fight," said Kliever. "They're keeping a lookout

126

for the police." He saw Frederick's expression. "When men fight each other these days, they're supposed to wear gloves," he explained.

"This is illegal?"

"In theory." Kliever looked around him. "But there are several policemen here, I'm sure. They enjoy a good scrap better than most." He walked through the crowd toward a small, rat-like man in a tweed suit, who was perspiring freely in the warmth of the evening. An ugly smile appeared on his face as he saw Kliever approach.

"Ah, Mr. Kliever," he said. "You'll have your usual wager, I presume? Today I can offer you a hundred to forty." His little eyes glinted. "*Very* generous, you'll agree."

Kliever grunted and produced his own bundle of notes. The bookmaker quickly counted the money and wrote him a receipt. He turned his attention to Frederick.

"And you, sir?" he asked. "Will you have the same?"

Frederick's fingers curled protectively around the money in his pocket and he silently cursed his stupidity. An unlawful bet! He shook his head. "I am sorry," he said stiffly. "I cannot wager my money. I do not even know who is fighting."

The man laughed. "You're unsure who

to back?" he chuckled. "Mr. Kliever, who would you suggest?"

Kliever looked away for a moment, his eyes searching for the boxing ring beneath the oak tree. Then he turned back to Frederick and said, "Me."

Moments later Frederick was following Kliever toward the ring, clutching the book-maker's receipt. He had been so surprised that he handed over all his money without another word of protest.

"This lad today is a local boy, very popular," Kliever was saying as he marched ahead. "Butcher's apprentice. He's strong and quick, but young. He's not done much fighting yet. Still learning." There was an unfamiliar steel in his voice. "I'll teach him a thing or two."

They arrived at the outer rope of the boxing ring, which was patrolled by a team of burly-looking men. All around them the crowd was raucous, fired up by excitement and the afternoon heat. Kliever took off his hat and threw it over the ropes. When it landed on the beaten-down grass in the inner ring, the crowd erupted, a huge roar in their throats.

Kliever stepped through the ropes and pulled off his shirt. The cries of the men around him were so loaded with venom and hostility that for a moment Frederick forgot about the money that he would never see again; instead he began to fear for his friend's life. Kliever looked calmly at the baying pack beyond the outer ropes. He produced a red and yellow handkerchief from his pocket and tied it to a corner stake of the inner ring. A moment later, a second hat landed in the ring. The crowd's attention quickly shifted from Kliever to the newcomer, who was climbing through the ropes, already stripped to the waist. The new arrival was a massive hulk of humanity, a sculpture of rippling muscle and menace. His body seemed designed for violence. His hands were the size of ham hocks. He pulled out his own handkerchief to delirious cries of approval. Kliever watched impassively as his opponent tied his colors to the opposite corner stake.

A third man stepped into the ring. He paraded around the perimeter with his hands in the air until the crowd had subsided into a restless silence.

"Good people," he cried, "there is nothing finer than the spectacle of two men fighting a bare-knuckled combat." The crowd murmured its approval. The man held up an imperious finger. "Now, mark my words.

There are those among us who believe that they know best how we Americans should comport ourselves. There are those among us who believe that it is their duty to decide what is right and what is wrong, what is good and what is not. There are those among us who seek to eliminate freedoms that are rightfully ours. I speak of those interfering busybodies who malinger in our state's legislative chambers." At this there was a chorus of enthusiastic booing. "As you know," continued the man, his voice rising, "our Congress, which represents no man *I* know, has outlawed this, our most cherished sport." The jeers grew louder. "Without ever seeing a punch thrown, the politicians *have banned our prize ring,*" shouted the man. "Those ignorant idiots have made criminals out of you and me. But we are here. And to that, these precious dandies of so many useless words have *no response.*"

The man moved to the center of the ring and stretched his arms out toward the corners where the two fighters stood. "Tonight we witness the glorious pugilistic traditions of these United States of America, pitted against the low cunning and devilish subterfuge that infests the prize ring on foreign shores." The man turned toward Kliever with a dramatic sneer. "Showing colors of red and yellow, known for his slippery German guile — the *Hun*."

The crowd howled its disapproval. Kliever stood motionless in his corner, listening impassively to the crescendo of hate. Frederick felt his skin crawl. The announcer allowed the crowd to vent its collective spleen before going on. "Against him, showing the colors of our hometown, a new young master of the fistic arts, our very own Butcher Boy, the still undefeated James McCready." Kliever's opponent raised his fists in salute, acknowledging the loud applause.

"We are not interested here in the prettified rules of engagement of that English fop, the Marquis of Queensberry," the announcer continued. "*This* fight shall be conducted in accordance with the London Prize Ring rules of 1838, to wit: no head-butting, eye-gouging, hair-pulling, or neck-throttling. The fighters have agreed that Mr. Abe Vanderzee will act as referee." The man took off his hat. "And now I give you — *the Butcher Boy and the Hun*." He clambered out of the inner ring, and Kliever and McCready approached the grassy center of the square. They shook hands amid a cacophony of booing and cheering. The referee, who was watching from the safety of the ropes, called for the contest to begin.

Frederick could barely bring himself to watch. The Butcher Boy came out with his huge fists swinging, two ferocious cyclones of menace. For the first few rounds Kliever weaved and bobbed, dodging the younger man's attacks with surprising agility. Mc-Cready would just need to land one square punch for the fight to be over. But as each round ended without a meaningful blow being landed, the Butcher Boy and his followers began to get restless. Spurred on by the crowd, McCready continued to attack Kliever, but his fists scythed through the air, chasing shadows. As his opponent stepped in close, Kliever began to pick off telling blows as McCready left his upper body undefended. Round after round, Kliever's punches were beginning to make themselves felt. The sustained ferocity of his initial offensive had exhausted the Butcher Boy. The crowd watched in sullen dejection as Kliever began to assert his superiority. In the seventeenth round his right fist caught McCready on the cheek, an inch below the eye, and opened a jagged wound. Blood began to pour down the young man's face and onto his chest. His left eye soon swelled into a gruesome blue-black envelope of mottled flesh. Dazed by the pain, the Butcher Boy began to bellow a forlorn lament like a stricken bull. His cries echoed across the field as he charged blindly at Kliever. The crowd watched in silence as Kliever's fists exacted their due. McCready staggered around the ring, blinded by his own blood. In between rounds his seconds pleaded with him to give up, but he refused, rising unsteadily to take more punishment. After ninety minutes of fighting, Kliever had begun to knock his opponent down at will, but on each occasion the Butcher Boy hauled himself back to his feet, refusing to concede defeat in front of his home crowd. Many in the audience, though, had seen enough. Men began to leave the field, shaking their heads.

Finally the Butcher Boy's seconds gave up talking to their man. Instead they moved around the ring and begged Kliever to finish the fight quickly. Kliever's face remained expressionless. The following round, he swiftly sidestepped McCready's next lumbering charge and caught the young man in a headlock. Then, with a succession of slow, deliberate blows, Kliever calmly pulverized his opponent's undefended face into a ghoulish hollow of crushed bone and decimated cartilage. Finally he released his grip and the body of the Butcher Boy fell to the grass. The referee did not need to conduct a formal count. He climbed into the ring and raised the arm of the victor into the air. It was only when Frederick saw the dark blood glistening on Kliever's knuckles that he remembered that he had won his bet.

On the journey back to Beatrice, Kliever explained how the system worked.

"I travel all over the state, and sometimes beyond," he said. "The fights are arranged by local bookmakers. The trick is to put forward a local man and talk up his prospects. People always want the next champion to be from their hometown. Once the whole place is chattering about his chances, the bookies can offer short odds on his winning, but they'll still have enough takers to make it worth their while."

"Then you turn up," said Frederick.

Kliever nodded. "They find a better fighter from out of town, someone that nobody knows. They offer long odds on him, so nobody is tempted to back him. When the local hero loses, they make a fortune."

"But *you* bet on yourself."

Kliever nodded. "Sometimes they offer to pay me a flat fee, but I prefer it this way. They give me generous odds. They can afford to."

The two men were silent for a while.

"I was scared," admitted Frederick.

"By the fight?"

"And the crowd."

"Oh, they're harmless enough. Men like to watch other men fight, that's all."

They stopped again in Jefferson City to redeem Jette's medal. That night, while his wife slept, Frederick returned it to its hiding place at the back of the chest of drawers. Then he added a fat roll of banknotes to the jar that lay hidden beneath the bedroom floorboard.

Frederick began to accompany Kliever to all his fights. Each time he bet larger amounts, taking whatever odds he was offered. Kliever continued to win. Before long he needed a second jar. Prizefights continued until one of the fighters was knocked unconscious or conceded defeat. Kliever could have won most of his fights in a matter of minutes, but the bookmakers wanted the contests to go on for at least an hour. Too obvious a mismatch would have been bad for business; they wanted the punters to believe that their man had stood a chance. And so Kliever would play with his unsuspecting victims like a cat toying with a mouse, until he decided to demolish them. Frederick was unnerved by the focused calm that descended on Kliever as he smashed his opponents into oblivion. He once ended a bout with a shower of blows of such brutality that his opponent was still lying where he had fallen an hour after the fight. A worried crowd surrounded the man's unmoving body as Kliever and Frederick climbed back into their buggy. Kliever had driven off without a backward glance. The journey home was made in silence.

Every dollar Frederick made was stained with the blood of the fighters who had been duped into climbing into the ring with Johann Kliever, blinded by false promises of victory and fame. But so fierce was my grandfather's desire to forge his own future that he learned to turn away from the gruesome cost of his good fortune — the beaten faces, ruptured organs, and crushed limbs of the defeated.

Punch by punch, fight by fight, his pile of money grew.

TEN

The cost of my grandfather's steadily accumulating nest egg lay not only in the bloody noses of strangers. A higher price was being paid closer to home.

Frederick could think of little else except the day that the Nick-Nack would be his. He spent all day and all night at the tavern, watching over his dreams, while Jette and the children waited for him to come home. He responded to his wife's attempts to engage him in any other topic of conversation with a peeved tolerance that drove her to despair. When she accused him of no longer caring about his family, Frederick was sullen and unapologetic. He had not abandoned them, he said stiffly; quite the opposite. He was investing in their future.

Soon they did nothing but fight. Resentment and disappointment soured even the simplest exchanges. Jette was unable to hide her scorn for Frederick's purported plan for the future. *What plan?* she demanded angrily.

It was a fair question. Frederick had not told her about all the money he had saved. He did not know how to explain where it had come from. He certainly did not want to tell her the truth.

He was ashamed of the truth.

Jette began to mourn the man she had fallen in love with, sadly remembering the bighearted beauty of his first words to her:

When it comes to dreams and fancies
and castles in the air,
I have the soul of a millionaire!

Now it seemed that dreams and fancies were no longer enough. Castles in the air could not compete with local real estate. Jette blamed America for hoodwinking Frederick with its empty, rotten promises.

Then a letter came from Hanover.

She did not recognize the handwriting on the envelope. She tore it open and scanned the single sheet of paper within. The letter was from a lawyer. The sentences came, one after the other, heavy with formal regret. From that unyielding thicket of dry, legal prose: her parents were dead.

Jette's mother had suffered a violent heart attack two months previously. Her father

138

had followed her shortly afterward, precise cause of death still unknown. The lawyer, charged by the court with the administration of the couple's estate, had discovered boxes of Jette's letters while compiling an inventory of their assets. Her mother had not thrown a single one away.

The news knocked the fight out of her.

There were no more angry confrontations. Silence descended on my family's house.

Joseph watched as his parents sank into their embattled stalemate. All he knew was that there was no more singing, no more laughter. Frederick had become a spectral presence, flitting in and out of the house under cover of night. Joseph stood at the closed bedroom door and listened to Jette sob into her pillow. He understood that the world as he knew it was coming to a messy end. He became a serious, unsmiling boy, haunted by his parents' sadness, sure that he was somehow to blame.

Once a month Frederick visited Frau Bloomberg's house for one of Joseph's music lessons. He listened to his son sing, with equal amounts of astonishment and pleasure. At the end of each session he stood and applauded, and then he opened his arms. This was the moment that Joseph waited for. He ran to his father and held on to him as tightly as he could. He would remember every sensation of that embrace — his face squashed against the rough fabric of Frederick's trousers, his almost unbearable happiness for those few, sweet moments — for the rest of his life.

Soon after Joseph's ninth birthday, Frederick and Riva Bloomberg decided that he was ready for his first public performance. They agreed that he should sing "Addio del passato," Violetta's mournful aria from *La Traviata,* at the Nick-Nack's next opera night. Joseph practiced for weeks, polishing every phrase of Verdi's melody until it shone. Thanks to Frau Bloomberg's inventive translations, he was under the impression that he was singing about a small dog that had fallen down a well, rather than the wreckage of a doomed love affair. Joseph was fond of dogs, as Frau Bloomberg knew. The plight of the fictional mutt added an emotional edge to his performance, and the effect was mesmerizing.

Frederick made Joseph and Riva Bloomberg promise to say nothing of their plans to Jette. He wanted to surprise her. Opera nights were now the only time she ever set foot in the Nick-Nack.

On the evening of the concert, Jette and

the children stood at the back of the room, watching Frederick perform. At the end of the recital, Frederick bowed to acknowledge the crowd's applause, and then held up his hands for silence. "Ladies and gentlemen," he began, "you are good enough to come here and listen to me sing my little songs. But tonight I am pleased to introduce you to a young man who has more talent in his little finger than I have in my whole body. He has never sung in front of an audience before." Frederick looked across the room and smiled. "Ladies and gentlemen, I present — Joseph Meisenheimer."

Joseph began to make his way through the crowd, his excitement growing with every step.

Over the course of the last few weeks, he had convinced himself that his performance that night would make his parents happy again. He would sing his song, and, overwhelmed with love and pride, Frederick and Jette would collapse into each other's arms. The miserable chill of the past year would be forgotten. It was the prospect of their reconciliation that excited him as he clambered up onto the stage. Joseph arrived at his father's side, shyly took his hand, and then, finally, turned with a hopeful grin toward Jette.

She was not there.

■ ■ ■ ■

As Jette had watched Joseph weave through the crowd, she knew at once that she could not, would not, watch him sing. She had no wish to see her son become another singer of songs before an audience of drunks. At once she began pulling Rosa toward the exit. A path cleared in front of her. As she reached the door, a hand touched her elbow.

"Jette," said Frederick. "Where are you going?"

"I'm not going to listen to this," said Jette angrily. "Don't expect me to —"

"Jette, please. Come back and hear your son sing."

She shook her head. "No."

"He has the most beautiful voice I've ever heard. I swear, the birds stop to listen."

Jette struggled to contain her fury. "Why didn't you tell me you were planning this?"

Frederick's face crumpled in disappointment. "I wanted to *surprise* you," he said.

Jette turned and looked across the room. Joseph stood in the middle of the stage, watching them. He had never looked so alone.

"Up there is no place for a small boy," she said.

"But his voice. It's a miracle. Up there is

where he needs to be."

"No, Frederick. Up there is where *you* need him to be." Before he could reply, she pushed open the door and left.

Frederick made his way back through the crowd to where his son stood.

"She's gone," whispered Joseph.

"But you'll still sing, won't you?" asked Frederick. He smiled weakly and put his hand on Joseph's shoulder. "We don't want to let these good people down, do we?"

The boy stared at the tavern door.

"Joseph?"

"Yes, Papa?"

"Are you ready?"

Joseph looked toward the piano, where Riva Bloomberg was eyeing him over the top of her music. The whole town was listening — except for the one person who mattered. He gave a small, mournful nod.

"Good boy." Frederick patted him on the back and retreated to the side of the stage. The opening notes of the piano accompaniment floated into the room. Joseph readied himself to deliver the first line.

When he opened his mouth to sing, no noise came out.

Riva Bloomberg faltered, and eventually subsided into silence. Prompted by Frederick's gestures, she tentatively played the introduction again. Once more Joseph took a deep breath, and again the audience watched the words form silently on his lips.

After four bars, Riva Bloomberg's fingers finally stilled. In the silence Joseph stared over the heads of the audience toward the tavern door. Finally Frederick stepped onto the stage and led his son away.

The following morning the citizens of Beatrice gravely addressed these events. People recounted the episode, shaking their heads at the strangeness of it all. The image of Joseph Meisenheimer, soundlessly opening and closing his mouth like a marooned goldfish, gripped the town.

The odd thing was that Joseph could still sing like an angel. He continued with his lessons, and in private his voice still made Riva Bloomberg weep. Joseph could not explain what had happened that night. A few months later, they agreed to try again, but the same thing happened. Joseph silently mouthed phrases, his chest heaving with effort. That was when Frederick decided that enough was enough.

Dr. Becker examined Joseph and concluded that there was nothing physically wrong with him. Of course there wasn't. It was simply that every time he was confronted with an audience, no matter how small, the memory of Jette's face looking at him across the crowd arose unbidden, and caught the notes in his throat. This was Joseph's tragedy: all that beauty, hidden from the world. It was our tragedy, too, in a way, for it was his silence that condemned us to our own peculiar musical fate.

Even though the rest of the town couldn't stop talking about it, Frederick and Jette never discussed what had happened that night. The house fell back into its old uncomfortable silence.

While Joseph was embarked on his futile attempt to engineer Frederick and Jette's reconciliation through song, his sister exploited her parents' disharmony to advance her own agenda. She played her parents with unblinking virtuosity, orchestrating conflict, whipping up maelstroms of guilt, agitating for favors. Frederick and Jette were too unhappy to realize what she was doing.

Rosa's manipulation of her parents was an act of desperation, not malice. The three years that separated her from her brother — three years that Joseph had had Frederick and Jette all to himself, in the full-beamed glare of their adoration — were a torment she could not stand. She believed herself second-best, an afterthought. In Rosa's imagination, her inferior status was as real as the fingers on her hand. And so she set about her family, pulling them this way and that, trying to make them love her more.

One afternoon a few months after Joseph's disastrous evening at the Nick-Nack, Rosa came in from playing in the yard, complaining of a headache. By the evening she was writhing in sheets sodden with sweat, her face as gray as stone. The following morning there were flecks of blood on her pillow and an angry rash across her chest. Dr. Becker was summoned. His sober diagnosis: typhus. Before long the only sound in the house was the rasp of air shuttling in and out of Rosa's fragile lungs as she fought for each breath. Every morning the doctor appeared by her bedside while Frederick and Jette hovered anxiously behind him. After his examination, the three adults would confer in grave murmurs. As the illness wrung her young body into exhausted defeat, here, finally, was the evidence Rosa had been craving, proof that her parents *did* love her, after all.

Dr. Becker had told Frederick and Jette that Rosa would be dead within a month, but he had not counted on my aunt's formidable willpower. Rosa was never going to allow herself to die — not *now*, after she had finally witnessed the love and affection that she had dreamed of for so long. She began to fight the disease. Three weeks later she was cheerfully sitting up in her bed, eating like a horse. Becker declared her a medical miracle. Rosa watched her mother's tears of gratitude, and felt a warm glow of happiness inside her.

It did not last long. Once she was healthy again, Rosa was appalled to discover that there were no more anxious bedside conferences, no more covert looks of worry, no more tears. She had much preferred the haunted, red-eyed look that her mother had worn during her illness.

Poor Rosa! She had been offered a tantalizing glimpse of everything she had longed for, only for life to return to its old, intolerable ways. Naturally enough, she did everything she could to make herself sick again. She foraged for toadstools in the woods and ate them where she found them. When that didn't work, she started licking anywhere she thought germs might be lurking — dirty floors, the soles of other people's shoes. More than once Joseph found his sister furtively running her tongue over mud-encrusted rocks from the yard, her eyes squeezed shut in hope and disgust. Every winter Rosa would stay outside in the snow as long as she could, woefully underdressed, courting influenza. She hovered outside Dr. Becker's consulting rooms, hoping to give a home to a stray virus. When, to her fury, she remained resolutely healthy, she tried a different approach, and began to concoct symptoms. Her first attempts at such medical dissembling were betrayed by an unchecked melodramatic streak that she had inherited from Frederick. The spectacle of her obviously healthy daughter thrashing around gibbering deathbed hysterics three times a week quickly alerted Jette to her scheme.

But even if her parents were not fooled, Rosa eventually began to believe her own fantasies. She became convinced that she really *was* ill. Dr. Becker's heart sank whenever he saw her in the waiting room, always with the same purposeful look on her young face.

It wasn't just her parents' affection that Rosa craved. She adored her brother, too. But while Frederick and Jette's indifference toward her was simply a figment of her imagination, with Joseph it was real enough. Rosa was a loud, complicating presence in Joseph's life, and he wanted nothing to do with her. His antipathy toward her manifested itself in a campaign of sly provocation. He pinched her, poked her, and pulled her hair. He called her names that he did not understand himself. He hid her toys, or put them in plain sight where she could not reach them.

Rosa suffered these cruel indignities in hurt silence. Joseph's antics frequently left her in tears, but not once did she run tattling to Jette — she did not want to get him in trouble. For she loved her brother more than anyone else, deeply and forever.

Joseph was perplexed to discover that there was nothing he could do to dampen his sister's affection for him. The meaner he was, the more she begged him to play with her. Rosa suffered his hostilities without a murmur of complaint, and he found that her occasional tears were an insufficient return for all the effort he put into making her miserable. And then, to his horror, those same tears began to make him feel guilty.

In the end, Joseph capitulated. He stopped pinching her and grudgingly began to accept her as a playmate. Rosa was in raptures. There was only one problem. While Joseph was prepared to play with his sister in the privacy of the little bedroom that they shared, he refused to let her join in his elaborate games with Stefan. They didn't need a pesky girl tagging along with them on their adventures through the woods. Rosa begged to be included, promising that she wouldn't get in their way. Stefan listened to her desperate entreaties with an amused glint in his eye, but said nothing. Joseph just waved her away, embarrassed and impatient to be off.

My aunt never gave up; she would continue to plead with the boys until they got bored with her. Then they would escape by running the length of the yard and disappearing into the forest with a gleeful holler of triumph. Rosa could never keep up with them. She chased them as far as the maple tree, but by then they were already long gone. She leaned against the trunk while she regained her breath, and used her shirtsleeve to wipe her tears away.

ELEVEN

In the summer of 1914, while Frederick and Jette struggled to maintain a grip on their own fragile peace, an assassin's bullet pushed Europe toward the abyss of hell. Even the *Beatrice Optimist,* proud peddler of parochial tittle-tattle, turned its gaze to the dark clouds gathering on the other side of the Atlantic. With every passing day its headlines grew starker, until one morning in August came the dread words WAR IN EUROPE.

As Germany mobilized its military and swept through Belgium and into northern France, President Wilson declared the United States' neutrality in the coming conflict. For three days in September the Allies defended the Germans' first drive into France, both sides sustaining dreadful casualties. Frederick could not look away. Men he had known, old colleagues and schoolmates, would be lining up to go into

151

battle. In neutral America, he cheered every German victory, willing his old country on.

And he was not alone. At prizefights, the Hun's arrival in the ring was now met with patriotic cheers as onlookers celebrated their German heritage. The bookmakers ended their arrangement with Kliever, their lucrative scheme spoiled by proud immigrants betting on the wrong man. War, it turned out, was bad for the fight business.

By that stage, Frederick had amassed sufficient funds to make Dr. Becker an offer both for the Nick-Nack and the house. The amount represented a good return on the doctor's original investment, and he agreed immediately. To Frederick's relief, he did not ask where the money had come from.

And so, on May 7, 1915, thanks largely to the illegal thuggery of Johann Kliever, Frederick became the sole proprietor of his own business, and a proud homeowner. That night at the Nick-Nack, William Henry Harris played the piano. Frederick refused to take a cent for drinks all evening. It should have been the proudest day of his life, but as he stood behind the bar and surveyed his prize, his heart was full of regret.

Jette was not there.

It was not her fault. She did not know what

he had done that day. Frederick had still not found a way to tell her.

The following morning, two words on the front of the newspaper changed everything, forever:

LUSITANIA SUNK

Frederick stood in the middle of the tavern and stared numbly at the headline. The British passenger ship had been attacked by a German U-boat eight miles off the coast of Ireland. A single torpedo hit the ship's starboard side. She sank in under an hour.

Over twelve hundred civilian casualties were reported.

One hundred and twenty-eight of them were American.

In the end there was no rush to war. Woodrow Wilson chose the diplomatic solution, demanding German assurances that the atrocity would never be repeated. The two countries brokered an uneasy truce, but everyone knew that the Germans were the enemy now. In Beatrice, people hardly knew where to look. The war was no longer a topic of animated conversation at the Nick-Nack; now men skirted uneasily around the subject. German was rarely spoken in public anymore.

For nearly two years the sinking of the *Lusitania* cast its shadow over the country. Then, in March of 1917, three American ships were destroyed by U-boats. On April 6, Woodrow Wilson announced that the United States was at war with Germany.

In Beatrice the news was met almost with relief. The townspeople were suddenly overcome by patriotic delirium. Overnight the streets became a fluttering sea of red, white, and blue. Merchants festooned their shops with flags and balloons. A seventy-foot flagpole was erected in the main square and Old Glory was hoisted into the sky, cheered on by a crowd of hundreds. A parade in support of the war marched through the town. Beneath the disapproving glare of Beatrice Eitzen, citizens assembled in front of the courthouse. The mayor praised the president's courage and fortitude; he gave thanks to the Lord for the freedoms that America had been blessed with; he roundly damned the Germans for their cowardly attacks, and vowed that with the might of the United States now amassed against it, the enemy would be crushed without pity or remorse. Frederick applauded every line. Next to him, Jette silently held Rosa's hand, paralyzed by fear. All around her, men threw their hats into the air, cheering the imminent destruction of her homeland.

The people's enthusiasm for the war effort did not abate. Sacrifices were willingly made. America now had troops to feed: farmers were encouraged to maximize production of crops and livestock for the hungry armies fighting in Europe. Families signed food pledges, promising to eat less. Empty stomachs rumbled proudly. Men invested their savings in government war bonds while their wives sewed patriotic garlands late into the night.

It did not take long for the atmosphere of hysterical patriotism to mutate into something more sinister. Fear was put to work. Leaflets encouraged citizens to inform on others who might harbor sympathies for the enemy. Americans fell upon their own language, hunting down sinister words. Sauerkraut was renamed Liberty Cabbage. Frankfurters became hot dogs. In St. Louis, a man defended Germany in an argument, and a furious mob stripped him naked and dragged him through the streets. Then they lynched him. The people of Beatrice shuddered and hung out another American flag.

Frederick decorated the Nick-Nack with yards of bunting, inside and out. The old

German folk tunes disappeared from the musical repertoire. Now people wanted songs forged in America, tales of frontier bravery and derring-do. Each evening ended with the national anthem. The audience would gravely stumble to their feet and listen as the night's band — no matter how unlikely the agglomeration of instruments — wheezed their way through "The Star-Spangled Banner." Frederick liked the version played by William Henry Harris the best. The pianist performed the tune straight and true, shorn of embellishment or syncopated trickery. Beneath his fingers it became stately and dignified, and bursting with hope. When he heard those first notes ring out through the room, Frederick would stand to attention and put his hand on his chest, and he could feel his heart beating its own celebratory rhythm within him.

Every day the newspaper was full of stories of the drive for new recruits. In June the United States Congress introduced the draft for all American men between the ages of twenty-one and thirty-one. By then Frederick was thirty-nine years old. In the opinion of the government he was too old to fight, but every day spent safely stationed behind the bar of the Nick-Nack weighed on his conscience. The words of Joseph Wall kept echoing through his head. Frederick wanted to be a good American.

One night at the end of the pier, he said, "It's strange to think that if I'd stayed in Hanover I would have spent the last three years fighting."

Johann Kliever looked at him sideways. "No, you wouldn't. You're too old. Children make better cannon fodder."

"You know what I mean. Over here, we're out of harm's way."

"Thank God. This lunatic war."

Frederick looked out over the water. "American boys are fighting now."

Kliever grunted. "Poor beggars."

There was a long pause. "We could always volunteer," said Frederick.

"I'm not volunteering for a damned thing," growled Kliever. "And neither are you."

"Our country is at *war,* Johann."

Kliever was silent for several moments. "You're serious," he said.

Frederick nodded.

"Well, if the Germans don't kill you," said Kliever with a grimace, "your wife surely will."

The following afternoon, Frederick came home early from the Nick-Nack. The children were playing outside. Jette was washing

157

clothes at the kitchen sink.

"You're home early," she said without looking around. As usual, she spoke in German. "Is something the matter?"

Frederick answered her in English. "Jette, we must talk."

She gave a small snort and continued to soap the clothes. Frederick watched her work for several minutes, saying nothing. He recognized every gesture his wife made, and yet he no longer knew this woman before him. A sudden sadness threatened to unstitch him, there and then.

"So talk," she said eventually.

Frederick sighed and switched to German. "I've been thinking about this war."

Jette paused for the briefest of moments, and then continued to scrub. "What about it?" she said.

"I feel so helpless."

"Helpless?"

"We're so far away from everything that's going on," said Frederick.

"Wouldn't you say that was a good thing?"

"Perhaps. But hanging out flags and singing the national anthem every night doesn't feel like enough."

She stopped her work and turned toward him. "What do you mean?"

"What I say. It's not enough."

"What more *could* you do?"

"I could volunteer. Sign up to fight."

Jette turned back to the sink. "You won't do that," she said.

Up until that moment Frederick had been cautiously circling the idea, unsure what he would do. But suddenly he knew. "Yes I will," he said sadly.

Jette turned to face him. "You cannot do this," she said. "You cannot bring us here and then *leave*."

"But Jette, I'll come back."

"Millions have died already. Why should you be any different?"

"Things will change now that America has joined the war."

Jette stared at him. "Do you think taking that oath made you *immortal*? You're still only flesh and blood. The bullets will still kill you." She stepped toward him and put a hand up to his cheek. "Where did you go, Frederick?" she asked. "Where's the man I fell in love with?"

He gazed back at her unhappily. "I'm still here."

Jette's hand dropped back down to her side.

They stood there in an agony of silence. Finally Frederick spoke. "Jette, I have to go and fight."

"But we need you *here*."

"Oh, let's not pretend. You don't need me for anything."

Jette began to cry. "And so you're running away?" she said, pushing an angry fist across her eyes. "If you're so keen to fight, why not stay and fight for your marriage?"

Frederick looked sadly at his wife. "Because I don't know if there's anything left to fight for." Without another word he turned and left the house.

Jette remained where she was. As she leaned heavily against the kitchen table, she knocked an empty bowl to the floor. Then, with one angry sweep of her arm, she pushed all the china off the table. Cups, saucers, bowls, and plates fell to the ground in a terrible crash. Not one piece remained intact. She sank to the floor, surrounded by the broken china, and let out a long wail of grief.

Joseph had been standing unseen at the kitchen door, listening. His mother's cry of pain was a sound he would never forget.

Frederick walked to the Nick-Nack, scarcely feeling the ground beneath his feet. He tried to bury his dismay beneath the drudgery of chores.

Jette didn't understand. Going to fight for his adopted country would root his family in this soil. America had welcomed him in, and had asked for nothing in return. But there was a debt to be paid, and he intended to pay it.

That evening Frederick walked back from the Nick-Nack alone. He had poured every drink as if it were his last. On his way home he stood at the end of the pier, listening to the waters of the Missouri rushing beneath his feet, and wondered whether he would ever hear that sound again.

When he arrived at the house, the front door was locked. He tried the door to the kitchen, but it would not yield, either. Frederick stood in the darkness and shivered. Jette had made her feelings clear. He crossed the yard and opened the door of the outhouse. He settled at an uncomfortable angle across the floor, his legs propped up against the wooden commode that he had installed during their first summer there. He lay awake for what felt like hours, staring at the ceiling.

By the time the first soft whispers of morning woke him, Frederick was so stiff that he could barely move. Gingerly he crept back to the house and tried the doors again. They were still locked. He peered through the window. There was no sign of movement inside.

"Jette!" he whispered, his face pressed up against the window. "Let me in, please."

There was no reply.

"I have to talk to you," Frederick said through the glass. "I need to make you understand."

Inside, Jette sat hidden in the shadows and watched her husband mouth words she could not hear.

Frederick finally gave up. He turned away from his home and made his way through the early-morning streets. A military recruitment station had been opened in an unused building behind the courthouse. The door was locked there, too. He had to wait for an hour before a clerk arrived, keys jangling, to let him in.

He spent the morning filling out forms, trying to forget his family waking up without him on the other side of town. He had never, he realized sadly, even said good-bye to his children. Well, he told himself, there will be plenty of time to explain when I return. I'll make it up to them then.

That afternoon he and a few other men were driven to the nearest railway station, where they joined conscripts from other small towns on a train that took them to Kansas City, where their military training would begin. Men stared out the windows, lost in their private thoughts. As the train rattled through the flat Missouri countryside, Frederick borrowed some paper from his neighbor and began to write a letter home.

TWELVE

After she had silently watched Frederick knock on the kitchen window and then disappear, my grandmother began to make plans.

A few hours later, she marched down to the doctor's office, where Dr. Becker received her with a smile.

"How nice to see you, Jette," he said.

"He didn't tell you, then?" she said flatly.

Becker frowned. "Tell me what?"

"Frederick has volunteered for the army."

"Pardon?"

Jette nodded. "He's gone off to fight in this awful war."

The doctor laced his fingers together and looked at her thoughtfully. "How extraordinary," he said.

"I'm sorry he didn't tell you before he left."

"So am I," said Becker. "I would have told him what a fool he was."

"Too late for that." Jette's face was grim.

"I'm here to ask if I can take over his job at the Nick-Nack. I know I have no experience, but without his salary we have no means of support, and I don't know how —"

To her surprise, Becker started to chuckle. She stared at him. "Is something the matter?"

"It looks as if your dear husband has been keeping secrets from both of us," said the doctor.

That was how Jette learned that Frederick owned both the tavern and their home. She sat in Dr. Becker's office and wept, stung by his deception. And then she realized that she had kept secrets, too — she had never told Frederick about the death of her parents. All that was left was the silence of their untold truths.

Her sadness took her breath away.

Later that morning Jette made her way to the Nick-Nack. Polk was sweeping the floor as she entered.

"Well," she said, "he's gone."

There was a pause.

"I'm sorry," said Polk. "Who's gone?"

Jette looked around her. The last time she had been inside the Nick-Nack was the night of Joseph's ill-fated opera recital. "I suppose you imagine you'll be in charge now."

Polk's face was blank. "In charge?"

"There's no need to pretend anymore, Polk," Jette said, sighing. "It's happened. Frederick has gone."

At this Polk leaned weakly on the handle of his broom. "Gone *where?*"

The look of bewilderment on the old man's face seemed genuine enough. "He's gone to join the army. To fight," said Jette, more gently.

Polk's face crumpled. "But what about this place?"

"That's what I want to discuss with you. Now, I have no idea when Frederick will return. But until he gets back I'm going to help you. You will continue to do what you do best, which is to serve drinks. I'll do everything else. If you agree, I'll double your salary, starting today."

Polk remained completely still. His knuckles had whitened around the end of the broom handle.

For as long as he could remember, Polk's life had revolved around alcohol — the making of it, the serving of it, and the drinking of it. There had been women once, but a long time ago. They had all escaped in the end. One had married a cattle farmer and gone to live in a big house in Cooper County, where she'd had eleven children.

166

Another departed for Topeka soon after a young and over-ardent Polk had left a necklace of walnut-sized bite marks on her neck.

Then there had been Loretta Heismoth. Loretta was a farm girl with a hint of a mustache on her upper lip and legs as solid as tree trunks. Over the course of one blissful summer, in a secluded spot in one of her father's cornfields, she let Polk do more than any of the other girls had ever done. His hands had been allowed to wander a little farther on each fevered excursion. He dreamed constantly of what lay beneath the seemingly inexhaustible layers of Loretta's undergarments. Progress was tantalizing but slow. As fall closed in, Polk began to worry that his time was running out. It turned out that he was right, although not quite in the way he'd imagined.

Early one September morning, Loretta's gelding, Buster, was stung by a wasp on his hindquarters while she was cleaning out his stable. The horse lashed out with his hind legs just as she was bending down to shovel his droppings into a bucket. When they found Loretta some hours later, there was a perfect facsimile of a horseshoe in the middle of her forehead. It had been a closed casket service. Polk had sat in the church behind Loretta's family, and wept along with them.

His tears were born more from frustration than grief, but they were just as heartfelt.

This was more than fifty years ago. Polk had given up on women after that. There was more fidelity at the bottom of a bottle, less chance of humiliation in the next morning's hangover. Polk hadn't thought about romance for years — until Jette walked into the Nick-Nack that morning and turned his life upside down.

Perhaps the shock of Frederick's departure had momentarily lowered the ancient bartender's emotional defenses. Perhaps there was something about Jette's physical heft that reminded him of poor Loretta Heismoth. Whatever the reason, as he leaned against his broom, Polk felt the fingers of God brush lightly over his soul. He had seen my grandmother many times before, of course. She had often come to the tavern for Frederick's musical performances. Then she had stood quietly at the back of the room, never emerging from out of her husband's shadow. Now, though! She had stepped into the light, a life force of impossible loveliness. Jette stood by the bar, impatiently waiting for an answer. Something slipped within him.

"Yes, Frau Meisenheimer," he croaked.

"Good. Thank you." Jette was calm, all business. "Let's see, we have a few hours before we open. Perhaps it would be best if we started with the prices."

Helpless to resist the quiet dignity of this little speech, Polk fell in love. Jette was twice his size, forty years younger, and married to his boss: the noble futility of it all was irresistible. He saw the chance for one final, doomed waltz with heartache.

In some ways, Polk was an incurable romantic. He understood that it was the act of loving, not of being loved, that mattered. He would keep his infatuation to himself. Besides, he had come to like and respect Frederick. Perhaps falling in love with his wife, if done correctly, might be considered a compliment. A beatific calm settled upon him. His unilateral adoration for Jette Meisenheimer would be a final, cleansing absolution. And, once in a while, he would bathe in the heroic misery of it all.

So Polk became a silent foot soldier of love, trudging onward with his exquisite burden. He spent the rest of the day explaining to Jette how the Nick-Nack was run. Her gaze made him stammer and blush like a young boy. Soon he was yearning for the first customer to walk through the door and rescue him. More than anything, he needed a drink.

When Polk collapsed at the end of that

first night, he fell further and harder than he had ever fallen before.

Jette had been sure that the Nick-Nack's customers would be horrified when they heard that Frederick had volunteered for the army. They would shake their heads and shuffle quietly away to their tables to contemplate her husband's irresponsible behavior. An air of sober reflection would descend.

By the end of her first evening behind the bar, as the loud, drunken crowd launched into their sixth joyful rendition of the national anthem, Jette stepped out into the alleyway behind the tavern and shed hot, angry tears. There had been no shocked silence at the news, no bemused outrage. Instead, Frederick's departure had been met with rapturous celebration. He had gone off to fight for the country he loved! He was a hero! Toast after toast was drunk. Rambling speeches were made, full of frank admiration.

After that, to Jette's dismay, the Nick-Nack became the town's war room. Men went there to talk about the latest news. Reports were analyzed, tactical developments discussed. Drinks were drunk — and so, inevitably, songs were sung. There were no German tunes now, of course. Instead the men swayed to "America the Beautiful," "The Star-Spangled Banner," and "The Battle Hymn of the Republic." Jette quickly came to loathe them all. She wondered what Frederick was doing. She was sure he was not singing.

When news reached the Nick-Nack of the death of a local soldier, an impromptu wake would be held. She hated those evenings most of all. Men sat quietly at their tables, raising their glasses to the fallen hero. It did not take long for the place to fall into an inebriated stupor. Those with the energy to fight often did. Jette watched this maudlin buffoonery with barely suppressed contempt. To make matters worse, the excessive consumption of alcohol, when combined with the contemplation of their own mortality, had a strangely libidinous effect on some of the Nick-Nack's clientele. It seemed that no man was immune to my grandmother's charms if he had enough drinks inside him, and poor Jette had to be constantly on her guard. I say "poor Jette," but she never regretted these encounters half as much as the fools who tried their luck with her. The punch that had floored Frederick at the moment of Joseph's birth was no fluke. She had a good eye and the size and strength to ensure that anyone she hit wouldn't forget it in a hurry. Although she only swung her fists in self-defense, every blow she landed bore the full force of her accumulated fury and frustration. Her victims would not return to the tavern for several days afterward, hiding their bruises. Heaven knows what they told their wives.

Jette's English improved dramatically when she began working at the Nick-Nack. During the day she would speak to Polk quietly in German, but when the doors opened she turned and faced the world with foreign words heavy on her tongue. She was a fast learner. Unlike Frederick, she did not study textbooks and newspapers; the Nick-Nack was her classroom. As a result, she was soon speaking with a splendidly idiomatic grasp of the vernacular that her husband never acquired, for all his diligence.

My grandmother continued Frederick's policy of booking bands, although for different reasons. Music could drown out the men's incessant talk about the war. Her booking policy was based largely on the volume of noise that the musicians were capable of generating. A really loud band could even stop the men from singing their stupid patriotic songs. She had only one rule: there was no more opera. The tunes that Frederick had made his own remained unsung.

While Jette struggled to come to terms with life without her husband, Joseph and Rosa were fighting battles of their own.

The children's lives had been turned upside down by Frederick's departure. Unfamiliar routines were forced upon them, now that Jette was working at the Nick-Nack. Each evening Joseph gravely led his sister to the tavern, where Jette fed them supper and put them to bed on improvised pallets in the back room. Joseph lay awake in the darkness, listening to the sounds of revelry through the wall, and thought about his father. At the end of each night, they made their weary way back home, Rosa asleep in Jette's arms and Joseph doing his best to hide his yawns, baffled by exhaustion and sadness.

Joseph was devastated by Frederick's desertion. He could not help believing that he was to blame. His attempt to reconcile his warring parents had failed — and now Frederick was gone. Guilt swarmed around him, blocking out the light. He clung to Jette's promise that Frederick would be home soon, and did his best to be brave. He tried not to think too much about where his father might be and what he might be doing, but it was a source of fascination for Stefan. Joseph listened numbly as his friend speculated endlessly about how many men his father had killed. He was unable to connect the steely, ruthless hero of Stefan's imagination with the gentle man he knew and loved.

Once a week my father walked across town to the Bloomberg farm, where he and Riva planned a grand recital to celebrate Frederick's return. Joseph felt happiest when he could disappear into the music and submerge himself in all that beauty. In between the songs, he told Riva Bloomberg how it would be: where Frederick would sit, how he would react to each piece. She listened with a sad smile on her face.

Rosa was too young to understand exactly where her father had gone. All she knew was that he was no longer there. Like her brother, she imagined herself responsible for his absence: she believed that Frederick had left because he did not love her. Her hypochondria worsened. Every week she was laid low by a fresh barrage of imagined ailments. But her broken heart was real enough.

One day in the early fall of 1917 Rosa looked out the kitchen window and saw a fat raccoon sunning himself on the roof of the outhouse. He lay on his back, quite still but for his long striped tail, which occasionally gave a languid flick in the warm afternoon air. He looked as if he did not have a care in the world. She went outside to get a closer look. At the sound of the kitchen door clicking shut, the raccoon slowly rolled over onto his belly and peered down at her from the roof.

"Hello," said Rosa. "What are you doing up there?"

The raccoon studied her unblinkingly for a long moment and then rolled onto his back again with what sounded like a deep sigh.

"Hey, I'm talking to you," said Rosa.

The raccoon sighed again, but did not move.

Rosa was used to having to work hard to get the attention of others. There was no reason why wildlife should be any different from her parents or brother. She went back into the kitchen, cut an apple into slices, and carried the fruit outside on a plate. She put it down on the grass and took a step backward.

"I brought you something," she said. "Are you hungry?"

The raccoon's head popped into sight again. He looked down thoughtfully at the fruit, and then vanished. There was an effortful scrabbling noise, and then the raccoon appeared from around the corner of the outhouse, heading for the plate. Rosa stood quite still and watched as the apple quickly disappeared. When he had finished, the raccoon picked up the plate and looked hopefully underneath it to see if there was any more to eat. Then he turned and looked Rosa in the eye for a moment before scurrying back to the outhouse. Moments later he was back on the roof, basking in the sun once more.

The next day the raccoon was sunbathing again, and the day after that. Each afternoon Rosa put a plate of fruit out for him, and watched from a distance while he ate. She decided to name him Mr. Jim.

The raccoon was extraordinarily fat and lazy. Not for him the joyous cavorting about of his peers. There was nothing Mr. Jim loved more than his long siestas on the roof of the family latrine. Each day, Rosa stood a little closer as she watched him eat his snack. Before long she was within touching distance of him. One afternoon she did not put the apple pieces on a plate, but held them out to him instead. To her delight, he shuffled closer and carefully took each slice from her fingertips.

Soon, much of Rosa's day began to revolve around the plump little creature. She spent hours watching him pad about the yard, casually sniffing out food and making himself at home. The only time he grew agitated was when other raccoons tried to eat Rosa's fruit. Then he quickly saw the intruders off, growling and snapping at them until they retreated. Rosa was pleased — Mr. Jim knew that the food was meant for him alone. Before long she was able to feed him sugar cubes out of the palm of her hand, and played with him like a regular pet.

The two of them quickly became devoted to each other. The minute Rosa stepped out of the kitchen door Mr. Jim would materialize, as if he had been waiting all day for her to appear. They would find a warm spot in the sun, and there Rosa would feed him and scratch his stomach. Mr. Jim lay on his back, his little legs akimbo, sighing blissfully.

One morning the little raccoon hobbled gingerly across the yard, and held his front paw up for Rosa's inspection. It was dark with blood. "Oh, you poor thing," whispered Rosa. "What did you do?" She went inside and fetched the family first-aid kit. Mr. Jim watched as she looked through Jette's box of home remedies. (My aunt, of course, was very well-acquainted with all of the various rubs and tinctures in that box.) She pulled out some alum peroxide and iodine. "Here, boy," she said. "Let's get you tidied up."

The raccoon did not move as Rosa cleaned

the wound and then tightly bandaged his paw in gauze. When she had finished, Mr. Jim limped cautiously around the yard with a mournful look on his face. Rosa went to fetch her mother.

"Look at him," she said. "He's too hurt to go back out into the wild."

Jette watched the raccoon shuffle lopsidedly by. "What are you proposing, Rosa?" she asked.

"Can't he come and live with us?"

"I thought he already did," said Jette dryly.

"No, but I mean *really* live with us," said Rosa. "He could be the family pet. We could take it in turns to —"

Jette shook her head. "I like Mr. Jim just fine, but he's not coming indoors."

"Just until he gets better," pleaded Rosa.

Jette sighed. "All right, look. If you want to make a little bed for him on the porch, that would be fine. Just until his paw gets better. But he stays outside."

They found a wooden crate, and Rosa spent the rest of the day transforming the box into a luxury raccoon accommodation. To her delight, Mr. Jim climbed right into the warm bed of straw that she had prepared for him. After that, Rosa dedicated herself to nursing Mr. Jim back to health. She checked and cleaned the wound every day and lavished double rations of fruit on the invalid.

Of course, that raccoon was no fool. He knew a good thing when he saw it. Even once his foot had healed, he returned to his comfortable crate every night. Jette had planned to throw the makeshift bed away, but she could see how much Rosa adored the little creature. In fact, she had grown quite fond of him herself. And so the crate was allowed to stay on the back porch, and my aunt continued to lavish all her untapped reserves of affection on the lucky creature. Thanks to Mr. Jim, Rosa finally found a way to escape her loneliness and heartache.

When Frederick's first letter arrived, Jette had been too angry to open it. During those first days without him, her fury had propelled her onward in a whirlwind of indignation, eclipsing sorrow. The next day, a second letter was delivered, and she dropped it unopened on top of the first. Another envelope joined the pile the next morning, then another.

After two weeks, Jette felt her resolve wobble. She moved the letters to the ledge above the fireplace, where she wouldn't have to look at them all day. Each morning a new envelope arrived. Jette found herself wishing that Frederick would miss a day, just once.

But he never did. The letters sat in chronological order beneath the terra-cotta angel's wing. Not one of them had been opened.

By the spring of 1918, however, Frederick's unswerving dedication to his epistolary task had begun to provide Jette with a measure of lonely comfort. Her anger had not survived the long winter nights. Now she simply missed him, and wanted him home again. She still did not open the envelopes when they arrived — it was too late for that — but now she began to dread the morning when the postman's hands would be empty. While the letters kept coming, she knew that Frederick was still alive. And so that unread library became a testament to hope.

THIRTEEN

When Frederick's train arrived in Kansas City, a committee of officers barked and cajoled the new recruits into straggling lines. They were led to a hall across from the station, where temporary lodgings had been established. Exhausted by his uncomfortable night in the outdoor latrine and the journey west, Frederick slept deeply, too tired to dream.

The following morning the men were woken before the sun had risen, and for the next three hours they paraded up and down a hastily cleared strip of land in their civilian clothes. A granite-faced captain screamed orders at them. By the middle of the morning the sun had risen high in the sky, baking the makeshift parade ground in stupefying heat. Frederick marched and spun to the left and right, his heart filled with foreboding. That night he lay on his bed and wrote another letter home.

Frederick was at least ten years older than all the other recruits. The men didn't know whether to laugh at him for his advanced years or respect him for volunteering. He passed the physical, but only just. The army needed men; it wasn't going to set the bar too high. After five days of marching and saluting, Frederick filed through the quartermaster's store and was finally handed his uniform. He was now an infantryman in the 35th Division of the United States Army. His platoon was moved out of their quarters and put on a train heading south.

For the next seven months, Frederick's home was a vast encampment of tents on a bleak, windswept plateau of rock, high above the Oklahoma plains. During that winter he forgot most of what he knew of himself, and learned how to be a soldier. He marched for miles across barren landscapes, buffeted by high winds and blinded by dust storms. He dug trenches in the frozen ground, unable to feel his frostbitten fingers. He rehearsed drills for poisonous gas attacks. He skewered countless sacks, practicing how to twist his bayonet into a man's stomach without catching the blade. He learned a number of ways to kill a man.

By springtime, Frederick was unrecognizable. Clean-shaven now, his face had lost its cherubic rotundity. His gut had vanished. An alien matrix of muscle grew across his chest and shoulders. Every evening he lay in his tent, shivering beneath threadbare blankets, and wrote to Jette, a single candle his only source of light and warmth. After a brief report on the day's activities, he would return to the old familiar themes as the cold seeped into his veins. Night after night he scribbled pages of explanations, arguments, and justifications. He wrote until his fingers were too numb for him to continue. The next morning he would take the letter — the envelope still unsealed for the censor's eyes — to the postal tent.

Not once did Jette write back.

As 1918 wore on, Frederick grew tired of the endless drills and exercises. He was ready for real opponents, not just the villainous figments of his commander's imagination. Finally his unit boarded a train east, to New York City, and one fall evening the liner *George Washington* set out from Pier 17 of the South Street Seaport. Frederick stood on the deck, watching the lights of Lower Manhattan twinkle into nothingness, and bade America good-bye.

The atmosphere on board the ship was celebratory. The men were part of the largest military operation in American history, and they were proud of it. None of them had fought in a war before. The *George Washington* made slow progress across the ocean, cautiously tacking one way and then another to avoid enemy submarines.

Frederick spent hours alone on the aft deck, gazing at the trail of churning white water that the ship left in its wake, edging its way back to old horizons. The moment he had stepped on board and felt the swell beneath his feet, memories of the voyage on the *Copernicus* rushed up in ambush. Retracing that journey alone, there was nothing to do but gaze back toward the family he had left behind.

When the ship arrived in France, the quayside at Brest was lined with crowds waving French and American flags. A brass band played and pretty girls blew kisses at the soldiers. A man with a huge wicker basket over his arm stood at the front of the crowd, handing out freshly baked pastries to the disembarking troops.

Frederick stared at the ground beneath his feet. The soil of mainland Europe: he was back where he had begun, ready to make good on a debt that nobody had asked him to repay. In that cheering crowd of strangers, he had never felt so lonely.

Many of the soldiers were directed immediately onto waiting trains to begin their journey to the front. Frederick's platoon was not due to depart until the following morning, and most of the men disappeared into the town, looking for excitement. Frederick carried his canvas bag to his appointed lodgings, sat down on his bed, and wrote another letter to Jette.

The following morning the platoon assembled at the train station. The soldiers waited on the platform, stifling yawns, their young faces drawn with exhaustion and pleasure. Frederick listened as they exchanged stories. The women of Brest had welcomed the Americans into their homes, and then into their beds. The men bragged to each other about their conquests, oblivious to the reason for the women's hunger: their own husbands had already been killed in the war they were now heading toward.

Frederick spent the day watching France unfold outside the train window. By mid-morning most of the men had fallen asleep, exhausted by the exertions of the night before. The carriage was silent but for the rhythmic clatter of the wheels as they pounded across the dilapidated rails. In the fields, children and women dressed in black toiled beneath the warm sun. A sea of purple thyme lapped up against the railway lines. As evening fell, they passed close to Paris. The train swept eastward through densely packed forests, dark with shadow. Hours later, they arrived at their destination, a deserted railway station illuminated only by a pair of dimly glowing gaslights. The soldiers peered out at the darkness. They remained on the platform for an hour, unloading equipment. A wooden cart piled high with apples had been left by the station entrance. In minutes all the fruit had disappeared into pockets. The clock above the platform read half past midnight by the time the group had assembled into long lines of men, guns, and horses. Frederick's bag felt heavy on his back. The procession shambled off into the darkness, led by two officers on horseback. Frederick was near the front of the line, among the infantrymen. The only sound was the thunderous tattoo of a thousand feet as they fell on the tarmac of a deserted country road.

After two hours, it began to rain.

The soldiers pitched their tents in a forest of closely packed spruce trees just as the sun was rising. The thick canopy of branches offered some respite from the rain, but by then it was too late. Frederick's uniform was sodden and cold against his skin. He could not remember ever being so wet.

They marched for five nights. Days were spent under the cover of woods or in abandoned farm buildings. Soldiers collapsed where they stood, grateful for the oblivion of deep-boned exhaustion. As the journey went on, the line became a ragtag congregation of listless, wandering souls. Each man walked with his head lowered against the incessant rain, alone with his thoughts.

As the convoy approached the front, they marched through a landscape of dead trees, the fractured bleakness punctuated only by the grim ruins of abandoned towns. The weary clump of marching feet echoed off the walls of half-destroyed buildings. The streets were empty, save for armies of feral dogs, thin-ribbed with hunger, which yowled at the passing soldiers. The men walked by, dead-eyed with exhaustion.

On the last night, they passed a bedraggled line of captured Germans marching in the opposite direction. The prisoners' uniforms were muddied and torn. Their hands were shackled in front of them. Frederick stared as the captured men shuffled by. Someone muttered *Amerikanisch,* the word fattened with fear and loathing. Frederick's heart was suddenly awash with sorrow. He was the enemy now.

At the front, they underwent final training to an unending chorus of explosions and gunfire from two or three miles farther north, a faint but persistent echo of death. There was little laughter now. That night in Brest seemed like a lifetime ago.

Frederick's unit was stationed in the southwest corner of the Argonne Forest in northern France. The battlefields of Europe were soon to fall silent, washed in the blood of a generation. By then the Germans knew that they were going to lose the war, but the tail of the dying beast was still lashing out, as fatal as ever. Enemy troops had scattered into the devastated countryside. They were savage, mutinous, and interested only in saving their own skins. Nobody wanted to be the last man to die. The United States First Army had been assigned the task of mopping up final pockets of resistance.

On October 13, in the first light of morning, Frederick finally stepped into the theater of war. His unit crept through the trees, the last of the year's leaves beneath their boots. The forest was softened by a fragile white mist. Every cautious step took them farther into enemy territory. They approached the first German post on their knees, inching silently forward, suspecting a trap, but all that remained was a devastation of barbed wire and broken concrete, deserted and desolate. The men wandered through the camp. A blackened pot still hung over the charred remains of a burned-out fire. It was the only recognizable thing in the place. Everything else had been broken into a thousand useless fragments.

The pattern repeated itself as the day wore on. Each camp they encountered had been abandoned with increasingly destructive fury. By the time the sun began to set, the men knew that there would be no Germans waiting to surprise them. Frederick could not help but be disappointed. He scoured the barren trees, still hoping for a glimpse of the enemy.

The leader of the unit was a carpenter from Joplin named Daniel Jinks. He was the only one of them who had a map. Their instructions were to spend the night in the forest, but when Jinks announced that there was a church nearby, the decision was unanimous, and they veered a mile or so off their projected course. When they arrived at the squat stone building, they saw that they were not the only ones who had been tempted by the promise of a night beneath a solid roof. Outside the church's front door, an American flag had been raised on an improvised pole. Soldiers leaned against the wall, rifles at their feet. Some smoked, others hungrily chased the last scraps of rations around their canteens. A row of small windows spanned the length of the building, warm with light from inside.

Candles were lit the length of the church's nave, casting shadows across the white-washed walls as the night stole in. Soldiers sprawled across the pews. Some men faced the altar, cleaning their guns. One or two were writing on scraps of paper, squinting at their words in the half-light. Others knelt or bowed their heads in prayer.

At the far end of the room a man was playing a piano, surrounded by a handful of soldiers. Frederick recognized the tune. It was an aria from *The Barber of Seville*. He walked toward the music. The piano player was a major — and, like Frederick, older than the other men. He wore thick glasses. Frederick watched for some minutes, and then joined in.

Ah, ah! Che bella vita!

At this, the pianist's face broke into a smile. He nodded at Frederick, inviting him to continue. When they had finished the Rossini, the pianist suggested some other pieces. It wasn't long before Frederick was up to his old tricks, striding up and down in front of the piano and gesticulating as he sang. The soldiers applauded, egging him on, grateful for the distraction from what tomorrow might bring. Frederick was happy to oblige. He hadn't sung a note since he had left Missouri. Now the joy of music coursed through him again. He hardly saw the men in front of him. He was performing for a private audience of three, half a world away. He sang his heart out.

Finally the major closed the piano lid, and waved away the protests of the soldiers. "You men need sleep," he cried. He smiled at Frederick. "You have a fine voice."

"Thank you," said Frederick. "You play very well."

The man shrugged. "I do all right. It's nice to find someone who can sing." He gestured at the men. "You would have thought a bunch of Irish Catholics from Kansas City would have been good for one decent singer, but no."

"You are from Missouri?" said Frederick.

The major nodded. "Born and bred."

"I, too, am from Missouri." Frederick beamed.

"You don't sound as if you've been there long."

Frederick frowned. "My accent is strong, yes. But I am an American citizen, and proud of it."

The pianist held up his hands. "I don't doubt it. I'm sorry. That uniform looks good on you, soldier."

Frederick saluted. "Meisenheimer, Thirty-fifth Division."

"Truman, Battery D."

The two men shook hands and were silent for a moment. "Have you been in France long?" asked Frederick.

"About six months," replied the major. "Long enough to be sick of it. I mean, don't get me wrong. France is a grand place for Frenchmen. I don't blame them for fighting for it. But I miss home." He looked at Frederick. "You seem a little old for all this."

Frederick stood up taller. "I volunteered," he said.

The pianist slapped his thigh in pleasure. "Me, too! But I wasn't just too old." He pointed at his glasses. "I had to cheat on the eye test. Memorized the chart." He chuckled softly. "Right now, there's nowhere else in the world a man could want to be. I'm proud of my country, proud of what it stands for, and I'm ready to fight for it. Not that my girl quite saw it that way," he added. "Here." He pulled a photograph out of his tunic pocket and offered it up for Frederick's inspection. "I'm going to marry her when I get home. Heart of gold, but a tongue of acid." He pulled a rueful grin. "Not afraid to make her feelings known, that one."

Frederick nodded. "My wife is the same. She could not understand why I had to come."

"You wait," said the major. "She will. One day people will look back and realize that this war was the most important struggle the world has known." He looked around him. "God knows how many of these men will make it through tomorrow, or the next day. But we're here for a reason. You and me, we'll be able to look back when this madness is over and say, we were there, we did our bit." He glanced at his watch. "And now I must make sure my men get a good night's sleep."

Frederick nodded. "Thank you," he said. "I have missed singing."

"You're good at it. Don't ever stop." The major removed his glasses and wiped them on his sleeve. He pushed them back onto his nose and winked at Frederick. "*Che bella vita,* eh?" The men shook hands warmly.

What a beautiful life.

Frederick found an empty pew, pulled out a piece of paper and a pencil from his kit bag, and wrote his daily letter home in the flickering candlelight. When he had finished, he folded the letter and slipped it into his shirt pocket. He stretched out along the hard wooden bench, and was soon asleep, borne into peaceful oblivion on the crest of all those rediscovered melodies.

The following morning Daniel Jinks led the unit back into the forest to continue their journey eastward. By mid-morning they reached the decimated remains of a small village. The townsfolk had fled months ago; the place had been used as a supply point for munitions and supplies for enemy troops to the west. The retreating Germans had destroyed as much of the place as they could. Frederick picked his way through the charred, cratered landscape that remained. He was in an irrepressible mood: music's flame had been reignited inside him, and he vowed to follow the pianist's advice. He wouldn't ever stop singing. Not again. He had spent the morning working his way with relish through the repertoire he had abandoned. As the unit made their way through the village, Frederick was singing the finale of *Così Fan Tutte,* gamely playing all the principal characters at once. He was not paying attention to the job at hand, and his overcoat got caught on one of the coiled lines of barbed wire that crossed his path. Still singing, he stopped and tried to pull himself free. His tugging only made matters worse, ensnaring the material more. Realizing that he was going no farther, he bent down to extricate his coat.

Such a big man, out in the open, momentarily still: Frederick was still singing when the hidden German sniper drew a bead on the back of his head. The sharp crack echoed through the empty streets.

Peter Kropp had been the postmaster in Beatrice for more years than anyone, himself included, could count. He had been enjoying a quiet retirement until his successor was conscripted in 1917. With the post office standing empty, Kropp was pressed back into service. He had been delighted to be back in his old job, until the telegrams began to arrive.

Now he walked somberly through the town, his hat held against his chest and his head cast down.

Jette had been standing at the window of the sitting room, gazing out at the street. When she saw the old postmaster hesitate at the gate, her world slipped silently into the long shadow of heartbreak. And then she was hurrying down the path to intercept the bad news, wanting to keep it out of the house. She wordlessly took the envelope from Peter Kropp's unsteady hand. A cold wind swept down the street. Jette's fingers curled tightly around the yellow square of paper as she dropped to her knees.

FOURTEEN

On the evening of Peter Kropp's visit, when there were no more tears left to shed, Jette took Frederick's letters down from the mantelpiece. She fumbled with the first envelope, the paper stiff after months over the fireplace. Frederick's handwriting was uneven, jagging sharply across the page. He had been writing on the train to Kansas City. My grandmother sat in an armchair by the fire and began to read.

As the night wore on, the sweet, funny man she had loved so dearly disappeared before her eyes. The early letters were full of tentative explanations and gentle pleas for understanding. But soon Frederick's new world had crowded in. His tone became more brittle, less willing to consider alternative views. Jette had read on in sadness as she watched the army sink its teeth into him. He filed reports of drills, mess hall politics, and military exercises. His letters became excruciatingly dull. Frederick was no longer interested in anything except the conflict that awaited him. He was eager to baptize his love for America in the blood of strangers. As she read, it felt as if Frederick were being killed all over again, each new letter a fresh bullet.

Her grief was too immense to hold on to. After so long without Frederick, waiting for precisely this news, she could only reflect numbly that today was really no different from yesterday. She was still alone. The yellow telegraph had announced a different fatality — the death of hope.

That evening, Jette returned to the Nick-Nack and served drinks and smiled, just as she always did. She listened to the men sing their songs. She told nobody what had happened.

For days she grimly batted away the news. The most dangerous time was in the mornings, just after she awoke. In those first unguarded moments of consciousness, truth lurked, ready to pounce. It's impossible to know how long Jette would have continued to bob along in this limbo of deferred grief had it not been for the letters.

As it turned out, Jette had been wrong to fear the day when the postman approached with empty hands. Frederick's missives from

Europe took weeks to make the long journey home, but news of his death had traveled faster, by official communiqué and telegram. And so after he died, Frederick's letters continued to arrive, a second slow creep toward the sniper's gun.

At first Jette was grateful; here was proof that nothing had really changed. Now, though, she tore open each envelope as soon as it arrived. Frederick was writing from northern France, just behind the front, waiting for his turn to fight. He wrote the date at the top of each letter. It was this slow countdown to the silence that she knew was coming that finally pulled Jette out of her denial. His words were strictly finite now.

The last letter arrived. Frederick never posted it; it had been found in the pocket of his tunic by Daniel Jinks, the carpenter from Joplin, who had sent it on himself. Jette opened the envelope, scarcely able to breathe. There was the date: October 13, 1918.

Curled up on a pew in that whitewashed church deep in the Argonne Forest, my grandfather handed Jette the key that would set her free. He did not write of his first day of engagement with the enemy — that long-anticipated confrontation. Instead he told her about the impromptu recital in the church with the kind pianist from Missouri. The music had woken up old memories and lifted his eyes beyond the bleak horizon of war. For the first time in months, he talked about coming home. Promises, crazy, impossible promises, spilled off the page, a glorious hymn to the future. Frederick was dreaming again. His last words to her were full of hope, of joy, of life.

Jette held the letter tightly in her hands. The man she had loved so dearly had returned to bid her a final farewell.

It was November 11, 1918, the day the Armistice was signed. The war had been won.

Now Jette could mourn properly.

She decided that there would be no funeral. She knew the crowd from the Nick-Nack would turn any memorial service into a mordant celebration, and she did not want that. Her husband was dead, his body abandoned in an unknown field on the other side of the world. The children had lost their father. They would stumble on, a lopsided trio, one corner of their perfect square gone forever. There was nothing to celebrate.

Instead she performed a little ceremony of her own devising. She built a fire in the backyard and burned all of Frederick's letters, except the last one. She held each piece of paper over the flames in turn, watching his words slowly disintegrate. She planted a young apple tree in the yard and sprinkled the ashes of the letters in the soil around the sapling. Frederick's words would enrich the ground he loved so much: new roots in America.

That afternoon, as the new apple tree swayed in the wind, she kissed her children's heads and told them that their father was dead. Joseph buried his face in the folds of her dress. Rosa covered her ears with her fists. The three of them clung to each other and sank to the floor.

Later that day Joseph stumbled to Frau Bloomberg's house. When she opened the door and saw his face, no words were needed. She knelt down on the doorstep and opened her arms. He clung to her, his shoulders heaving in wordless grief. Riva Bloomberg gently pried his fingers from around her neck. "Joseph," she whispered. "Come with me." She stood up and led him down the corridor to the music room.

Joseph looked away from the piano. "I won't sing," he said. "Not without him here."

"But he *is* here," said Riva Bloomberg. She gently placed her hand on Joseph's chest. "He's in here. Your father is part of you, and he always will be. If you sing, he'll hear you.

I promise." She sat down on the piano stool and waited with her hands folded on her lap.

Joseph stood there for an age.

In the end, all his hard work did not go to waste. The recital took place, exactly as he had planned it, except that the songs were no longer songs of welcome, but a final good-bye. His voice, sweet and lovely, filled the empty room.

That evening, the mood in the Nick-Nack was ecstatic. People were celebrating. The Armistice had been signed. Victory was secured. The singing grew louder as the night went on. Jette stood behind the bar and listened. Toward the end of the evening, after a particularly boisterous rendition of "Keep the Home Fires Burning," she climbed up onto the counter and clapped her hands for attention.

"Gentlemen, please!"

A sea of happy faces turned toward her.

"Our beautiful hostess!" called out a drunken voice.

"How about a victory dance?" shouted another. The crowd laughed.

Jette waited for the noise to die down. "You are all celebrating tonight," she began. There was a cheer. "You want to honor the men who have fought for this country."

There was a low rumble of approval. "American heroes!" called a voice from the back of the room.

Jette's eyes were dry as she looked around the room. "Well, I have news about one American hero." She took a deep breath and relinquished her secret. "My husband is not coming home. He was killed by enemy fire in France."

In the stunned silence that followed, she climbed down from the bar, straightened her dress, and walked out the back door of the tavern. Not one person moved as she went.

Alone in the deserted alleyway, Jette slumped against the wall. Her chest tightened in a vise of melancholy. As she fought for breath, one of her legs gave way beneath her, and she stumbled forward into the darkness. She collapsed onto her knees, her body felled by tears.

A memory drifted back to her. During those long walks through the streets and gardens of Hanover, Frederick would tell her the plots of the operas he loved so much. There had been talking statues, deals with the Devil, megalomaniacal dwarves. She had laughed at the improbability of it all. But she reserved her greatest scorn for the absurd heroines who threw themselves about in twittering fits of melodrama, forever threatening to kill themselves for love. But whoever really died of a broken heart? she had asked him with a smile. Oh, he had replied, entirely serious, you'd be surprised.

So he was right all along, she thought. Grief began to smother her.

Then she heard the singing from the other side of the tavern door.

Jette propped herself up on one elbow and listened. "The Star-Spangled Banner" was seeping into the cold night air — but there was none of the usual celebratory pomp. Instead the men were singing softly in tribute to Frederick, their voices joined in gentle unison. When they reached the end of the fourth verse, there was a long silence. Jette gazed up into the starless sky. She wondered where she would ever get the strength to pick herself up.

The answer came there and then.

The men inside began to sing "The Star-Spangled Banner" again. This time, though, all restraint had vanished. The usual lusty bellowing had returned, more spirited than ever, fueled by the euphoria of victory. America had won! To the victor the spoils!

Jette thought of her grandfather, directing his troops to slaughter from the safety of his ridiculous balloon. She realized then that nothing would ever change. Men would repeat the same stupid mistakes again and again, slowly wiping themselves off the planet. She clambered to her feet, her grief eclipsed by fury, and made herself listen to the revelry inside the Nick-Nack. She wanted the sound of the celebration scratched into her memory, an indelible scar.

Men would never curb their lust for blood. Even Frederick — sweet, gentle Frederick — had been hypnotized by all that violence. As Jette listened, she knew that the idiots in the Nick-Nack's choir had learned nothing, and never would.

So then: the salvation of the human race lay in the hands of women.

Mothers would not send their children off to die.

The following morning, Jette made a placard out of a large piece of wood. On it she painted the phrase:

SAVE OUR CHILDREN. NO MORE WAR.

While the paint dried, she dressed in widow's mourning. She kissed her children and walked slowly toward the main square, holding her handmade sign in front of her. She made quite a spectacle, this towering vision in black. People peered quizzically at her as she passed. In front of the courthouse steps lay the debris from the previous day's victory celebrations, a tattered landscape of red, white, and blue. Jette began to march slowly around the building. Before long, every window of the courthouse was filled with curious spectators. A crowd gathered on the sidewalk to watch her progress. She ignored them all.

Halfway through the morning, Nancy Ott fell into step next to her. Her family ran the grocery store on Main Street — the store whose German sign Frederick had noticed moments before Jette's waters broke. Nancy Ott sat next to the till, where she rang up purchases and dealt in prurient, low-grade gossip. Jette had shopped there for years. Over the course of their long acquaintance the two women had never quite become friends, but the relationship had always been cordial. Now, though, the shopkeeper was scowling ferociously.

"Have you no shame?" she hissed.

Jette continued walking, looking straight ahead.

"Think of your poor husband, Jette. He must be turning in his grave, may God rest his soul." Nancy Ott was struggling to keep pace with Jette's long strides. "This is an insult to everything he fought for."

"I loved my husband very much," Jette replied calmly. "I miss him with all of my heart. He was a good man, and a brave man, too. But he was also an idiot. He chose to go to war, and he got himself killed. Now my children must grow up without a father, and I must go to the end of my days a lonely woman."

"But the war is won."

"Well, forgive me if I don't share your joy. It won't bring Frederick back."

"This display of yours won't bring him back either," snapped Nancy Ott.

"That's true," agreed Jette. "But it might save others. And that is no insult to his memory, whatever you may think. Now, if you'll excuse me." With that she quickened her pace a fraction, and effortlessly left the older woman trailing in her wake.

"You're no longer welcome in my store," called Nancy Ott in fury.

Jette disappeared around the corner of the courthouse without looking back.

"Traitor," cried Nancy Ott.

At midday Jette returned home. It was November 12, 1918 — perhaps not the most obvious day to wear a sign saying NO MORE WAR, but to her it made perfect sense. The first day of a new peace was precisely the time to begin her campaign. The sacrifices of the fallen were already fading from people's memories, obscured by the complacency of victory. Jette knew it would not be long before the same mistakes would be repeated.

My grandmother might have understood what she was doing, but nobody else did. Word spread quickly through the town that she had lost her mind to grief. Wives shook their heads in sympathy. Men grumbled that mourning should take place in private. The whole spectacle, it was agreed, was in shocking taste.

That night at the Nick-Nack, the atmosphere could not have been more different from the celebrations of the previous evening. Jette's presence behind the bar smothered good cheer like a wet blanket on a small flame. By then everyone had heard about her confrontation with Nancy Ott, and the sinister menace of the old woman's final insult had grown with every whispered echo on the lips of others. People looked away as they ordered their drinks, words of condolence caught in their throats.

By chance William Henry Harris had been booked to play that evening, but the little pianist only added to the somber mood. Rather than his usual up-tempo selections, he just played mournful tunes. At the end of his set, he left the piano and walked to the middle of the stage. He looked out across the room and waited patiently for silence. Finally the room fell quiet, all eyes on the dapper pianist who, up until that point, had never uttered a word in all the years he had been playing there.

"I ain't no poet," he began. "I say what I have to say with my fingers, not with words. I got one more song, though, and I want to dedicate it to Mr. Frederick Meisenheimer. We never did have that much to say to each other, him and me, but he was a good man. He loved this music, and he loved this bar, and he loved this country." The pianist sat down at the keyboard. "The national anthem," he announced.

Rather than the simple, somber rendition that Frederick had so admired, this time William Henry Harris let loose a swaggering, finger-snappin' stomp. His hands were a blur as the melody raced ahead, skipping and weaving through jazzy bass lines and strange harmonies. Notes flew from the piano at a ferocious clip, scattering in all directions. It was "The Star-Spangled Banner," all right — red, white, and drenched in the blues. When he finished, William Henry Harris stood up and quickly left the stage.

In the surprised silence that followed, Jette

saw her chance. She climbed onto the stage and faced the crowded room.

"My husband came to this country and fell in love," she began. "He adored this place. He loved the ideas that this nation was built upon. Tolerance. Opportunity. And, more than anything, freedom. He loved them so much that he was prepared to sacrifice his life for them." Jette looked around the room. "We made this place our home. Our children were born on this soil. This is my country," she declared. "And I am a good American."

A low murmur spread around the room.

"I am as thankful as anyone for this victory," Jette continued. "I am grateful that the war is won. But my children's hearts have been broken." She paused. "When I march through the town I mean no disrespect, to my dead husband or to anyone else. I am frightened, that is all. I am frightened that there will be more wars. More good men will die. And if that happens, then Frederick's death will have been for nothing. That is why I march." She looked at the faces in front of her. "I know many of you disagree with me. That is your right. But I beg you, in the name of the freedoms that my husband died for — let me say what I have to say."

With that, Jette turned and left the stage.

It was a tremendous performance. And,

astonishingly, it worked.

We Midwesterners are a reasonable lot. If you argue your corner, you'll get a fair hearing. And so it was: the citizens of Beatrice listened to Jette, considered the merits of her argument, and they decided that perhaps she had a point. The following morning, when she appeared outside the courthouse dressed in black, people bowed their heads as she passed, only now they did so as a sign of respect, not disgust. Even if people weren't exactly *happy* about her protest, they recognized her right to make her feelings known.

As she marched, my grandmother — that reluctant American — was shining a small light on our country's freedoms.

FIFTEEN

Winter wrapped the countryside in its cold embrace. Snow came in the first week of December, but still Jette appeared each morning for her lonely vigil at the courthouse, her black uniform stark against the glistening white of the town's deserted streets.

But something far more ominous than snow rode in on the cold fronts that swept across the country that winter. A deadly strain of influenza was spreading, hastened over continents by the troops returning home. It was the war's final shake of its monstrous fist. Death came quickly, victims dying in agony as blood seeped darkly from their noses, ears, and mouths. Their lungs filled with treacherous liquid, drowning them from within. Men returned home from the war, pleased to have survived, and then dropped dead, felled by a more lethal foe. In the end, the pandemic killed more people than all the bullets and bombs and poison gas combined.

The first reports of the disease came from Fort Riley in Kansas, only a few hundred miles away, but in its rush to devastation, the deadly virus passed Beatrice by. The towns-folk monitored the horror in the newspaper and took no chances. Strangers were no longer welcome. Every time a child coughed, Dr. Becker was hastily summoned. Rosa no longer had to concoct fictional illnesses — now there was a genuine reason for her to worry. She became convinced that she would be the first to perish. She took to walking everywhere with a thick scarf tied over her face and obsessively monitored her own symptoms, or lack of them. Most of all, she worried about who would look after Mr. Jim when she died.

Inevitably, death finally came to our little town, and when it did, it brushed close enough to my family to make me wonder how different our own story might have been.

After the war Johann Kliever had resumed his prizefighting career, traveling across the state and beyond to clobber the life out of unsuspecting opponents for cash. A day after his return from a bout in southern Illinois, he fell ill. He writhed on his bed, blind with delirium. Anna held his hand, but she did not call the doctor. She knew that there was nothing to be done. The disease spared nobody, and inviting Becker into their home would merely hasten its spread across the town. She wiped her husband's brow and waited sadly for the end.

Kliever was still an ox of a man, and immensely strong. He fought the virus with the same ferocity that he dispensed with those foolish enough to clamber into the prize ring with him. Astonishingly, he was still alive a week after the disease had risen up to claim him. After ten days, the fever relinquished its grip, and he slowly began to recover. As his huge body lay limp on the bed, Anna began to wonder whether she might dare to hope.

But hope is for fools. That night, as she lay next to her sleeping husband, the virus lay siege for a second time. Anna's life slipped away as Kliever slept on, too weak to be roused by her fevered cries. By the following morning her screams had stopped.

The deaths of Frederick and Anna drew their sons closer together. Both Joseph and Stefan had discovered that the world was not the perfect place that they had once imagined it to be. It was knowledge that neither of them could ever escape. They weren't ready or able to talk about the pain of their loss, but each knew that the other understood. Their bond of shared grief was all the stronger for never being put into words. Those deep, inarticulate ties gave the boys comfort and strength. Alone, either might have collapsed beneath the weight of his grief, but together they propped each other up and staggered on toward the future.

The old games that had so absorbed them in the past were long forgotten. Instead they discovered new distractions. Sometimes Stefan borrowed one of his father's shotguns, and the boys would trudge up to Tillman's Wood and shoot at animals. They never killed anything, but that didn't matter. The heft of the gun in their arms, the sharp recoil against their shoulders, the whiff of cordite in the air — that was what was important. Their wayward bullets ripped through the undergrowth and splintered old tree trunks. Joseph and Stefan found comfort in those small trails of destruction. They were imposing a measure of control over the chaos that had overturned their lives. The deafening ring of gunshots in their ears obliterated their loss, at least for a while.

Jette was devastated by Anna's death. First she had lost her husband, now her best friend. She felt increasingly lonely and remote. There was nobody left but the children, and without them she feared that she would float away. Each morning she looked out the window at the naked boughs of the young apple tree she had planted in Frederick's memory. It occurred to her that it was time to put down some roots of her own.

While Frederick was alive, it had been easy for Jette to despise the Nick-Nack. But his death demanded a rewriting of what had gone before. Every note he had sung still echoed in the old bricks. The place became a memorial to him, and Jette threw all her energies into honoring his legacy. She began to book more bands, and made plans for the future. But history conspired against her: in January of 1919, Missouri was one of five states to ratify the United States Congress's bill outlawing the sale of alcohol. Those five votes were enough to ensure that the ban on liquor would become law exactly twelve months later.

The last year of the Nick-Nack's life was an extended good-bye party. People drank as if every evening would be their last. Business had never been better. Polk and Jette struggled to cope with the extra workload, so Joseph began to help when he could, sweeping floors, clearing tables, and washing glasses. The customers were kind to him. They slipped small coins into his pocket and pressed crumpled cigarettes on him with a benign wink. Joseph began to understand that the tavern traded in more than simply drink. Other commodities were also on offer: companionship, community, and the comfort of ritual. He became familiar with the nightly rhythms of hope and despair, as the world slowly collapsed around the men who drank there. They wept, fought, slept, and stared longingly at his mother, before stumbling out into the darkness at the end of each night.

Joseph was proud to call himself a workingman. He devised a small ritual: at the end of every week, Jette gave him a dollar bill, thanking him for his hard work. Joseph put the money in his pocket, relishing the touch of the paper beneath his fingers. Then he pulled the note out again and gravely handed it back, his contribution to household expenses. It was this transaction, the responsibility and sacrifice of it, that gave him the most pleasure of all.

Meanwhile, there was music everywhere. The Nick-Nack was reveling in a marvelous swan song. Just about anyone who walked through the door with an instrument under his arm could secure a night's work. There were brass ensembles, string quartets, an endless procession of guitars and fiddles.

William Henry Harris still played regularly, his elegant fingers weaving syncopated spells to bewitch the listening crowds.

Joseph enjoyed the bands, but it was the singers he remembered the most. A woman came from Quincy, Illinois, squeezed into a tight satin dress, a slash of scarlet across her mouth. She winked and hollered her way through a honky-tonk repertoire of old bordello songs, bursting with lewd innuendo. She had the saddest eyes Joseph had ever seen. There was a huge ogre of a man, nearly seven feet tall with a long black beard down to his chest, who carried his double bass onto the stage as if it were a child's violin. He glared furiously at the audience, and then began to croon plaintive love songs in a screeching falsetto, accompanying himself with occasional low percussive thwacks on the bass strings. Identical twins from Moberly hunched over their banjos and sang mournful songs of longing and regret. The long necks of their instruments pointed away from each other, slender horns on a double-headed beast.

During these performances, Joseph moved among the tables, delivering fresh drinks and picking up empty glasses, but always listening to the music. One night, four men dressed in brightly colored jackets walked quietly onto the stage. There was no band to accompany them. They huddled closely together, almost turned in on themselves, paying no attention to the audience. Then, without warning, the air was filled with delicious sound. Their four voices merged to form a perfect chord, brilliant with promise. Joseph stood, his tray limp in his hand. It was the sound he had been waiting for his whole life.

Once they had the audience's attention, the quartet launched into "You're the Flower of My Heart, Sweet Adeline." The lead singer sang the main line while his three companions wove intricate patterns back and forth around the melody. They swooped and rumbled, creating layered confections of a cappella harmony, cross-pollinations of sweet notes and tones. Their voices would stack up with exquisite precision for a dazzling instant; then they would move on, tearing down the edifice they had just created and constructing another of equal wonder in its place. For an hour they sang folk songs, spirituals, and ballads. Joseph listened, spellbound. Frederick used to call the human voice God's first instrument, and here it was in all its unadorned beauty, four times over. Their last note, a big, fat sunbeam of harmony that refracted through the room in warm shafts of beauty, rang out for several beats too long, the singers reluctant to bring the music to an end.

Joseph never forgot that night. The shadow it cast would be a long one.

Amid all the elegiac revelry at the Nick-Nack, Prohibition was drawing nearer. On January 16, 1920, the tavern would close its doors for good. Jette gazed at the calendar like a condemned prisoner staring up at the glinting blade of a guillotine. She watched helplessly as the months passed, too paralyzed by the impending calamity to come up with an alternative plan.

Around that time, new neighbors arrived in the house next door. Like Jette's own lopsided family, the Leftkemeyers were missing a parent. There were just two of them, a short, serious-looking man, and his daughter, who was about Joseph's age. Martin Leftkemeyer had come to Beatrice to run the town's bank. Every day he wore the same three-piece suit and pristine brown homburg. Joseph watched him as he trotted down the steps of his house on his way to work. Amid the town's farmers and laborers he seemed more like an exotic bird of paradise than a bank manager.

The bank occupied a large building on

Main Street, just opposite the tavern, but Martin Leftkemeyer never came in for a drink. Instead he went home every night to eat a quiet supper with his daughter. This allowed everyone else to gossip about him freely, but the lack of any ascertainable facts meant that people resorted to idle speculation, not all of it generous.

Jette listened to these rumors and kept her own counsel. She had knocked on the Leftkemeyers' front door a few days after their arrival, a basket of freshly baked *roggenbrot* under her arm. She had stayed as long as she could, trawling indiscreetly for information.

"What a tragedy," she said when she returned home. "The poor man could barely look me in the eye. Wouldn't smile. So serious. His wife died in the influenza epidemic. He's come here from Kansas City to start a new life." She was silent for a moment, as she contemplated the impossibility of her ever attempting a similar escape trick. She was rooted here now, and she knew it.

Joseph, though, wanted to hear about the daughter.

"She's a skinny thing, that's all I can tell you. She sat the whole time with her hands folded neatly on her lap and didn't open her mouth once."

"Is she pretty?" asked Joseph. He knew the

answer to this already, but wanted to hear it from someone else.

"Pretty?" sniffed Jette. "I didn't notice."

Joseph hid his disappointment. He had been unable to take his eyes off the girl next door. She offered a fragile allure that was quite alien to him. Thanks to all that German food, most of the females in Beatrice had lost their gamine figures by adolescence. But there was almost nothing to Joseph's new neighbor. He was bewitched by the graceful contours of her slender arms. Every day she wore a different color of ribbon in her hair. Joseph had already begun to lie awake at night and think about those ribbons.

"What's her name?" he asked, staring at his fingernails.

"The girl? She's called Cora."

Cora!

Joseph began to loiter at the living room window for hours, hoping for a glimpse of Cora Leftkemeyer. During the day she was a cyclone of domestic industry, forever hanging out washing in the yard, sweeping the back porch, or cleaning windows. Every afternoon she put on her bonnet and walked to the shops with a wicker basket on her arm, returning a little while later with groceries for dinner.

More than anything, Cora loved to spend

time planting and tending her vegetable garden. In this she was always meticulous and methodical. Joseph watched with interest as she carefully staked out the perimeter of the area with string and tall poles. She spent hours turning over the soil with a pitchfork that probably weighed as much as she did. She planted seeds in precisely measured lines, smoothing over each tiny hole with the back of her trowel. At the end of each furrow was a stick with a yellow piece of paper pinned to it — a reminder, Joseph supposed, of what she had planted. She watered every morning and evening. She often sang as she worked. Sometimes she simply wandered up and down the neat lines of topsoil with her hands on her hips, a look of quiet satisfaction on her lovely face. By the time she had finished her work, her cheeks were often smudged with soil. Joseph had never been so enchanted.

Every evening after dinner, Cora and her father walked arm in arm around the neighborhood. Neither talked as they made their way up and down the streets of the town. Joseph dreamed that one day it would be *his* arm that Cora took before setting out on her stroll.

There was a certain purity to my father's adoration. He was still young enough to be awed by the intoxicating force of his own passion. Everything was brilliantly illuminated by his ardor. Each beer-stained table he wiped, each glass he collected and washed, each sweep of the broom across the Nick-Nack's dirty floor — it was all for Cora. He tripped happily through his days, his heart a large, silent incubator of innocent devotion.

Joseph knew better than to discuss his fascination with Cora Leftkemeyer with Stefan. Their gruff discussions about females were willfully coarse (as well as anatomically inaccurate). Joseph had no business falling in *love* — he knew that much. A confession of how he felt about his pretty neighbor would provoke nothing but scorn from his friend. Consequently he maintained his usual mask of bored disenchantment whenever the topic arose with Stefan. Joseph made no attempt to hide his love-struck mooning from Jette, though. As she watched him keep his vigil by the window, my grandmother's heart flooded with memories of Frederick. She knew that the aria that had ambushed her from behind the hedge in the Grosse Garten had been a long time in the making. Now Jette watched her son as he fell under a stranger's spell with the same intensity, and she couldn't help but worry.

Unlike Joseph, my grandmother was unimpressed by Cora's cool demeanor. She thought the girl was too wrapped up in her Kansas City sophistication to be interested in a country boy like him. When Jette looked at Cora, all she could see was the person who was going to break her son's heart.

Which she duly did, although not in the way that Jette had imagined.

Sixteen

As 1919 drew to a close, the mood in the Nick-Nack grew increasingly despondent. People drank as much as they could while it was still legal to do so. Jette stopped booking music acts. Customers no longer listened. Instead they turned their backs and muttered about the fools in Washington who passed such idiot laws. Every night people begged Jette to ignore the ban.

There was no chance of that, though. The town's police chief, Walford Scott, promised her that he intended to enforce the new law vigorously. He dropped by once or twice a week and hungrily inspected the tavern's remaining stocks of alcohol, taking note of what had been consumed. Jette knew that he and his deputies would confiscate whatever bottles remained undrunk. She also knew that any seized contraband would be poured directly down their throats, and was determined that there would not be a drop left for them. She resolved not to take a cent for drinks on the final night.

January 16, 1920, the last day of the Nick-Nack's existence, dawned crisp and clear. Joseph walked toward the tavern, cheerfully humming "Sweet Adeline." He was not worried by the Nick-Nack's impending closure; he was still young enough to believe that everything would work out all right in the end. Besides, he was (as usual) preoccupied by his thoughts of Cora Leftkemeyer. As he made his way through the town, he concocted fantasies about how she would finally notice him and how, the thunderbolt unleashed, she would adore him as much as he adored her.

To Joseph's surprise, there was a tall man lying on the ground in front of the Nick-Nack. His head was resting on a small case and a battered hat covered his face. Two large black hands lay folded peacefully across his chest. He appeared to be asleep. Joseph gingerly stepped over him and inserted his key into the front door. Just then a hand gripped him by the ankle.

"Little man," growled a low voice. "You gonna ask me in?"

"I thought you were asleep," said Joseph.

"Fat chance. Your Missouri ground ain't as soft as some." Joseph tried not to stare as

227

the man slowly got to his feet. He brushed dirt off his arms and legs, and waited patiently as Joseph fumbled with the key. A generation on, my father was as tongue-tied as Frederick had been when William Henry Harris had first appeared at the Nick-Nack's door. Finally the two of them stepped inside.

"I heard you hire musicians," said the man, looking around.

"We used to," said Joseph. "But we're closing down. Tonight is our last night."

"Prohibition?" The man put his hands into his pockets. "You actually gonna do what that dumb law says?"

Joseph nodded. "What do you play?" he asked.

The man bent down and opened his case. Inside there was a cornet. He put the instrument to his lips and blew a streaky run of quarter notes. "You like that?"

Joseph had no wish to upset the enormous stranger. "It's very nice," he said.

The man put his head to one side. "You ever been to New Orleans?" he asked.

"I've never left Missouri," admitted Joseph.

"Well, New Orleans is famous for three things: gumbo, carnivals, and cornet players. We got cornet players coming out of our asses down there." He played a bright little phrase. "There's one kid blows the rest of us halfway down the street. Louis Armstrong, his name is. They call him Satchelmouth, on account of his big fat face. You could stuff his horn into that mouth of his and never know where it went." The man shook his head. "That boy can charm the moon down from the sky, he plays so hot." He walked over to the stage and opened the piano lid. "Too hot for me, at any rate. Every night folks ask me how come I don't sound more like that flashy little motherfucker. Fact is, that's just not how I like to play." He perched his enormous frame on the edge of the piano stool, and softly played a chord with his left hand. With his right hand he raised his cornet to his lips and played a couple of mournful notes. His fingers moved across the piano keys, a sparse and haunting accompaniment. He sat back on the piano stool. "That hot stuff isn't for me, see? I like to play sweet and *low*." He looked at Joseph. "So you gonna give me a gig?"

Joseph coughed uncomfortably. "Like I said, it's our last night."

"All the more reason. One night only. Catch it while you can."

"I'll have to ask my mother," said Joseph. "She'll be here later."

"Your mother, huh." The man leaned over

the piano and picked out another chord, strange and melancholy. "Mind if I wait around?"

Joseph shook his head. He fetched the broom and began to sweep the floor while the man watched him from the stage. Occasionally he would turn to address the piano keys and concoct another foreign chord that hung in the air, dissonant and unsettling.

About an hour later, the front door opened and Jette walked in. When she saw the man at the piano she stopped abruptly. Immediately he stood up, hopped off the stage, and walked toward her. "Good morning, ma'am," he said. "Your son was good enough to let me in to wait for you. I heard you have music here in the evenings, and —"

Suddenly he stopped talking. "I know you," he said.

"I beg your pardon?" said Jette.

"I *know* you," repeated the man. "I seen you before somewhere."

Jette shook her head. "No, I don't think so," she said.

"Never forget a face," said the man. "I seen you before. You ever been to New Orleans?"

"No," said Jette.

"Not *ever?*"

"Well, I was there once, for less than a day,

but that was a long time ago, and anyway, there's not the slightest —"

The man snapped his fingers. "The train station. There was flooding up the line. I spoke with your husband. Got you on a boat upriver."

Jette frowned. "There *was* a man —"

"You was expecting." The man turned and looked at Joseph and whistled. "This the boy?"

Jette was still struggling to make sense of this unexpected arrival. New Orleans was another world away. "Yes, but —"

"Lomax. The name is Lomax."

"Mr. Lomax," said Jette weakly. "It's been a very long time."

"And how is your husband?" asked Lomax. "I remember he liked Buddy Bolden." He turned to Joseph. "Buddy Bolden was another cornet player. The real deal. That cat could play Louis Armstrong's raggedy little ass off. Your daddy heard him play. That was how we met."

"My husband was killed in Europe, Mr. Lomax," said Jette quietly. "In the war."

"I'm sorry to hear that."

After a moment's silence Joseph said, "He wants to play tonight."

Lomax turned and pointed toward his cornet that was sitting on top of the piano.

"I told him it's our last night," said Joseph.

"Would you play something for me?" asked Jette.

"Happy to," said Lomax. He sat down at the piano and picked up his cornet.

As Jette listened to the languorous unfurling of melody, she remembered her brief time in New Orleans. Lomax had been the first friendly face they met in America. Without him they might never have made it to Missouri. She wondered what path her life might have followed if the man on the stage had not appeared when he did. The thought occurred to her that, like the improvised melodies that Lomax was spinning from the bell of his horn, every life was a galaxy of permutations and possibilities from which a single thread would be picked out and followed, for better or for worse. When the music ended, Jette made a choice of her own that sent our family careening down an unlikely path that only now has acquired the reassuring gloss of inevitability. By such delicate threads do all our existences hang.

She smiled. "Joseph, Mr. Lomax was very kind to your father and me, a long time ago. Of course he can play."

Lomax grinned. "*Never* forget a face," he said proudly.

In truth Jette did not much care for Lomax's maudlin music, but she knew that Frederick would have approved: here was a stranger from across the years, arrived just in time to help administer the last rites to her husband's dream.

As it was, nobody complained about the music at all, because Lomax's tender ballads were difficult to hear above the hysteria of the tavern's final night. The whole town wallowed in a riot of nostalgia, fueled by an ocean of free drink. Determined not to leave a drop for Walford Scott and his thirsty minions, Jette kept pouring drinks until the final bottle had been emptied. By then it was three o'clock in the morning, and the Nick-Nack was still half-full, although only a few customers were conscious. Men snored fitfully in their chairs. Some had crawled onto the stage and were sleeping next to the piano.

For the last time, Jette and Joseph walked home from the Nick-Nack, leaving the front door unlocked and the passed-out drinkers in peace. Lomax followed them, Rosa fast asleep in his arms.

"So, Miss Jette," said Lomax as they walked home. "What happens next?"

Jette looked up at the stars. "I've been wondering that for months." She sighed. "And I still have no idea. The Nick-Nack is all I have."

"People are always going to want their liquor," said Lomax quietly.

"No," said Jette firmly. "I won't do that. I won't become a criminal."

They walked on in silence.

"Miss Jette," asked Lomax after a while, "can you cook?"

"I suppose so. Why do you ask?"

"Well," said Lomax, "even if people can't drink, they still have to eat."

Lomax spent the night on the floor of the sitting room, sleeping in front of the fireplace, beneath the terra-cotta angel wing. When Joseph woke up, he found their guest sitting outside on the porch, his long legs stretched out in the sunshine.

"Was I dreaming," said Lomax, "or was there a *raccoon* sleeping in that crate?"

"That was Mr. Jim," said Joseph.

"He didn't look too pleased to see me. Gave me a mean old look as he slunk off." Lomax laughed softly to himself. "Mr. Jim," he said.

Joseph sat down next to him. "What's it like, living in a city?"

"What's it like? It's loud, for one thing. Everyone lives so close to each other. And you know, down there, in Louisiana, with all them bayous and swamps —" Lomax pinched his nose. "But this." He turned toward Joseph. "You know what the air around here smells like to me? It smells like *freedom*."

"I liked your playing last night."

"You did, huh. Well, thanks. I think you were about the only one payin' any attention," said Lomax without bitterness.

"Where will you go now?"

"Kansas City, most likely. Bennie Moten's got a band there. Figure he might need a cornet player. And if he don't, I'll find other work. Plenty of good music going on there right now."

"The girl next door is from Kansas City," said Joseph.

Lomax raised an eyebrow. "She your girl-friend?"

"I've never spoken to her."

"You haven't? Why not?"

Joseph blushed. "I don't know what to say."

Lomax nodded sympathetically. "My friend, you are not alone. There are fellas been around a lot longer than you who still have no idea how to talk to the ladies."

"What about you?"

"Oh, I got an idea."

"So tell me, then. What should I say to her?"

"Aw, you know." Lomax sucked in his cheeks. "My, what a pretty dress you're wearing today. Excuse me, but you have the most beautiful eyes. Tra la la."

Joseph gave Lomax a look.

"Or, okay. You could give her something. Pick her some flowers. Write her a poem."

Before Joseph could reply, Jette appeared at the door. She winced as she blinked into the morning sun. As a rule she never drank when she worked, but last night she had been swept up in the sentimentality of the occasion. She looked as if she was regretting it now. Jette shaded her eyes and squinted at Lomax and Joseph.

"Mr. Lomax, I've been thinking about what you said last night," she said. "And you're right. People still need to eat."

"Yes, ma'am, they do," said Lomax.

"You're going to open a restaurant?" asked Joseph excitedly.

"I don't know." Jette sighed and looked at Lomax. "Do you really think it could work?"

"If you can cook, then it'll work." Lomax looked thoughtful. "You already got most of what you need. You got a place, you got tables and chairs. You got a clientele."

Jette looked up at the sky. She had lain awake most of the night, thinking about the idea. It was the only plan she had. "Mr. Lomax," she said, "would you be interested in earning a little extra money?"

Lomax got to his feet. "Ma'am, I'm *always* interested in earning a little extra money."

Thirty minutes later, Joseph and Lomax were standing in the middle of the deserted Nick-Nack. They had shaken the last slumbering drinkers awake and sent them on their way. Now they surveyed the wreckage of the night before. There were mountains of unwashed glasses. Chairs had been up-ended and abandoned where they fell. Hats and shoes littered the floor.

They spent the morning clearing out everything that wouldn't be needed. In the alleyway behind the building they lit a bonfire and watched while memories burned. They upended tables and chairs and began to file down the legs so they no longer wobbled. While they worked, Lomax talked. Joseph could have listened to his deep, rolling voice for the rest of his life. His language glittered with mystery, enriched by Southern patois and an impressive lexicon of cusswords. Lomax wove his tales into a rich tapestry of food, heat, women, and music — Buddy Bolden, King Oliver, Louis Armstrong, an army of cornet players. New Orleans shimmered in the background of his stories, a mirage.

Lomax had grown up in the Third Ward, the eldest of six children. His mother worked as a seamstress. She made a little money on the side practicing voodoo, casting hexes on enemies, a nickel a curse. He never knew his father. His first job, at eight, was delivering five-cent buckets of coal to the prostitutes on Bienville Street. His childhood was hungry but happy. Every Sunday he and his brothers followed the marching bands as they paraded through town. The musicians looked so fine in their pristine uniforms, instruments gleaming in the sun. He told Joseph about catching crawfish off the pier at Algiers, about stealing jars of honey off traders' wagons. He recalled sneaking backstage at the Funky Butt Hall on Perdido Street to watch the beautiful dancers shimmy beneath the bright lights.

Joseph listened, agog at news of this alien world. The only black man he had ever spoken to was William Henry Harris. Lomax's life in the Louisiana delta was exotic, steamy, and cruel, a universe away from the vanilla, landlocked borders of Missouri.

As they walked back to the house at the end of the day, Joseph was exhausted. His body hummed with the ache of a day's work, and he was filthy with dirt and grime, but he was happy. He was looking toward the future, and saw nothing but mystery glimmering just beyond the horizon.

His euphoria did not last long. When he pushed open the front door, Jette was sitting at the table, her head in her hands. She looked up as they walked into the room.

"Something terrible has happened," she said.

Despite the audience's apparent indifference to Lomax's performance the previous evening, those pretty melodies had lain siege to an unexpected heart.

Polk, the ancient bartender, had listened to the music, and a heavy melancholy had descended upon him. Ever since he'd been struck by Cupid's unexpected arrow the day of Frederick's departure for war, his devotion to Jette had never faltered. In the intervening months he had remained more or less constantly drunk. With enough whiskey inside him he could still achieve a sedated equilibrium, at least for a while.

But Polk's precariously balanced existence was knocked disastrously off-kilter by the sweet sounds that crept out of Lomax's cornet. He listened in dismay to the truth and beauty in those sad notes. The music clustered around his beleaguered heart, extinguishing hope. Only when he crashed to the ground later that evening was he finally able to escape its spell.

When Polk awoke in the alleyway behind the Nick-Nack some hours later, he opened his eyes and stared up at the stars. Inside, the tavern was silent. He gingerly pulled himself to his feet.

The hopelessness of Polk's love for my grandmother had given him a certain grace, but not any longer. His feelings had been betrayed by the purity of Lomax's music, exposed for what they really were: shabby, second-rate, and compromised by his own timidity. He walked sadly through the deserted streets of the town.

Even before Lomax's cornet had sliced him open, Polk had been teetering on the brink of despair at the prospect of the tavern closing its doors. There would be no more exquisite proximity to Jette, and no more liquor to soften his nightly crucifixion. Over the past few months Polk had been pilfering bottles from behind the bar and hiding them beneath his bed, but he knew that he was merely postponing the inevitable. A future without alcohol or Jette Meisenheimer was waiting for him, and he did not know how he was going to survive.

The old bartender heard the quiet pulse of the river nearby, and turned toward it. He walked to the end of the pier and stared out into the night. *Such a shame,* whispered the rushing water beneath his feet, *such a shame.* With a small sigh, Polk stepped forward and allowed his body to fall into the water's embrace. There was barely a ripple as the river closed over the old man's head, bearing him onward into darkness.

It was one more departure, another good-bye.

Polk had been found a little way down-river, his tired, bedraggled body washed up on a muddy bank. Cap in hand, a somber Walford Scott had delivered the news personally to my grandmother.

Jette had grown very fond of the old bartender. She sat at the kitchen table and wept for him. Chief Scott did not know whether he had jumped or fallen into the river; the evidence was inconclusive.

Still, no amount of fruitless conjecture would ever bring Polk back. The Nick-Nack was gone, and its tottering talisman with it.

SEVENTEEN

That evening Lomax sat down to dinner with Jette and the children. The four of them ate in silence. Usually Rosa dominated mealtime conversation, but she was perfectly silent, her eyes never leaving the dark-skinned stranger sitting across the table from her. Jette had made a thick potato soup laced with sauerkraut. Lomax ate thoughtfully.

"Is this the sort of thing you were thinking of serving in the restaurant?" he asked.

Jette nodded. "Do you like it?"

"Oh, well. It's very good, yes." Lomax stirred his spoon, not looking up.

"It's German," said Jette. "It's traditional."

"Uh-huh. Traditional. Well, okay then." Lomax returned to his silent contemplation of his soup bowl.

Jette remembered their first meal in New Orleans, the hotel table laden down with all that spicy food. "Perhaps you think it's a little bland," she sniffed.

Lomax put his hands up. "I never said that," he protested. "It's very nice."

Jette's eyes narrowed. *"Nice?"*

"Absolutely. Delicious, in fact." Lomax tried a worried smile. He knew he was in trouble.

Jette put down her spoon. "Perhaps you have some suggestions as to how I might improve it?"

"Oh, no, no, no," muttered Lomax, shaking his head. "I wouldn't —"

"Really," interrupted Jette. "Please." Although it was not a request.

"Well." Lomax looked uncomfortable. "You might add a little cayenne."

"Cayenne? I've never heard of it."

"Cayenne pepper. Give it a little zing."

"A little *zing,*" repeated Jette.

"Or, um. Maybe some dried basil," said Lomax, his voice small.

There was a long silence.

"Are you a cook yourself, Mr. Lomax?" asked Jette eventually.

"I don't know that I'd call myself a *cook,* but I've worked a few different kitchens in my time," he answered. "That place I met your husband? Chez Benny's? I worked there for a while. I learned a thing or two along the way."

"Well, then, perhaps you could show me

243

how *you* would do it."

"You want more zing?"

Finally, Jette smiled. "Yes, I want more zing."

The next few weeks were a riot of industry. Lomax agreed to stay until the Nick-Nack's metamorphosis was complete. He slept in the back room of what was to become the new restaurant. During the day he and Joseph worked together, slowly erasing the years of liquor and smoke. They whitewashed the walls and polished the floors until they shone darkly underfoot. The old mirror that had hung for years behind the bar was removed, cleaned, and rehung. The piano was pushed back into the same corner where Frederick had first discovered it, silenced once more.

My father and Lomax had plenty of time to talk while they painted and cleaned. Joseph loved to hear his new friend's tales of New Orleans, but what really made the two of them as thick as thieves was Cora Leftkemeyer.

Lomax was fond of boasting about the trail of brokenhearted women he had left in his wake. His bragging convinced Joseph that he had finally found the person to help him unlock Cora's heart, and he peppered

Lomax with questions. Seeing the desperate look on his young friend's face, Lomax's soliloquies on the manifold complexities of the female became more thoughtful. The two of them discussed tactics and techniques. They practiced opening conversational gambits. Lomax would flutter his eyelashes and respond to Joseph's questions in an arch falsetto. Joseph became upset when Lomax could no longer contain his laughter. He mumbled his lines, his face a mask of terror. No amount of coaching could hide his fear. When it came to Cora Leftkemeyer, there was simply too much at stake.

While Lomax and Joseph worked, Jette ordered pots and pans, a mountain of new plates, glasses, and cutlery, and a new stove. She visited local farmers and negotiated daily deliveries of vegetables and meat. She bought tablecloths and candles.

There was no rest in the evenings. Jette and Lomax discussed menus and stood over the stove, experimenting with recipes. From somewhere Lomax had procured a selection of herbs and spices that Jette had never seen before, and he showed her how to use them. My grandmother was a good student. Soon the kitchen was a rainbow of paprika, bell peppers, okra, and sweet potatoes. Saucepans of fragrant, dark stock bubbled on the stove, filling the house with their dangerous, delicious aroma. Every fresh concoction now had plenty of zing. Occasionally there was *too* much zing — Lomax was sometimes reduced to coughing fits when Jette was too heavy-handed with those new, potent ingredients. Every night he would taste my grandmother's latest attempt at gumbo, red beans and rice, or shrimp Creole. Jette made notes of whatever improvements he suggested, and would try again the next day.

One evening Lomax put a forkful of chicken étouffée into his mouth. It was Jette's fifth attempt in three weeks. On each previous occasion he had shaken his head; this time, though, he closed his eyes and a wide smile appeared on his face.

"Oh, that's it," he breathed, "that is *it*." My grandmother stood there, a wooden spoon in her hand, blushing like a schoolgirl. "Miss Jette" — Lomax grinned, his mouth still full — "you just took me home."

Jette beamed at him.

Throughout all this, the rest of the town looked on. Jette's decision to open a restaurant was a matter of mild interest, but it was Lomax's continued presence that scandalized the gossips. A black man in the house! What's next? people wondered. Well, this, came the reply: he would murder them all in their beds soon enough. They watched Lomax go in and out of the Meisenheimer home as if he owned the place. They watched and waited.

Jette decided that they needed a new name to go with the new venture. The Nick-Nack held too many memories, not all of them good. It was time to move on and start afresh. She ordered a new sign, which Lomax nailed over the door.

The sign read FREDERICK'S.

On the first Sunday in April, the new restaurant opened its doors for its inaugural lunch service. There was a healthy line of hungry guests at the door, still dressed up in their churchgoing best.

Jette had invited Mathias Becker to be the guest of honor. The doctor was never one to turn down the offer of food, and he happily accepted. Joseph led him to the best table in the room. "This is quite delightful," he said to my father as he sat down. "I can't wait to see the menu!"

"Actually, there is no menu," said Joseph.

"No menu? How can you have a restaurant without a *menu*?"

"You've got two choices," explained Joseph.

"Just two?" pouted Dr. Becker.

"We've got either pork chops and sauerkraut or jambalaya and jalapeño corn muffins."

The doctor stared at him. "What did you say?"

"Pork chops —"

"No, no. The other one."

"Oh. Jambalaya and jalapeño corn muffins."

"Goodness. That sounds like an illness, not something you eat," said Dr. Becker.

"Oh no, it's delicious. It's got smoked sausage, chicken, rice, and tomatoes in it. And lots of spices."

The doctor's nose wrinkled. "Spices?" He stared long and hard at Joseph, who smiled affably back. Finally the doctor came to a decision. "Pork chops," he harrumphed.

It had been Jette's idea to offer only two items a day. She knew her limitations as a cook. In addition, she wanted to be in the dining room while the restaurant was open, so the food needed to be prepared in advance. Lomax was stationed in the kitchen, ready to plate up orders from the bubbling pots. Each day there would be one traditional German dish, bland and monumental, and one more exotic. As that opening sitting progressed, however, Jette began to wonder whether she might have miscalculated. Joseph was carrying plate after plate of pork chops across the room. Not one person ordered the jambalaya. Finally Joseph came out of the kitchen, looking worried.

"We've run out of pork chops," he told her.

Jette let out a deep breath. "All right, then," she said.

The next people waiting to be served were Bucky and Minnie Rohrbacker. Bucky was the best cattle auctioneer in the county. He'd been known to knock back a drink or two at the Nick-Nack in his time, and he was gazing around the room with an astonished look on his face as he lowered himself into his chair.

"Sure looks different in here now," he said, a little wistfully.

Minnie Rohrbacker beamed at Joseph. "And look at you, all grown up!"

"The thing is, we've run out of pork chops," said Joseph.

"That's all right," said Minnie kindly. "What else do you have?"

Joseph stood on one foot. "Jambalaya and jalapeño corn muffins."

Minnie Rohrbacker's smile slipped a little. "Jamba— ?"

"Jambalaya. And jalapeño corn muffins."

"That sounds interesting," she said uncertainly.

"It's better than the pork chops."

Neither of the Rohrbackers looked convinced. "Don't you have anything else?" asked Bucky.

Joseph shook his head.

Bucky looked at his wife. "Well, we're here," he said, sighing. "We may as well try the — What was it again?"

"I'll bring it right out," said Joseph.

A few minutes later he delivered two steaming plates of jambalaya to the table. The Rohrbackers sniffed and prodded cautiously at their food. Finally Bucky shoveled a forkful of rice and sausage into his mouth. He chewed thoughtfully for a moment. Then he took another bite. And another. Then he took a small bite of a corn muffin.

Jette watched all this from across the room until she couldn't help herself any longer. She went up to the table. "How is everything?" she asked.

By then small beads of sweat had begun to appear on Bucky Rohrbacker's forehead. "Good God, Jette," he gasped. "What's in this? My throat feels like it's on fire."

"Don't you like it?"

Bucky shook his head. "My head may be about to blow off, but I believe it's the

250

best goddamned thing I've ever put in my mouth." He wiped his napkin across his brow. "Could I have another glass of water?"

You don't become the most successful cattle auctioneer in Caitlin County by being a shy and retiring type. Bucky Rohrbacker was used to making himself heard over the agricultural ruckus of a busy auction yard and a crowd of squabbling farmers. He was blessed with a *very* loud voice, and his profane opinion was heard by everyone in the restaurant.

Thirty minutes later there was no food left in the kitchen.

The following day Jette prepared Wienerschnitzel with pan-fried potatoes and a devilish chicken gumbo. Reports of the new restaurant's unorthodox menu had spread quickly through the town, and although there were still many diners (including Dr. Becker) who chose the more familiar fare, this time orders for both dishes were evenly matched. Jette had to turn disappointed customers away when the food ran out.

That night she and Lomax planned out a schedule of menus. There were two dishes for each day of the week — fourteen recipes in total, before the cycle began again.

By the end of the first week, people had

begun to wait in line thirty minutes before the restaurant opened, just to be sure to get a table. It did not take long for many of the Nick-Nack's old customers to return to their old haunt, albeit for more sober communion.

Joseph enjoyed taking orders and clearing plates. He developed a knack for describing Lomax's culinary creations in particularly mouthwatering terms, so that even the most cautious of the town's eaters were unable to resist them. He ferried plates back and forth between the dining room and the kitchen while Jette took the money and poured gallons of iced tea. She bought a till, which gave a satisfyingly heavy *ching* every time the drawer slid open. In that metallic chime she heard the echo of promise and hope.

Jette was bombarded by pleas from customers to open for dinner in the evening, but she always refused. Frederick's opened at eleven o'clock each morning, and was always closed by two. Jette and Lomax spent the afternoon preparing the next day's food, while Joseph and Rosa washed dishes and swept the floors. By six o'clock the work for the day was done. After supper with Lomax at a small table in the kitchen, Jette took her children home.

While the restaurant was open Lomax stayed in the kitchen, hidden from view. He was well aware of the unease that his presence might cause. He was used to the fear of strangers. It was as familiar to him as the sound of his own voice. He knew that this town was not for him.

But days and weeks passed, and still he did not go.

The fact was, Lomax couldn't leave. He found himself skewered in place like a butterfly wing pinned to a collector's board. The fierce love of Jette's family kept him there long after he should have been on his way.

·

EIGHTEEN

At about the time that Joseph began work at the restaurant, Stefan started to help his father on the farm. As a result, the two friends saw less and less of each other, but every so often they would still escape up to Tillman's Wood with Johann Kliever's rifle. They hid in the undergrowth and waited for unsuspecting wildlife to wander into their path. Their aims gradually improved. Stefan in particular had a good eye and was able to hit his target more often than not. They often walked back to Joseph's house with a collection of dead animals in a sack, but not all outings were so successful. One hot afternoon in early summer, the boys had bickered at each other the whole time they lay hidden, and as a result they had missed everything they shot at. After two hours they trooped back down the hill, their bag still empty, both in foul moods. Each blamed the other for his misses. Stefan stormed through the forest with his father's gun over his shoulder. Joseph hung back, seething in silent fury. He wanted no more to do with Stefan that day. As he made his way down the hill toward the house, Joseph realized that he now preferred Lomax's company to Stefan's.

When they approached the bottom of the hill, Stefan was so far ahead of Joseph that he was only just visible through the trees. Suddenly Stefan stopped moving. After a moment, he reached for the gun. "Oh, boy. Just wait until you see this!" he shouted. "Sitting target!"

"What is it?" called Joseph.

"Fat little beast," said Stefan. "I think he's *sunbathing*." He raised the shotgun to his shoulder.

"Wait," said Joseph, quickening his pace. Stefan appeared to be aiming directly into his backyard. "Don't shoot anything until I —"

But Stefan did not wait.

The shot cracked through the air. Stefan lowered the weapon and yelled in delight. "Got him!"

By now Joseph was running as fast as he could. "What did you do?" he gasped.

"Down there on the roof," said Stefan triumphantly.

My father squinted through the trees, cold

dread clawing at his gut. On top of the old outhouse lay a familiar gray ball of fur. There was a dark stain on Mr. Jim's exposed belly where Stefan's bullet had scored a direct hit.

For three days Rosa would not leave her bedroom. The little house echoed with her grief. That fat little raccoon was the best friend she'd ever had, and now he was gone. My aunt wept and wept, inconsolable in her loss.

In the end, it was Lomax who rescued her.

One afternoon he knocked on the door of the bedroom and peered inside. As usual, Rosa was sitting on the bed, her face stained with tears.

"I got something for you," he said. Under his arm he was carrying a flat piece of wood with black and white squares painted on it. He laid it down in the middle of the floor. "You know what this is?"

Rosa shook her head.

"This here is a chessboard. You ever heard of chess?"

Rosa shook her head again.

"It's the greatest game in the world." From his pocket Lomax produced a small bag. Inside were thirty-two tiny chess pieces. He tipped them onto the board and began arranging them in their starting positions.

Rosa watched closely, not saying a word. "I carved these myself," he said. "Want me to show you how to play?"

Rosa wiped her eyes, nodded, and clambered off the bed.

For the rest of the afternoon, Lomax showed her how each piece moved. My aunt did not blink as his long fingers glided across the board, pushing the two armies into war.

Finally Lomax groaned a little and stretched his arms above his head. "I tell you what. Sitting on the floor all afternoon is hard work when you've got bones as old as mine." He looked out the window at the approaching twilight, and then back at my aunt. "I have to go now."

For the first time in hours, Rosa moved. She reached out and grabbed his wrist. "Come back tomorrow," she begged.

Lomax's eyes twinkled. "I'll be here."

Every day after that Lomax sat on the floor and explained a new technique — the pin, the fork, the sacrifice. Rosa listened and watched. He never had to explain anything twice. Chess made complete sense to my aunt. She was hypnotized by the tapestry of patterns that could be spun by those wooden pieces. Within the game's limitless permutations she found a means of expressing herself. She improved with mesmerizing speed, fueled by natural flair and ferocious determination.

Chess was always more than just a game to Rosa. She waged war over that board. After a while Lomax stopped giving her lessons and they just played. As kindly as he could, he thrashed Rosa day after day, but each loss just made her more determined to win the next time. She spent hours alone with her chess set, learning the secrets hidden within those sixty-four squares.

With his homemade chessboard Lomax opened up a whole new world for Rosa. There she could escape the sadness of her loss. Little by little, the light returned to her eyes.

After the shooting, Joseph and Stefan did not go hunting again.

Perhaps it was inevitable that the boys' friendship would not survive the incident undamaged. Joseph was angry with Stefan for what he had done, even though his friend hadn't known that Mr. Jim was Rosa's pet. It didn't help that Stefan was unrepentant about what had happened. To him the episode was nothing more than a fine piece of marksmanship. When Joseph explained about Rosa's attachment to the raccoon, Stefan laughed in his face and then marched down the hill, the gun slung over his shoulder. Joseph stood there and watched him go.

They did not see each other for several weeks after that. When Stefan finally appeared and shrugged a lazy apology, Joseph knew that things would never be the same again. He could still hear the harsh bark of his friend's mockery in his head. Perhaps inevitably, he turned more and more to Lomax for comfort and advice. Whether Lomax was qualified to dispense the kind of wisdom that Joseph was hoping for is perhaps questionable; but he was there, and he was willing. Joseph sought Lomax's opinion on a wide variety of topics, but in the end his questions would always circle back toward Cora Leftkemeyer.

Joseph and Lomax now found themselves disagreeing about what should be done about Cora. Lomax maintained that further theorizing was useless. It was time for Joseph to put all that talk into practice. Joseph knew that Lomax was right, but by then his infatuation was so all-consuming that the prospect of rejection was unthinkable.

Lomax saw the despair in his young friend's eyes, but he was losing patience. "You think that girl's gonna wait for you?" he asked.

"You think she's tellin' all them other fellas to skit, 'cause she's waiting for her little neighbor to summon up the courage to talk to her?" He shook his head. "She don't even know you *exist,* Joseph. Every time you see her comin', you start off in the other direction as fast as you can go."

This was true enough. Cora and her father had visited the restaurant the previous week and Joseph had been so terrified that he hid in the kitchen and begged Jette to take their order.

"I'm just not ready," he told Lomax.

Lomax sighed. "You keep this up and you won't need to worry about being *ready.*"

Every night Joseph tossed and turned in his bed, miserably awake, unable to escape his tortured thoughts of his beautiful neighbor. One evening, as he stared into the darkness, unable to sleep, he decided to go and see Lomax. Even his friend's grouchy disapproval had to be better than this. He quietly pulled on his clothes and slipped out of the house.

The streets were quiet. An almost full moon bathed the town in a ghostly light. As he approached the restaurant, Joseph heard Lomax's cornet floating through the still night air, cushioned on a soft piano chord. He stopped and listened. It was difficult to imagine a life without Lomax now.

Just then Joseph heard approaching footsteps. Not wanting to be caught out so late, he stepped into the shadows cast by the restaurant wall. A moment later a trio of dark silhouettes appeared, moving stealthily and with purpose. The men walked right past him, unaware of his presence, and vanished around the corner of the building. Joseph stood frozen. There was no reason for these men to be here, so late at night.

He heard a soft knock at the back door, three brisk raps and then two slower ones. The music stopped. A moment later there was a low murmur of voices, but Joseph couldn't make out what was being said. He remained hidden in the darkness, his stomach a churning pit of apprehension. Finally Lomax's mysterious visitors began to walk back down the alleyway. My father held his breath as they passed by him for a second time, walking more quickly now. After a moment Lomax resumed his quiet music-making at the piano.

Joseph stood in the shadows, lost in thought. Then he crept down the alleyway, took a deep breath, and knocked on the door — three quick thumps, two slow. Moments

later the door opened. He heard Lomax before he saw him.

"You folks must be thirsty tonight if you
already — Aw, shit."

They looked at each other in silence.

Finally Joseph found some words. "What
are you *doing,* Lomax?"

Lomax crossed his arms. "I might ask you
the same question. Why aren't you in bed?"

"I couldn't sleep, so I came to see you.
Who were those men?"

Lomax blinked. "What men?"

"The ones who just knocked on your door.
The ones you thought were *thirsty.*"

The word hung between them. Lomax
studied Joseph for a moment and then
shrugged his shoulders. "Man's gotta make
a living," he said.

"A living?"

"People can't buy liquor anymore, but
they're still thirsty."

Joseph frowned. "So you're —"

"Making a little moonshine, that's right.
Little trick I learned long time ago." Lomax
gestured behind him. "There's a whole
kitchen back here," he explained. "Seemed
a shame not to use it."

"But what if you get caught?" asked Joseph, fretful.

"Caught by who?" Lomax asked. "The

chief of police, that Mr. Scott, he's my best customer. He already drunk the rest of the town dry, and now he got himself a little taste for it." Lomax laughed softly. "I ain't worried about him." He paused. "You know who I *am* worried about?"

"Who?"

"Your mother. If she hears about this, she'll whup my behind and send me packing so fast my head'll spin." He eyed Joseph. "You gonna tell her?"

More than anything, Joseph didn't want Lomax to leave. He shook his head.

And so Lomax continued to operate his clandestine business from the back door of the restaurant under cover of darkness. The diners seemed oblivious to all that illicit late-night trade, but they weren't, of course. Many of them would quietly return at night, skulking down the dark alleyway in search of a bottle of Lomax's fearful brew.

Since Frederick's departure for the war in Europe, Jette and her children had struggled through each uncertain day. Lomax became a new sun around which to orbit, and their unsettled existence finally came to an end. Joseph was learning to be a man. Rosa had found solace and reward at the chessboard. Jette's new business was under way. She was finally able to imagine a new future for them all.

It was Lomax who was the curator of these dreams. This stranger brought hope to my family, and with it, peace.

NINETEEN

By then Joseph was sixteen years old. He enjoyed being a workingman, and was pleased that his job at the restaurant meant he no longer had to go to school. His favorite time of the day was early in the morning. He quietly performed his chores, folding napkins, cleaning silverware, and setting tables. He relished the solitude. When the doors opened and the outside world swept in, he would not have another moment to himself.

Alone, he often sang to himself. His angelic treble had deepened to a warm and rich tenor, just like his father's. Joseph had begun to sing the songs and arias that he had heard Frederick perform in that same room. The music had been buried somewhere deep within him, and now it emerged, note-perfect, after years of silence.

One morning he was singing snatches of *Rigoletto* as he swept the floor of the dining room. Lomax emerged yawning from the kitchen, and leaned against the door frame, watching. When Joseph finally noticed him, he stopped at once.

"You never told me you could sing," said Lomax.

Joseph looked sheepish, and then grinned.

"You ever thought about serenading your pretty little neighbor?"

"Cora?" Joseph looked doubtful.

Lomax nodded. "She might like to hear that."

Of course, Joseph knew the story of Frederick's musical ambush of his mother, that Sunday afternoon in Hanover. He stood in the middle of the floor, lost in thought.

That night Joseph crept out of the house just before midnight. Lomax was waiting for him by the gate.

"You ready?" he asked.

Joseph shook his head. "Not really."

Lomax patted him gently on the back. The Leftkemeyers' house stood in darkness. They walked around the side of the building until they were standing beneath a window. "This the one?" whispered Lomax.

Joseph nodded. "I think so."

"What you goin' to sing, anyway?"

" 'Nessun dorma.' "

Lomax looked at him.

266

"It's Italian," explained Joseph. "It means 'Nobody sleeps.'"

"You don't know nothin' in *English?*"

"But this is from *Turandot*."

"Look, it could be from Tallahassee for all I care. But this girl don't speak Italian, far as I know, and —"

Joseph touched Lomax's arm, suddenly calm, confident. Puccini had pedigree when it came to this sort of thing. "I think it'll work," he said.

Lomax shook his head. "Nobody sleeps, huh. Well, let's hope you got that bit right." He squeezed Joseph's shoulder. "I'll be over there." He pointed to a nearby tree. "And remember, don't say *nothing*. Just let the music do the work."

"So I just sing the song and then disappear?"

"Right."

"And what if she doesn't recognize me?"

"Oh, don't you worry about that." Lomax grinned. "Now go sing." And with a wave he retreated into the darkness.

The night air was warm and still. Joseph gazed at the sky, wondering whether Frederick was up there somewhere, willing him on. Finally, he turned toward Cora's bedroom window, quietly humming the opening bars of the aria to make sure he had the pitch about right. He crossed his fingers and took a deep breath.

Lomax couldn't see anything from behind the tree. As he stood in the darkness, waiting for Joseph's song to begin, it occurred to him that none of the women *he* had ever known were at their sweetest or most romantically inclined when unexpectedly woken up in the middle of the night. As the minutes passed, he became increasingly apprehensive. Finally, he poked his head around the tree trunk and squinted toward the Leftkemeyer house.

Joseph stood in a patch of moonlight beneath Cora's window. His body weaved in gentle rhythm. One hand rested on his chest, the other was raised up to the heavens. Lomax watched as his lips formed all those beautiful Italian words.

Not one sound came out of my father's mouth.

The next night they tried again. And the next. For a week Lomax watched as Joseph fought for control of his mutinous vocal cords. Each night my father would finally retreat, his face hot with tears. Not even the ardor of first love could free him from his old phobia of public performance. Perhaps that should have been no surprise. Cora

Leftkemeyer was the most important audience of all.

Joseph was devastated. His silence became a prison from which he could not escape. The strain of his nightly frustrations began to show. His eyes became ringed by dark shadows of exhaustion. He yawned as he took orders and ferried plates to and from the kitchen, his mind still trapped beneath Cora's window. To make matters worse, his father's ghost had settled on his shoulder. Joseph wanted to live up to Frederick's legacy. He longed for his own story to tell about Puccini.

Lomax was soon wishing he had never suggested the idea. He loved Joseph, and he couldn't bear to watch him suffer. Joseph continued to make his nightly pilgrimage alone. The hopelessness of the situation revealed a stubborn streak within him. He had no plan except to carry on, in the hope that one night his voice would finally emerge from his throat, fluttering into the night air like a magical bird in a fairy tale.

Luckily, Lomax didn't believe in fairy tales.

It was a Sunday afternoon in September. Joseph had been singing silently beneath Cora Leftkemeyer's bedroom for almost a month, and he looked wretched. He was sweeping up the first fall of leaves from the maple tree at the bottom of the yard, and he sang as he worked. Lomax and Jette watched him from just inside the kitchen door, where they could not be seen.

"He has a fine voice," said Lomax.

"Just like his father," murmured Jette.

They were silent for a moment as they listened. "Miss Jette," said Lomax, "why are you hiding?"

She turned to look at him. "Didn't you know?" she said. "Joseph can't sing in front of people."

"He can't?"

"Not if he knows they're there."

"He never told me that," said Lomax thoughtfully.

"It's a long story." Jette was silent for a moment as she remembered storming out of the Nick-Nack before Joseph's first public performance. No measure of regret could ever unpick the past. All that beautiful music was inside him, and she had trapped it there for good. She had always considered her furtive listening penance for what she had done. "His voice is so beautiful." She sighed. "Where are you going?"

"Be right back," said Lomax.

A few minutes later Lomax was leading a

wide-eyed Cora Leftkemeyer across the yard toward her future.

He motioned for her to stop behind a small row of tightly clustered spruce trees. He held his index finger in the air. "Listen," he whispered. Joseph was invisible behind the wall of green, but his voice floated through the air. The melody was sweet and clear and true. The two of them stood silently behind the trees, listening to my father sing. They must have looked an odd sight. Lomax towered over the girl, whose skin was as white as his was black. He wore his usual old shirt and tattered overalls. Cora was still dressed in her best church clothes. After a while Lomax pointed to a spot where she could look through a small gap in the trees. Cora moved forward and stared through the branches. Then she did not move for some time.

Finally she stepped back and turned to Lomax. "Why have you brought me here?" she asked. Her cheeks were flushed.

"Miss, do you know who that is?"

"He's my neighbor's son."

"Your neighbor's son, that's right." Lomax nodded. "His name is Joseph Meisenheimer. He's a friend of mine."

The two were silent for a moment as they listened some more.

"Why have you brought me here?" asked Cora again.

"Go to your bedroom window at midnight tonight," said Lomax softly. "Look outside. See what you see."

That night, Cora Leftkemeyer hid by her bedroom window and watched Joseph perform his silent tribute. She stood quite still, her fingers coiled tightly around the fabric of the curtain. It was a cloudless evening, and in the light of the moon Cora could see his lips moving soundlessly. She remembered the voice she had heard that afternoon, rich and clear, full of beauty and hope.

The following evening, Cora knew that sleep was a million miles away. She made a careful chink in the curtains and stared out of it, waiting. The Leftkemeyers' garden was cast in ghostly shadows, as still as the clock on her wall.

When Joseph finally appeared beneath her window, she felt her heart tumble. Once again, when he opened his mouth, no sound emerged. But it no longer mattered.

Cora Leftkemeyer could hear his song.

TWENTY

That first night, as Cora had stared down at the strange young man weaving silently below her bedroom window, bathed in silver moonlight, a whole new world suddenly burst into view. Joseph's display of devotion ignited a flame deep within her. The following morning she stood furtively by the kitchen window, waiting for a glimpse of Joseph as he left for work. She gazed at him as he yawned down the street toward the restaurant, and was unable to think about anything else.

They had never spoken a single word to each other.

Joseph would have probably gone on singing silently beneath her bedroom window for the rest of his life, but Cora was in no mood to wait. She watched him sing for one more night. The next evening she marched across the lawn.

Lomax had not told Joseph about his conversation with Cora, and so when my father opened the door and saw her standing there, he stared at her in mute amazement. Cora stared right back. In the moonlight Joseph's features had been largely hidden by shadows. When she gazed into his astonished face, any lingering doubts that she may have had vanished. She took a step forward and held out her hand.

Joseph reached for her fingers. "You're here," he said.

"I've been watching you," breathed Cora. "I've been hearing you sing."

The time that followed was rich with the unsullied bliss of first love. Cora and Joseph spent every evening together, going for long walks through the woods or sitting on the back porch drinking iced tea. They talked forever, an endless river of conversation, meandering across whole worlds. When it was time for Cora to cross the lawn back to her house, they lingered endlessly, reluctant to give each other up to the solitude of the night.

Each day Joseph found himself mesmerized afresh, agog at the news that Cora was here, with him.

She begged him to sing the song he had performed beneath her window. He refused at first, sure that the music would never come, but he was helpless to resist her entreaties for long. One evening he reluctantly agreed to try. He stood up, cleared his throat, and looked into her eyes. A deep breath — and then the melody emerged, ringing with crystalline beauty. Cora gazed up at him in delight. When he had finished, she stood up without a word and kissed him softly on the cheek. After that he sang for her every day — the same songs that Frederick had performed twenty years earlier, as he had serenaded Jette on the streets of Hanover. Cora listened, enchantment illuminating her beautiful face.

After years of silence, love set all that music free.

When Jette finally learned the details of Joseph's unorthodox amorous campaign beneath Cora's bedroom window, she could not help feeling proud of him, despite her misgivings. Lomax was a different matter, though. When she discovered that the nocturnal serenades had been his idea, and that it was he who had led Cora across the yard that Sunday afternoon, she confronted him.

"How are you going to feel when she breaks his heart?" she reproached him.

Lomax was unrepentant. "Who says she will?"

Jette shook her head. "This will end badly, you'll see."

"Have you seen how happy he is, Miss Jette?"

Jette snorted. "That's what worries me. He can't think straight. And they don't even know each other!"

"You didn't know your husband when he sang through the hedge at you."

"Well," said Jette, "that was different."

"Hmm. Funny how it's always different." Lomax scratched his head. "Look, Miss Jette, I love your boy," he said. "I don't want to see him hurt any more than you do. But I seen the look in his eye when he talks about that girl. He's pinned his whole life on her. Right or wrong, that's how it is. Smart or dumb, that's how it is. Not for me to judge. So what was I supposed to do? Turn away and let his dreams go up in smoke?"

"You could have told me what was going on."

Lomax shook his head. "It was already hard enough for Joseph to do what he did. If you had told him no, he never would have even tried." He paused. "I won't say I'm sorry for what I did. But I didn't do it to hurt you. Matter of fact, I wasn't thinking about you at all. I was thinking about *him*."

"But what if this is all a terrible mistake?"

"Miss Jette," said Lomax softly, "you got to let him *go*."

Understanding hit Jette like a low punch to the gut: from now on her relationship with her son would be defined by her inability to save him from his own mistakes. She resolved to accept Joseph's choice, bravely and without fuss. Her own mother's refusal to welcome Frederick into their family had chased them halfway across the world. She promised herself that she would not make the same mistake.

And so, as the romance between Joseph and Cora shyly blossomed, Jette dived gamely into the fray, extending invitations left and right. Every week the two fractured families ate together at her dinner table, where she served up her most popular dishes from the restaurant.

Jette did her best to like Cora, but maternal instinct clouded her view. The prim little girl from next door still struck her as cool and aloof. But weeks passed, and then months, and her bleak predictions of her son's heartbreak did not materialize. She had to admit that she had never seen Joseph so happy. When he announced one evening that he had asked Cora to marry him, and that she had accepted, Jette had the grace to admit (at least to herself) that she might have been mistaken.

Instead a new fear clouded the horizon. Jette was sure that Cora thought herself too grand for a small town like Beatrice. She became convinced that as soon as the young couple was married, Cora would announce her desire to return to Kansas City, or beyond.

Martin Leftkemeyer's concerns were quite different. He was not worried about the prospect of imminent abandonment, nor was he unhappy with his daughter's choice of mate. In fact he liked Joseph a great deal. It was the rest of his family that was the problem.

My grandfather had come to Beatrice in search of sanctuary. He needed to escape the memories of Cora's mother that lingered in the large, sad house in Kansas City where they had lived. He had stayed by his wife's bedside and watched as the influenza extinguished the light from her eyes. There was nothing he could have done to save her, and his powerlessness against the random brutality of fate flattened him almost as much as the loss of the woman he adored. Suddenly he was a frightened man. The busy streets outside his front door now hummed with invisible threat.

Our quiet little town had seemed a perfect antidote to the violent clamor of the big city.

His desk at the bank was always immaculately tidy. He paid meticulous attention to detail. The never-changing paperwork offered comfort in its bland functionality, a dour buttress against unpredictability. Boxes ticked, blank spaces filled: this, at least, he could control.

Unsurprisingly, then, Jette's capacity for benign chaos made Martin fretful. Her cheerful exuberance put his careful, well-ordered existence under threat. Those weekly festivals of starch at the Meisenheimer dinner table were a particular torment. He suffered quietly through Jette's effusive hospitality, and would stagger home at the end of every visit, giddy with relief to have survived. Martin loved Cora more than anything in the world, and he wanted her to be happy. But her marriage to Joseph sounded the death knell for any lingering hopes he may have had for a tranquil life.

Jette's reservations about the union were mild in comparison to Rosa's first flagrant hostility toward Cora. Nobody would ever be good enough for Rosa's darling brother. My devoted aunt had spent her whole life trying to get Joseph to love her back, just a little, and she could not stand the thought of being eclipsed completely by the pretty girl from next door. And so she hated Cora, unable to forgive her for stealing Joseph away.

One day Cora and Joseph arrived at Jette's house while Rosa and Lomax were immersed in one of their afternoon chess games. Cora watched them play. Rosa ignored her, frowning at the board in concentration. Lomax, though, grinned at her. "You ever play chess, Miss Cora?" he asked.

"I used to," said Cora. "But a long time ago."

"Perhaps the two of you should play." Lomax sighed, gesturing at the pieces before him. "She's beating up on me. Again."

Rosa looked up for the first time. "Would you like to play?" she asked Cora.

Cora smiled at her. "Finish this game. You and I can play tomorrow."

Rosa spent the next day imagining the look on Cora's face as she inflicted a crushing defeat on the unwelcome interloper. Victory at the chessboard would never win Joseph back, but it would be sweet, all the same. When Cora sat down opposite her, looking uncertainly at the pieces, there was a merciless glint in my aunt's eye.

Half an hour later, Rosa surveyed the board in disbelief. Her forces had been decimated. Cora had played with stunning, sustained aggression. Rosa had been unable to mount a single attack of her own. To her horror she felt the hot prickle of incipient tears behind her eyes. Cora hadn't just outplayed Rosa, she had *destroyed* her. My aunt had been completely outclassed, and she knew it. Her tears were tears of envy and admiration.

Rosa would have preferred to go on loathing and ignoring Cora as before, but this complicated matters. There was little in the world that was more important to Rosa than chess. She looked down at the board, marveling at the elegance of Cora's game, and knew that she would do anything to be able to play the same way. She cleared her throat, unsure if the words she wanted to say would emerge. She pointed at the board.

"Could you teach me?" she asked.

In the following months Rosa discovered new worlds. Cora taught her opening sequences and their variations, wily defenses, and other fiendish gambits. Rosa learned them all by heart. Chess pieces danced patterns in her head, an atlas of exotic names: the Italian, the Sicilian, the Catalan, the Indian. Cora was a generous and patient teacher. Even though Rosa would never be able to forgive her completely for stealing Joseph away from her, much of her antipathy dissipated in a quiet haze of gratitude over the chessboard.

Only one photograph was taken on my parents' wedding day.

I have it in front of me as I write. The newlyweds stand in the center of the picture, side by side, holding hands. Cora looks calm, resolved, quietly satisfied. And radiantly pretty, of course. Joseph is grinning like an imbecile. It is ten months since Cora interrupted his silent recital beneath her bedroom window, and he still cannot quite believe that any of this is actually happening.

Similar expressions of disbelief, although not so beatific, appear on the faces of the wedding guests who flank the happy couple. Jette Meisenheimer and Martin Leftkemeyer share the same faraway look as they gaze vaguely toward the camera. Rosa hovers by her brother's shoulder, clutching a small bouquet of flowers, her face an unreadable mask. Only Lomax, proud architect of the union, appears to be enjoying himself. He is on the far right of the picture, dressed in a suit purchased for the occasion. He is laughing as the photographer presses the button.

TWENTY-ONE

On his wedding night, Joseph packed his bags and made the short journey across the yard, where he joyfully installed himself in Cora's bedroom.

Now it was Jette's turn to spend hours peering wistfully across that narrow expanse of grass, just as her son had done. She gazed at the Leftkemeyers' house, wondering when Joseph would leave her.

In fact, the idea of leaving Beatrice had never occurred to the newlyweds. Joseph would have followed Cora to the ends of the earth, of course, but she had no intention of abandoning her father.

Jette was astonished when, a week or so after the wedding, Joseph suggested that Cora should start work at Frederick's. "This is a family business, and she's family now." He grinned. "Besides, she's much prettier than me. She can take the orders and charm the customers, and I'll stay in the kitchen with Lomax."

"I could use the help." Lomax nodded, looking pleased. "It gets kind of lonely back there, you know."

Jette looked uncertainly at her new daughter-in-law. "If you're sure," she said. "It's hard work."

Cora smiled at her. "I'll work as hard as anyone else, I promise you that."

And she did.

Cora quickly took control of the dining room. She mastered the restaurant's peculiar, ever-changing menu. She glided back and forth from the kitchen laden down with plates and glasses, never dropping a thing. When the last customers had been served, she rolled up her sleeves and got to work with whatever needed to be done to get ready for the following day. She polished silverware, mopped floors, and chopped anything put in front of her — and all this tireless industry was performed with a wide smile on her lovely face.

My grandmother had the grace to acknowledge when she was wrong; Cora was not the prissy girl she had taken her for. Before long the two women worked the dining room in harmonious tandem.

Cora was not the restaurant's only new

recruit. It was around that time that Rosa also began to work on weekends, busing tables and cleaning dishes. Jette watched her daughter as she worked. Rosa was a pretty enough girl — perhaps not a real beauty like Cora, but she had an open face and big brown eyes that shone with sharp intelligence. Her hair was long and straight and as dark as mahogany. She was tall for a teenager, but did not possess her mother's robust physical heft or confidence. Instead she moved with awkward caution, as if she couldn't entirely trust her body to do her bidding. She did her best to smile at the customers, but Jette could tell that it was an effort. Rosa would have preferred to go about her business untroubled by the cheerful parade of diners who marveled at how she had grown and peppered her with well-meaning inquiries. Even back then my aunt's distaste for the spotlight was apparent. She would always prefer to remain hidden from view. (One day I would discover just how hidden.)

In the kitchen, Lomax taught Joseph how to cook. At first my father tried to take notes, but soon gave up. Lomax's idiosyncratic approach to culinary instruction meant that the recipes changed each time he cooked them.

"It's not about exact measurements or ingredients," shrugged Lomax, when Joseph complained. "Good food is about *feeling*. Cooking is an art, not a science. You got to have soul to feed people right." He smiled. "That's what this is. Soul food."

Joseph frowned. "Yes, but how many —"

"Just go with your instincts," advised Lomax. "Improvise a little." He held an imaginary cornet up to his lips and blew. "No shame in making it up as you go along. You'll get a feel for it, I promise you."

And sure enough, Joseph did. Under Lomax's loosey-goosey tutelage he developed an intuitive grasp of how food should be prepared. Not once in his culinary career did my father ever use a measuring cup or scales. He discovered a flair for creating fresh combinations of flavors. He began to concoct his own variations on Lomax's recipes. Unshackled from the rigid prescriptions of cookbooks, Joseph became a poet in the kitchen.

With both Lomax and Joseph at the stove, Jette began to offer more choices each day. Business continued to grow. People began to visit from neighboring towns. Jette bought a safe for the restaurant's takings — much to the chagrin of Martin Leftkemeyer, who couldn't persuade her to open a bank account. She also took her grandfather's military medal from its hiding place at the back of her chest of drawers and put it in there, too. She was pleased to have the medal finally out of the house. Her guilt at her theft retreated, just a little.

At Lomax's suggestion, Cora began to use her vegetable patch behind the house to supply the restaurant with produce that couldn't be found elsewhere. She grew several varieties of peppers and chilies that Lomax and Joseph used to add spice to their dishes. There was an inverse corollary between size and kick; the smaller and more withered the vegetable, the more caution was required. Cora grew Jalapeños, Jaloros, Anaheims, Habaneros, Costeño Amarillos, Cayennes, Apaches, and Cherry Bombs. Lomax's favorites were Bangalore Torpedoes, long craggy things as viciously hooked as a witch's finger and about as ferocious, if you put one in your mouth.

Cora and Lomax tended their unusual harvest together. Their horticultural double act was always accompanied by gales of laughter. Joseph liked to watch them as they worked, warmed by their obvious fondness for each other, and hoped that they weren't laughing about him.

Married life brought about one other big change for Joseph. He began to go to church.

Neither Jette nor Frederick had ever had much time for religion. Much of Jette's childhood had been spent shivering in the shadows of Hanover's austerely grand cathedral, while her mother peered around to see who else of consequence was there. It had gradually dawned on Jette that her family's faultless attendance record had nothing to do with faith. Church was a social occasion, not a spiritual one. She had taken to stomping around the Grosse Garten on Sunday afternoons as a means of shaking off the cobwebs of that morning's dose of hypocritical piety. Frederick's own Sunday mornings had usually been spent in bed with a pillow over his head, recovering from the excesses of the previous evening.

Joseph had inherited his father's cheerful agnosticism rather than Jette's visceral disdain for the whole business, and so when Cora asked him to attend the First Christian Church with her, he went along happily enough. Each week he donned a freshly starched shirt and walked proudly to church with his wife on his arm. He knelt and stood and sang along with everyone else, and listened to the sermons with polite interest. He saw the devout shine in Cora's eyes, and wished that he shared her faith.

Every Sunday morning Joseph stood by Cora's side and kept his eyes squeezed shut as he pretended to pray. It was the only lie he ever told her.

Twenty-Two

When she wasn't busing dishes at Frederick's, Rosa was plotting her escape.

Formal education was of minimal interest to our little community of farmers back then. The town's school had been run for years by Heidi Schlatt, who had watched several generations of children stumble through its doors. She believed that her role was more pastoral than strictly educational. More precisely, her job was to make sure that the children made it to the end of each day without hurting themselves, or anyone else, too seriously. On any given day, there might be thirty or so children milling around the schoolroom, ranging in age from five to sixteen. None of them really wanted to be there.

Except, that is, for Rosa.

Most children in the town stopped attending school as soon as they were old enough to start work or get married. My aunt had grown used to the sight of girls not much older than her, hunched over in exhaustion from long days helping in the fields and the burden of a household to run. Often they trudged through the town, wearily pushing baby carriages ahead of them. Rosa was determined not to suffer a similar fate. She continued to attend school every day, long after all her friends had stopped. By the time she was seventeen she had read every book in the (admittedly paltry) library, many of them twice. Each afternoon she brought an armful of books home with her and barricaded herself behind a fortress of words.

When my aunt looked up from the page, Jette would often be gazing silently across the yard toward the Leftkemeyers' home. Rosa watched this wistful surveillance, wishing that her mother would turn around and notice *her*. But Jette's eyes remained fixed on the house next door. This was a bitterness that my aunt had not expected: even in his absence, Joseph still eclipsed her. There was, Rosa concluded sadly, nothing left for her here.

In the spring of 1926, with Heidi Schlatt's nervous assistance, Rosa secretly applied for a place as an undergraduate at the University of Missouri, Columbia. If her family no longer wanted her, she would seek out a different life somewhere else.

The day that her letter of acceptance arrived, Rosa did not know whether to laugh or cry. In the intervening months she had vacillated between hoping that she would get to go to university — and praying that she would never have to leave. She breathlessly read the short, formal paragraphs of congratulation, and immediately told herself that she wouldn't go if Jette wanted her to stay.

Later that afternoon Rosa handed her mother the letter and watched her face as she read. Jette remained quite still. Finally she looked up.

"But, Rosa, why did you never say anything about this to me?"

"I didn't know what you would think," said Rosa quietly.

"But this is, this is —"

Jette stopped talking, and began to cry.

At the sight of her mother's tears, Rosa's heart flooded with relief. She smiled. "It's all right, Mama. I've already decided. I won't —"

"— this is *wonderful*."

Rosa stared at her.

"University. You." At this Jette began to cry again. "I'm so proud I could die."

"So I should accept?" whispered Rosa.

Jette threw her arms around her. "Of *course* you should accept." She squeezed her tightly. "This is the happiest day of my life." Without Jette's strong arms around her, Rosa might have collapsed to the floor in shocked dismay. She buried her face in her mother's shoulder. Rosa and Jette clung to each other, their quiet sobs a tender duet. But my aunt's tears were tears of sadness.

Rosa spent the rest of the summer hoping for evidence that Jette was at least a little sorry that she would soon be moving away. But my grandmother's delight did not abate. If anything, as the start of the new term grew closer, her mood became even sunnier. She bought Rosa a brand-new trunk in which to pack her belongings. My aunt began to worry that she'd made a terrible mistake. At least while she was still in Beatrice, her mother could not forget her completely.

"Won't you feel lonely here all by yourself?" she asked.

"Oh, don't you worry about me," answered Jette cheerfully. "I'll keep myself busy. I've got Lomax to keep me company. And Joseph and Cora just next door."

Rosa nodded sadly. That, she knew, was all that really mattered. She could be a million miles away, as long as Joseph was close.

The day of Rosa's departure dawned bright

and clear. The family gathered around the carriage to see her off. Rosa passed between them, kissing and hugging and weeping. Jette waited for her at the carriage door, the last in line to say good-bye. Rosa stopped in front of her. Their fingers touched, then laced tightly together.

"Mama," whispered Rosa, "I don't want to go."

"I know," said Jette, drawing her close.

Rosa could hardly breathe. "Should I stay?"

There was a long silence. Rosa closed her eyes as tightly as she could.

"No, my darling," said Jette softly. "You should go."

Rosa sniffed. "But I just want to stay here with you."

"And do what? Wait for a husband to put you to work?"

"I could work in the restaurant."

They looked at each other for a moment. Jette patted her arm and smiled at her. "Time to go," she said. "It's a long ride." She kissed her on the cheek.

Rosa turned and climbed the steps into the waiting carriage. As the horses began to move slowly off down the street, she turned to watch all the people in the world that she knew and loved. Lomax called out something, but she could not make out the words over the noise of the clattering wheels. Joseph and Cora stood side by side, holding hands, watching her go. At the center of them all stood her mother, her arm raised in cheerful salute. The carriage turned the corner at the end of the street. Rosa slumped back in her seat, her cheeks wet with stunned tears.

Rosa looked out at the passing countryside, but all she could see was the joyful smile on Jette's face as she had waved good-bye.

That smile had not lasted long. As the carriage vanished from view, Jette's waving hand went to her face, and the tears she had been fighting back began to fall. She stood in the middle of the road and wept. She had lost Frederick, then Joseph, and now Rosa. And now she was alone.

There had been nothing in the world Jette had wanted more than for Rosa to stay, but she would not deny her daughter the chance to escape. Finally Lomax stepped forward and placed a gentle hand on her shoulder. She allowed herself to be guided back inside.

After that, Jette's gaze fell with increasing frequency on the house next door. Joseph's angel wing still hung above the fireplace, a silent reminder of all that she would never be able to recapture now. My grandmother stared at the treacherous walls of her empty home, wondering how they had allowed her family to escape.

It was Lomax who rescued Jette from her sadness. Every evening he made his way to her house, and the two of them talked, long into the night. Lomax missed Rosa, too, and their shared loss created a new bond, transforming years of polite banter into a deeper friendship. For the first time, they began to speak about themselves, rather than simply the children. Jette told stories about her childhood in Hanover. She told him about her grandfather, watching military carnage unfold from the safety of his balloon. Lomax's tales of growing up poor in New Orleans made her eyes shine with tears. Murderous German generals and children scrabbling around for forgotten lumps of coal in the squalor of the Third Ward — it was hard to imagine two more different people, but before long each came to rely on the other's quiet companionship.

During this time Lomax's illicit alcohol enterprise was booming. As word of his lethal concoction and its stupefying effect spread, demand began to outstrip supply, and he had to turn away customers from the alleyway. Sometimes there were fights. Men who had purchased bottles began to strike deals with those who had not been so lucky, selling their liquor on for an immediate profit. Lomax watched as his customers doubled their money by these quick resales, and decided to up his prices.

It was his first mistake. Born while the embers of the war fought for his freedom were still glowing across the country, Lomax had spent his life negotiating the perils of his black skin. He had survived thanks to his ability to spot trouble early, but he had grown too comfortable for his own good in our little town. His finely calibrated defense mechanisms had grown rusty. Men were prepared to pay Lomax for his liquor, but now they muttered angrily to each other as they waited in line in the shadows behind the restaurant. An uneasy standoff continued, until Lomax made his second mistake.

One of his regular customers had been out of town for several days, and had not heard about the price increase. On the first night of his return, he appeared, as he always did, with exact change for one bottle of brew. Lomax counted the man's coins and calmly told him that he did not have enough. The matter might have ended there had he agreed to the man's offer to pay him the balance next time, but he refused to extend any credit. Thirsty as he was, the man was not going to plead with a Negro in front of an audience, and he stormed away. Lomax watched him go, and then turned his attention to the next customer.

Two days later, the man came back.

Jette and Lomax sat in front of the fire, picking through their childhoods, plundering memories. When the stories stopped, they sat in companionable silence.

"Thank you, Miss Jette," said Lomax after a while.

"For what?"

"For letting me love your family like my own."

"Well, love is a two-way street. You get as much as you give, don't you think?"

"Yes indeed. I'm a lucky man. A *very* lucky man." He stood up and stretched. "I just wanted to say, you know."

Jette looked at him for a moment. "May I ask you a question?"

"You can always *ask*."

"What's your first name? The one your mother chose for you?"

Lomax chuckled. "Shoot, Miss Jette, I can hardly remember. Nobody's used it since I was six years old. I been plain old Lomax for too long now to change back again."

"I don't want you to change anything. I'd

just like to know."

He stood there for a moment, considering the request. "It's James." The word escaped him like a sigh.

Jette tilted her head to one side. "James," she said softly.

"Now promise me you won't ever call me that."

She smiled. "I promise."

The only sound in the room was the warm crackling of the fire in the grate.

"Well, good night," he said.

Jette got to her feet. She took Lomax's hands in hers and kissed him on the cheek. They stood there, as still as statues in the flickering shadows of the fire. Then her fingers let him go, and without another word he pushed open the door and stepped out into the night.

It was cold beneath the winter stars, but Lomax scarcely noticed. The memory of Jette's embrace protected him from the chill, warming him from within. He walked down the town's empty streets, in no hurry to return to his lonely room. He turned toward the river. The moon's pale reflection danced on the dark water as it rushed eastward into the Mississippi's fierce embrace. From there the current turned south, all the way back to New Orleans. Lomax was glad that he was upriver now.

It was after midnight when he turned into the alleyway behind the restaurant, finally ready for sleep. He stopped when he saw the door hanging off its hinges. The wooden panels had been smashed repeatedly, splintered craters of violence. Lomax stood quite still and listened. No sound came from within. Then there was a soft whistle from the end of the alleyway.

There were ten of them, their faces hidden by scarves. Lomax stared into the row of eyes, trying to make out someone he knew, but all he could see were dark pools of hate. The pack approached, the dull scrape of their boots across the ground loaded with menace. Each man carried a weapon. He saw the clubs and brickbats, and the narrow flash of a silver blade in the moonlight.

He swallowed his fear and spoke. "Help you?"

"It's time someone taught you a lesson, boy," called a voice, high-pitched with excitement.

The alleyway was a dead end. There was nowhere to run. Finally one man stepped forward from the rest of the group. In his hands was an iron bar.

"What makes you think you can come to

this town and rob us all blind?"

Lomax shook his head. "Didn't rob no-body."

The man snorted. "You parade about like you're the goddamned king of England. You put up prices for your liquor and then you refuse to accept our money. But we're proud men, see? No nigger's going to treat us like that."

"Proud men?" growled Lomax. "If you so proud, why won't you show me your face? You scared I'll come back and haunt you?"

The man did not answer, but took two steps closer. "We should've done this a long time ago," he said, and then he swung the iron bar as hard as he could against Lomax's knees.

It was three days before Lomax was found.

His naked body was hanging by the neck from the bough of an old cypress tree in the woods behind Jette's house. His arms and legs had been broken too many times to count. The skin on his back was ripped open, a savage matrix of lacerations where he had been flogged before he died. Every one of his ribs had been smashed. His hands and feet had been hacked off and left to rot beneath the body. By the time he was found, they had been picked clean of flesh. His eyes and mouth were black with the swarm of insects.

News of the lynching electrified the town. Whispers swept through the streets like a chill wind. People swapped stories with their eyes cast low, wondering who knew more. When asked, Walford Scott, the police chief, muttered vaguely about ongoing investigations. Nobody was surprised when weeks passed and nothing happened. Not one clue was announced. Not one lead was pursued. The guilty men still walked free.

If the police had made any attempt to catch the men who had lynched Lomax, the gossipmongers would have been kept occupied for months. But inevitably, given the lack of new developments, the story went cold.

The town, in other words, moved on. But my family did not. For Jette and Joseph, the death of Lomax stopped all the clocks.

TWENTY-THREE

Nothing would be the same again. The world had broken, smashed into a million pieces. All that remained was baffled misery.

Sometimes Joseph remembered Lomax as he had been in life, cheerful and kind, those big warm hands reaching out toward the world. But mostly it was his mutilated, rotting corpse swinging from the tree that haunted his dreams. Sweet memory had been poisoned by the obscene violence of his death. There was nothing else left to remember Lomax by. Even his cornet was gone, stolen by the killers.

Walford Scott refused Jette's entreaties to deliver the body to her for a proper burial, insisting (while avoiding her eye) that the corpse was needed as evidence. Instead one morning in early December, Jette, Martin, Joseph, and Cora trudged into the woods to the spot where Lomax had been found. They breathed white clouds into the cold forest air as they said their good-byes. Cora and Joseph stood side by side, holding hands, remembering that Sunday afternoon when Lomax had knocked on the Leftkemeyers' front door and politely asked Cora whether she could spare a few moments of her time.

After that Jette simply withdrew, forced into retreat by the knowledge that murderers were strolling freely down the streets of the town. The world outside her front door became a pit of suspicion, her neighbors a repository of collective guilt. She became unable to leave the house.

When Frederick's opened again for business, it was my parents who stood proudly at the helm, Joseph at the stove and Cora managing the front of the house. Joseph guiltily abandoned the German dishes that Jette loved so much, and built a modest, thoroughly American menu. There was meat loaf, fried chicken, tuna salad, cheeseburgers. Everything came with French fries and a pickle on the side. The blue plate special was always one of Lomax's exotic creations, potent with the kick of chilies from Cora's vegetable patch. Joseph cooked these dishes in sad memorial to his friend. Every pungent cloud of spice brought Lomax back to life as vividly as if he were standing beside Joseph at the stove. But when my father turned around, he was still alone.

The new menu allowed Joseph to keep his overhead and his prices low, but the volume of contented diners passing through every day meant he was still able to turn a good profit. But it took an immense effort of will for Joseph and Cora to open the doors every morning. Lomax's murder still cast them deep into shadow.

Cora watched the faces of her customers, searching for evidence of knowledge or guilt. Everyone in the town ate there; somebody had to know something. People still joked and gossiped with her, but she could barely bring herself to smile as she took orders and refilled coffee mugs. The simplest pleasantries stuck in her throat. Joseph stayed out of sight in the kitchen, quietly dreaming of revenge. How easy it would be, he thought. A pinch of something deadly in the eggs would do it.

Up until Lomax's murder, Reverend Kellerman, the pastor at First Christian Church, had been given to delivering quiet, thoughtfully constructed homilies on abstruse theological points. Now, though, appalled by the attack, he flayed his congregation with the full fire-and-brimstone treatment. Nobody was innocent, he thundered. Someone must know something, and the price of silence in this world, he vowed, would be eternal damnation in the next. The clergyman almost launched himself out of the pulpit as he fretfully invoked the Almighty's vengeance on those godless souls who had committed the crime. Some of the culprits, he knew, were sitting before him in the congregation, and this realization drove him into a storm of fury. The following week, the pews were crammed with an expectant audience, hoping for more ecclesiastical fireworks. Reverend Kellerman gave the same sermon again, and then again the week after. The more people came to enjoy the spectacle, the angrier he got. With each performance his delivery became more hysterically splenetic. Soon Sunday morning services became standing-room only.

(So it was that Lomax's death transformed the fortunes of First Christian Church. For years there had been an intense three-way competition between First Christian, the Baptists, and the Lutherans for the town's floating worshippers. Up until that point many people chose their church based on the length of the sermon — the shorter the better — and the quality of the fried chicken at church socials. Reverend Kellerman's brand of fiery polemic changed all that. People didn't care how long a sermon went on for, if it kept them entertained. The congregation shivered appreciatively as the pastor shook his fist at them, promising that they would rot in the flames of hell for all eternity. Offertory takings soared. It didn't hurt that they had Lotte Heimstetter doing the fried chicken, either.)

Every week Jette wrote to Rosa, but she was unable to tell her the terrible thing that had happened. Instead she buried her sadness beneath bland news bulletins. Rosa's replies, when they came, bustled with youthful self-importance and enthusiasm. She was studying hard and relishing university life. If she noticed that her mother no longer mentioned Lomax in her weekly reports, she never asked why.

It was only the following summer, when Rosa returned to Beatrice at the end of the academic year, that Jette told her about Lomax's death. Rosa wept for two days, numb with sorrow. She had adored Lomax more fiercely than anyone, and could not believe that he was gone. When she was finally able to look up from her grief, she was shocked to see the toll the news had taken on her mother. Jette had begun to wither in stooped defeat. She languished for hours in her chair, staring sightlessly at the angel wing that still hung above the fireplace. The lynching had cleaved through all Jette had known. She shuffled through the house like a ghost, sad and listless. She was unable to muster the enthusiasm for even the simplest projects. Had it not been for Rosa's worried nagging, she would never have pulled herself out of bed from one day to the next.

As fall approached, my aunt realized that she would not, could not, return to Columbia for her second year of study. When she announced her decision to stay, Jette simply wept quiet tears of gratitude. Rosa knew then that she had made the right decision.

That September, my aunt returned to the school that she had left little more than a year previously — this time as a teacher. Heidi Schlatt greeted her with a grateful hug, and promptly retired.

The schoolhouse was a small, whitewashed building with a shingled roof and a bright red front door. Beyond it lay an untended pasture where the children played during breaks until called in by the ringing peals of the teacher's handbell. The single classroom within smelled like a church, all wood polish and old books. An old flag hung limply on a pole next to the blackboard.

With her single year of university education, Rosa was, by some distance, the most qualified teacher who had ever taught there. After so many years of Heidi Schlatt's benign but ineffective stewardship, nobody was ready when my aunt swooped down on the school like an avenging angel. She barked out commands with the ferocity of a parade ground sergeant-major. She meted out draconian punishments with such dead-eyed calm that even the most cantankerous children thought twice before crossing her. It was not long before she had transformed the schoolroom into a model educational environment, full of silent, hardworking, and utterly terrified students. Children began to come home with books under their arms. Some parents complained about the homework, but that didn't last long. They were as scared of the new teacher as their children were.

Rosa expanded the curriculum, setting her sights beyond mere competence in reading and writing. She taught history and geography, mathematics and literature. She gave those children their first glimpse of the world that lay beyond Caitlin County. To her own quiet astonishment, my aunt discovered that she was born to teach.

■ ■ ■ ■

While Jette and Rosa gingerly picked a way through their sorrows, a new sadness came knocking for my parents. Since their wedding, Cora had suffered two miscarriages. The second of these had come on Christmas Day of 1926. After that, nothing. It was as if her body had taken matters into its own hands, determined to spare her further heartbreak.

Cora continued to work at the restaurant, but a light had gone out inside her. The bright, vivacious girl Joseph had married slowly disappeared from view, her existence reduced to wretched monthly cycles of hope and despair. Dr. Becker could find nothing wrong with her. *Keep trying,* he would gravely suggest, patting her hand in sympathy. *Everything happens for a reason. Keep trying, and just when you least expect it, your little miracle will arrive.*

It began to seem as if a miracle was precisely what was required. At church Cora and Joseph got to their knees and prayed for God to bless them with a child. As they knelt together in the pew, Joseph would glance sideways at his wife and watch her lips move in desperate supplication. Neither of them could look beyond the impossible promise of the next four weeks. The future was for people with the luxury of hope.

But the future came looking for them, all the same. In the spring of 1927 the Mississippi burst its banks in the worst flood in human memory. All along the great river, from Leeville to Cairo, the levees collapsed and sent tidal waves crashing across the cotton fields of Louisiana. The Missouri River rose in sisterly sympathy, with catastrophic results. In Beatrice, half the streets were submerged beneath a lake of stinking brown water. Anything that could not be raised out of harm's way was destroyed. Pets and livestock drowned. Crops were decimated. Every day Joseph waded to the restaurant and bailed sludge out onto the street.

Jette's house was built on elevated ground, and the water stopped two blocks away from her front door. When the river finally retreated, a crusted waterline of dirt marked the walls of the town's buildings, showing the high point of the flood. Jette stepped out of her house for the first time in months and walked through the town, inspecting the damage. The pungent odor of rotting food and dead animals was everywhere. To Jette it was the sweet smell of revenge. Lomax's murderers might have gone unpunished, but this collective retribution had been administered instead. Her grief loosened its grip.

Despite all of Joseph's efforts, the flood had devastated the restaurant. It seemed that no amount of scrubbing or cleaning could eradicate the lingering stink of putrid floodwater. The old tables and chairs had been submerged for too long, and had begun to rot. The kitchen equipment was beyond rescue. The old piano that Lomax had loved to play was ruined forever. My father gutted the interior, knocked down the wall between the dining room and the kitchen, and waited for his insurance check to arrive.

Two months later, the restaurant reopened for business. It was scarcely recognizable. A long chrome countertop ran down one side of the room. Behind it lay a gleaming grill. In front of the counter there was a row of stools crowned with bright red leather cushions. High-backed booths with pristine banquettes ran around the periphery of the room; smaller tables were crammed in between.

Joseph proudly showed Rosa and Jette the improvements. "It all looks so bright and shiny and new," said Jette, remembering the shadowy decrepitude of the Nick-Nack. "So *American*."

"Well, that's what we are," said Joseph agreeably.

"Yes, I suppose so," conceded Jette.

"I think it's very nice," said Rosa, sitting down in one of the booths. "It's a lot bigger. Won't you need more help now?"

Joseph nodded. "We'll probably have to find another waitress."

"Did you hear that, Mama? They'll probably have to find another waitress."

Jette looked crossly at her daughter. "Honestly, Rosa, you have the subtlety of an elephant."

Joseph looked at Jette. "If you want a job here, you only have to ask," he said.

"Who says I want a job?" sniffed Jette.

"*I* do," said Rosa. "You've been cooped up in that house for far too long."

"Nonsense," said Jette halfheartedly.

"I'd love it if you would," said Joseph.

Jette looked between her two children. "I suppose a few shifts wouldn't hurt," she said.

And so, thanks largely to my aunt's shameless bullying, Jette stepped cautiously back into the world.

In addition to making the cosmetic changes, Joseph and Cora now opened the restaurant's doors at six o'clock every morning and fed the citizens of Beatrice breakfast. Three new coffee machines stood at one end of the kitchen, fueling diners with an endless supply of caffeine.

Each morning Joseph took delivery of dozens of fresh eggs from local farms, and by lunchtime every single one of them was gone. There was nothing my father enjoyed more than cracking an egg against the side of a hot skillet and watching it cook. He loved the swift metamorphosis from limpid translucence to opaque, wholesome goodness. Poached, over easy, sunny-side up, it didn't matter — each one slid perfect from his pan, yolks as rich and runny as liquid gold. He produced glistening clouds of creamy scrambled eggs. He created omelets as light as air. He cooked other things during that morning shift — crisp rashers of bacon by the pound, fistfuls of sausage, tottering piles of pancakes, crunchy mountains of hash browns — but he was a magician with those eggs.

My grandmother did not approve of all the changes that Joseph and Cora had made to the restaurant. She certainly didn't enjoy the early breakfast shift, and would yawn pointedly as she toured the room, filling up coffee mugs. She missed seeing her favorite dishes on the menu. But she was pleased to have escaped the prison that her home had become, and had the grace to keep her thoughts to herself.

■ ■ ■ ■

Two and a half years after the flood, further calamity came calling, this time of the man-made variety. The stock market crashed and the black clouds of economic disaster swept across the country. In the cities, jobs vanished and people starved. Things were no better in the countryside. The price of corn tumbled, but farmers were still unable to sell what they had. Vast surpluses of crops and livestock rotted unwanted on farms. Thousands of acres of cotton stood unpicked in the fields of the South, the cost of harvesting far exceeding any price that could be got for it. The weather did not help. A succession of summer droughts was as devastating as the flood that had submerged the same fields a few years earlier.

There was no money anywhere. People were staying home to eat. The restaurant became a sea of empty tables. Worried, Joseph slashed his prices. Then he slashed them again, and he kept slashing them until it was cheaper for people to eat at Frederick's than to buy the food and cook it themselves. Slowly, customers began to stop by again. Joseph was barely making enough to live on, but as businesses across the country went into bankruptcy, my father managed to keep the restaurant open, but only just. Over the years he had amassed a respectable nest egg, which he kept in the safe in the back room. He had inherited Jette's distrust of banks, and preferred to keep his money where he could see it. From time to time he liked to pull out the bundles of notes just to feel their heft. He loved the smooth feel of the paper beneath his fingers.

Cora's father became the busiest man in town, reluctantly repossessing farms across Caitlin County. Every week there was a new foreclosure. Martin Leftkemeyer was a compassionate man, and his new line of work made him miserable. Proud farmers begged him for one more week to make payment, and he could only shake his head in regret. There was nothing he could do. Up and down the country banks were going under. The order had come down from the boardroom to call in every defaulting loan.

It did not take long for Martin's unpleasant duties to take their toll on him. People did not understand that he was only following instructions, and they blamed him for the bank's unyielding position. At first men grumbled behind his back, but as the foreclosures multiplied, they no longer hid their hostility. Former friends and customers coldly turned away from him as he walked down the street.

Reverend Kellerman, who had developed a keen sense for crowd-pleasing topics, began to use his sermons to harangue the mortgage lenders for driving families to ruin. Martin sat stiff-backed in his pew, his face flushed red with anger and shame. His gentle temperament left him ill-equipped to withstand this sort of vilification. He did his best to make amends, inviting the families who had lost their farms for dinner, but these invitations were ignored or angrily declined. By 1931 he bore the undeserved resentment of the entire town on his weary shoulders.

During the fall of 1932, the handsome and urbane governor of New York crisscrossed the country in his campaign for president. Rosa persuaded Jette to travel with her to Jefferson City to hear Franklin Roosevelt speak in front of a cheering crowd on the steps of the Capitol. The result of November's election was never in doubt. Roosevelt took office the following March. He cajoled and bullied Congress into passing bill after bill to provide relief for the country's starving poor.

It was a monumental effort, but it was too late for some.

One evening in the late summer of 1933, Joseph heard cries in the street outside the house. He opened the door to see people hurrying past, talking excitedly to one another as they went.

"What's happening?" he called out to a young boy who was racing by.

"Fire," the boy yelled back. "At the Kliever farm. The barn's gone up."

Joseph went back inside to fetch his hat. Cora and her father were in the kitchen. "Johann Kliever's barn is burning," he told them.

Martin went very still. "I was there this afternoon," he said. "We foreclosed on the property. It belongs to the bank now."

Ten minutes later Joseph arrived at the farm. A crowd had gathered, watching the flames that engulfed the charred frame of the barn. The screams of terrified livestock could be heard from inside the burning building. In front of the silent crowd, standing alone, was Stefan. Joseph approached him.

"Stefan, thank God you're all right. What happened?"

"They took the farm," said Stefan, not taking his eyes off the flames.

"I heard. I'm sorry."

"It's all gone. There's nothing left."

Joseph looked at the burning building. "Where's your father?"

That was when Stefan turned to stare at him, his eyes full of sorrow.

Suddenly there was a mighty crack as one of the barn's twin doors collapsed off its hinges. The huge slab of burning wood fell forward, sending a cyclone of sparks cascading into the evening air. A wave of heat rolled outward through the hole where the door had been, sending the crowd scuttling backward.

Joseph and Stefan did not move. They stared into the blazing interior of the barn. Behind the wall of fire, half-hidden by the dancing flames, was a long, blackened body, dangling from the end of a rope.

TWENTY-FOUR

Johann Kliever's suicide nearly finished Martin Leftkemeyer off. It was one thing to withstand the scorn of his neighbors, but having a man's death on his conscience was another matter. My grandfather became ashen-faced with guilt. From the haunted look in his eye one would have thought that he had set a torch to the place himself.

Stefan disappeared after the fire. Every day Joseph walked to the Kliever house and banged his fist against the door, calling his friend's name. There was no response.

Then one evening Stefan appeared at Joseph's house. A week's beard shadowed his hollow cheeks. His eyes were darkened with grief.

"Stefan," said Joseph with relief. "I've been looking for you."

"I know," replied Stefan. "I heard you knocking every day."

"Then why didn't you answer?"

"I couldn't come to the door. No fit state." He paused. "Nobody else came," he said. "Nobody else stopped by."

"Perhaps you didn't —"

"And now they've taken everything." Stefan's voice was empty. "It's all gone. The farm, the equipment, the lot. They came by today and took the keys to the house. As good as threw me out onto the street."

There was a long silence. "Tell me what I can do," said my father softly.

"I need a job. And somewhere to stay."

That night Stefan Kliever slept on the sofa in my parents' living room. Early the next morning he followed Joseph and Cora through the town's empty streets to the restaurant. Once he had eaten a plateful of eggs and sausage, Stefan sat on a stool at the end of the counter and watched Joseph cook breakfasts for the next several hours.

There was something beautiful about watching my father work. He moved with exquisite precision between the pans as he juggled multiple orders simultaneously. Joseph used to tell me that being a short-order cook is like dancing with ten girls at once, but he always made that complex choreography look effortless. He worked with his back to the room, filling plate after plate, fueling the town for the long day ahead. Occasion-

ally he would look up from the grill long enough to welcome a customer with a cheerful greeting over his shoulder, but he never took his eyes off the arsenal of bubbling pots in front of him.

When the breakfast rush ended, Joseph turned to Stefan with a tired smile. "Still interested?" he asked.

His friend sipped on the cup of coffee he had been nursing all morning. "Think you can teach me how to do all that?"

Joseph handed him an apron. "Only one way to find out," he said.

Stefan spent the rest of the week standing in front of the hot plate, flipping burgers. Joseph showed him how to move the patties around the cooking surface to speed up or slow down the meat's progress, and how to press down on the beef with his thumb to see if it was cooked right. Each morning Stefan ground up pounds of seasoned chuck steak and sculpted the meat into neat disks. He cut thick slices of tomato, washed the lettuce, and split open each bun. He sliced and fried mountains of onions for garnish. His sandwiches were juicy, architectural wonders, gravity-defying edifices of meaty goodness. Cheeseburgers quickly became the most popular item on the lunch menu.

Joseph was delighted. "You're ready to

learn something else," he told Stefan one day, but his friend shook his head and gestured toward Joseph's pots and pans.

"I don't know if I could do what you do, and cook a thousand things at once. I'd rather do one thing well."

Joseph grinned. "All right, then. I'll be the jack-of-all-trades. You can be the master of one."

During breakfasts Stefan helped by grilling toast and cooking the bacon and sausage. The two men moved easily around each other in the confined space behind the counter. Joseph was pleased to have Stefan by his side, but Cora and Jette were not so enthusiastic. "Times are so hard," Cora told him. "Now isn't the time to take on a new employee."

"We won't pay him much," said Joseph. "Food and a bed is what he needs most right now, and we can give him that." Stefan had taken up residency in Lomax's old room at the back of the building. "Besides, think of how good his parents were to us when we arrived in town. Who knows what would have happened if it hadn't been for their kindness. Don't you think we owe him this, after what's happened with the farm? Stefan has lost everything."

"We hardly make enough to survive as it

is," said Cora.

"He'll make us money in the long run, you'll see," said Joseph. "Everyone loves his cheeseburgers. Takings are already up."

"Hmm," said Jette. She had tried one of Stefan's cheeseburgers, and it had been delicious, but she would have preferred schnitzel and sauerkraut.

Rosa was also doubtful about Stefan's arrival, but for different reasons. It was Stefan who had first taken Joseph away from her when they embarked on their boys-only adventures in the woods, and she had never trusted him since. Throughout Rosa's childhood Stefan barely noticed her, but she had always been pitched in undeclared war against him. She had instinctively known that he was her adversary — even before he shot her raccoon. Now when Rosa saw Stefan working at the grill next to her brother, she thought of poor Mr. Jim, murdered while sunbathing on the outhouse roof, and a flutter of uneasy excitement arose from somewhere deep within her.

The economic situation continued to worsen over the next few years. Not even Mr. Roosevelt could work instant miracles. Families who had lived in the town for generations packed up and left, looking for work and a square meal. Most of them never returned.

The restaurant continued to survive, but only just. Stefan's cheeseburgers helped. As time went on they acquired an enthusiastic local following. Soon he was busier than my father during the lunchtime rush, and Joseph found himself helping Stefan, rather than the other way around. They put up a large sign outside the building: CHEESEBURGERS OUR SPECIALTY.

Jette thought wryly that at least her husband would have approved: Frederick's was all-American now. She and Cora continued to take orders and pour coffee all day. Each night Jette and my parents would walk wearily home, leaving Stefan alone in the small room at the back of the restaurant.

Joseph did not know how Stefan spent his evenings, but he sometimes smelled stale alcohol on his friend's breath in the morning. Stefan never spoke much while they worked; instead he bent over the grill, completely focused on his work. Joseph did his best not to mind. He supposed that Stefan was trying to bury the pain of recent events beneath all that ferocious industry.

During that time, Jette grew increasingly worried about what was going on in Europe. A long shadow of terror had fallen across Germany as Adolf Hitler reshaped the country in his ghoulish vision. Jette read the newspaper every day, shaking her head. Hitler was building an *army*. What did these people think he was intending to use it for? She wrote to the president, explaining the threat to world peace posed by the Nazi regime. Her letter received a polite response, assuring her that Mr. Roosevelt was grateful for her thoughtful analysis. Encouraged, she wrote again, and again, and then again.

She did not receive any more replies.

In late August 1935, Joseph and Cora crossed the path to Jette's house. Cora's hand rested gently over her belly. Their faces were stunned starbursts of hope.

After all the years of heartbreak and disappointment, Cora's pregnancy took everyone by surprise. Jette gave up writing letters about the Nazis and took up knitting instead. Channeling the energy that had previously been directed toward bringing down the leader of the Third Reich, my grandmother produced more tiny sweaters, cardigans, and hats than one child could ever need.

Those months of waiting for the baby to arrive were the longest they had ever known. Cora bloomed and suffered in equal measures, shuttling between disbelieving happiness and wretched fear that her body would betray her yet again, but finally she allowed herself to believe that this time she would become a mother.

The regulars at Frederick's were delighted by the news, and congratulated my parents warmly. The horrors of fatherhood immediately became a favorite topic of conversation among the men who ate at the counter. Joseph listened to their stories of paternal suffering with growing anxiety. He wanted to hear about the hope, the unending parade of love, all that, but his mischievous customers continued to serve up a diet of unremitting gloom about the trials that awaited him.

It was left to Stefan to break my father's heart, just a little. He would not share Joseph and Cora's happiness. It was as if their joy was more than he could bear. Instead, he turned coldly away. He scowled through every jolly conversation about fatherhood, a jagged fault line of grief and resentment running just beneath his angry silence.

But not even Stefan's hostility could dampen Joseph's joy for too long. He even discovered the first cautious flickerings of faith within him. After so many years of bruising despair, Cora's pregnancy really *did* seem like a miracle. At church he bowed his head in prayer, and offered up his thanks.

My brother, Freddy, arrived into the world

in much the same way as he would carry on thereafter: obligingly punctual, and without undue fuss or drama. Cora's labor lasted all of an hour before the baby slithered out into Dr. Becker's waiting hands and lay there, staring up at the old physician with an apologetic look in his eye, as if he were sorry for causing all this trouble.

That night, the family crowded around Cora's bed and gazed in wonderment at the infant as he slept peacefully in his mother's arms. Jette and Martin stood at the end of the bed, blinking at the grandchild they had believed would never come. Rosa knelt by Cora's side and silently stroked the baby's soft head. Joseph watched them all, becalmed by a new, profound contentment. Finally, he had a child to adore. His world was complete.

Or so he thought.

TWENTY-FIVE

One morning, a few months after Freddy was born, Joseph kissed his wife and sleeping son good-bye and set off for the restaurant. He strolled down the empty streets, singing happily to himself, already looking forward to returning home to his family at the end of his shift.

To his surprise, the front door was locked. By the time he arrived Stefan had usually switched the lights on and fired up the grill. Joseph got out his key and opened the door. The place was still dark.

"Stefan?" he called out. Joseph had noticed that his friend had begun to drink more heavily in recent weeks, and he wondered whether he was sleeping off a particularly bad night. "Stefan, wake up!" He turned on the lights and knocked on the door of Stefan's room. When there was no answer, he pushed it open. The room was empty.

Joseph went through the restaurant. The

old kitchen where Lomax had taught Joseph to cook was now used as a storage area. Two large refrigerators hummed quietly in unison. On the table in the middle of the room were neatly stacked piles of plates, ready for the day ahead.

Then he noticed that the door of the safe was hanging open. With a cry he ran forward.

His money was gone. The Kaiser's medal was gone. Stefan had taken everything.

Numbly Joseph stood up and walked back into the restaurant. By the grill lay a piece of paper. On it Stefan had scrawled:

NO MORE.

Just then the front door opened and Jette walked in, yawning as usual.

"Stefan's gone," Joseph told her.

"Gone? What do you mean?"

"He's left. Disappeared." Joseph handed her the note.

"No more *what*?" muttered Jette.

"He opened the safe," said Joseph. "He's taken everything." He sat down heavily on a chair and looked at her. "What are we going to do?" he asked.

Jette reached for her apron. "We're going to do what we always do," she said. "We're going to feed people breakfast."

And that is what they did.

For the next few hours Joseph escaped into his work, a solo performer once more. If the food took a little longer to appear that morning, nobody seemed to mind. It was only as he scoured the grill clean after the breakfast rush that Joseph was hit by Stefan's treachery. This was how he was repaid for his kindness! A flash of wordless, white-hot fury seared through him, obliterating reason, demanding action. The grill was still scorching hot. Carefully, slowly, Joseph pressed his forefinger down on one of its cast-iron ridges, and held it there. The pain was terrible, but he did not move. He closed his eyes, wanting to remember the sensation forever. When Joseph finally lifted his hand away, whole worlds of agony had entered his body through the inch-long gash of blackened skin on his fingertip.

By the time he closed up the restaurant that afternoon, the pain had smashed his anger into a fragmented mosaic of humiliation and regret. He walked home slowly. When he told Cora the news, she reached for him and held him tight. Not one word of rebuke passed her lips.

"I'm sorry," he mumbled into her shoulder. "I should have listened to you."

331

"Hush now," she whispered. "It doesn't matter."

"But Cora, he took *everything*."

She gently pushed him away and looked at him. "Listen to me, Joseph." She lay a finger on his chest. "Nobody can take away what really matters." She turned and looked toward the cot where Freddy lay.

Joseph looked at his sleeping son and knew that his wife was right, at least in part. Stefan's theft was easy enough to calibrate. In time he would be able to replace every dollar that he had stolen. But that was not the loss he mourned. Stefan had taken something much more precious than his life savings and his mother's old medal. Joseph was left to pick his lonely way through the shattered fragments of thirty years of friendship.

Although it turned out that Stefan *did* leave one thing behind.

After Stefan's disappearance, Joseph's days at the restaurant were long and difficult. On his own once more, he was exhausted by the end of each day. The burn on his finger ached for weeks afterward. The pain was strangely comforting, an apt accompaniment to his grief. The scar calcified into a cratered memorial of Stefan's betrayal. Decades later, when Joseph was a very old man, its ghoulish ridges were still clearly visible on his ancient, paper-thin skin.

At least he had a means to escape his dismay. Whenever Joseph held his newborn son, his pain at Stefan's desertion was eclipsed. He could gaze down at that small face until the end of time and never tire of it.

Frederick Lomax Meisenheimer had been named on the assumption, not unreasonable in the circumstances, that Joseph and Cora would only get one shot at nomenclatorial tribute. When, to everyone's astonishment, I arrived less than a year later, there was some debate as to what I should be called. As she rocked me in her arms for the first time, Jette told my parents about her conversation with Lomax on the night of his death, and his quiet confession of a first name. After that, it was easy: I was to be James Martin Meisenheimer.

If Freddy was a happy miracle, then I was a freak, a billion-to-one shot. (My arrival also vanquished any lingering religious doubts that Joseph had. Now he was first to his knees every Sunday morning.) Still, for all that our presence in the world was in apparent defiance of biology, we were both sickly boys. Our puny bodies were pummeled by tides of germs and disease. We sniveled and coughed our way from one medical condition to the next, but even so my brother and I brought my family into the light once again. Cora's eyes began to shine with their old confidence. Not even the sight of German troops marching through the Rhineland could diminish Jette's joy in us, her snot-ridden, puking grandsons.

When Cora fell pregnant again at the end of 1938, she became something of a medical sensation. The third pregnancy was difficult, however. For the first few months she walked out into the yard every morning and noisily emptied her stomach into the bushes. When the vomiting finally abated, she had already begun to swell up like a balloon.

Freddy and I had been angels in the womb, but the new baby left Cora too exhausted to move. Jette and Rosa performed child care in shifts, ferrying Freddy and me back and forth between the two houses. They fed us and wiped our noses and kept us out of our mother's way while she languished in bed.

Joseph was the one person in Beatrice who had stopped marveling at Cora's sudden and extraordinary fecundity. He had decided that it was God's will, and that was good enough for him. It did not occur to him that all those years of miscarriages and dashed hopes meant that Cora was now well beyond usual childbearing years, and that with each new pregnancy, no matter how miraculous, came increased risk. By then he had begun to believe that higher forces were looking out for them — and that, as a consequence, nothing could possibly go wrong.

On September 1, 1939, as German troops crossed the Polish border at Dirschau and fired the first shots in the bloodiest war in human history, Cora went into labor. It took two days for England and France to declare war on Germany. It took three days for Cora to give birth. For much of that time Dr. Becker — who by then was a very old man — hovered uncertainly at the end of the bed, scratching his chin.

For there was not one baby, but two.

When the twins were finally born, they immediately began screaming at each other at the top of their tiny lungs — a dialogue that would continue in much the same way for the next twenty years or so. Unlike Freddy and me, they were big, hearty boys, exuding rude health from the moment they appeared. Dr. Becker wrapped them in blankets and sent a startled-looking Joseph downstairs with them.

Jette was waiting in the kitchen, warming

milk on the stove. When Joseph appeared with two bundles in his arms instead of just one, a hand shot up to her mouth.

"Oh, heavens," she breathed.

Joseph beamed at her.

Jette raised her voice to make herself heard over the twins' yells. "Are they . . . ?"

"Both boys," answered Joseph happily.

But while Jette and Joseph blinked at each other in disbelieving joy, the miracle of Cora's fertile loins morphed into tragedy. As she lay in the bed that had been her prison for so many weeks, her exhausted, pulverized body finally gave out. Something broke deep within her, and she began to bleed uncontrollably. Her whimper of warning into the sodden pillow went unheeded by Dr. Becker, who was in the bathroom, washing off the grime and sweat of three long days by her bedside. By the time he noticed the dark blood that had begun to pool around Cora's midriff, the hemorrhaging had become unstoppable. Life gushed out of her.

The old doctor knew there was nothing he could do. He held Cora's hand in sad silence and watched her go.

When Becker finally made his way down the stairs to examine the babies, his feet were leaden. He heard the newborns before he saw them, their lusty screams floating through the house. He pushed open the kitchen door. Joseph and Jette were sitting at the table, each holding one of the babies.

They looked up at him, their eyes shining.

TWENTY-SIX

My mother was the only woman Joseph had ever loved. He had adored her from the moment he first laid eyes on her. Cora was the crucible where all his hopes and dreams had been forged. Her sudden absence untethered him absolutely. He staggered through the house, seeing her everywhere. She would not let him go. Or was it he who could not relinquish her? She haunted his thoughts as he stumbled numbly through each day, but it was the wishful trickery of his dreams that he dreaded the most. Night after night his subconscious duped him with fresh phantasms of hope, cruelly resurrecting Cora's ghost. There she was, as beautiful as ever, us boys in her arms, laughing and smiling. The hope of that vision lingered on in each new dawn, but never for long. Even before Joseph was fully awake, the bitter truth crashed over him. He lay in the empty bed, pinned in place by the weight of his loss, and wept at the prospect of another day without Cora by his side.

Joseph might never have gotten out of bed at all if it hadn't been for me and my brothers. As it was, the world outside his stilled heart was more chaotic than ever, thanks to our collective pandemonium. There were four small lives to nurture and care for. Nights were punctuated by the twins' hungry wails, which sent him blearily downstairs to warm milk on the stove. Freddy and I were too young to understand what had happened, but Cora's absence disturbed us. We had both taken to wandering through the house in the middle of the night, looking for her. Joseph took our hands and coaxed us gently back to our beds.

Jette saw the despair in Joseph's eyes, and remembered her own sorrow at the prospect of a life without Frederick by her side. Twenty years had done nothing to dull the ache of her own loss, and now she felt her heart break all over again. She feared for us, growing up without a mother's embrace to warm and protect us, and she did everything she could to fill the hole that she knew could never be filled. She bathed us, fed us, held us close. She crooned old German lullabies. She kissed us, again and again and again, and tried not to fear for the future too much.

A week or so after the twins' birth, Jette gently pointed out to Joseph that the babies would need names. He looked at her blankly. He and Cora had both been so sure that the new baby would be a girl that they had not even considered one boy's name, let alone two. He asked Jette if she had any ideas. As it happened, she did; and so the twins were named in honor of two of my grandmother's political heroes — who were not brothers themselves, but did come from the same family. Theodore and Franklin Meisenheimer took to their presidential names with ease. From an early age they behaved as if they were already accustomed to the privileged entitlements of high office, as they imperiously squawked at the rest of the family (and each other) to do their inarticulate bidding.

The family quickly improvised new routines. During the day, Jette looked after us while Joseph hauled himself across town to open the restaurant. He hired Mrs. Heimstetter, doyenne of fried chicken at First Christian Church, to take orders and pour coffee in Jette's absence.

When Rosa returned from the schoolhouse in the afternoon she assumed control of our carelessly marauding existences, and Jette retired to her armchair to calm her ragged nerves. Mealtimes were never the most joyful of occasions back then. Teddy and Frank screamed indignantly throughout. Freddy and I sat in our high chairs and made as much noise as we could, just so we could be heard above the twins' racket. The adults watched us, battered by sadness and exhaustion. After the dishes had been cleared away, a tired convoy made its way back across the grass to our home. Joseph bathed us, all four boys in the bath at once, and put us to bed. Once he had tucked us in, he would lie on the floor between the cots and tell us a story. He concocted epic adventures in which our family had the starring role. Of course, in these tales there were not five of us, but six. Each night Joseph wistfully brought Cora back to life, and it was always she who single-handedly saved us from danger. Without her, we would have perished every time. We listened, deaf to the catch of fear in our father's voice. One by one, the four fidgeting bundles around him would subside into stillness. Sometimes he didn't notice that we had fallen asleep, and would carry on with his tale long after there was nobody left to hear it, bewitched by his own fantasy. He often fell asleep where he lay, lulled by the gentle rhythms of our sleep.

With us, Joseph was always as gentle as

a lamb, but a smoldering anger was creeping up through the cracks of his sorrow. As Dr. Becker had stood in the kitchen doorway and told him that his wife was dead, my father's faith drained out of him in one sickening, lurching evacuation. No matter how miraculous Cora's pregnancies might have appeared, he knew at once that divine intervention had nothing to do with it, after all. No deity would grant his wife's wishes and then kill her for them — not even the snarling, unforgiving deity that Reverend Kellerman liked to invoke in his sermons. It was all a sham, Joseph saw. There had been nobody up there listening.

One evening several weeks after Cora's death, Reverend Kellerman appeared at the front door, a basket of freshly baked rolls under his arm. Joseph stood on the threshold with his arms crossed, unwilling to let him into the house.

"We've missed you at church, Joseph," the pastor said, a look of friendly concern on his face. "You know, it's at times like this, when your heart is heavy with grief, when you need your faith more than ever. There's solace in worship."

My father said nothing. Reverend Kellerman cleared his throat. "The Lord moves in mysterious ways, Joseph. I don't know why

He chose to take Cora from us, but He had His reasons. He always does. Ours is not to reason why."

Joseph stepped forward and took two warm rolls out of the basket.

"There's more nourishment in the love of Christ than in a million of those rolls," said Reverend Kellerman with a smile.

By way of response Joseph threw one of the rolls at his visitor. It hit the preacher squarely on the nose, bounced off, and landed near his feet. Both men looked at it for a moment.

"I understand that you're angry right now," said Reverend Kellerman, "but don't allow your grief to eclipse God's love." The next roll hit him on the forehead, more forcefully than the first. Joseph stepped forward and took the basket. Reverend Kellerman relinquished it and folded his hands in front of him. "Cora loved Jesus," he said. "She wouldn't want you to turn your back on Him." The next roll hit him just below the eye. "Well," sighed the minister, brushing some crumbs off his cheek, "I should probably be going now." He turned stiffly and made his way back down the garden path. An aerial bombardment showered down on him as he went. By the time he reached the gate, the basket was empty, and our front yard was littered with sweet-smelling grenades. Joseph stood on the front porch and watched the pastor retreat. He had not said one word.

To Reverend Kellerman's credit, he was not put off by my father's fusillade of baked goods. The next day, a Saturday, he appeared at the restaurant just before closing time, a sheaf of papers in his hand. He sat quietly at the farthest booth from the door with a cup of coffee and a slice of cherry pie, and began to make notes. Joseph watched him suspiciously from behind the counter. The last diners left the restaurant, until only Reverend Kellerman remained. When Mrs. Heimstetter hung up her apron and bade them both good night, the minister looked up and smiled at Joseph.

"Will you join me?" he asked.

Joseph picked up the coffeepot and brought it over to the table. He refilled the pastor's cup and poured one for himself before sliding into the booth. "I suppose you have something more to say," he said.

Reverend Kellerman gestured to the papers in front of him. "I'm working on my sermon for tomorrow," he said. He took a sip of coffee. "I know these are difficult times for you, Joseph. I can only imagine the pain you're feeling. You'll need strength to get you through."

"I'm strong enough, thanks."

"God is the source of your strength."

My father shook his head. "Not mine."

"Yes, Joseph. Yours, too. Everything comes from the Lord. And just as he gives it, he can take it away. Think about Samson. God gave him the strength of a hundred men. He killed a thousand Philistines with the jaw-bone of an ass. But when his hair was cut, he lost that strength." Reverend Kellerman sat back. "Do you see? His power was a gift from God. And God took it away."

"You're saying that if I lose my faith, I'll lose my strength."

"If it happened to Samson, why not you?"

"But he lost his strength because Delilah cut his hair."

The minister frowned. "Look, Samson was weak. He told Delilah his secret. That was his downfall."

Joseph folded his arms and said nothing.

Reverend Kellerman changed tack. "You remember the parable of the lost sheep. Matthew, chapter eighteen. There was a shepherd who looked after a hundred sheep. One of them got lost in the mountains. The shepherd left the rest of his flock and went to look for the one that was missing. He did everything he could to find that one little sheep."

"Let me guess," said Joseph. "I'm the lost sheep."

The minister smiled at him. "Not for long, I hope."

"And you're the shepherd?"

Reverend Kellerman shrugged. "It's my calling."

"You'll do whatever it takes to rescue me?"

"Whatever it takes."

"You're a brave man."

"I have strength of my own."

"Which God gave you."

"Of course."

Joseph stood up. "Well, Reverend, I hope God doesn't take your strength away, too, like he did with Samson. Because I'll warn you now, I'm one stubborn son of a bitch."

That night Reverend Kellerman had difficulty getting to sleep. He was unable to put his conversation with Joseph out of his mind. The minister was profoundly bothered by my father's indifference at the prospect of being saved. He heard the mockery in Joseph's voice. *I hope God doesn't take your strength away, too.*

When he finally drifted off into an uneasy sleep, his dreams were foggy echoes of their exchange in the restaurant. There was long-haired Samson in chains, pulling down the pillars of the Philistine temple; Reverend Kellerman himself, carrying a gnarled staff, the good shepherd, heroically seeking his missing sheep; and Joseph Meisenheimer, coffeepot in hand, turning away from him.

In the middle of the night the minister awoke and sat bolt upright in his bed. He blinked rapidly in the darkness, filled with a sense of wonder. Careful not to wake his sleeping wife, he pulled back the covers and went to his study. He threw away the notes he had been making the previous afternoon and excitedly began to write a brand-new sermon for that day's service. The minister scribbled away excitedly, not stopping to consider whether the brain wave that had shaken him out of his sleep was really (as he fancied) a gift from God, or instead the result of some disastrously muddy nighttime thinking.

The next morning, Reverend Kellerman's eyes were shining as he climbed into the pulpit. He told the congregation how Delilah betrayed Samson to the Philistines by cutting off his hair. Then he related the parable of the shepherd and his lost sheep. Joseph Meisenheimer was his very own lost sheep, he declared. It would require faith and determination to rescue him, he declared. It would require *strength*. He would not be weak — like Samson. Then Reverend Keller-man drew himself up tall, and vowed loudly before God and the people of Beatrice that until he had brought Joseph Meisenheimer back into the fold of the church, he would not cut a single hair on his head.

The congregation sat there uneasily, unsure if they had heard him correctly. Everyone was too polite to point out the profoundly il-logical nature of his proposal. What had left the minister blinking in sleep-addled awe the previous night made no sense at all in the cold light of that Sunday morning, but Reverend Kellerman was too swept up in the drama of it all to notice. He beamed down triumphantly at his flock, mistaking their collective bewilderment for hushed admira-tion.

Word quickly spread about the sermon. When Joseph heard about the clergyman's peculiar vow, he simply shrugged his shoul-ders. But the next time Reverend Kellerman came calling, he refused to speak with him. And the next.

The minister soon realized that he had made a horrible miscalculation. He had woefully underestimated my father's limit-less reserves of obstinacy. Every morning Reverend Kellerman stood in front of his bathroom mirror and scratched his growing beard, ruing the day he had ever taken Joseph on.

It soon became apparent that neither man was going to give in, so the rest of the town settled back to enjoy the fun. Reverend Kellerman's flowing locks became a public index of our family's godlessness. After a year or so, the shaggy-haired preacher who climbed up the pulpit steps every Sunday to deliver his sermons with an increasingly manic gleam in his eye seemed far more eccentric than the trim, mild-mannered cook whose soul he was so determined to save.

The unbending forcefulness of my father's atheism surprised everyone. It was one more thing that distinguished us from the other kids in Beatrice. Most people's lives revolved around the twin suns of extended family and church. We had neither. We were cocooned in those two little houses on the outskirts of town, an uneven mishmash of three generations. I'm sure we were rich material for the town's rumor mill, but none of us cared. We were just trying to muddle through and make it to the end of each day in one piece.

TWENTY-SEVEN

It sounded as if the war that was unfolding in Europe was being waged inside our
house. Freddy and I had been quiet babies,
but Frank and Teddy rampaged through
the house with the devastating force of an
invading army. Nothing was too trivial to
merit full-scale engagement. The sustained
intensity of their fighting was such that none
of the grown-ups ever had much time for
Freddy or me.

The twins really were identical. The only
way to distinguish one from the other was
a small mole that Teddy had just above his
right ankle; Joseph and Jette were always
rolling down their little socks to see who was
who. As the years passed, each remained a
perfect replica of the other.

In December 1941 the Japanese attacked
the naval base at Pearl Harbor and President Roosevelt solemnly told the nation that
America was at war, once again. By then the

twins were two years old, and their talent for mayhem was reaching its first apex. I, at the grand old age of four, was mired in sibling-inspired ennui, dreaming of the day when there would be nobody left but me.

It was difficult for me, this sudden demotion in the family ranks. Freddy had the consolation of being the eldest; nothing could ever rob him of that. Also he didn't seem to *mind* being ignored. During that first year, before I came along, his every twitch and fart had been cataloged and marveled at, and that was probably enough attention to last anyone a lifetime. I, though, was unable to relinquish the limelight so easily. Sandwiched between serenely untouchable Freddy and the twins' dazzling commotion, I became sullen, resentful, and overly sensitive to every perceived injustice.

I wasn't the only casualty of all that domestic chaos. My poor grandfather was suffering mightily, too. Martin Leftkemeyer was still mourning the loss of his darling daughter, and his nerves were being flayed daily by the brutal cacophony that had descended on his house. In the summer of 1942 he moved to a small apartment above the bank where he could grieve in peace.

We were now a household of five men, none of us especially well house-trained.

Jette and Rosa's best efforts could not halt the calamitous mess that our undomesticated existences created. No sooner was one discarded toy picked up than another would be carelessly deposited elsewhere. The house was booby-trapped with sharp items lurking underfoot, just out of the lines of adult vision.

After a long day at the grill, Joseph was too tired to tolerate sibling squabbles when he got home. Evenings became death by a thousand cuts, every high-pitched shriek another livid wound. He winced his way through supper, balefully eyeing the clock as it crept toward our bedtime.

Finally he thought of a way to combat our endless bickering. One night he arrived home with a large box in his arms. We watched as he carried it into the living room and placed it on the table.

He turned to us. "Boys," he said, "I finally worked out what this house was missing."

"What?" asked Freddy.

"*Music,*" said Joseph. "Look."

Inside the box was a beautiful radio, constructed out of polished walnut with a vast, single speaker squatting in the middle of its elegant façade. Five narrow chrome bars spanned the mesh from top to bottom. They reminded me of a lion baring its teeth.

"What does it do?" I asked.

By way of response, Joseph squatted down in front of the machine and switched it on. A soft hiss of static emerged from the beast's ferocious maw. He turned a fat knob and the needle on the central display shifted a little to the right. "I don't know quite — Ah, here's something." A creamy chorus of trombones and saxophones oozed into the room, as smooth and polished as the radio itself. Joseph grinned at us. I couldn't remember the last time I'd seen him smile. "That's Glenn Miller," he said. "'Tuxedo Junction.'" When the tune ended, Joseph fiddled with the dial again. There was more static, then a thunderous blast of timpani and strings. He shook his head and moved on. For thirty minutes we surfed the airwaves, randomly alighting on snatches of melody and then taking off again.

Each night after that, we sat in front of the radio and bathed in whatever oases of sound my father's fingers discovered on that dial. The ritual silenced our petty bickering, at least for a while. We were discovering music for the first time, but for Joseph every tune crackled with old memories. Caruso sang the same arias that Frederick had performed in the Nick-Nack. And in the rousing stomps of Duke Ellington, Fletcher Henderson, and

Artie Shaw, he heard the distant, blues-tinged echo of Lomax's cornet. Sometimes we would catch a crisp blast of four-part barbershop. It was still the sound my father loved the most. As he listened to those swooping tags and perfect chords, he looked at us, his own fractious quartet, and wondered if our squalling discord could ever be transformed into such harmony.

In the years that followed, Joseph's grief over Cora's death did not abate, although its volume changed, from center-stage howl to a soft chorus of melancholy, whispered from the wings. Everything good was tempered by the knowledge that it would have been even better with Cora by his side. His mourning became a one-way stream of private telegrams, each one laced with tender regret: *You would have loved this. How you would have laughed at that.* After her death, Joseph was smothered by a fresh blanket of silence. He never sang another note, his beautiful voice locked within him once more.

My mother's presence lingered on in the house after she was gone. There were photographs of her everywhere. I sometimes caught Joseph reaching out to touch one of those pictures in wistful communion. I wished that I missed her as much as he did.

I watched him disappear into his memories, and wanted to join him there. But I could not remember her. There was nothing for me to hang my remorse upon. Cora's clothes still hung in her wardrobe in mothballed memorial, and from time to time I crept into Joseph's bedroom to examine the cloistered rainbow of brightly patterned dresses. I buried my nose in the soft folds of fabric and inhaled deeply, hoping to unearth long-buried memories, but my mother remained out of reach, a distant ghost.

In April of 1945, as the war was heading toward an Allied victory, President Roosevelt died. We all sat around the radio and listened to the live broadcast as the vice president was sworn in as the thirty-third president of the United States. It was a proud day for all Missourians. Harry Truman was the first man from our state to make it to the White House.

Jette still had Frederick's last letter to her, the one he had written in that little whitewashed church in northern France. She did not know it, but the man taking the oath of office was the same piano-playing major who had accompanied Frederick in his last recital, and had sent him singing into the woods on his last morning on this earth.

My grandfather's passion for his adopted

country had been boundless. I can only imagine how proud he would have been if he had lived to see that moment. To have sung with the president of the United States!

One evening in late 1946 Joseph walked to the farmhouse where Riva Bloomberg still lived. Nearly three decades had passed since he had last made that journey. Frau Bloomberg, now a tiny, white-haired lady in advanced old age, welcomed Joseph with a joyful hug and shuffled painfully down the corridor to the room where they had spent so many hours together at the piano. When he explained his proposal, Riva Bloomberg began to weep. Her fingers, once strong enough to strangle chickens and keep up with Frederick's impetuous tempi, had been frozen by arthritis, and the piano had not been played for years.

Joseph wanted to buy it so that he could teach us to sing.

He offered a generous price, but Riva Bloomberg waved the figure away. She would not accept any payment. Another generation of Meisenheimers learning to sing at her piano was reward enough for her, she told him. Joseph kissed her softly on the cheek and promised her that she would be guest of honor at their first public performance.

Jette greeted the piano's arrival in the house with certain misgivings. It was, after all, a machine designed to produce noise, and as such it appeared somewhat redundant. But she saw the look in Joseph's eyes, and knew better than to protest too much.

Every evening Joseph sat at the piano and constructed simple arrangements of songs he had heard on the radio. He hummed to himself as his fingers poked at the keys, piling up chords. We flew around him as he worked, whooping and hollering, ignoring all that thoughtful prodding.

When he had completed a handful of arrangements, Joseph beckoned Freddy toward him. My brother stood obediently next to the piano and sang the patterns of notes that Joseph picked out. By then I was obsessively monitoring every family transaction for further evidence of my own irrelevance, and so I hovered suspiciously by the door, watching and listening as Freddy's faltering treble floated through the room. My surveillance lasted two nights before I asked if I could join in.

It was immediately apparent to Joseph that our voices would never possess the luminous quality that his own once had, but we did okay. When he first heard us pipe out "Stars Fell on Alabama" in simple two-part harmony, his smile warmed us like sunshine. Basking in the glow of his approval, we began to learn new songs, and our repertoire slowly grew.

One evening Joseph invited Jette to listen to us sing. Our grand finale was "When the Red Red Robin Comes Bob-Bob-Bobbin' Along." Freddy and I performed this with a little dance routine of our own devising that was supposed to represent the afore-mentioned robin, duly bob-bob-bobbin'. We sang and bobbed with such serious looks on our faces — this was our big moment, our first proper audience, and we were both concentrating madly — that at the end Jette had to sweep us into her arms and cover us with kisses to hide her laughter. Just at that moment, Teddy ran around the corner. He saw his grandmother bend down to hug us, her face lit up with pleasure, and came to an abrupt stop. Seconds later, Frank hurtled into the room, crashed into his brother, and sent them both sprawling forward in a heap. The twins gazed up at the three of us locked in our delicious embrace, and I knew right away that that was the end of that.

Sure enough, the following night Frank and Teddy joined the huddle around the piano, demanding to be included. Freddy and I complained in a halfhearted way, but we knew that there was nothing we could do to stop them.

What I hadn't anticipated was how completely the twins would eclipse us.

I will never forget the night I first heard Frank and Teddy sing. Joseph asked us to repeat our recital of the night before, and we awkwardly stumbled through the songs while the twins sat on the floor, listening. By unspoken agreement, there was no bobbin' of robins this time. If we were going to go down, we would go down with some measure of dignity preserved.

When we had finished, Joseph beckoned the twins toward the piano and began to play some simple melodies for them to sing. From the moment they opened their mouths, it was clear where our grandfather's musical legacy had come to rest. The twins' voices were as pure and as sweet as morning birdsong. As each perfect note emerged from their untutored throats, Freddy and I shrank further into the wall.

My father's face was illuminated with something leagues beyond joy.

The twins had no idea of the effect they were having on the rest of us. When Joseph finally closed the piano they hovered for a second or two and then ran howling out of the room, throwing punches at each other as they went. Freddy and I were left in silence with our father. He looked at us.

"Well!" he said.

That night I cried myself to sleep.

Joseph had originally supposed that Freddy would sing the lead melody in our little quartet, and I would sing the second part. Frank and Teddy would be consigned to the nether regions of harmony, the unglamorous tonics and humdrum fifths, while Freddy and I stole the show. After that first night, though, we all knew that those plans would have to change. Joseph did his best to cheer us up when he explained this to us. He told us that the lower parts were musically more challenging. That was certainly true, but if anything it made matters worse, given the imbalance in our abilities. Frank and Teddy only had to listen to an arrangement once for the music to be hardwired into their musical circuitry. After that they could reproduce each of the four separate parts, effortlessly unpacking the tune's complex harmonic structure.

Freddy and I, by contrast, had to work devilishly hard. Singing the melody was one thing; delving deep into each chord to forage for underlying harmonies was quite another. Each note felt as if we were stepping into a void. To our young ears these new parts seemed untethered from the tune. We had to listen, listen, and then listen again as Joseph patiently played our parts on the piano. We stood and practiced until those alien notes finally stuck in our heads.

Joseph taught us all the barbershop favorites. The lyrics might as well have been in Latin for all the sense they made to us. Some sight we must have made, four young boys declaring their love for a procession of faceless girls with names like Dolly, Nelly, Suzy, and, of course, Adeline. We offered up hymns to this gal and that gal, your gal and my gal, a legion of babies, sweethearts, and dolls. We sang a lot about walking down streets, in the rain, on the sunny side — actually, in just about every meteorological condition imaginable. And we sang an awful lot about Dixie, without ever being sure who or what Dixie was. There was unsurpassed silliness and cheap sentimentality in abundance. Still, on we sang, learning how to blend our voices into one.

Freddy and I labored away at the underbelly of the tunes while the twins soared effortlessly above us, and occasionally our harmonies coalesced into something rather beautiful. But as our singing improved, the nightly sessions around the piano became more fractious: it did not take long for the music to become just one more thing for Frank and Teddy to fight about. They began to bicker and squabble about who should sing the lead. Soon our rehearsals became the forum where the twins' loathing of each other was refined to its purest, most poisonous form. I couldn't tell their voices apart if I closed my eyes, and perhaps that was the problem: the burden of being indistinguishable from each other, even on such a sublime level, must have been unbearable. If they were not singing in perfect harmony, they were pinching and kicking each other. While the twins fought, Freddy and I toiled. Very often nobody was having an especially good time.

But there were glimmers of delight that kept us coming back for more. We discovered the quiet pleasure of being buried deep within that music. The twins may have hogged the melodies, but my own notes fattened those tunes into glistening slabs of sweet harmony, and that was enough for me. Our individual voices were subsumed into a delicious aggregation. When we got it right, the sound that spilled into that room was just beautiful. Joseph sat at the piano and listened, a proud smile on his face. And that remained the most precious reward of all.

For months our nightly rehearsals were private affairs. When we finally made our first public performance, Joseph kept his promise to Riva Bloomberg that she would be the guest of honor — although not in the way that either of them would have liked.

TWENTY-EIGHT

One afternoon in the fall of 1947 Joseph knocked on the door of the schoolhouse, where the four of us now spent most of our days being cowed by Rosa. (Not even Frank and Teddy were a match for our terrifying aunt. They may have run riot at home, but the moment they stepped into that schoolroom they were as meek as lambs.) Rosa opened the door and looked at Joseph.

"What's wrong?" she asked. Only an emergency could have made him close the restaurant early.

"Riva Bloomberg died," he said. "I need the boys."

Rosa eyed him suspiciously. "Why?"

"She left a note. She wanted them to sing 'Amazing Grace' at her funeral."

"'Amazing Grace'? You do realize that's a *hymn*?"

Joseph rolled his eyes. "Thank you, yes."

"And that the funeral will be in the church?"

"Look, it's for Riva. It's the least I can do."

Rosa look amused. "Has anyone told Reverend Kellerman?"

"I haven't got time to worry about him," said Joseph. "We've got to start practicing right away. They've never sung a hymn before."

"No, I would think not," said my aunt, amused.

For the rest of the afternoon we applied ourselves diligently to learning the hymn. We were excited at the prospect of our first public performance, and the hostilities that usually accompanied our rehearsals were momentarily suspended. We were focused on the music, riding the crest of each phrase as one, united in spirit and purpose. We were no longer just four boys singing. Finally we became a quartet.

The following morning Joseph and Jette argued all the way to the church. My father may have been prepared to let us sing, but there was no way he was going to attend the service himself. He did not want Reverend Kellerman to claim his appearance as any sort of victory in their ongoing feud. Jette begged and pleaded with him to change his mind, but he was adamant. We trailed a few steps behind them as they squabbled, humming "Amazing Grace" under our breaths and tugging nervously at our collars.

At the front door of the church, Joseph squatted down and drew the four of us into his arms. He kissed each of us, told us to sing our hearts out for Frau Bloomberg, and promised to wait outside. We walked into the church and settled down in the back pew. Jette sat next to us, keeping watch.

Freddy nudged me. "Did you see the coffin?" he whispered.

I shifted position and squinted through the crowd toward the front of the church. In front of the altar, surrounded by a glade of lilies, a small casket sat on a pair of trestles.

I frowned. "What about it?"

Freddy gripped my sleeve. "Do you think she's in there?"

"Of course she is," I muttered.

I glanced sideways at the twins to see if they'd heard Freddy's dumb question. They hadn't. Frank was sitting with his head tilted back, gazing up at the ceiling and blowing a spit bubble between his lips. Teddy was idly scratching a buttock, looking around the church with interest. Freddy poked me in the ribs again.

"What?" I glared at him.

"Look at the coffin," Freddy whispered.

"I just did."

"Look at the *lid*."

With a sigh, I looked at the lid.

It was open.

I sank back into the pew and we looked at each other in horror. We had never seen a dead body before.

"Do you think her eyes are open?" whispered Freddy.

Before I could answer, the doors at the back of the church opened. We clambered to our feet and watched Frau Bloomberg's nine sons walk up the aisle, followed by Reverend Kellerman, who clasped a Bible between his hands and kept his head bowed as he walked. I watched him as he passed by the coffin. He did not stop and stare at the dead woman lying there. I could feel my heart thumping against my ribs. A dead body! I closed my eyes tightly and hummed my part.

Riva Bloomberg's sons were cattle farmers. They were big, heavyset men with a reputation as hard-bitten, no-nonsense types, but they were also highly emotional, God-fearing folks. The highlight of Bloomberg family meals was the grace, which would be long, high on drama, and by the end would have half the assembled company sobbing into their chests. The Bloombergs loved nothing more than a good funeral, and by the end of the scripture reading, the pews were filled with quietly weeping mourners.

Reverend Kellerman climbed into the pulpit to deliver the funeral address. He pulled his straggly gray hair (which by now was well past shoulder-length) out of his face and peered down at the rows of black-clad children, grandchildren, and great-grandchildren of Riva Bloomberg, their cheeks shining with fresh tears. His gaze finally fell on the four of us at the back of the church. He stared at us for a moment before beginning his sermon.

It was a point of some pride for the minister that he did not tone down his usual hell-and-damnation rhetoric for funerals. He did not do comforting introspection, fond memorializing, that sort of thing. Instead, he told the listening congregation that for all of her apparently saintly behavior, Riva Bloomberg had been as bloated with sin as the rest of us, and was thus condemned to languish in the ravaging pits of eternal hellfire. Even as we are gathered here praying for her soul, he thundered, the diabolical flames of damnation are consuming her. By the time he had finished, the church had been stunned into silence.

"And now," said Reverend Kellerman, "*at the departed's special request*" — his eyes rolled — "Frederick, James, Franklin, and Theodore Meisenheimer are going to sing 'Amazing Grace.'" His tone made it clear that the four of us were destined for an even worse fate than Riva Bloomberg's.

Jette stood up and ushered us along the aisle. I felt the gaze of the congregation on my back, but I was far more worried about the open coffin at the front of the church. Freddy was in front of me. I could see the fear coiled between his shoulder blades. The carpet beneath my feet seemed to be tugging at my shoes, holding me back, but on I went, until I was standing next to my brother, peering down at the old dead lady.

Frau Bloomberg lay with those famous chicken-strangling hands crossed gently over her chest. She wore a simple black dress, black stockings, flat black shoes. Around her neck hung a small silver cross. Her eyes, mercifully, were shut, but I was unable to look away from her soft, still face. She seemed so peaceful. It was hard to believe that at that very moment her soul was being feasted upon by the devil himself. The thought occurred to me that I never, ever, wanted to die.

There was a pointed cough. I looked up. The whole church was watching us as we stood paralyzed in front of the coffin.

Teddy and Frank were waiting impatiently. I moved toward the twins, and after a moment Freddy followed. Finally we turned to face the congregation. I stared blindly at the people in front of me. All I could think was: she's never coming back.

Teddy, who was singing the lead, counted us in with a whispered four. As one we took a deep breath.

Amazing grace! How sweet the sound.

We nailed it. Every harmony, every inflection and nuanced dynamic that we had slaved over — it all came off perfectly.

As for what happened next, I can only imagine that my recent encounter with Riva Bloomberg's dead body must have left me in a state of heightened emotional sensibility. I began to cry at the beauty and sadness of it all. This was not, unfortunately, a compassionate tear or two trickling discreetly down my cheek, but a fully fledged bawl. Suddenly I was fighting for breath, gulping air into my lungs. I stood there silently, my mouth opening and closing like a demented goldfish. As I struggled to regain control of my lungs, I realized that Freddy had stopped singing, too. Instead he was looking at me, his eyes full of concern. Not for the last time, my brother's bighearted compassion got the better of him. We may have had a job to do up there, but Freddy, bless him, was more worried about me than the music. Which just made me want to cry even more.

So there we were, two of us singing, two of us not. At least the right two were still going. The twins carried the melody onward, their voices intertwining perfectly. Freddy and I just stared at each other, quite lost. There was no way either of us would be able to pick up our parts midway through the tune.

As public debuts go, it was a disaster. It could have been a fatal blow to our musical career, but for what happened next. It turned out that there was a reason why Riva had wanted us to sing "Amazing Grace": it was the Bloomberg family hymn. By the end of the second verse the congregation had recovered from the shock of Reverend Kellerman's sermon, and were ready to reclaim the service as their own. As Frank and Teddy began the third verse, everyone else in the church joined in, bellowing the words as loudly as they could, trying to drown out the echo of the preacher's words. The twins' voices could no longer be heard as the congregation sang and swayed in their grief. Freddy remained motionless, his gaze flickering between me and the open coffin. I just stood there with my head in my hands, quite overcome.

The hymn soon degenerated into a chaotic free-for-all. Even the drunks who used to raise the roof of the Nick-Nack with their marching songs were more disciplined than the Bloomberg clan in mourning. Everyone, it seemed, had his own idea about how the tune went. Faced with a churchful of contradictory opinions, each singer just sang a little louder. The result was a catastrophe, musically speaking, but by the time the congregation had stumbled to a messy conclusion (several bars separating the first ones home from the stragglers), every face had been lit up. That was when I finally understood what my father and grandfather had known all along. That crowd of tone-deaf cattle farmers showed me what music, however imperfect, can achieve. They taught me the redemptive power of song.

The other thing that a good sing-along can do, apparently, is erase memory banks. After the service, word quickly spread that we had sung magnificently. I suppose those present were grateful for our help in chasing Reverend Kellerman's words out of the building. Whatever the reason, we were the beneficiaries of some generous collective amnesia. Reports focused on those first few moments before everything fell apart. People clucked admiringly. Such precocious talent, they said. Those who remembered Frederick nodded sagely. It's in the blood, they said.

We continued to gather around the piano each evening to learn new tunes. A month or so after the funeral, Dale Fruhstock came into the restaurant and asked Joseph if we would sing at his daughter's wedding.

And so, rather than falling at the first hurdle, our musical career was launched.

After Sandra Fruhstock's wedding (which passed smoothly enough, the bride and groom getting hitched without any more emotional meltdowns) we became a popular fixture on the Beatrice social scene, such as it was. Four cute boys with bow ties and high-pitched harmonies — what was not to like? Soon we were performing regularly at weddings and the Saturday night dances that took place each week around town. We even did a few more funerals. I learned to tamp down my emotions. The trick was to cut myself off from the dramas unfolding before us. We witnessed many pivotal moments in other people's lives, but by the age of eleven I was a cynical, world-weary pro. Retirement parties, baptisms, family reunions: it didn't matter to me. It was just another gig.

As we began to try more complicated arrangements, Joseph's limited ability at the piano began to cause problems, as he was unable to show us how our parts fitted together. To our delight, he solved the problem by asking Morrie Knuckles to stop by and play the piano.

Morrie's parents ran the pharmacy in town. He was a year older than Freddy. Everyone loved Morrie. He was extremely tall for his age and ridiculously good-looking. He possessed big dark brown eyes and perfect, brilliant teeth, and was unburdened by the usual nettled insecurities of adolescence. I don't ever remember hearing him say a mean word to anyone. I always felt a little warmer, walked a little taller, after Morrie Knuckles had taken the time to tell me a joke or ask me how things were going. We always loved it when he came to play our piano and listen to us sing.

Joseph never accepted a dime as payment for our services. We didn't mind. The applause, the indulgent smiles, the occasional toe-curling peck on the cheek from a grateful bride — that was enough for us. Joseph stood in the shadows at the back of the room and watched us sing — except when we performed in church, of course. Then he would loiter in the parking lot, hands buried deep in his pockets, no matter how filthy the weather. He must have made a strange sight, this lonely man standing quite still beneath the large stained-glass window, listening intently. For when our father heard the four of us sing, he could think only of Cora. For him our voices chanted a never-ending hymn to her memory. Our harmonies sent him to a place where we would never find him, somewhere pooled with old stories and sweet regrets.

TWENTY-NINE

While we were growing up, so was America. Another war had been won, but the cost of victory was still being calibrated. A new enemy was rising in the East. The evil threat of Communism cast a chill shadow across our homes. We had seen the carnage caused by the *Enola Gay* and its deadly cargo over the skies of Hiroshima. Now people began to wonder how long it would be before the Soviets aimed such terrible weapons at us. Americans buried their fears beneath a mountain of gleaming household appliances. New cars rolled off production lines in Detroit, bodies long and sensuous, sharp lines flashing chrome. People scurried out of the cities, needing somewhere to put all that *stuff*. Sprawling subdivisions appeared on the fringes of towns, brand-new houses as chillingly uniform as the endless rows of white crosses freshly planted in the fields of northern France. Those new streets had no fulcrum, no heart, just house after house after house. Community was replaced by commute. Every morning the country climbed into all those sparkling new automobiles and drove off to work.

Not that suburbia made it to Beatrice back then.

We were still a town of farmers, mostly. There was no need to build new homes. The exodus from Beatrice that had begun during the Depression continued in the years after the war. People were moving away, and they wanted to go much farther than the first empty field.

We weren't going anywhere, though. The four of us roamed through the town, as comfortable in its streets as we were in our yard. Back then, there were no curfews, no worried parents waiting by the telephone. We were lucky to have all that freedom, even if we didn't know it. We spent the long summers of our childhood in the same giant oak in Tillman's Wood that Joseph and Stefan Kliever had so loved. The tree sheltered us from the unforgiving sun and kept us dry during the thunderstorms that punctuated the relentless summer heat.

Sometimes I left the others to their fun and climbed away from them, as high as I could. Alone among the tallest branches, there was nobody in the county higher than me. Up there the leaves were caressed by a cooling breeze on even the stillest of days. I peered over the edge of the cliff and watched the Missouri River far below me. The sun's reflection caught the crests of the gently rippling water. The dazzling quilt of light appeared quite still, as if time up there were frozen.

Long after the oak had stopped being our communal playground, I continued to return there alone. I still visit it now, from time to time. I'm too old to climb it these days, of course, but when a certain melancholy steals over me, one that cannot be banished by more traditional means, I will slowly make my way up the hill to Tillman's Wood. The tree has been colonized by a new gang of escape artists these days. These kids have taken to hacking their initials into the old trunk. The letters run into each other, an extended, primal howl encircling the tree. I sit on the ground, leaning against the trunk so I cannot see them. I breathe deeply. The smell of the soil and the damp bark at my back trigger a thousand memories, and I escape.

As we grew older, Freddy and I stopped visiting Tillman's Wood, but the twins continued to play there for years afterward. They spent every moment they could outdoors. The war still loomed large in our young imaginations, and both Frank and Teddy enjoyed leading platoons into bloody battle with each other. These games were punctuated with technical disputes about the accuracy of each other's shooting, and how many bullets it took to kill a man. It was usually Frank who raised these objections; he found that tormenting Teddy with pedantic queries about whether or not he was really dead was more fun than peppering him with imaginary bullets. Their weapons, after all, were just pretend, but there was nothing imaginary about his brother's fury at all the interruptions. Frank calmly disputed everything until Teddy lost his patience, at which point he would administer a brief but violent beating. Frank was usually laughing too much to bother defending himself, and his mocking guffaws hurt Teddy far more than his fists ever could. It would be days before they went back into the woods to kill each other again.

Jette watched the twins' growing dislike for each other with concern. She suggested to Joseph that it might be a good idea to channel some of their enthusiasm for physical confrontation toward more positive pursuits, and so my father signed them up for every sporting activity available. They excelled at everything, but baseball was their passion. (Frederick, our family's proudest American, would have been delighted.) With its limitless capacity for statistics, the game allowed the twins to compete against each other even when they were playing on the same team. After the games they would argue about who had done best, qualifying and parsing the unforgiving numbers on the page.

The boys became the stars of the Beatrice Little League team. They went in to bat at numbers one and two, and between them they threw every pitch of every inning. For the first time in living memory, the team began to win more games than it lost, and suddenly there were more than just bored, anxious parents in the crowd. The whole town began to flock to the diamond behind First Christian Church to watch the games.

Family life soon pulsed to the gentle rhythm of the Little League fixture list. I spent the warm Friday evenings of my childhood summers perched on peeling bleachers with my nose in a book, while my younger brothers brought glory to Beatrice. By that time I had embarked on two simultaneous love affairs that, sixty years on, have yet to relinquish me from their grip. One was with a game; the other was with a middle-aged Englishman. My aunt introduced me to both.

One afternoon at the height of summer, Rosa appeared at our house wearing a white straw hat with a wide rim. She smiled at me when I opened the door.

"James. The very person."

"Hello, Aunt Rosa. You look very nice. Are you going somewhere?"

"I hope so." She eyed me speculatively. "Are you busy?"

"Me? Not especially."

"Good. Come on, then." At once she turned and walked back down the path. After a moment's hesitation I reluctantly followed her. Rosa may have been my aunt, but she was also the despot who terrorized us at school each day. I was used to obeying her instructions.

"Where are we going?" I asked.

"I'm going to buy you some ice cream," she told me.

I brightened considerably at this news. "At the restaurant?"

Rosa's nose wrinkled. "I thought we might try the new ice cream parlor."

"Oh," I said. I had never been to the ice cream parlor.

"I thought we'd have a bit more privacy there," explained Rosa.

"All right," I said, suddenly anxious.

Rosa strode briskly ahead, talking brightly, while I struggled to keep up. At the ice cream parlor Rosa ordered me an ice cream sundae and a strawberry milk shake. She ordered an iced tea for herself. We settled into a booth and she watched me eat.

"What do you think of the milk shake?" she asked.

"It's wonderful," I said. "Would you like to try some?"

"Oh, no thank you. I can't. I think I may be chronically allergic to dairy products."

I frowned. "Chronically — ?"

She leaned forward, entirely serious. "Your milk shake might kill me if I drank it."

I was shocked. "Really?"

Rosa nodded soberly. "Best not to take any chances."

I took a tentative, guilty sip.

"Is it better than your father's?" she asked.

My father's milk shakes were pretty good, but this was, without question, better than any I'd ever tasted before. My cheeks flushed with guilt as I nodded mutely.

"Don't worry," said Rosa cheerfully. "It'll be our little secret."

I looked up at her. The scowling, chalk-throwing persona that my aunt adopted so convincingly in the schoolhouse had vanished completely, replaced by this kind woman I hardly recognized. I didn't know what I had done to be singled out for this special treatment, but suddenly it didn't seem like such a bad thing. Here we were, just the two of us, and it felt good.

"Everyone needs secrets," she told me. "It keeps you from going crazy."

"Do *you* have secrets?" I asked her.

She looked down at her iced tea and swirled the straw around the glass. "Lots, actually," she said.

I didn't believe her. "Tell me one, then."

"If I told you, it wouldn't be a secret anymore."

"Just a small one."

"A small one." Something unreadable passed behind Rosa's eyes. She drummed her fingers on the tabletop. "All right, then. But you have to promise not to tell anyone."

"I promise."

She made a show of glancing about her and then leaned toward me across the table. "Sometimes this town drives me nuts," she whispered.

I looked at her in astonishment.

"You wait," she told me. "You'll see what I'm talking about, once you leave yourself."

"Once I *leave?*" The idea had never occurred to me.

Rosa took a sip of her tea and nodded. "You'll leave. And then one day you'll come back, and everything that you used to love about the place will drive you a little bit crazy."

"Did *you* leave?" I asked.

She nodded. "I went to college, but only for a year. And then later on I left again, for a little while." She smiled at me, a little sadly. "But each time I came back."

I thought about this. "Why?"

"Love," she answered simply.

"Really? Love?"

She nodded. "You, your father, your grandma. Home is where the heart is, James. I can't leave Beatrice any more than I can cut off my own arm."

"But you don't like it here?"

Rosa sighed. "Oh, most of the time I like it just fine, I guess. Maybe not as much as some people. Still, life would be boring if we all liked chocolate ice cream, wouldn't it?"

I stared down at my half-eaten sundae, unsure what she meant.

Later we walked home in silence. We stopped in front of Jette's house. "Well, thanks for the treat," I said. "That was fun."

Rosa cocked her head to one side. "Can

you come in for a minute?"

I followed her inside. In the drawing room Jette was dusting the mantelpiece. My father's angel wing still hung in solitary splendor, high up on the wall. She turned toward us as we entered. "There you are," she said.

I gave her an awkward wave. "Hi, Grandma," I said. It felt strange to be here without my brothers. I felt a little furtive, as if I were secretly trying to gain some illicit advantage over the rest of them.

Jette looked first at me, and then at Rosa. "Did you have a nice time?" she asked.

"Very," said Rosa. She and my grandmother exchanged looks.

"Well, it's all ready," sighed Jette.

"What's all ready?" I asked.

"Over here." Rosa led me across the room. A chessboard had been set up on the dining table.

"Chess," I said. I remembered finding my mother's old board stashed away in the back of a cupboard once.

"Fancy a game?" said my aunt.

"I don't know how to play."

"Not *yet*." She beamed at me.

385

THIRTY

It was only as I lay in my bed that evening, thinking about my strange afternoon with Rosa, that I realized why my aunt had taken such a shine to me. She had grown up in Joseph's shadow, and so she probably felt a certain kinship with me — the next generation's forgotten child. Perhaps she thought that a little extra attention from her would boost my confidence and make me feel loved. I was unsure what to think about this. I liked my aunt, but I wasn't sure if I wanted to spend my free afternoons having my confidence boosted on a regular basis — even when there were ice cream sundaes on offer.

As it turned out, I didn't have much of a choice. Rosa came calling for me again a week or so later, and after another trip to the ice cream parlor we returned to Jette's house to continue my chess education. Over the months that followed, Rosa showed me moves and tactics, just as Lomax and Cora had taught her. An unfamiliar light shone in her eyes as she watched my fingers hover hesitantly over the pieces. I loved to hear about the games she had played with my mother when she was younger. Every so often she would nod approvingly and tell Jette, "He's got his mother's talent."

Jette said nothing.

Before long I began to look forward to my afternoons with Rosa. She was a willing and discreet confidante. Over a succession of milk shakes and sundaes I confessed all manner of petty grievances against my brothers, my father, and my life in general. She listened to it all, her head cocked thoughtfully to one side. Not once did she offer me advice, but that was all right. I did not want advice. I just wanted someone to listen to me.

During those afternoons, Rosa also told me lots of good jokes. Even better, she taught me how to tell them. Boys tend to race through jokes, desperate to get to the punch line. My aunt taught me to slow down. She showed me how each joke was put together — where to pause, what to emphasize, how to deliver the payoff. She made me practice the same routine over and over again, and then sent me home to perform it for my brothers. The sound of their laughter was sweeter than any harmony we'd ever sung.

Encouraged, I began to study the professionals. Jette had a radio in her living room, and we would listen to the first superstars of comedy while we leaned over the chessboard: Abbott and Costello, Amos 'n' Andy, George Burns and Gracie Allen, Edgar Bergen. Rosa liked Jack Benny best, but Eddie Cantor was my favorite. I adored his fast-talking, wisecracking delivery, but what I liked most of all was that he was a monologue merchant. The other comedians worked in teams and played off each other, but Cantor's comic momentum was sustained by nothing more than the sheer, unrelenting force of his wit. Singing in the quartet had jaded my enthusiasm for group endeavors.

The next stage of my education in comedy began in the spring of 1950, on my thirteenth birthday. Rosa appeared at our house while we were still eating breakfast. "Here," she said, thrusting a small package into my hand. "It's time to introduce you to the master." I eagerly tore off the wrapping paper and then had to try to hide my disappointment as I held up the gift for general inspection.

My aunt had given me a book.

I was at an age when covers were the only thing I ever thought of judging a book by, and this one did not look promising. There was a picture of a young man dressed in a tuxedo, leaning back against a table with an anxious look on his face. He had raised one elegantly clad leg, at the end of which dangled a small dog, hanging on to the man's trousers with its teeth. In the background was a woman in a red dress, her hand raised to her face in consternation. I took all this in, dubious. At the time my tastes in fiction were limited to cowboys, aliens, and wartime derring-do. I gazed at the man in the tuxedo suspiciously, but it was the presence of the woman that really set the alarm bells ringing. I could not imagine why I would ever want to read a book with female characters in it. At that point in my life, my knowledge of women was derived exclusively from the lyrics of barbershop songs, and as a consequence I regarded all females with deep suspicion. They were to blame for all the mushy drivel that we had to sing week in and week out. Girls were to be serenaded, put up on a pedestal, and worshipped. Much of our repertoire was really no more than elaborate begging: *Won't you please be mine? Dream a little dream of me! Let me call you sweetheart!* Women made men act like idiots, I knew that much. And I was pretty sure they wouldn't be much use in a shoot-out, of either the intergalactic or terrestrial variety.

"Thank you," I said politely.

"Funniest thing I've ever read," Rosa told me.

The book was called *The Code of the Woosters,* by P. G. Wodehouse. Again, this was far from promising. I did not know if this P. G. Wodehouse was male or female. I turned the book over, looking for clues. "P. G. Wodehouse," I mused. I pronounced it Woad-house.

"Wood-house," corrected my aunt.

"That's not how it's spelled," I objected.

"Yes, well, he's English, you see," said Rosa, as if that explained everything.

I greeted this news with mixed feelings. Everything I knew about the English I had learned from dime-store paperbacks whose stories were set in wartime Europe. It was not uncommon for a brave but stupid English pilot who had been shot down over France to stumble in halfway through the narrative and complicate matters for the gutsy American hero who was single-handedly trying to save the Allied war effort. The Englishman's principal dramatic purpose was to introduce an element of levity. His attempts to help the gutsy American hero would be benign but hapless, and invariably ended up making things worse. Still, at least the English always acted honorably — which was more than could be said for the French.

That afternoon I settled down on a quilt in the backyard, the sun warming my back, and began to read. By the time Jette called me in for supper, I was lost in another world.

The plot of *The Code of the Woosters* is so convoluted that any attempt at summary is doomed to failure. It is a story of policemen's helmets, antique cow-creamers, and temperamental French chefs. There are splenetic magistrates, weak-chinned aristocrats, doe-eyed maidens, and a would-be fascist dictator who designs ladies' underwear. There is theft, burglary, and blackmail. All this is delivered in Bertie Wooster's trademark high-narrative style. His rhetorical flourishes rained down on me like a shower of mud, obfuscating meaning. The combined complexities of plot and language made for a confusing but compelling read. By the time Bertie had left London on a mission to help his friend Gussie Fink-Nottle out of a romantic predicament, I was ensnared by the peculiar foreignness of it all. The world I had jumped into was so unrecognizable to me that it might as well have been about the aliens I was so fond of.

By the following afternoon I had finished the book. I put it down, walked thoughtfully around the yard once or twice, and then picked it up again and turned back to the beginning. Rosa had been right. It *was* hilarious. The trouble was, I wasn't sure why. A slight fog lingered over matters as I finished the last page, which led me to suspect that I had sailed past large parts of the story without really grasping what was going on. Subsequent readings clarified certain plot points, and I soon stopped worrying about precisely *why* people behaved in the way they did. Instead I just reveled in the jokes, all those deftly delivered one-liners that I didn't quite understand. Bertie describes Roderick Spode, his nemesis, as having an eye that could open an oyster at sixty paces. I *knew* that was funny, but I didn't have the faintest idea what it meant.

After three rereads, I had more or less worked out what was going on. *The Code of the Woosters* finally dispensed with, I asked my aunt for more. Delighted, Rosa sent me home with my arms piled high with Wodehouse. These were the books that I escaped to during those long Friday evenings on the baseball bleachers. While my brothers were heroically engaged in the quintessential American pastime, I was half a world away, swept up in the misadventures of silly English aristocrats.

I enjoyed all of Wodehouse's creations, but I loved Bertie Wooster the most. I adored his loyalty to his feckless chums; his eloquent, if occasionally baffling, turns of phrase; and his manifest idiocy. I fancied we had much in common, he and I. In particular, we shared the same suspicion of women. (Bertie's aversion to romantic commitment has often made me wonder whether he, too, had sung in a barbershop quartet while he was up at Oxford.) The books teemed with females, legions of them, and Bertie's entirely sensible attitude was to stay as far away from them as possible. He left the mooning around to his imbecilic male friends, who were forever falling in love. I was grateful that the romances that drove many of the stories forward were devoid of the ghastly sentimentality that I had feared when I gazed down at that first cover. Hand-holding and the whispering of sweet nothings were largely conducted off-page. Instead amorous entanglements were more like business transactions. In Wodehouse's world, falling in love was about far more than two people sighing sweetly at each other — that was the easy part. Every romance involved a series of knotty negotiations with an army of third parties, usually old and cantankerous family members, who seemed, for reasons that I could never readily fathom, to have the ability to kill the affair stone dead. It was years before it dawned on me that having two people simply fall in love just isn't very funny. I wasn't sure whether to be comforted or saddened by the news.

Over time I became more adept at parsing Bertie Wooster's tortured way with metaphor, but there was nobody except for Rosa with whom I could share these linguistic glories. We developed our own dialect of in-jokes, and I delighted in the baffled looks on other people's faces when we traded these one-liners. I loved to tease her with Bertie's little speech to Jeeves: *"It's no use telling me there are bad aunts and good aunts. At the core, they are all alike. Sooner or later, out pops the cloven hoof."* She always laughed at this, albeit with a slightly pained expression on her face. We created our own little patch of Bertie's Mayfair, right here in the middle of Missouri, and nobody but us could gain admission. P. G. Wodehouse forged a bond between my aunt and me that was stronger than one of Jeeves's miracle hangover cures.

I soon shared her passion for chess, too. At the end of each lesson of drills and exercises, we would play a game or two. Of course, Rosa thrashed me every time, but I didn't mind. In fact I adored the elegance of the checkmates that she inflicted on me. I would stare down at the board, taking in the treacherous pattern of pieces, and a smile would break out on my face. Not even the most felicitous of Wodehouse's jokes could match the pleasure I got from those bloodless kills. My aunt would watch my beaming face with a frown. She did not wholly approve of my enthusiasm for her victories.

"It wouldn't hurt you to mind losing just a *little*," she said after one especially devilish checkmate.

"But that was so clever," I replied.

Rosa sighed and shook her head. "You'll never be a decent chess player if you don't have a hunger to win."

In fact, this was not true. Despite the fact that I had never won a game of chess in my life, Rosa was a good teacher, and I had become pretty adept. When I discovered that one of my classmates, Magnus Kellerman, also played, I challenged him to a game after school one day. I beat him so easily that I didn't know where to look. After I checkmated him, Magnus looked at the board for a few moments and then stuck his hand out across the board. We shook solemnly.

"Play again tomorrow?" he said.

Luckily for me, Magnus did not mind losing. He was grateful to play at all.

Magnus was the only child of Reverend

Kellerman, my father's would-be spiritual savior. A lifetime of being told by his father that he was going straight to hell had equipped Magnus with a well-developed sense of his own miserable worthlessness, but not much else. He didn't have much going for him in the first place. He was, for one thing, extremely fat — the result, possibly, of too many of Mrs. Heimstetter's famous fried chicken dinners. Even in our awkward crowd of preadolescent misfits, he was painfully shy. He did his best to fade unobtrusively into the background, which was difficult, given his size. He scuttled about with his eyes lowered, the next whispered apology always forming on his lips. He never raised his hand in class. At lunch he sat behind the schoolhouse and watched the rest of us as we ran and yelled through the meadow and chased away the boredom of our morning lessons, sure that we would not want him to join in our games. About this, he was right.

Magnus must have known about our fathers' peculiar feud. By then Reverend Kellerman's face was scarcely visible behind a shaggy forest of gray whiskers, and it's hard to fathom what reserves of courage Magnus must have plumbed to sit down with one of Joseph Meisenheimer's boys every day, even for something as innocent as a game of chess. It was a profound act of rebellion. I was just delighted to find someone else to play chess with, someone I could beat. Rosa had given me a small chess set that I took with me everywhere, and when school was over Magnus and I would settle down to play. I moved quickly and aggressively. Magnus, by contrast, pondered everything at length, his face a pained knot of worry. When he finally reached down to pick up a piece, a small sigh of regret would escape him. He knew he was going to lose, but the inevitability of the outcome didn't matter to him. Defeat beckoned on so many fronts for Magnus Kellerman that he probably regarded getting thrashed by me as its own small victory.

I had other friends I liked to pal around with at school, but I never connected with any of them in the same way that I did with Magnus. In chess we found a bridge over which we could flee together. The lure of those sixty-four squares was irresistible, and soon, to my surprise, I saw more of Magnus Kellerman than any of my other buddies. He and I didn't talk much. There wasn't an awful lot to say. During our games the rest of the world kept its distance, and for this we were each grateful to the other.

■ ■ ■ ■

My brothers and I were becoming increasingly busy with singing engagements. Our brand of syrupy romance was especially popular at weddings. We kept the congregation entertained while the bride and groom signed the marriage register. We were usually invited to the reception after the ceremony. The Knights of Columbus Hall had cornered the wedding reception market in Beatrice. As soon as the ceremony was over, guests hurried down the street to get in line for the buffet, which always consisted of boiled beef, boiled potatoes, and boiled green beans. During the meal the happy couple would tour the tables, greeting their guests. The bride always led the charge. Her new husband would trail a few steps behind, thoughtfully chewing his gum, wondering what on earth he had gotten himself into.

These weddings were never the best advertisement for the joys of matrimony. The spectacle of two young people embarking on their lives together gave the older couples in the congregation an opportunity to reflect on their own unions. Once that process had begun, the slow accumulation of grievances, disappointments, and resentments was as unstoppable as the Kansas City Express. By the end of the night everyone had found something to fight about. Couples sat slumped in defeat, husbands tugging dejectedly at their ties while their wives, prim and thin-lipped, looked the other way.

The most exciting part of the festivities was the cutting of the cake. These were elaborate confections, festooned with pink and yellow roses made of frosted sugar. The younger children would demolish their portions in seconds and, their bodies hijacked by the ensuing sugar rush, would charge screaming through the hall. At Maria Hulshoff's wedding, the bride's six-year-old cousin Lenny was so hopped up on marzipan that he ran straight into the wall by the back door, knocking himself out cold in the process. There is still a small dent in the plaster just below the light switch.

When the four of us weren't singing, we worked with Joseph at the restaurant. Just for once, being second eldest was an advantage. Freddy was expected to stand by the grill and watch Joseph as he worked. My father kept up a running commentary as he flipped burgers and cracked eggs, scrupulously explaining every facet of the process. Every so often he would hand Freddy a wooden spoon or spatula and invite him to try for himself. Freddy would step wearily toward the grill and prod the cooking food with undisguised reluctance. He understood what all this meant. As the eldest son, it was both his right and his duty to inherit Joseph's gastronomic dynasty. My father was already looking forward to the day when Freddy would stand alongside him and they would feed the town together.

The rest of us were mercifully unburdened by such grand paternal expectations. It was my job to help Mrs. Heimstetter take orders and ensure there was always fresh coffee in every guest's cup. I soon got to know all the regulars — which was about the whole town — and actually came to enjoy my shifts at the restaurant. I was the only one of us who did. The twins bused empty plates, washed mountains of dirty dishes in the back room, and swept the restaurant floor, bickering incessantly at each other as they did so.

Sometimes Joseph would glance up from the food in front of him and watch us as we worked, an unreadable look in his eye. Freddy was already as good as chained to the grill, but Joseph was wondering what the future held for the rest of us.

THIRTY-ONE

For as long as I could remember, my brothers and I were a constellation of four. We occupied places collectively — restaurant, house, schoolroom, stage. My brothers were reference points by which I could plot my own coordinates and ground myself accordingly. I always knew that one day our little unit would be broken up, and that a new means of navigation would be required, but I still wasn't ready for the schism when it came.

In the fall of 1951, Freddy began high school. While the twins and I remained under Aunt Rosa's tutelage in the old schoolhouse, I watched in silent envy as my big brother set off each morning on his own. The year yawned endlessly before me until the day when I would be walking there with him.

Freddy soon began hanging around with Morrie Knuckles, who still came to our house each week to play the piano during our rehearsals. The twins and I were mightily impressed by this, particularly since it afforded him a degree of access to Morrie's older sister, Ellie.

Eleanor Knuckles was eighteen years old, utterly beautiful, and the object of more adolescent fantasies in Caitlin County than any Hollywood starlet. Morrie's parents owned the town pharmacy, and Ellie worked there, too. Even with her lustrous mane of fragrant, honey-blond hair tied back in a ponytail and dressed in an unflattering white coat, she was still impossibly alluring. We knew that she was way, way out of our league. The years that separated her from us were our salvation, in a way. We knew that our devotion would never be reciprocated, but the older boys in town were not so lucky. For them, there was the faintest glimmer of hope, and this was their downfall. The pharmacy had been a theater of heartbreak for countless would-be paramours. There had been many whispered declarations of love between the shelves of aspirin and nasal decongestant, but none had ended well.

After our rehearsals Morrie and Freddy would stroll off into town, laughing or talking earnestly as they went. I watched them walk down the street into some exciting future where I was not, and felt my heart beating blackly within me. *My* best friend was Magnus Kellerman — fat, unpopular Magnus. Our chess games were always conducted in out-of-the-way places, where nobody would interrupt us — and where nobody would see us. I never invited him home, fearful of my brothers' mockery.

Of course, it wasn't Magnus's fault that Freddy was friends with someone as glamorous as Morrie, but I blamed him for it all the same. I exacted revenge the only I way I knew: I joined in the taunts and teasing of the other kids, finding guilty comfort in the collective venom of the crowd. I look back on these idle cruelties with shame, now. Magnus suffered it all without complaint. He was too grateful for any crumbs of kindness I chucked his way to complain when I acted like everyone else.

The following fall, I finally began at Beatrice High myself. The school was a single-story, monolithic sprawl of red brick and whitewashed concrete. It couldn't have been more different from Aunt Rosa's quaint little schoolroom. Long corridors crisscrossed the building, a lattice of low-ceilinged, windowless chutes that funneled students past a thousand identical doors. We scurried through the maze, lost and late for class, our worried faces lit by the fluorescent glare overhead. We resembled nothing more than a pack of lab rats, caught in a monstrous experiment.

Suddenly I was a stranger in the town where I had lived my whole life. The school drew students from several smaller villages nearby, and I had never seen a lot of my classmates before. Many of the boys in my class were the sons of farmers, huge for their age from a lifetime of work in the fields. They sat at the back of the room, taciturn and terrifying. I remember once, at the St. Louis zoo, watching a lion sun himself on a flat rock, his large head sunk low to the ground. He surveyed the gawking crowds through heavily lidded eyes. These farmers' sons watched the rest of us with a similar bored detachment. There was also the same sense that they could have swatted us out of existence with a casual swipe of their giant paws. At least the threat that they posed was more or less quantifiable. With the girls — well, with one girl in particular — it was different.

You can't fight genetics. Falling deeply in love with strangers was in my family's blood. Frederick had worshipped Jette from a distance as she clomped around the Grosse

Garten; Joseph had adored Cora while she tended her vegetable patch. My father's and grandfather's stories were beautiful, bursting with romance, ripe for telling to future generations.

Mine, not so much.

For it was my bad luck to fall head over heels in love with Miriam Imhoff.

I can still remember the very first time I saw her. It was my first day at Beatrice High. I was sitting in our homeroom class, waiting for the bell to sound, fiddling with my pens in an effort not to look too anxious. The door opened, and in walked the most beautiful girl I had ever seen in my life. A delicate spray of freckles kissed both her cheeks and the top of her cute little nose. She had huge, deep green eyes. But it was her hair that really caught my imagination, a lustrous mane of russet curls, which shone coppery gold in the sunlight.

She walked right past me and sat down at a desk near the back of the room. I spent the rest of the class surreptitiously trying to steal glances toward her. Subsequent surveillance confirmed my initial impression that she was utterly perfect. Every time I looked at her I felt a peculiar yawning sensation in my stomach. I wasn't sure whether I wanted to gaze at her forever or to run away, as far

and as fast as I could. By then I was familiar
enough with Bertie Wooster's idiotic friends
to know what was happening to me. I was
falling in love.

The Imhoffs lived in a large house just
off the main square. Her parents were rich,
at least by local standards. Miriam had not
attended Rosa's school with the rest of us;
instead, a private tutor had come five mornings a week to teach her French and Latin
and trigonometry. Her parents had decided
that once she was old enough to attend Beatrice High, she should mingle with the community at large, agricultural riffraff that we
were. She walked up and down the school
corridors with the sort of confidence that
I supposed only a private tutor could teach
you. Every day she arrived at class perfectly
turned out, as deliciously winsome as a
china doll. My classmates swarmed around
her, an admiring chorus, but I didn't dare
approach, sure that I would make a fool of
myself if I stepped into her heavenly orbit.
Instead, thick-headed with infatuation, I
became the class show-off. I spent all day
cracking bad jokes, misbehaving, acting the
clown. There was no level of love-struck
buffoonery to which I would not sink to get
Miriam Imhoff's attention. Of course, she
always ignored me, but the boys at the back

of the room watched me closely. They were probably planning to take me down a peg or two, but I didn't care. I would have happily traded some retributive whacks across the head for an appreciative giggle or two from the object of my devotion. On I went, making an ass of myself. Every morning I bounced out of bed at the prospect of another day spent in the delicious proximity of the beautiful girl who wanted nothing to do with me.

I thought about Miriam all day, and I dreamed about her all night. I began writing very bad poetry, just for her, gushing tributes to her unassailable perfection. Unfortunately all those barbershop songs had left their mark on me: I could not escape their mawkish ideas of sugary romance. Overwrought metaphor tangoed with inexcusable cliché. I stashed every completed ode beneath my bed, the growing pile of terrible verse testament to my inarticulate ardor.

To complicate matters further, my body was being battered by a relentless typhoon of hormones. Back then nobody talked about that sort of thing. All I knew was that a lot of the time there was an embarrassing lump in my pants. Following weeks of trouser-bound experiment, I finally figured out what to do about it. Then it became difficult to think about anything else. Suddenly any door with a lock on it glimmered with erotic promise. The cubicles in the boys' locker room were just too tempting to resist. I would retire there several times a day and furtively whack off. Not once on those excursions to the toilet stalls did I think about Miriam Imhoff. My passion for her was too noble to sully with my adolescent lust. Instead I thought, perhaps somewhat ungallantly, about the other girls in my class. But as much as I was enjoying myself, I knew that what I was doing was wrong. Guilt and shame gnawed away at me, until salvation of sorts arrived.

One morning I crept into the locker room and quietly slid into my usual cubicle. As I pulled the bolt into place, I heard heavy breathing from a few doors down. I sat down on the toilet seat and listened, thinking: *I am not alone.* There was a small groan, followed by some hasty tugs at the toilet roll. A moment later, furtive footsteps padded past my door.

The next thing I heard was the quiet hiss of running water. I squinted through the tiny crack between the door and the cubicle wall.

Even from behind, the rotund physique was unmistakable.

"Magnus?" I whispered.

■ ■ ■ ■

It took me five days to get Magnus Kellerman to admit what he had been doing.

Although we were in different classes at the new school, we had continued to meet for our daily chess games. After our encounter in the locker room, the thoughtful silence that usually descended while we played was punctuated by my incessant accusations. I prodded and cajoled him, obnoxious and persistent. We played every afternoon in a far corner of the cafeteria, well out of earshot of our fellow students. On the fifth day after the incident, Magnus did not appear. As I waited for him, alone with my chessboard, I realized forlornly that he was the only real friend I had at school. When I finally saw him make his way across the room toward me, I wanted to throw my arms around him in relief, but he stood in front of me, grim and business-like. "I'm not going to play chess with you anymore," he told me.

I sat there, stunned. "Why not?" I demanded.

"Because of all the crap you've been giving me about the restroom," he said.

"Magnus, please," I said. "Sit down."

"I don't want to sit down."

"At least let me explain."

His eyes were thick with suspicion. "Explain what?"

"Look, there's something I didn't tell you." I paused.

"What?" Magnus frowned.

I sighed. "I was — Well, I was doing that thing, too."

Magnus ran a worried hand through his hair, suspecting an elaborate ruse to humiliate him further. "Really?" he said.

"Really. Several times a day, sometimes." I felt the color rise in my cheeks. Magnus saw it, too. He knew then that I wasn't kidding.

"Huh," he said.

He sat down.

Our shared hobby opened new conversational doors for Magnus and me. Now that we knew each other's darkest secret, there seemed little point in holding back on anything else (although I never confessed my devotion to Miriam Imhoff). Our chess games were no longer conducted in silence. Ideas had been fermenting within us, and our muddled internal monologues needed an audience. In each other we found a willing listener.

Magnus told me that he longed for the day when school would be over. The afternoon he graduated, he told me, he was going to pack his bags and leave Beatrice forever. He had it all worked out. He would take a coach to St. Louis, find a job there, and begin a new life, finally free of his father's judgmental glare.

I listened to all this, unsure what to make of it. Part of me was disappointed by the poverty of his ambition. I wanted to say, *St. Louis?* Why not New York? Or Europe? Or at least somewhere where the weather is more pleasant? But I kept my thoughts to myself, since the idea of leaving town had never even occurred to me. I nurtured no lingering resentments. I harbored no secret plans. I thought I was perfectly happy where I was.

I still felt guilty about my constant trips to the school toilets, but Magnus made me feel better about it. He informed me that everyone — he pointed a stubby finger at me to reinforce the point: *everyone* — whacked off. How did he know? I asked, wide-eyed. His father had told him so, he said. It was one of the many reasons why we were all going to hell.

It transpired that Reverend Kellerman had caught Magnus jacking off in his bedroom some months previously. There had been much thundering and imprecation, and dire, end-of-the-world threats if Magnus

were ever to disgrace the house with such
depraved behavior again. Since then the
pastor had taken it upon himself to protect
his son from further temptation. Magnus
had been forbidden to shut his bedroom
door, ever. His father had taken to creeping
down the corridor in the dead of night to
listen for signs of illicit nocturnal frottage.
Once, Magnus had found him in his bedroom on his hands and knees, searching the
wastepaper basket for balls of malodorous
tissue paper.

Magnus told me all this with sober resignation one afternoon as we sat in the cafeteria, the chessboard between us.

"So what do you do?" I asked.

"At home, nothing," he replied.

"Nothing?" I breathed. I shared my bedroom with my three brothers. Magnus was
an only child. He had a room all to himself,
open door or not. The very idea made me
dizzy.

"Not in the house."

I looked at him. "Not *in* the house?"

Magnus shrugged.

"Where then?"

Magnus contemplated me for a long moment. "The pier," he said finally.

The Kellermans' house was two blocks
from the river. I frowned, trying to work

it out. "But how do you . . . ? Where do you . . . ?"

"I sit on the end of the pier."

"In *full view*?"

He rolled his eyes. "I only go out at night, James. It's *dark*. Nobody can see me. And when I finish, it just falls into the water."

I was hugely impressed by this. There was something heroic about my friend's determination to feed his habit while also technically complying with his father's apocalyptic prohibition.

"Don't you ever worry about being caught?" I asked.

Magnus shook his head. "I wait until it's late. There's never anyone about. Although I take a fishing rod with me, just in case."

I wondered whom he thought he might fool, dragging a fishing rod through the town in the middle of the night.

"Besides," he added, "I'm never out there for very long."

Later it would become apparent that the real danger in Magnus's nocturnal excursions had nothing to do with being caught.

As the year wore on, the novelty of my infatuation with Miriam Imhoff faded, and with it disappeared the cocoon of blissful hope that had first protected me from the shrapnel of unrequited love. My joy at the fact of Miriam's existence slowly morphed into bleak despair. Family history settled heavily on my shoulders. I thought of Frederick hiding behind the privet hedge, of Joseph standing beneath my mother's bedroom window for night after night, and I knew that I would never have the nerve to serenade my beloved with a song of my own. Instead I floundered in silent anguish, unable to quell the storm of defeated self-loathing that was growing inside me. I no longer bounced out of bed in the mornings. Now I trudged to school, my head hung low, resigned to another day of torment.

Meanwhile, Miriam triumphantly conquered the school. She was top of our class, she won the lead part in the annual play, and she was always surrounded by an admiring gaggle of girls and boys. She floated down the corridors, serene, untouchable, and completely unaware of my existence. I loved her more with each passing day. And the more I adored her, the more I knew I would never do a thing about it.

I did my best to distract myself with regular trips to the locker-room stalls. While Miriam remained strictly off-limits, I began to broaden my palette beyond my lovely classmates. By far the most interesting addition to my erotic smorgasbord was the school music teacher, Mrs. Fitch.

Freddy and I both took extracurricular singing lessons with Mrs. Fitch. Every Tuesday afternoon she sat at the piano and coaxed a little more out of my limited talent. Mrs. Fitch had also taken over the piano-playing duties at First Christian Church when Riva Bloomberg's arthritic fingers could no longer cope. She had always looked rather dour as she sat at the piano grinding out hymns, but away from church she was all sauce. She sashayed foxily down the school corridors, swinging her hips like a showgirl at Radio City Music Hall. We all looked on, agog. She was tall, blond, and perhaps slightly overweight. I suppose she must have been in her early forties. She favored brightly colored sweaters that were a size too small. I glimpsed whole universes in the taut promise of all that angora wool. Now on my trips to the locker room I had to make a delicious choice between my classmates' coltish allure and Mrs. Fitch's more mature charms. Both worked.

In her youth, Margaret Pfaff (as she was back then) had been one of the beauties of the town. She had been pursued by a legion of ardent young men, and she had rejected them all. In her early twenties she disappeared to Ohio. She returned three years later, with a new name and a husband in tow. That alone would have been enough to set half of the town against Rankin Fitch. But he was also an attorney.

Until Rankin Fitch's arrival in Beatrice, the Caitlin County courthouse resembled a convivial gentlemen's club more than a bastion of justice. Every morning the judge and the lawyers ate breakfast together at Frederick's. Over plates of my father's ham and eggs they went through the day's docket and decided who was guilty, who was right, who was wrong, who would get what. Then they would troop back to the courtroom and perform their prearranged roles for the benefit of their unsuspecting clients. Justice had been administered in this way for as long as anyone could remember.

Rankin Fitch changed all that. He refused to go to Frederick's for breakfast. He had the extraordinary notion that his clients deserved better than to have their fates decided in private by a cabal of lazy attorneys who wanted to get home in time for dinner with their wives.

His courtroom manner also provoked a good deal of attention. There were none of the pompous circumlocutions that the other lawyers were so fond of. Fitch prowled around the courtroom while he delivered his arguments; he harangued the jury, interrupted the other attorneys, and muttered abuse at the judge. He routinely savaged opposing witnesses on cross-examination, leaving them to be led away in tears.

The other thing about Mrs. Fitch's husband was that he was a dwarf.

Rankin Fitch stood three and a half feet tall in his little stockinged feet. His body was the size of a child's, but he possessed none of a youth's limber ease. Thick, foreshortened limbs emerged at peculiar angles from his compact torso, and he moved with an awkward, staccato stiffness. On top of his tiny body sat, disconcertingly, a full-sized adult head. Behind his thick, purplish lips were crammed irregular yellow teeth. His long nose was mottled with dark moles. Lustrous tufts of black hair curled from his nostrils and ears. His eyebrows sprouted in fierce, untended abandon above small, dark eyes, which squinted suspiciously out at the world.

The town's amateur psychologists discussed at length the extent to which Rankin Fitch's physical flaws drove him to the success he found in the courtroom. The mesmerizing effect he had on juries was due, at least in part, to the extraordinary spectacle he presented. The jurors couldn't take their eyes off him. He wore tiny patent leather shoes and three-piece suits. His undersized diaphragm gave his voice a nasal, high-pitched twang, which added to the bizarre drama of his performance. Whether it was because they were fascinated, or intimidated, or because they just felt sorry for him, juries responded to Rankin Fitch's theatrical entreaties on behalf of his clients. He had a phenomenal success rate at trial.

For a while Rankin Fitch had driven a shiny, bright red Cadillac with white leather seats, modified so that his short legs could reach the gas pedal and the brake. When we saw the car gliding through town, it seemed as if it were driving itself. You had to look closely to see Rankin Fitch's little hands on the steering wheel, his eyes glinting malevolently through the windshield. He drove as aggressively as he litigated, which, given his physical limitations, was something of a problem. After his fifth accident in the space of a few months — clipping a fire hydrant behind the courthouse, which he couldn't see in his rearview mirror — the insurance company refused to underwrite him anymore. After that he sold the Cadillac and rode to court on a child's bicycle instead, suit trousers tucked into his socks. He flew through the town with a ferocious scowl on his face, his custom-made coattails flapping behind him. A dwarf from Ohio: he couldn't have been any more alien if he had arrived in a spaceship.

They made quite a couple, the statuesque blond bombshell and her miniature husband. Standing side by side, Rankin Fitch's head barely made it to his wife's midriff. The mechanics of the Fitches' marital relations was a favorite topic of conversation among the regulars at the restaurant counter. Diagrams were sketched on napkins with possible solutions to what appeared to be a — literally — insurmountable problem. But the guffaws provoked by those crude drawings hid the room's collective envy. They could mock the tiny attorney all they liked, but Margaret Fitch was still his.

All this gave my fond thoughts of Mrs. Fitch in the school toilets an extra frisson. I would occasionally find myself imagining Rankin Fitch's ugly face bobbing up and down in helpless fury while he watched me ravish his wife. After that, whenever I saw him barreling down the streets on his little bike, I felt a chill of apprehension. Mr. and Mrs. Fitch taught me that fear can lend an additional charge to sexual encounters. I have been largely terrified ever since.

THIRTY-TWO

I was not the only one undergoing a profound physical metamorphosis back then. My father was counting the days until Freddy graduated from high school and joined him at the grill. He was looking toward the future, and was determined to haul the restaurant into the modern age. He installed a blazing flash of red neon above the door that could be seen from a block and a half away:

FRED'S DINER

Joseph ordered laminated menus, complete with touched-up photographs of his most popular dishes. I no longer had to memorize what was on offer, but simply dealt out pieces of plastic to hungry customers.

A less fortunate facet of my father's grand plan to modernize the place was his idea that the waitstaff should wear uniforms. Now, at the start of every shift, I reluctantly clipped on a cheap red bow tie and pinned a badge onto my shirt pocket that read, idiotically in my opinion, MY NAME IS JAMES. Worst of all, I had to wear a little paper hat that sat at a perky angle on my head. This ridiculous outfit would have been embarrassing at the best of times, but Joseph compounded my adolescent agony several times over when he invested in a jukebox.

The jukebox stood by the door, as fluted and flashy as any automobile. Every couple of weeks a man would appear to add new selections and take out the old 45s that nobody listened to anymore. The words "Seeburg Select-O-Matic" were printed in elegant, fluid chrome on the curved glass hood. Now the place was always filled with music, and to my horror, the diner (we were no longer allowed to call it a restaurant) became a popular destination for the town's youth.

I began to dread going to work. My shifts — which I used to enjoy, in earlier, hatless days — became a brutal form of torture for my anxious, teenage soul.

My nadir came one busy Saturday afternoon when, to my horror, I saw Mrs. Heimstetter lead Miriam Imhoff and a coven of her pouting acolytes to one of the big corner booths. I knew at once that I would never win Miriam's heart if she saw me in my stupid uniform.

I pulled my hat down over my eyes and slunk toward the back of the room, as far away from Miriam's booth as I could be. The next time Franklin passed by I grabbed him. His arms were full of dirty plates.

"Frank, I need you to do me a favor," I whispered urgently.

"Yeah, bit busy right now," said Frank, trying to pull away.

"There's money in it for you," I said.

Frank stopped. "How much?"

I hastily calculated the price of eternal happiness. "Two dollars," I said.

Frank appeared interested. "What do you need?"

"You see that booth in the corner? Go and take their order for me."

Frank turned and looked in the direction of my surreptitiously pointing finger. Then he laughed. "You want me to wait *Miriam Imhoff's* table?"

"You know Miriam?"

"I know *of* Miriam," answered Frank, an enigmatic smirk on his face.

"So, well, great. Will you do it?" I asked anxiously.

"Hell, no," laughed Frank. "Watch out, brother. Those girls look *hungry*."

I trudged across the room, ready to bid my dreams of grand romance good-bye. I now regretted all the hours I had spent trying to draw attention to myself in the classroom. Miriam would recognize me at once, take one look at my stupid hat, and that would be that — my hopes dashed forever. My bow tie felt like a noose around my miserable neck as I approached the table.

All the girls were laughing at something Miriam had said as I pulled my order pad out of my apron pocket. I began to take orders for milk shakes and sundaes, slowly working my way around to where Miriam was sitting. When it was her turn, she raised those beautiful eyes to meet mine, and asked for a club soda and a grilled cheese.

There wasn't the faintest glimmer of recognition on her lovely face.

A new generation of American soldiers was fighting abroad, this time in the swampy deltas of Korea. We sang at the funeral of two local boys who were killed during the Battle of Triangle Hill. They were best friends and had enlisted together. Their coffins lay side by side in the church, each draped in an American flag. The whole town was crammed into the pews that day.

It was around this time that my grandmother bought a television. She grimly watched the death toll mount as the Allied campaign in the Far East ground to a bloody halt. For months there was a military stalemate; the only news was of casualties. Jette angrily shook her head as she listened to President Truman warn of the Communist threat, half a world away. She knew it was all a charade. Men had to have their wars. They would always find an enemy to fight.

Of course, my brothers and I didn't want to know about the war; we wanted to watch *The Ed Sullivan Show* and *Martin Kane, Private Eye*. The four of us made the pilgrimage across the lawn to Jette's house whenever we could. Morrie often came, too, as his family did not have a television.

Something strange was happening to Morrie. He had always been tall, but he had kept growing. Now he was massive — not just taller, but bigger in every respect. There was just an awful lot more of him than there had been when he'd first come to play the piano. He was too large to fit comfortably on the sofa. Instead he lay on the floor, his long legs stretched out toward the television screen, vast expanses of pale skin on display — his trousers were always too short for his ever-growing legs. He was still as kind as ever, but he laughed less than he used to. His movements became more ponderous as he struggled to keep those outsized limbs under control. I began to realize that he wasn't simply a big kid. There was something wrong with him.

I asked Freddy about it.

"Good grief, James, did you just notice?" he said.

"Well, he was always tall," I answered. "But he's just kept growing. It's like he's never going to stop."

"That's just it," sighed Freddy. "He's *not* going to stop."

"What do you mean?"

"His pituitary gland isn't working," said Freddy.

I frowned. "His . . . ?"

"Pituitary gland. His body doesn't realize it should stop growing."

"So he's just going to keep on getting bigger and bigger? That's crazy." I laughed. "Is he going to be the tallest man in the world, then?"

Freddy shook his head. "He'll probably die first."

I looked at him, horrified.

"Bodies aren't supposed to *be* that big," explained Freddy. "The heart can't cope. Too much strain."

"But that's — When will that happen?"

"Could be next week, could be next year. Nobody knows."

Just like that, Morrie Knuckles was transformed from a gentle freak into a lumbering human tragedy.

As the months passed, Freddy and Morrie became closer than ever. They walked home together each day after school, Morrie's vast frame towering over Freddy and leaning on him gently for support. His giant hands and feet grew so remote from the rest of his body that he had difficulty getting the blood to circulate. Freddy sat and rubbed those huge fingers and toes while they talked, as if it were the most natural thing in the world. I looked on, dumbfounded by the two of them. I knew that I would have run as far as I could from Morrie Knuckles's broken pituitary gland and the havoc it was wreaking. But it never occurred to Freddy that he might bail out on his friend. They did everything together. Strangely, there was rarely a somber moment. Freddy cracked endless gags and did impressions of teachers from school. Morrie smiled and laughed at my brother's antics. Their unguarded kindness toward each other was beautiful. They were just boys, unequipped to bear the weight of Morrie's tragedy, but the shadow it cast burnished them with an exquisite grace. The two of them waited for the end together, Morrie gentle and brave, my brother dignified and hilarious. Their friendship was the only defense they had, but within its cocoon they seemed at peace. Together, they were immune to the sadness that they knew was waiting. It was only late at night, when he thought the rest of us were asleep, that I heard Freddy weep quietly into his pillow.

The strange thing was that, as I listened to my brother cry himself to sleep, I was jealous of him. I envied Freddy his central role in the drama. I longed for the chance to perform such heroics myself. I coveted his friendship with Morrie, but it was his new maturity that I wanted most of all. While I was still furtively grabbing myself at every opportunity, Freddy had embarked on a mission of beautiful, noble futility, and in the process he was becoming a man. I began to wish for a tragedy of my own.

And then, by golly (as Bertie Wooster would have said), I got one.

One Saturday morning in late April of 1953, in the middle of a busy breakfast shift, Billy Florscheim appeared at the door of the diner, out of breath. Billy was the First Christian Church's choirmaster. "James,

James Meisenheimer," he cried, the moment he saw me. "There you are. Have you seen Magnus Kellerman today?"

I shook my head. "We played chess after school yesterday afternoon. That's the last time I saw him. Why? What's happened?"

"He's disappeared," gasped Billy. "His parents are mad with worry. They're forming a search party."

"Magnus has *run away?*" I said.

He looked at me sharply. "Did he say anything to you?"

I thought of my friend's cherished plans to begin a new life in St. Louis. My eyes grew as big as saucers. "No," I said hollowly.

When I told Joseph what had happened, he didn't hesitate for a moment. We closed the diner as quickly as we could and hurried off to help with the search. A large crowd was milling outside the church. Reverend Kellerman was organizing groups, sending volunteers off to search in different parts of town. When he saw us approach, he abruptly stopped what he was doing and walked over. He and my father hadn't spoken in fourteen years. The minister's hair had turned as white as snow by then. It fell, rich and lustrous, halfway down his back. His whiskers had grown into a long, uncontrollable thicket; even his eyebrows had begun to sprout in splendid, bushy abandon. He had begun to bear a startling resemblance to the Almighty himself. The two old adversaries looked at each other for a moment.

"Heard about your boy," said Joseph. "We're here to help."

"Thank you." Reverend Kellerman's voice was soft, quite unlike his usual delivery from the pulpit.

"I'm not coming back, though," warned my father.

The pastor's eyes creased into a small smile.

The two men shook hands.

We were sent to search the woods behind our house. For the next five or six hours we went up and down the hill, calling out for Magnus. I searched and shouted along with the others, even though I was sure that he had hitched an early-morning ride out of town and was now heading toward his dreams, bound for St. Louis.

It seemed that everyone was growing up except for me.

As evening drew in, we finally gave up our search and returned to the church. We walked back along the riverbank, tired and hot, our voices hoarse from yelling. As we passed by the pier, I noticed that the far end of the wooden walkway looked strange. I went to investigate. As I approached the end of the pier I saw that some of the old planks had splintered into rotten fragments and fallen into the water. My throat tightened in sudden, wordless sadness.

I walked slowly back to the church.

We're all sinners, Reverend Kellerman used to tell us. Week after week he had promised his congregation that they would all burn in Lucifer's flames. As it turned out, his own dose of damnation arrived early; hell had come to visit him on earth.

His son's body was found later that evening, a mile or so downriver. Magnus was floating facedown in the water, a few feet from the riverbank. His naked buttocks shone pale in the moonlight. I don't suppose, given his monumental girth, that he was a very strong swimmer at the best of times, but he didn't stand a chance with his trousers around his ankles. Some of the material had snagged on an underwater root, halting his progress.

In the end, he never even made it as far as St. Louis.

THIRTY-THREE

We did not sing at Magnus Kellerman's funeral, because there *was* no funeral. His parents left Beatrice two days after his body was found, taking their dead son with them. To this day I have no idea where Magnus is buried.

Nobody could understand why the Kellermans fled as they did, when there was a whole town ready to offer them help. I suspect that they could not face such an effusion of well-intentioned sympathy and Christian charity.

There was no escape for me, though. I waited for the yoke of grief and suffering to descend upon me and bestow its grace, just as it had for Freddy. To my dismay, though, I felt no beatific glow of anguish for me. I hoped that I might be in shock, that my friend's death just hadn't sunk in. But as the weeks passed, I still failed to register the kind of soul-enriching remorse that I had been hoping for. This prompted a degree of melancholy, but for me alone: Why, I wondered miserably, couldn't I have been fond of Magnus the way that Freddy was devoted to Morrie?

I realized sadly that I'd never been much of a friend to him. Finally, shame sharpened my loss into something resembling pain.

Soon after the Kellermans left town, a new minister arrived at First Christian Church. Beatrice was Arthur Gresham's first professional posting. He was young and extraordinarily devout. He was also very handsome, with a chiseled jaw and neatly cropped dark hair. He did not possess the fiery rhetoric of his predecessor, but after two decades of splenetic predictions of eternal damnation, the congregation was ready for a change of pace. People were relieved when Reverend Gresham plowed a less hysterical furrow in his sermons. He spoke thoughtfully and calmly, his delivery rarely rising above his normal speaking voice. He would take a theme from the day's scripture, expand upon it briefly, throw in a few telling anecdotes, and then — just as people were settling back into their seats for the long haul — announce the next hymn.

Attendance at the ten o'clock service increased, swelled by rumors of the new minister's good looks and the brevity of his weekly address. The town's unmarried young women began to cram themselves into the front pews. They batted their eyelashes at him, provoking a scarlet flush in the young clergyman's finely sculpted cheeks as he led his flock in worship. With Reverend Gresham in the pulpit and Mrs. Fitch at the piano, now everyone in the congregation had something to distract them during the services. Poor Reverend Kellerman was not much missed.

Death danced all around us back then. On Christmas Eve, my grandfather, Martin Leftkemeyer, passed away in his sleep. He died as he had lived, quietly and without fuss. He had limped through the years since my mother's death, a baffled, lonely wreck of a man. We could not cry for him. He was happy at last, reunited with the two women he had adored. A month or so later, Dr. Becker, who by then was in his nineties, suffered a massive stroke. He was discovered sitting in his favorite armchair, the *Optimist* neatly folded on his lap, a puzzled look on his face, as if he had been pondering his own final diagnosis.

Jette was buffeted by the loss of her old friends. She stopped working shifts at the diner, and in the months that followed she aged visibly, as if time had finally caught up with her. She spent her days in her armchair, watching the flickering television screen with the curtains drawn. We often went round to watch with her, and she was always glad to see us. When all four of us went, we sang for her, and this was what she loved the most. She would settle back in her chair, her white hair fanned out against the cushion, and close her eyes. A small smile would appear on her face as she listened, warmed by distant echoes that only she could hear.

By then it was Freddy's senior year at school. When he wasn't with Morrie he spent a lot of time alone on our back porch, listening to radio broadcasts of baseball games that were being played hundreds of miles away. I watched him through the door. He would sit for hours, his chin in his hands, staring out into the yard, never moving, listening to the low tones of the commentators and the excited cheers of the distant crowd. The strange thing was that Freddy didn't even *like* baseball. I suppose the sedate rhythm of the games, the slow crawl toward an irrelevant conclusion, ball after ball after ball, was a balm against whatever storms were raging inside him. I assumed that he was thinking about Morrie, wondering when his friend's mutinous body would give up on him, but it turned out that there were other things on his mind, as well.

My brother graduated from Beatrice High one morning in early June. That afternoon we sat around the kitchen table eating a celebratory lunch with Rosa and Jette. Joseph was in an expansive, expectant mood.

"So," he said, smiling at Freddy, "when do you want to start work?"

"Monday," Freddy replied.

Joseph laughed. "Excellent! You're keen to get started, then."

Freddy didn't blink. "Mr. Niedermeyer says they've been short-staffed for months."

There was a terrible silence around the table. Finally my father found his voice. "*Oscar* Niedermeyer?" he croaked.

Oscar Niedermeyer ran the town's funeral parlor. Freddy nodded.

"He's offered you a *job?*"

"I asked him for one," corrected Freddy.

"But you already *have* a job. With me."

Freddy put down his knife and fork. "I don't want it."

Joseph stared at him. "Why not?"

"I want to do something else."

"Something else? What's wrong with being a cook?" choked my father.

"It's the onions," said Freddy.

My father looked stricken. "The *onions?*"

Freddy shrugged. "I hate the smell of fried onions," he said. "They stink. Did you never notice?"

Joseph was too mortified to speak.

"You can come home and scrub yourself raw, but it doesn't make any difference. The smell gets into your clothes and under your skin and just *stays there.*"

The two of them looked at each other across the table.

"Besides," said Freddy, "there's more to life than feeding people breakfast."

"More to *life?*" thundered my father. "What's that supposed to mean?"

Freddy stood up. "I want to do something else, that's all."

"Where are you going?" demanded Joseph. "We haven't finished discussing this."

"There's nothing more to discuss," replied Freddy, his voice steady. With that he walked out of the room.

"Joseph," said Rosa gently.

If my father heard his sister's warning, he ignored it. A moment later he was out of his chair. Rosa and I followed him to the back porch. Freddy was sitting in his usual spot, listening to a game between the Braves and the Phillies. We watched through the screen door as my father turned off the radio with an angry swipe of his fist and demanded explanations. Freddy answered him quietly. More questions followed, my father's arms flying about in agitation. Freddy listened, and then shook his head. Finally Joseph turned his back on his son and walked into the yard. There he stood quite still with his hands on his hips, staring up at the cloudless sky.

"Well, well," murmured Rosa. "I never knew Freddy had it in him."

"Neither did I," I said.

"He didn't tell you anything about this?"

I shook my head. "Not a word."

Working in a funeral parlor made a certain sense for Freddy, I could see that. His best friend was dying, after all. The somber atmosphere at work would match his mood exactly. Freddy sat on the porch for a moment, watching Joseph. Then he reached over and switched the radio back on.

My aunt put a hand on my shoulder and squeezed softly. "You know what this means, don't you?"

I turned to look at her. "What?"

She smiled at me sadly. "You're next."

Freddy began work at Niedermeyer's the following week. He took a bus to Jefferson City and bought two black suits. The atmosphere

437

in our house was glacial for weeks afterward. At breakfast Freddy and Joseph sat at opposite ends of the table, ignoring each other. The rest of us hunkered down in between the two workingmen, keeping a cautious eye on both.

There was one upside to Freddy's new job: we saw an increase in funeral engagements. He was now in a position of some influence with the families of the recently departed. He was able to suggest — discreetly, of course, and with appropriate dollops of hand-wringing compassion — that perhaps a musical tribute might be in order at the ceremony. Perhaps some four-part harmony, madam?

None of this helped me, of course.

Rosa had been right: I was next.

Thirty-Four

My own senior year at high school — a time,
supposedly, of carefree, youthful innocence
— was cast into bleak shadow by the fate
that now awaited me on graduation. Mostly
it passed in a haze of baffled dismay.

The hot plate was waiting for me. I was to
be a short-order cook.

More than anything else, I remember feeling lonely that year. After Magnus died,
I didn't make any more friends; I was too
busy working. I had less than twelve months
to learn what Joseph had been teaching
Freddy for years. Each morning I reluctantly
tied on my apron and helped my father with
the early breakfast rush before grabbing my
books and staggering to school. Freddy had
been right about the fried onions. I quickly
came to detest them, too. As I sat in class I
could smell them on my clothes and in my
hair.

The twins were freshmen by then, but of

course they wanted nothing to do with their boring, smelly older brother. I was left to contemplate my dreary fate alone. I remembered Rosa's quiet confession of wanting to escape our little town during that first trip to the ice cream parlor. *You'll leave,* she'd told me. *And then one day you'll come back, and everything that you once loved about the place will drive you a little bit crazy.* Well, my aunt had been wrong. I would never leave, not now. Even poor old Magnus had escaped farther than I ever would.

While I was busy cooking eggs and frying up mountains of Texas toast, everyone else at school began to pair off. Suddenly there were couples everywhere. From the pretty cheerleaders to the math club nerds, they all found a lid for their pot. The heady whiff of hormonal overdrive was palpable. Everyone was at it. Everyone except me.

Worst of all, Miriam Imhoff was at it, too.

One Monday morning in early spring Kevin Kinney, the school's star linebacker, arrived at school and began telling anyone who would listen what Miriam Imhoff had let him do to her in the back of his car the previous Saturday night. By Tuesday, everyone had heard the rumors, and for the rest of the week fresh details of Miriam's wanton depravity percolated through the school.

I listened along with everyone else, but I knew better than to believe such filthy lies. By then I considered myself something of a connoisseur of pornographic fantasies, but some of her alleged stunts sounded improbable, even to me. I knew Miriam would never do such things, especially not with a lumbering knucklehead like Kevin Kinney. I waited for her to refute the whole story.

But Miriam didn't deny any of it. In fact, she appeared to be relishing the attention. Girls swarmed around her, scandalized and eager for information. Boys kept their distance, watching her furtively. During the course of that week, speculation about her nymphomania grew to fever pitch. I did my best to pretend that none of it was happening. Then on Friday Miriam arrived at school with Kevin's lettered football jacket around her shoulders, and my heart broke into a million tiny pieces.

In the evenings, while my classmates felt each other up in the backs of their parents' cars, I went to visit Rosa. Earlier that year, having finally saved up enough money to buy a place outright, she had moved out of Jette's home and into a house of her own. Rosa cooked me dinner and then we listened to the radio and played chess. Our tussles over the board were less one-sided now. Sometimes I even won. While we played, our conversations invariably followed the same pattern. She would begin by telling me of her most recent illnesses, describing each symptom in unnecessary detail and then offering up a variety of morbid diagnoses for my consideration. Over the course of that year Rosa suffered enough chronic diseases to kill her several times over. Every part of her body was riddled with cancer; mosquito bites throbbed with fatal menace; the mildest rash prompted predictions of a long and hideous death. More than once she made me swear that I wouldn't let her suffer too much when the time came. She loved nothing better than burrowing through her encyclopedia of infectious diseases. Her pulse raced in fear and excitement as she triumphantly checked off the symptoms of yet another murderous illness that had her in its grip.

Since Rosa was feeding me each night, it seemed rude to point out that she appeared as healthy as ever (which she did). All she really wanted from me was a sympathetic *ooh* at some of the more gruesome bits of her prognosis, and I was happy enough to oblige. When my aunt's apocalyptic medical ruminations were finally exhausted, it was my turn to moan. My litany of ills never varied much.

I remained devastated about Miriam Imhoff. It was painful enough to imagine her with anyone else — but why did she have to hook up with *Kevin Kinney,* of all people? I was dismayed and outraged by her lack of taste. He was an oafish moron with a military buzz cut, a dumb laugh, and a neck as thick as my thigh. I began to speculate that perhaps Miriam hadn't been out of my league after all, if she'd been willing to go out with *him.* I replayed in my head dozens of moments when I might have flashed a shy smile, instead of always running blindly in the opposite direction. But it was too late now.

Miriam was not the only source of my abject self-pity, though: when school was over, I would be grilling burgers for a living. Rosa was not as sympathetic about this as I would have liked, frankly. She told me that it would be nobody's fault but my own if I took a job that I did not want. When I protested that I had no choice in the matter, she snorted and told me that if Freddy could stand up to my father, then so could I. But I knew that wasn't true. I wouldn't have been able to bear the weight of Joseph's disapproval for more than a minute. I think Rosa realized this, too. She knew the insecurities of the second born. Still, that didn't mean she was going to give me an easy ride.

As I watched the calendar creep slowly forward, a defeated inertia crept over me. I numbly ticked off the days to graduation. When the posters went up on the school bulletin boards announcing the senior prom, I took no notice. As far as I was concerned, there was nothing to celebrate. Besides, I had no wish to watch my fellow graduates paw at each other's fancy clothes before they slunk off for slugs of vodka and steamy bouts of heavy petting. And the prospect of watching Miriam and Kevin dancing together as newly crowned king and queen of the prom was too appalling to contemplate.

I never would have gone if we hadn't been booked to sing there.

A week before the prom, the gym became a hive of industry as an army of seniors began its transformation to an elegant venue for the grand soiree. The room had acquired the funky whiff of perspiring adolescents that no amount of balloons or bunting could ever shift, but nobody seemed to mind. A makeshift stage was constructed over the bleachers at one end of the room, behind which a huge purple banner emblazoned with the words GOOD-BYE, CLASS OF '55! had been hung.

As they worked, the girls discussed how far they might be prepared to go with their dates if things went right. The boys watched them from the other side of the room. As the big day approached, the febrile atmosphere of sexual anticipation grew. While I moodily contemplated my father's pots and pans, my classmates were considering their own induction into adulthood in altogether different terms.

I spent the day of the prom standing next to my father, helping him with the Saturday lunchtime rush. At three o'clock I escaped the grill and walked morosely up to Tillman's Wood. There I clambered through the limbs of the old oak tree one last time, a valedictory tour. Most of my classmates were impatient for school to end, but I was clinging desperately to what remained of my childhood. I watched the sun as it inched westward across the sky. There was no stopping the dull trudge of time.

That evening the four of us gathered in the kitchen. We wore dark suits, white shirts, and thin black ties. This was our standard uniform for funerals, which struck me as appropriate, since we were there to witness the death knell of my youth. Frank was the last of us to appear. As he walked into the kitchen a pungent aroma wafted from him.

I frowned. "Is that *cologne* you're wearing?"

My little brother inclined his head toward me. "It is."

"Did you take a *bath* in it?" asked Freddy, wrinkling his nose.

The thought occurred to me that I could have used a splash of cologne myself to mask the lingering odor of fried onions, but I said nothing. Frank extracted a comb from his inside pocket and ran it through his hair, which, I now noticed, was shining with a recent application of Brylcreem. "It's the senior prom, fellows," he said. "You snooze, you lose."

"It's not *your* senior prom," I pointed out.

Frank waved away my objection.

"I believe," declared Freddy, "that young Franklin thinks he's going to *score*."

Teddy immediately looked worried. "That's ridiculous!" he barked.

"Do the math." Frank pointed at me. "There are boys going without a date. There'll be girls without a date, too."

"But you're a freshman," said Freddy. "No girl is going to throw herself at you, just because she hasn't got a date."

Frank sat down at the kitchen table. "It's

their senior prom," he said simply.

"Besides, that cologne is awfully strong," I said. "They won't get within ten feet of you without gagging."

Frank put on a pair of dark glasses. "Mock me all you like, James," he said coolly. "Like you said, it's *your* prom. But we'll see who's laughing at the end of the night."

I understood my brother's thinking. The fables of bacchanalian excess that surrounded previous prom nights had cloaked the event in irresistible erotic mystique. I didn't have the heart to tell him that a posse of teachers prowled the school all evening, which meant that the interesting stuff would take place after the dance, in the backseats of cars out at Gants Bluff. And Frank did not have a car.

We practiced our set list for that evening. We were doing the usual crowd-pleasers, and for the finale I had penned some snappy new lyrics to "Toot, Toot, Tootsie," which said good-bye to school, innocence, happiness, hope, that sort of thing.

As we walked to school we were passed by a slow-moving fleet of cars filled with my classmates. The boys lounged behind steering wheels, doing their best not to look awkward in their rented tuxes. Their dates sat next to them, checking makeup in their compacts and smoking furiously. The couples weren't talking much, nervous about the evening ahead. Seeing their anxiety cheered me up a little, and for a while I managed to camouflage my misery behind a veneer of haughty condescension.

In front of the school, prom-goers were milling about. Girls squealed and kissed one another. They admired each other's dresses and exchanged final words of encouragement. Boys gave each other last-minute pep talks. Most of them had hip flasks hidden in their jackets, the liquor siphoned off from their parents' drinks cabinets. They all looked as if they could do with a swig right then, but the booze wasn't for them. It was for their dates. Everyone knew that alcoholic lubrication would be required if the evening was to end as hoped.

We made our way toward the gym. Streamers had been hung across the room, crisscrossing above our heads. On the stage, a solitary microphone stand stood gleaming beneath a bank of bright spotlights. The rest of the room was plunged into shadow, illuminated only by a rotating mirror ball that had been hoisted high above the painted lines of the basketball court. A constellation of tiny squares of light floated across the floor. In one corner of the room lurked a crowd of grim-faced teachers, none of whom looked happy about sacrificing their Saturday evening to police a crowd of randy teenagers. We were not due to sing for over an hour, and so we gathered by the side of the stage and watched as the gym began to fill up. Frank inspected every girl with interest, although he was still wearing his dark glasses, which meant that he couldn't see much. Most of the activity was near the punch bowl. The teachers hovered nearby, hawkishly watching for attempts to sabotage the mix with alcohol.

Just before eight o'clock, Eugene Jurgenschlitter, the chairman of the prom organizing committee, approached us. He was wearing a lime green plaid tuxedo. His date was a heavyset girl called Julie Tippet, who was squeezed into a scarlet dress that was a couple of sizes too small for her. She stood two paces behind Eugene and smiled at us. The lights from the mirror ball bounced off the orthodontic strips on her teeth. I could smell the alcohol on their breaths. I figured Eugene would need to be pretty well oiled if he was going to contemplate sticking his tongue into Julie's industrial-grade metalwork.

"You guys ready?" asked Eugene.

Since it was theoretically my prom, I had

been designated spokesman for the night. "Absolutely," I replied.

"You'll sing for thirty minutes?"

I nodded. "Maybe a bit longer, if we get encores."

Eugene grinned. "Encores, right."

Frank spoke for the first time. He had been examining Julie Tippet with undisguised interest. "We get encores," he said, looking directly at her over the top of his dark glasses.

Julie Tippet giggled and let out a small hiccup.

"Hey, Eugene," I said, "are you going to introduce us?"

"Sure thing," said Eugene. He took a small flask out of his inside pocket and took a quick swig. He smacked his lips together and winked at us. "Show business, eh?" he declared. With that he turned and clambered unsteadily up the steps and into the glare of the spotlights. At once the crowd began cheering and whistling, relieved that matters were about to get under way. Eugene squinted out at the audience and waved his arms for silence.

Next to me, Frank turned toward Julie Tippet. He whipped off his dark glasses and gave her an unambiguous look. "We also do *requests*," he said. Julie giggled again.

Eugene finally got the crowd quiet. He

made a few brief announcements about the evening's schedule and then introduced us. We filed onto the stage. There was some polite applause and we launched into "Brown Eyes, Why Are You Blue?"

By then we had been singing together for so long that we no longer worried about getting the music right. We had begun to focus on other aspects of our performance: certain numbers now came with little dance routines, and we jazzed up our tunes with swinging finger-snaps. We followed our opening number with a languorous version of "Over the Rainbow." Beyond the glare of the spotlights I could make out the silhouettes of young couples standing close together. I looked anxiously for a flash of Miriam's gorgeous, flame-colored hair, but she and Kevin were nowhere to be seen. Julie Tippet stood alone by the wall, watching us. I wondered where Eugene had disappeared to.

A prom audience is a very different beast from a funeral congregation. That night everyone had other things on their minds besides us, and after a couple of tunes people sauntered off to refill their cups of punch, or went outside for a cigarette. Our finale was "Toot, Toot, Tootsie." With my clever new lyrics and a rousing last chorus crammed full of impressive vocal pyrotechnics, I had been hoping for a rousing send-off, but instead, as our final chord ended, we were greeted with slightly bored applause from the few prom-goers who remained.

So this is how it ends, I thought sadly. My brothers quickly left the stage, but I lingered there for a moment, looking out across the empty room. I didn't want to relinquish my final moment in the spotlight, even if there was nobody watching me.

Finally I trudged off the stage and went to find my brothers, who were waiting for me outside.

Freddy looked at me, concerned. "You okay?"

"Someone might have stayed to *listen*." I couldn't keep the bitterness out of my voice.

Frank looked around him and put his dark glasses back on. "I'm going back inside," he announced.

"You're not coming home?" said Teddy.

"Business to attend to," said Frank.

"Don't worry, Ted," I said. "He'll be home five minutes behind you."

"What is it, James," said Frank, "can't you bear the thought of someone else having fun?"

That was pretty much it in a nutshell, but I wasn't about to admit it, least of all to him.

Frank turned and sauntered back inside. We watched him go.

"He's not *really* going to *score,* is he?" asked Teddy after a moment.

I shook my head. "Of course not. Even I have more chance of getting laid tonight than he does."

Which was an interesting remark, given what happened next.

Part of me wanted to leave the prom as quickly as possible, but I was unable to pull myself away. I knew that when I headed for home, I would be bidding my childhood good-bye. The future would be coming for me in the dim light of morning, and so I went back inside for one final waltz with my past.

I made my way back to the gym. The corridors thronged with excited seniors. There were one or two girls sobbing in the shadows, but even they were being consoled by a sisterly arm wrapped around their shoulders. Nobody was alone. Nobody except me.

"James Meisenheimer."

I turned at the sound of my name and saw Mrs. Fitch walking toward me. "Heard you up onstage just now," she said, smiling. "Nice job."

I grinned at her. "Thanks. I couldn't have

done it without you." We had had our final singing lesson together the previous week.

She looked pleased. "So how's prom night treating you?"

I put my hands into my pockets. "All right, I guess."

Mrs. Fitch cocked her head to one side. "No date?"

"No date," I said, as brightly as I could.

"Want to keep me company, then? I'm on patrol."

"Patrol?"

"Keeping an eye out for illicit activity," she explained, arching an amused eyebrow.

I shrugged my acquiescence. We walked down the corridor in companionable silence. After three years of singing lessons, Mrs. Fitch and I knew each other pretty well. By then I had more or less gotten over my earlier infatuation with her. I wondered what her husband was doing tonight.

We passed the science labs. Mrs. Fitch opened each door and peered into the darkness. In the final classroom, I saw her stiffen. "There's someone in here," she said over her shoulder. She stepped inside and switched on the light. I followed her in. Beneath the blackboard, a curled-up figure had collapsed in a heap next to a pool of vomit. I heard a faint groan. "Do you know who that is?"

asked Mrs. Fitch. "I can't see his face."

Neither could I, but the lime green tuxedo was unmistakable. "That," I told her, "is the chairman of the prom committee."

"Eugene *Jurgenschlitter*?"

Hearing his name, Eugene's groans grew a little louder.

Mrs. Fitch looked cross. "Oh, heavens. I suppose we should do something," she sighed. We hauled Eugene upright. He was in bad shape. His jacket had been torn in a couple of places and he stank of stale puke. A crust of dried vomit had formed down one side of his face. He blinked at us miserably.

"Where's Julie?" he mumbled.

I had a pretty good idea where Julie was, but I figured poor Eugene had enough to deal with just then. We propped him up against the wall with his head between his knees and told him to wait for someone to come and fetch him.

"I'll send one of the faculty to take him home," said Mrs. Fitch as we closed the door behind him.

Just beyond the science classrooms were the music rooms. As we reached the room where she taught, Mrs. Fitch turned to me. "Have you got a moment?" she asked. "I've been on my feet all evening, and these shoes are killing me. I could do with a sit-down."

"Of course," I said.

She smiled at me and pushed open the door. Inside we each unthinkingly assumed the positions we took each week — Mrs. Fitch on the piano stool, me standing to one side. She took off her shoes and began to rub her feet.

"So," she said, "the diner awaits." For the last twelve months Mrs. Fitch had sympathetically listened to my complaints about my fate after graduation.

"Like the grim reaper," I agreed.

"It won't be that bad," she said.

"Right now it sure feels that way."

A small smile played around her lips. "You're not looking forward to the joys of adulthood?"

"Should I be?"

"Oh, it has its moments." Mrs. Fitch stood up and walked over to the door. She slipped the bolt across and sat back down on the piano stool. Outside the room's small window, it was completely dark. The corridors were silent. We could have been the last two people on earth.

"James," she said, "there's something I need you to do for me."

"Of course," I answered.

"Come here." She reached out and took my hand. I watched in mute astonishment as my fingers touched the hem of her dress. She pulled my wrist upward. When the tops of her stockings came into view I let out a small cough of disbelief. As the dress continued to ride up her thighs, she opened her legs.

Finally I chanced a look at Mrs. Fitch's face. Her mouth was slightly open. She was still gripping my wrist, more tightly now. She nodded at me gently and guided my fingers higher. When I touched her for the first time, she let out a small gasp. I froze.

"Are you all right?" I asked.

She smiled at me then, and shifted her weight forward on the piano stool. I felt my fingers press up against her more firmly. "I'm just wonderful," she whispered.

The next thing I knew, I was on my knees, her fingers in my hair.

A while later — I lost all sense of time — she pushed me away and stood up. She turned around and motioned to the back of her dress. "Help me out of this, will you?" she asked. I pulled down the zipper and watched hungrily as she stepped out of her clothes. She stood in front of me wearing only her stockings and a bra, a miracle of cantilevered wonderment.

"Now," she said, taking a step closer. "Let's see about you."

No more words were spoken, until, about a minute later, I said, "Oh!"

"Oh," said Mrs. Fitch.

Then I said: "Sorry."

She patted me gently. "That's all right," she sighed.

I thought quickly. Mrs. Fitch hadn't had time to take her bra off. I desperately wanted to see her breasts, but I was unsure how to ask politely. I wiggled my eyebrows suggestively.

"Couldn't we do that again?"

Mrs. Fitch shook her head.

"It's just that, you know, in a minute I'll be —"

She put her hand up to my cheek. "James, please. Stop talking and get off."

I did as I was told. Without looking at each other we quickly put our clothes back on. She went over to the door and pulled back the latch. I was being dismissed.

By the door I stopped. "Good-bye, James," said Mrs. Fitch, patting me on the shoulder.

I nodded reluctantly, and trudged off.

"Enjoy the rest of the party," she called.

THIRTY-FIVE

The following day I started work.

There was no fanfare, no grand ceremony. I just tied my apron around my waist and began peeling potatoes to make hash browns for the town's hungry churchgoers. Nobody who came in that morning saw anything different; there we were, my father and I, slaving away at the grill, just like always.

But that Sunday morning felt very different, at least for me. All there was before me now was a future filled with eggs, bacon, and toast. And a universe of cheeseburgers. I was to spend my life fulfilling the greedy whims of strangers, one order at a time.

Just in case all that wasn't enough, I also had Margaret Fitch to think about.

As I pushed sausage links up and down the hot plate, I contemplated my encounter in the music room, beset by a variety of conflicting emotions. There was, of course, dazed disbelief that it had happened at all.

459

Then there was an intense frustration that there was nobody I could brag to about it. (I'm ashamed to say that it was at this point that I *really* began to miss Magnus Kellerman.) I felt guilty, too — I knew that my behavior was unworthy of my grand feelings for Miriam Imhoff. And there was a profound regret that I had missed my chance to see Mrs. Fitch's breasts.

Most of all, though, I was just plain terrified.

As I began to consider the implications of what we had done, my thoughts inevitably turned to Rankin Fitch. I knew that if he ever discovered that I had screwed his wife, however ineptly, he would wreak an apocalyptic revenge that would ruin my life forever. My imagination ran riot. I saw myself being sent down for a stretch in the state penitentiary, framed by the wily lawyer for a crime that I did not commit. I began to obsess about the Fitches, and what they might do to me. Such an obviously unhappy marriage, I thought, unable to suppress the lump rising in my throat.

That was when it hit me.

Mrs. Fitch — poor, sweet, lovely, sexy Mrs. Fitch! — had fallen in love with me.

Suddenly everything began to make terrible sense. Her advances in the music room that night had been a desperate plea to be rescued from her loveless union with her miniature husband. She had probably adored me for years, but knew that she could not declare her devotion until we were no longer teacher and pupil.

It was all very flattering, but I knew that I wasn't going to be Mrs. Fitch's knight in shining armor. There would be no heroic showdown on the courthouse steps between the ardent young lover and the cuckolded husband. Instead I decided to slink away and leave them to their lives together.

After that I began to dread singing at First Christian Church. Mrs. Fitch often played the piano at weddings, and she smiled bravely at me when we caught each other's eye, but I could see the sadness and disappointment in her face. I wasn't proud about abandoning her, but I knew it was the right thing to do. Yes, I wanted to see her breasts, but not *that* much.

Instead, I did my best to focus on my exciting new culinary career. In the absence of other options, I decided to try to be the best short-order cook I could possibly be. I immersed myself in my daily chores. By concentrating on the details of each task, I was able — for a while, anyway — to ignore the overall bleakness of my prospects. I discovered a measure of quiet satisfaction in small jobs well done. Nobody but me knew how precisely and efficiently I had chopped that day's quota of green peppers, but that was all right. It helped me get through each long shift.

Once lunch had ended, Joseph and I got to work prepping for the following day. I enjoyed these afternoons alone with my father. He showed me how to layer up trays of lasagna, watched as I carefully followed his secret recipe for meat loaf. Now that I had officially joined him at the grill, Joseph proudly boasted about me to the regulars who ate breakfast at the bar each morning, telling them all that I was a natural. When he pointed an egg-covered spatula at me and called me his partner, it almost made the whole thing worthwhile.

Soon after I began working full-time, Rosa started to come in every morning for a cup of coffee on her way to school. She sat at the counter and sipped her drink, watching me as I fried bacon and buttered mountains of toast. No matter how much I whistled, no matter how loudly I laughed at the customers' jokes, she persisted with her silent scrutiny over the rim of her cup. I didn't fool her for a minute.

When Joseph and I had finished work for

the day, I would sometimes stay behind in the diner and switch off all the lights. The lingering smells of the day's cooking took on a warm intimacy in the darkness. I sat at the counter, enjoying the solitude. Every so often I would feed a fistful of nickels into the jukebox. My nighttime listening back then was Bill Haley and His Comets, Pat Boone, the Four Aces, and some young punk called Elvis Presley. I allowed my mind to wander, adrift on a sea of bright, uncomplicated melody. As the music washed over me, I wondered how I might clamber out of the black hole that I had inadvertently tumbled into.

A few months after graduation, Miriam Imhoff and Kevin Kinney got married. By then Miriam was about seven months pregnant.

We sang at the wedding, of course. Miriam's father glowered furiously throughout the ceremony next to his silently weeping wife. Their daughter had been supposed to go to university a long way from here — Harvard, Princeton, somewhere like that. They hadn't paid for all those private tutors to have her knocked up by some sweaty, bone-headed jock. The groom's family, in contrast, thought it all a tremendous lark. The swelling in the front of Miriam's wedding dress was a source of loud sniggers and admiring nudges. The Kinneys smirked and the Imhoffs shuddered through the service, the two families barely looking at each other. But I may have provided the oddest spectacle of all as we stood at the front of the church and sang "You're Nobody Till Somebody Loves You." I stood ramrod straight, chest puffed out, and sang my broken heart out as tears ran steadily down my cheeks.

Two months later, Miriam gave birth to twin girls. I grew accustomed to having my heart crushed every time I saw them roll by in their enormous station wagon. The fact that Miriam was now married and a mother to boot did nothing to diminish my silent devotion. I had adored her so completely, worshipped her so devoutly, that I couldn't simply turn those emotions off. I was unable to turn away and look elsewhere. It was enough just to have Miriam close by, if only to gaze upon from a distance. So when, the following year, Kevin Kinney joined the army and moved his family to Kansas, I was devastated. All of a sudden there was a gaping, Miriam-sized hole in my life. I had come to define myself, at least in part, by my hopeless love for her, and her absence threatened to unravel me completely.

One easy avenue of escape still lay in my aunt's library of Wodehouse novels, although the refuge provided by those daft aristocrats and steel-eyed maiden aunts was only temporary. Soon I would be reluctantly pressing the pages back together, bracing myself for reentry into the world I was trying so hard to escape. But from the bliss of all that reading, an idea took root inside me.

I decided to write a book myself.

Without telling anyone, I saved up and bought a portable typewriter. It came with a sturdy carrying case that clipped neatly onto the base of the machine. I kept it hidden beneath a bench in the back room of the diner. Every night I lugged the typewriter to one of the booths, where I would insert a sheet of blank paper and stare thoughtfully at the keys, waiting for inspiration to strike. I should have been trying to decide what to write about, but it was more fun to dream about what would happen once my novel was published. I would move to New York and embark upon a life of celebrity and glamour. I dreamed of bohemian parties in brightly lit Manhattan apartments, of cocktail-fueled brilliance and beautiful women. I knew that P. G. Wodehouse now lived on Long Island, and I supposed that he and I would become fast friends. We would compare notes on current projects, and nonchalantly toss off wickedly funny plot twists over long, martini-drenched lunches. He would dedicate his next Jeeves and Wooster novel to me. I, the grateful young apprentice, would acknowledge his influence in my next acclaimed blockbuster. Critics would note this in their rapturous reviews, and ponder in print whether one day I might even surpass the master.

For now, though, I was stuck in Beatrice, Missouri, chained to an unforgiving hot plate and reeking of fried onions until I could think of something to write about. Then one day my novel crystallized before me: I would just tell the very story I was so desperate to live. My hero would be a humble young writer from the rural Midwest whose brilliant first novel thrust him into the literary limelight and brought him fame and fortune in New York.

Now that I had my subject, the words flew out of me. I named my fictional alter ego Buck Gunn — a strong, unpretentious name, I thought, manly and indisputably American (unlike, well, *Meisenheimer*). I gave Buck all the adventures I wanted for myself, dispatching him into the jungle of Gotham, where he encountered an army of eccentric geniuses, jaded celebrities, and exotic goddesses, all of whom wanted to sleep with him. He'd had a girl back home, of course, a beautiful redhead, his high school sweetheart. She had begged him not to go east. Did Buck Gunn listen to her tearful entreaties to stay? Did he stop to console her in her sorrow? He did not. He simply patted her on the cheek and rode out of town, not once looking back at her as she lay on the sidewalk, prostrate with grief.

I enjoyed writing that scene.

Every evening I hauled out the typewriter and wrote long into the night. I did not tell a soul what I was doing; this was my little secret. I was unconcerned with tedious stuff like grammar and spelling; that, I reasoned, was what editors were for. Besides, I did not want to dilute my raw talent by worrying about humdrum concerns with syntax, and the like. Gradually, the pile of pages grew.

As a result of my literary endeavors, my days at the diner became easier to bear. I consoled myself with the thought that this would not last much longer. The stories that I spun each night were a buffer against the dread tedium of my existence. The staccato rim shots of the typewriter were a percussive hymn to my future life, far away from here. I bashed away at the keys like a man possessed, every downward jab freighted with boundless, impossible hope.

■ ■ ■ ■

In the spring of 1956, Freddy moved out of the house. Joseph had never been able to forgive him for his decision to go and work for Oscar Niedermeyer, and the atmosphere at home had remained arctic ever since. The rest of us had been tiptoeing around the two of them for so long that we were relieved when Freddy finally carried his suits across the lawn and moved in with our grandmother next door. By then Jette was seventy-seven years old. A few months earlier there had been a small fire in her kitchen after she had set a pan of grease to heat on the stove and then fallen asleep in front of the television. The house stank of scalded fat for weeks afterward. She moved slowly now, her limbs tight with arthritis. Her eyesight had deteriorated. Too much television, she would cheerfully explain to us all, but we all knew the truth: she was getting old.

Although she would never have admitted it, Jette had always been fondest of Freddy. She saw the kindness in his eyes, and worried about him as a result. The twins had no need of anyone's sympathy or concern, and I was well hidden behind my own defenses. Freddy's big heart left him ill-equipped

to deal with life's dangers and disappointments, and his grandmother loved him a
little more for it.

Each morning Freddy prepared breakfast
for them both and read the front page of the
Optimist out loud to her — her eyes could no
longer bear the strain of all that small print.
It was Freddy who picked Jette up when she
stumbled. It was Freddy who cooked for her
and bathed her. Before long, there were precious few secrets between those two.

Little by little, with Freddy there to look
after her, Jette's grasp on the world loosened. Later we would discover that her brain
had been ravaged by postencephalitic Par-
kinson's disease. All we knew back then was
that sometimes her universe slowed to an
impossible crawl. Tasks that had once taken
a moment to perform now took an entire
morning. Freddy once returned from work
late in the afternoon to find Jette sitting at
the kitchen table, quite motionless, a forkful
of lunch in her hand, frozen halfway to her
mouth.

Thankfully, Jette was unaware of the
unsettling spectacle she presented: as her
brain changed gears, it hoodwinked itself.
She had no idea that her internal clock was
crawling forward a thousand times more
slowly than the rest of the world. She began

to mumble disjointed German phrases, a mournful echo of long ago. Her brain staged a full retreat from the horrors of old age, and her punctured body mirrored that inert collapse. Now she was just a mess of enfeebled limbs, chaotically arranged in her favorite chair.

When he wasn't looking after his grandmother, Freddy spent as much time as he could at Morrie's house. By then his best friend was nearly eight feet tall, and could barely move. He spent most of his time on the floor of his parents' living room — he had grown too large for beds or sofas — splayed out on a makeshift pallet of rugs and cushions. His immune system was so fragile that even a common cold posed a serious threat. His overburdened heart still beat on, but there was no hope left.

My brother was twenty years old, too young for all this. He spent his days at the funeral parlor, shepherding strangers through their grief. Then he returned home to tend to his own dying loved ones. By then both Jette and Morrie were just waiting for the end. There was nothing Freddy could do but wait with them. There was no consoling hand on the shoulder for him when he mourned, no softly whispered words of comfort. He faced his sorrow alone.

■ ■ ■ ■

Even with Freddy gone, our bedroom was
still crowded.

In the fall of 1957, Frank and Teddy began
their senior year. They were the undisputed
stars of the varsity football and baseball
teams, although by then they were far more
interested in chasing girls than sporting
glory. The subject had been a sore spot between the two of them ever since the night of
my senior prom. Frank had returned home
long after midnight. The next morning his
neck and lower lip bore evidence of substantial bruising and abrasions. It was the sort of
damage that could only have been inflicted
by the metalwork on Julie Tippet's teeth. Ac-
cording to Frank, he had found Julie alone
and drunk in the gym. It transpired that it
was Julie who had borrowed a car that night,
not Eugene, and before long she and Frank
were on their way to Gants Bluff, in convoy
with a score of other lovebirds. Julie hiccuped
morosely as she drove, which caused the car
to swerve precariously into the middle of the
road. Frank had been scared out of his wits,
but the journey was a risk worth taking.

I lost count of the number of times I listened to Frank brag about what he and Julie
Tippet had done in the back of that car.

Teddy, of course, poured scorn on Frank's story, disputing every detail. He desperately did not want any of it to be true.

Just as with everything else, chasing after girls became a matter of intense competition between the twins, but they soon realized that the female of the species represented an adversary far more potent than each other. Sometimes at night they put their competitive instincts to one side, and a spirit of cautious cooperation would descend as they compared notes and swapped advice.

They would usually still be discussing the manifold mysteries of the female when I got home after another night's typing at the diner. As I listened to them talk, I thought about Mrs. Fitch. My brothers were discussing girls, but I had made love to a real woman, who was passionate, sensuous, and experienced. Quality, not quantity, I told myself — that was the important thing. As a tactic, it worked pretty well, until the late spring of 1958. Then everything began to go wrong.

Thirty-Six

One afternoon, a few weeks before the twins were due to graduate, Frank barreled into the kitchen. I had just arrived home after a long shift and was making a sandwich. Teddy sat at the table, idly flicking through the *Optimist* and yawning loudly.

"Teddy, Teddy, Ted," panted Frank. "You won't believe it." He pulled out a chair and sat down. "This afternoon. Holy smokes. The most incredible thing." He paused for a beat. "Mrs. Fitch."

My world imploded messily in on itself.

Teddy put down the newspaper. "What about her?"

"After my singing lesson. In the music room. Unbelievable."

I stood by the refrigerator, frozen in horror. "What happened?" I croaked.

Frank didn't need any more prompting. "We were about finished with my lesson, and she beckons me over. 'Franklin,' she says, 'there's something I need you to do for me.' Then she takes my hand and sticks it up her skirt, just like that."

Teddy sat quite still. "No she didn't," he said after a moment.

"It's true."

I said nothing, too appalled to speak.

"Anyway, there I am, touching her, you know, and she starts to moan."

"No she didn't," said Teddy, a pink flush now creeping up his neck.

"Oh, but Ted, I'm afraid she did."

"And I suppose then the two of you went at it over the piano stool," said Teddy scornfully.

Frank nodded, closing his eyes. "It was incredible. She's got these amazing big brown nipples."

A hiss of inarticulate indignation escaped me. Frank had seen Mrs. Fitch's tits!

Fear and doubt clouded Teddy's eyes. "You're a lying son of a bitch," he said.

"I suppose her husband can't satisfy her much," mused Frank. "Perhaps his cock is as tiny as the rest of him."

"Shut up," said Teddy.

Frank sniggered. "Dwarf-cock."

Teddy shot out of his chair. "I said shut up!" he yelled.

The look on Frank's face was one of pure

delight. "Why, Theodore," he drawled, "I do believe you might be jealous."

Teddy was done talking. He lunged across the table and smacked Frank across the face. Moments later the two of them were rolling around on the kitchen floor, trading blows. I left them to it, and walked out into the yard. My sandwich was dry and tasteless in my mouth as I negotiated the wreckage of my shattered illusions. I had built up substantial emotional equity in my encounter with Mrs. Fitch, but now it was hard to avoid the conclusion that she probably hadn't been in love with me, after all; she'd just been horny for some young flesh. She wanted a properly proportioned penis after all that dwarf-cock.

For the next few days Teddy moped around in a miserable funk, until one afternoon — the afternoon of his own singing lesson — he bounced into the kitchen, all grins. The moment I saw his face, I knew what had happened. His eyes were shining in dazzled triumph. It seemed that Mrs. Fitch had used the same lines and gestures that she had used with me and Frank. I found this lack of variety a little insulting. I began to wonder whether she actually derived any pleasure out of these carbon-copy seductions, or if she was simply collecting youthful scalps with the needy but joyless monotony with which a drunk pours the next shot of liquor down his throat.

Teddy didn't care about any of that, though. He was jubilant. Frank was surprisingly magnanimous about it. The twins compared notes in awed tones, and a grudging parity was quickly achieved.

I, meanwhile, felt too stupid for words.

My disappointing discovery about Mrs. Fitch marked the start of what proved to be an eventful summer.

Freddy and I may have stayed rooted in our town after we finished school, but the twins had long been contemplating a future beyond the Caitlin County line. A year earlier, without telling anyone, Frank had applied for a place at Duke University, and had been accepted. I believe that every day during the intervening months my brother had thought about the eight hundred miles that he would shortly be putting between himself and the rest of us. He already had his eyes on a place at law school, three years down the road. His plan of escape was simple: run early, run fast, and run far.

Teddy's strategy, characteristically, was a little more prosaic. He had applied for a place at the University of Missouri. Still, from either school the rest of the world would inevitably heave into view, and I knew that they would soon be lost to us.

The summer of 1958, then, had an elegiac quality about it. We were all aware that a chapter was drawing to a close. For one thing, there would be no more singing. The prospect filled me with dread. I was still bewitched by the harmonies we made together. Those perfect chords still offered a means of escape from the tedium of everyday life, and I was not yet ready for silence. I increased my literary efforts, writing longer and longer into the night. Soon those dreams would be the only ones I could turn to.

It was a long, hot summer that year. Whenever we could, the four of us spent time by the river. Our favorite place to swim was where the old pier used to stand. After Magnus Kellerman's death, the town council declared the structure a hazard, and voted to remove it. To save money, they cut down its wooden legs rather than remove them completely. The tops of the poles sat six inches below the surface of the water, invisible from the riverbank beneath the rippling crosscurrents. We liked to dive off the shorn-off struts into the cool water.

Of course, Freddy and I had our jobs, which limited our swimming time, but Frank and Teddy spent hours soaking up the sun's rays even at the height of the long, humid days, when most people preferred to retreat indoors to escape the heat. After swimming, they would dry off by standing on one of the pier's hidden poles. They basked in the sun's warm embrace while their ankles remained in the water, keeping them cool.

But even such simple pleasures would not last the whole summer. In June, Morrie's condition began to deteriorate rapidly. Freddy went over to visit him each evening after Jette had gone to bed, and the two of them talked long into the night. They both knew that time was running out. Freddy often fell asleep on the sofa, and would wake up just in time to get home to make Jette's breakfast and then appear, yawning, at the funeral home.

Just as Freddy had feared, Morrie's heart had not expanded at the same preposterous rate as the rest of him. It could no longer cope with the strain of keeping his huge body alive. There was simply too much of him.

One warm evening in July Freddy fell asleep, holding his friend's hand. When he woke before dawn the next morning, he felt the cool stiffness in Morrie's giant fingers. He gently rested his friend's hand on his still chest, and went upstairs to knock on Mr. and Mrs. Knuckles's bedroom door.

Despite all the time we had had to prepare ourselves, the news of Morrie's death shocked us all. The completeness of his absence — after all that excess of flesh and bones, suddenly nothing — left us numb with grief. Only Freddy, it seemed, was able to function properly. He submerged his sorrow beneath a sea of professional rectitude, and took care of everything. That morning the body was removed to the funeral parlor. (It had to be transported in a truck. The Niedermeyer hearse was too small.) By lunchtime Freddy had called a coffin manufacturer in St. Louis to order the outsized receptacle that would be needed for the burial. Morrie and Freddy, it transpired, had been planning the funeral arrangements for some time. My brother had promised to give his friend exactly the farewell he wanted. That project, maudlin though it was, gave him the focus he needed to remain composed while the rest of us fell apart. By nightfall the service was booked, the hymns chosen, the announcement sent to the *Optimist*. Pallbearers had been contacted. The coffin was so huge that twelve men were needed to carry it. The twins and I were among those Morrie had chosen for the task. We could not have been more proud.

Teddy took the news the hardest of anyone. He had quietly adored Morrie, but he had cloaked his hero worship in a fog of willful ignorance. He had managed to convince himself that one day Morrie would get better. It had been a triumph of frightened obstinacy — at least until Freddy came home and told us that his friend was dead. Suddenly there was nowhere for Teddy to hide from the truth. He retreated to the old oak tree at the top of the bluff and waited for his tears to stop. Teddy was not a boy much given to thoughtful introspection, but his comfortable existence had suddenly been tipped headlong into squalling, savage uncertainty. Morrie Knuckles was dead, and my brother's casual assumption of his own invincibility, his blithe belief that everything would always turn out fine in the end, had been smashed into oblivion. As he hid in the tree, Teddy began to reevaluate everything he knew. Before long his tears were not for Morrie, but for himself. For the first time in his life, doubt and self-pity crowded in, obscuring the golden future that he had always taken for granted. What, he began to wonder, did Fate have in store for *him*?

As it happened, at that very moment Fate was slowly making its way toward Tillman's Wood, wheezing up the steep hill behind our house.

THIRTY-SEVEN

It was a hot day. Exhausted by his tears, Teddy finally fell asleep in the tree, where he dreamed of his own funeral. In his dream the church was empty save for a single mourner, who stood alone in a faraway pew, sobbing into a handkerchief.

A cool breeze caressed him awake. As he opened his eyes, he realized that he could still hear the quiet weeping that he had heard in his dream. It was coming from the bottom of the oak tree. Teddy leaned forward and looked down through the leaves.

Rankin Fitch was sitting on the ground next to his tiny bicycle, fingering the barrel of a pistol. Long, awful sobs escaped him. He was dressed for court, spruced up in one of his tiny three-piece suits. My brother stared down at him as unholy terror clawed at his throat. He knew at once what this meant: Rankin Fitch had discovered what Teddy and Mrs. Fitch had done in the music room, and now he was here for revenge. The two of them were alone on top of the hill. Nobody would hear the gunshot.

Teddy remained frozen in fear as he listened to the weeping coming from beneath him. Rankin Fitch's tears grew more sinister with each miserable sob. My brother began to panic. There was no escape. He shut his eyes tight and began to pray. *Get me out of this, Lord,* he breathed, *and I'm yours. I'll be a pilgrim, a priest, whatever. I'll go to Africa and be a missionary. Just don't let me die today. Don't let that crazy midget son of a bitch shoot me.*

The next thing Teddy heard was a loud *click,* followed by a howl of anguish. He cautiously peered down. Rankin Fitch was shaking the gun in fury. Then he put the barrel against the side of his head, closed his eyes, and pulled the trigger.

Another click.

The dwarf wasn't going to kill Teddy. He was trying to kill himself. My brother slumped back against the tree trunk, giddy with relief. There was another click, followed by more cursing. Teddy risked another look. Rankin Fitch was getting back onto his bike, shaking his head in disgust. Teddy watched as he pedaled out of sight.

It was a moment before he realized that

the little attorney had headed off in the wrong direction.

Teddy slithered down the tree as quickly as he could. He reached the ground just in time to see Rankin Fitch, shoulders hunched forward and feet pedaling furiously, propel himself and his bicycle over the edge of the cliff. A terrible, mournful cry floated across the still summer air.

As he hurtled into nothingness, Rankin Fitch called out his wife's name.

When the dwarf's broken body was discovered floating in the Missouri River, it was the most exciting thing to happen in Beatrice in years. The rumormongers fell on the suicide like a pack of starving wolves. It became apparent that I was not the only one who had regarded Rankin Fitch with dread suspicion. His strange death was all the license people needed to give full vent to their jaundiced opinions about him. Amid all the whispering in the days that followed, not one syllable of sympathy was uttered. People were too busy speculating about what had made him do it.

Teddy knew, though. He wandered about with a haunted look on his face. He could still hear the dead man's final cry as he had pedaled off the bluff, and was nearly paralyzed by guilt.

We now had two funerals to prepare for. They were scheduled for the same day. Morrie's was to take place in the morning, Rankin Fitch's in the afternoon.

The twins and I arrived at First Christian Church early for Morrie's service. Freddy was already there with the Knuckles family. When he saw us, he pointed toward the room at the back of the church that Reverend Gresham used as an office. We pushed open the door and peered inside.

The two coffins lay side by side beneath the window. Morrie's was the size of a small car, all gleaming teak and polished gold handles. Rankin Fitch, in contrast, had fitted nicely into one of the inexpensive coffins for children that Niedermeyer's offered. Lying in the shadow of Morrie's enormous custom-made marvel, his coffin looked like a miniature, morbid plaything.

Morrie's service was predictably well attended, the pews overflowing with family and friends. Mr. and Mrs. Knuckles sat in the front pew with Ellie, who looked more beautiful than ever in her grief. Freddy sat next to her. Reverend Gresham led the congregation in an opening prayer. Then Freddy got to his feet and walked slowly toward the altar.

My brother did not say much, but his words held a universe.

"Morrie Knuckles was the best friend anyone could wish for," he said. "He was sweet, and he was kind, and now he's gone." Mr. and Mrs. Knuckles propped each other up, their eyes closed. "What do you say about a boy who died so very young?" asked Freddy. "I don't know. But I wish with all my heart he hadn't gotten sick. I wish he hadn't died."

I glanced across at the front pew. Ellie was crying, her mascara gently running toward those heavenly cheekbones.

"We all knew this day would come," Freddy continued. "Morrie always told me that he wanted this service to be a celebration. He thought that he'd had a good life, a full life, and he was grateful for it." My brother looked down at his shoes. "I'll be honest with you, I'm kind of mad at him about that. Because I don't feel like celebrating right now. He was my friend and I loved him, and it's all so damned unfair. But then I guess it doesn't much matter what I think." He nodded at us. "Morrie always loved this tune," said Freddy, as the twins and I joined him in front of the enormous coffin. "This is what he wanted sung at his service. So we're going to sing it, whether we really want to or not."

We belted out the song's chorus with gusto, although none of us believed a word of it.

You got to ac-cent-tchu-ate the positive
Eliminate the negative
Latch on to the affirmative
Don't mess with mister in-between!

When we finished, the church was completely silent. Then Mr. Knuckles stood up, raised his hands toward us, and began to clap. After a moment, his wife stood up next to him and joined in. Then the pew behind got to their feet, too. Within moments, everyone in the place was standing and applauding. A huge, pulsing crescendo of love and regret rolled like thunder toward the front of the church. The noise was astounding. If Morrie wanted a celebration rather than mourning, then that was what the assembled company would give him. They clapped and they hollered and some even stamped their feet, a sustained tribute to the huge, gentle boy who had touched so many with his kindness.

Freddy stood there and listened, a small, sad smile on his face.

The afternoon service was a more subdued affair. I eyed Rankin Fitch's coffin as it sat in front of the altar. It occurred to me that the dead man would not have cared about the size of his coffin. He *knew* it was going to be small. It was only the rest of us who were forever being surprised by how tiny he was.

And finally I understood. The fact that Rankin Fitch was a dwarf was not, in the end, his story. He was a man who had cycled off the edge of a cliff. *That* was his story.

Suddenly I was staggered by what he had done. I could not imagine the depths of his misery — a misery so bleak and absolute that it had kept his legs going, against all natural instincts, propelling him on toward his death.

After Reverend Gresham's sermon, we performed "Abide with Me." As we sang, I devoutly hoped that Rankin Fitch wouldn't be abiding with me. I had been terrified of him while he'd been alive, but the prospect of being haunted by his vengeful ghost was even worse. Teddy had told me, owl-eyed, about the dead man's final cry, his wife's name on his lips as he fell through the air. Now both of us were wondering if we might be to blame.

As it turned out, we were not alone. In addition to the local legal crowd, there was a different constituency of mourner skulking at the back of the church. Still in their suits and ties from the earlier service, most of the town's young males had returned, all with the same guilt-pinched expression on their faces. All eyes were fixed on the grieving widow, who sat alone in the front row. Once again I found myself having to reappraise the extent of Mrs. Fitch's extracurricular activities. By then I had reconciled myself to the fact that our union in the music room was not the rhapsodic episode I had once supposed it to be, but looking at the massed ranks at the back of the church, I was astonished by how extraordinarily *comprehensive* Mrs. Fitch appeared to have been. Jocks from the football team sat next to bespectacled members of the after-school math club. A whole generation of Beatrice males had come to offer apology and seek forgiveness for their sins.

If Margaret Fitch was aware of the parade of her sexual conquests in the pews behind her, she gave no sign of it. She remained dignified and calm throughout the service, and seemed quite unperturbed by the peculiar circumstances of her husband's death. Widowhood suited her, I thought. She looked absolutely sensational in black.

THIRTY-EIGHT

Rankin Fitch's peculiar death continued to send ripples of unease through our little town, causing turbulence in unexpected places. At the funeral it wasn't just the boys at the back of the church who were haunted by guilt. There had been someone else present who was thoroughly spooked by the whole affair.

Ever since his arrival in Beatrice, everyone had been waiting to see which of his lady parishioners handsome Reverend Gresham would choose for his wife. But he had shown no interest in any of the young ladies who came to hear him preach every Sunday morning. Various uncharitable theories were propounded as to why this might be, but none were close to the truth. In fact, like the rest of us, the minister had also fallen under Margaret Fitch's alluring spell. During services he watched her play the piano, perturbed and intoxicated by the inappropriate thoughts that kept popping into his head.

It all was innocent enough at first. After all, she was a married woman. Just as we had all been free to fantasize about Eleanor Knuckles because she was so obviously unattainable, so Reverend Gresham had license to dream about Mrs. Fitch without feeling *too* bad about it. The young clergyman knew that no harm could come from his idle ruminations.

After a while, though, Margaret Fitch's marriage stopped being a bittersweet escape valve, and instead became simply a torment. As he became increasingly smitten with her, Reverend Gresham found himself wishing, quite explicitly, that Rankin Fitch would vanish off the face of the earth. So when he heard the news of the attorney's death, the first thought that popped into the pastor's mind was *Margaret Fitch is no longer married!* But any elation that he might otherwise have felt at the news was swept away by the tidal wave of guilt that came crashing down on him moments later: he had prayed for this very thing to happen. Reverend Gresham's guilt threatened to smother him completely. And yet, as he sat with the mourning widow to comfort her, he could not extinguish the small flame of hope that had been ignited within him.

It was a very disturbing state of affairs. Each night he got down on his knees and prayed for guidance, but none had been forthcoming. Sometimes during the day he needed to escape from the church and go for a walk to try to clear his head. During these excursions, Reverend Gresham had discovered a measure of consolation in my father's blueberry pie. He knew that adding Gluttony to his list of sins wasn't going to help him atone for what he'd done, but those generous wedges of succulent, gooey sweetness helped soothe his soul just a little.

One afternoon, a few weeks after the funerals, Reverend Gresham was walking toward the diner for his daily dose of restorative pie. He turned the corner to walk the final few blocks along the river, deep in troubled thought.

Frank was idling away the afternoon alone by the riverbank. He had just finished his swim, and was standing on one of the hidden struts of the old pier, drying off beneath the sun. But what Reverend Gresham saw was this: there, a good thirty feet from the shore, in the middle of the onrushing current of the Missouri River, was one of the Meisenheimer twins. The pastor blinked, and looked again. He was not mistaken. *The boy was standing on the water.* His eyes were shut, and his arms were flung outward from his body, forming the shape of a cross.

The blueberry pie was forgotten. Reverend Gresham turned and stumbled back the way he had come. At the church, he flung himself to his knees at the steps of the altar and began to pray.

Early the following morning, Teddy trudged to the church. He had a great deal on his mind. My brother had undergone an abrupt yet profound religious conversion following his strange encounter with Rankin Fitch in Tillman's Wood.

The facts, as my brother saw them, were incontrovertible. As he had shivered in terror halfway up the oak tree, waiting to die at the tiny attorney's hands, he had prayed to God for mercy — and here he was, still breathing! It was a miracle, there was no other word for it.

No matter that it was a strange kind of divine intervention, saving one life at the expense of another; all of a sudden the blissful yoke of spiritual certainty settled upon Teddy's shoulders. Joseph had raised the four of us to be staunch atheists, but now my little brother had more faith than he knew what to do with. God's love shone down on him, bathing him in grace and covering him in confusion.

For one thing, he had profound misgivings about the bargain he had hastily struck with the Almighty while he was hiding up the tree. Strong as his newfound religious convictions were, Teddy did not want to go to Africa and become a missionary. He wanted to see if it might be possible to renegotiate, or at least clarify, some of the terms of the deal. As a result he had spent a lot of time praying, but — never having prayed before — he was unsure if he was doing it right. His surreptitious conversations with the Lord had been disappointingly one-sided so far, and had left him none the wiser, so he'd decided it was time to seek some professional guidance.

Teddy pushed open the door of the church and looked around. The place was empty. Just as he was about to leave, he heard someone snoring. He tiptoed up the aisle. Reverend Gresham was lying in front of the altar, his hands clasped tightly together in prayer. He was fast asleep.

"Reverend?" whispered Teddy. He put his hand on the sleeping man's arm and gave him a gentle shake.

Since seeing Frank sunbathing the previous afternoon, the clergyman had spent every waking moment in fervent and alarmed prayer. He knew what he had witnessed by the riverbank: Christ crucified, walking on water, back among his flock once again. And he had little doubt that the Messiah's return had something to do with Rankin Fitch's death, and Reverend Gresham's feelings toward his wife. So when he opened his eyes and saw the newly risen son of God looming over him (he, of course, had no way of telling the twins apart), the potent cocktail of ragged exhaustion and apocalyptic neurosis made him scream in terror. Teddy stared down at him, alarmed.

"Don't worry," he said. "It's me, Teddy Meisenheimer."

By then Reverend Gresham had struggled awkwardly to his feet, not taking his eyes off Teddy. He bowed his head, and said, "I know why you have come."

My brother's eyes grew as large as saucers. "You do?"

The minister swallowed. "This is about Rankin Fitch, isn't it?"

Teddy took a sharp intake of breath. So God truly *was* all-knowing. There was no other way that Reverend Gresham could have known about the deal he'd struck while he'd been hiding up the tree. He hadn't told a soul about it. "Yes it is," he said in quiet awe.

"What do you have to say?" asked Reverend Gresham apprehensively.

"I was hoping you'd be able to help me," said Teddy.

The clergyman's eyebrows twitched. "You want *me* to help *you*?"

"That's right," said Teddy.

There was an awkward pause.

A weak smile creased the corners of Reverend Gresham's mouth. What could the Messiah possibly want from *him*? "Exactly how can I be of service?" he asked politely.

"Well." Teddy plunged his hands into his pockets. "I was wondering whether we might be able to work something out. Find a solution."

"A solution?"

Teddy nodded. "One that didn't, you know, involve sacrificing my whole life."

A strange choking sound emerged from Reverend Gresham's throat. Jesus had already died once for the sins of mankind. Now he seemed ready to do it all again, just because of *him*! "I hardly think the sin warrants it," he stammered.

"The sin?" said Teddy.

"Exodus, chapter twenty, verse fourteen,"

said the minister. " 'Thou shalt not commit adultery.' "

"Oh," said Teddy. "*That* sin."

"Or perhaps I should say, 'Thou shalt not covet thy neighbor's ass.' Since, as you know, it's not as if anything actually ever —"

"Excuse me," interrupted Teddy. It didn't seem right, standing in church discussing Mrs. Fitch's ass, which was what he was pretty sure they were doing. "You're saying that you don't think I need to throw everything away because of this?"

"Oh, absolutely *not*," said Reverend Gresham.

Teddy brightened. So he wouldn't have to spend the rest of his life in Africa after all! "Do you think it would be all right if I stayed in Beatrice?"

Reverend Gresham considered my brother for a moment, and wondered whether this was some sort of test. "If that's what you choose to do," he said carefully, "I'd be honored if you'd attend our church every Sunday."

Teddy's face fell. "Ah."

"Is there a problem?"

"Well," said Teddy, "I'd love to, of course. It's just that my father —"

"Oh, don't worry," laughed Reverend Gresham anxiously. "I know all about your Father!"

"Really?" said Teddy, surprised.

"Of course," said the minister. "I know Him well."

"Well, in that case you'll understand my concern."

Reverend Gresham understood no such thing, of course, but he nodded anyway. "Your Father's capacity for forgiveness is infinite," he said, hopefully.

"Do you think so?" asked Teddy.

"I *know* so." The clergyman beamed. "So you'll come?"

Teddy had been worrying about how he was going to tell Joseph about his newfound faith. At least Reverend Gresham's invitation would force the issue. "Sure," he said, and stuck out his hand. The two of them shook.

"There *was* one last thing," said Reverend Gresham. "That whole business with Mr. and Mrs. Fitch."

The two of them looked at each other for a long moment.

"Yes?" said Teddy.

"Shall we agree to say no more about it?"

"That would be fine," replied my brother, trying to hide his relief. "My lips are sealed. You'll hear no more of it from me, I can promise you that."

Reverend Gresham looked pleased.

"Well, good-bye, then," said Teddy.

"Anything I can do to help," said the minister, "just let me know."

Teddy gave the thumbs-up sign. "See you on Sunday." And the two most confused people in Missouri that morning went their separate ways.

That evening Margaret Fitch visited Reverend Gresham and told him that she had decided to leave Beatrice. The town had too many painful memories for her, she explained. As the young clergyman listened, any doubts that may have lingered about my brother's divinity (he hadn't expected the risen Christ to be quite so *goofy*) were swept away. Finally, God had responded to his prayers. And how! A quiet cyclone of awe tore through him. After Mrs. Fitch left, he fell to his knees and began praying all over again.

THIRTY-NINE

That strange summer of 1958 finally drew to a close. At the end of August the twins left town. We all drove with Frank to Jefferson City and watched him board his train east. He waved as his carriage pulled away from the platform, a grin of dazed relief on his face. My father drove Teddy to Columbia, the back of the car piled high with everything my brother owned. Joseph was heartbroken at the vast geographical buffer that Frank had so carefully interposed between us and his new life in North Carolina, but the shorter journey was just as painful for him. He was proud of his boys, of course, but he knew that he had lost them both.

We missed the twins, but after a while those of us who remained in Beatrice adapted to their absence and found a gentler rhythm to our newly compact existence. There was Joseph and me in our house; Jette and Freddy next door; and Rosa in defiant solitude, two blocks away. When I wasn't working at the diner, I shuttled between these three hubs. I played chess with Rosa several times a week and visited my grandmother when I could. I sat and held Jette's hand and talked and talked until my throat hurt. She smiled at me, vaguely aware that I was someone she had once known. Most of the time her rheumy eyes gazed sightlessly across the room, her mind tucked safely away, out of reach. On I plowed, relentless and bright. She seemed comforted by the sound of my voice.

I missed our singing more than I missed the twins themselves. I was smothered by the silence. Without the quartet, I was drifting away on the quiet tide of my own irrelevance. I often belted out our old tunes into the morning air as I walked to work, but my voice, shorn of fraternal support, sounded lonely beyond measure.

Now that my brothers had left, I longed to escape more than ever. I thought constantly about Miriam Imhoff, and wondered where she was now. Every discussion about cattle feed at the diner's counter was an unwelcome reminder that I was still here, marooned in Missouri. I found myself wishing that Jette and Frederick had taken a boat to Ellis Island, like everyone else. Cooking eggs in Brooklyn or the Bronx might at least have been bearable, with the shimmering promises of Manhattan only a train ride away. I worked in long-suffering silence. I was as tethered as the cows my customers talked about at such intolerable length.

Still, there were small compensations. With the twins gone, I finally had a bedroom to myself. I carried my typewriter home and set it up on a makeshift desk in the corner of the room. Every night I escaped into my novel, seeking solace in the unlikely adventures of Buck Gunn. When I finally switched off the light, I stared into the darkness and tried to imagine what adventures Teddy and Frank were enjoying, so far away from our little town.

I was twenty-one years old, and had never seen the ocean.

Joseph had been dismayed when Teddy told him that he was going to return home every weekend so he could attend the Sunday morning service at First Christian Church. He took Teddy's conversion to Christianity as a personal affront. I often heard him stomping ill-naturedly around the house, talking to himself about Teddy, wondering where he had gone wrong, trying to work out how this could have happened. (My brother, probably wisely, had not explained to Joseph that his Road to Damascus moment had come about as he cowered in the limbs of the old oak tree, believing he was about to be shot dead by a cuckolded dwarf.)

As a result of my father's displeasure, Teddy's weekend visits home were strained affairs. He arrived on the bus late Saturday afternoon, and we all ate dinner together at our house. Freddy and Aunt Rosa peppered him with questions about college life, while Joseph harrumphed his way through the meal, muttering that Teddy should be out chasing girls and drinking beer on a Saturday night. The following morning Teddy put on a coat and tie and tiptoed through the house like a thief. He slunk through the town toward the church, guilt pinching his shoulders.

It wasn't just our family who came to view Teddy's trips home with misgiving. Reverend Gresham quickly came to regret his invitation to the risen Messiah to attend his church every Sunday. Of course, the young clergyman was grateful that the awkward situation with Margaret Fitch had been resolved, but my brother's presence still put a huge strain on him. Teddy always sat in the same pew toward the back of the church, and Reverend Gresham found himself watching him as he delivered his sermons. In the past the minister had sometimes recycled old ideas and favorite themes, but he didn't dare try any of those tricks now. While we were sitting in uncomfortable silence around the dinner table, Reverend Gresham was hitting the books, anxiously drafting and redrafting the next day's message. He often didn't get to bed until the early hours of Sunday morning, and would appear at church with dark rings of exhaustion around his eyes. To make matters worse, sometimes Teddy lingered in the church after the service, a meaningful look in his eye. Reverend Gresham didn't know if he was going to offer criticism, advice, or something else, but nor was he willing to find out. Instead he crept out the back door and scuttled home to pray for forgiveness. Private apologies to the Almighty were easier than enduring the wide-eyed scrutiny of His son.

In fact, Teddy wasn't waiting for Reverend Gresham at all. As he sat and listened to the sermons that the minister had worked over so slavishly for his benefit, my brother's eye fell with increasing regularity on the pretty young girl at the piano. Darla Weldfarben had taken over the musical duties at the church when Margaret Fitch left town. Her hair was always tied back in a prim ponytail, and a small cross hung on a silver chain around her neck. Teddy found himself thinking about that cross during the week as he sat in lectures and labored over his coursework. On Sunday mornings he offered to help her collect the hymnals. The two of them chatted amiably while they did their chores. When she smiled her thanks, Teddy felt something slip inside him.

My brother embarked on a suitably monk-like existence during the week. He kept a polite distance from his fellow undergraduates. The other students regularly left the campus in search of beer and local girls, but he went to bed early and read his Bible. At the end of each night he knelt down by the side of his bed and prayed about Darla Weldfarben.

And lo, it came to pass that God saw fit to answer Teddy's prayers for a second time. By the Christmas holidays, he and Darla were an item. Now we had an extra place to set at our Saturday evening meals. If Darla noticed the way that Joseph glowered suspiciously at her cross, she chose to ignore it.

Even if Teddy's visits home weren't quite the happy family occasions that we might have hoped for, at least he *did* come home — which was more than could be said for his brother. Frank seemed determined to stay in North Carolina as long as he possibly could. At the end of each semester, an affable but infuriatingly vague letter would arrive explaining why he had to remain on campus during the holidays. He had found a new job; he had extra studies to complete; he couldn't afford the ticket home. We had no way of knowing whether any of it was true. The only thing I was sure of, reading between the lines of those bland evasions, was my little brother's glee at having escaped. I wrote to him, demanding point-blank when he was going to return. About a month later a postcard arrived, addressed to me. On it Frank had written simply:

WEDDINGS AND FUNERALS ONLY.

He was true to his word. During his time away, he came home twice — for one of each.

During the final months of Morrie's life, Freddy had become as much a member of the Knuckles family as he was of ours. He spent many nights sleeping on the couch next to his friend, and he ate at their table more often than he did anywhere else. Shared grief erased the usual walls of polite Midwestern formality. Morrie's parents treated Freddy like another son. This metamorphosis seemed entirely natural; everyone was too focused on the dying boy sprawled across the living room floor to worry about much else.

After Morrie died, Freddy continued to visit the Knuckles home. He could no more stop knocking on their front door than he could stop breathing. Mr. and Mrs. Knuckles escaped their grief by working longer hours at the pharmacy, reluctant to face the now-empty space in the middle of the living room floor. As a result, Freddy often found himself alone in the house with Ellie. The two of them sat at the kitchen table and talked for hours, drawn together by the urgent need to remember the brother and friend they had lost. From the depths of their shared sorrow sprung a new intimacy. This was Morrie's legacy, his final gift to those he loved. In his death they turned toward each other, and found fresh reason to hope.

It was Ellie who worked it all out. She woke up one morning after a fitful night's sleep, and was astonished to discover that she had fallen in love with my brother. As she brushed her teeth, she gazed at her reflection in the bathroom mirror and watched tears of happiness brim in her lovely eyes. That evening, when Freddy knocked on the front door, she was ready for him.

The person most surprised by this turn of

events was Freddy. (Although I was not far behind.) He had been burdened by the same innocent infatuation with Eleanor Knuckles as the rest of us. Now here she was, holding his hand and telling him that she adored him. When she was finally through talking, the two of them stared at each other for several moments, both scared out of their wits. Then she took a half-step toward him. The kiss that followed was awkward and clumsy, but it did the trick.

I suppose Morrie's death had taught them that there was precious little time to waste. Their wedding was set for the spring of 1959, just a few months after that first kiss in the hallway (they had not even made it to the kitchen). Freddy asked me to be his best man. I accepted with mixed feelings. We both knew that I was his second choice for the job.

The wedding took place on a Saturday afternoon at the First Christian Church, with the usual reception afterward at the Knights of Columbus Hall. The evening before, I drove to Jefferson City to pick Frank up from the railway station. We didn't talk much on the journey home. He parried my questions with bored grunts and stared out the window in thoughtful silence. When we arrived in Beatrice, there was not a flicker of emotion on his face as we passed the town's landmarks, unmovable stars from which the arc of our childhoods could be minutely charted. He turned away from the memories that lingered on every corner. Frank was looking only forward now. He did not want to be here. I felt sad for him, and for us.

The service itself passed smoothly enough. Eleanor Knuckles was utterly, transcendently, beautiful. Freddy was handsome and suave. Reverend Gresham's sermon was short and to the point. I managed not to lose the ring. And for the first time in twenty years, Joseph stepped inside a church.

After the happy couple had exchanged their vows, the four of us sang "Wedding Bells Are Breaking Up That Old Gang of Mine." As the familiar embrace of our harmonies warmed me, I watched my father smile to himself, and wondered where our voices had taken him. He could have been sitting downstairs in the dark after our mother had died, listening to barbershop tunes crackle through the evening static. Or further back: clearing tables at the Nick-Nack on the night he heard four-part harmony for the first time, perhaps, or holding Jette's hand in the shadows as he listened to his own father sing. But then I realized that his memories would not be of other people's voices, but his own. He, after all, could sing more beautifully than any of us. At that moment, I understood: when Joseph listened to us, he could hear the distant echo of his own sweet song.

At the end of it all, my brother walked out of the church a married man, his beautiful bride on his arm. It seemed preposterously grown-up of him. Once again, Freddy had quietly outflanked us all, confounding expectations. It had been a long time since I had seen him smile. After everything he had been through, capturing the heart of Eleanor Knuckles didn't seem like an unreasonable reward.

The following day, Frank returned to North Carolina. We didn't see him again for over a year.

FORTY

After the wedding, Ellie moved in with Freddy and Jette next door. I began to shuttle between the two houses more frequently. I was fascinated by the spectacle that my brother and his new wife presented. The two of them were simply brimming with happiness. It was beautiful to see.

I did invite some girls out on dates back then. I even drove a few of them out to Gants Bluff in my father's Oldsmobile with half a bottle of gin stashed under the passenger seat. But even as we wrestled halfheartedly in the backseat, I couldn't help thinking how tawdry and immature it all was in comparison with Freddy and Eleanor's grand romance. It didn't help that whenever I kissed a girl I was assailed by wistful thoughts of Miriam Imhoff, and what might have been. As a result I was unable to muster the necessary enthusiasm, and soon we would be driving back into town in strained silence.

After a few of these difficult evenings I decided to give up on girls for a while, and instead began living vicariously through the amorous entanglements of Buck Gunn. One of the advantages of confining relationships with the opposite sex to proxy encounters within the pages of my novel was that — unlike my interactions with actual, breathing females — I was always in complete control of the situation. The risk of humiliation was eliminated entirely. The beautiful women Buck flirted with at parties all laughed at his jokes, swooned at his good looks, and were *always* ready to put out. Best of all, when I (or Buck) grew tired of them, they would obligingly disappear, usually with a cheerful wave and a grateful smile.

My novel was protecting me from more than just girls. It was an incubator for my secret dreams, my ticket out of town. I focused all my energy on completing it. The steady aggregation of pages had continued throughout 1959, and by Christmas it was finished. I spent a week contemplating the thick stack of paper on my desk, reading a paragraph here and there, profoundly impressed with myself.

I wondered what to do next. On a fresh page I typed out a dedication.

■ ■ ■ ■

To Miriam, for everything, forever

I looked at the words for a long time. Then I tore the page into tiny pieces and put a new sheet in the typewriter.

To Rosa, with love

It was my aunt who had first sparked my enthusiasm for literature with *The Code of the Woosters*. She was my teacher and my best friend. The next evening I presented her with the manuscript and asked if she would do me the honor of being the first person to read it. She read the dedication page and went very still. For the first time that I could remember, Rosa appeared to be lost for words. She leaned over and gave me a kiss on the cheek and stood up.

"Where are you going?" I asked.

"To bed."

I frowned. "I don't quite —"

"Best place to read," she said.

"But what about dinner?" I asked.

"Fix it yourself, if you want some," said Rosa briskly. She brandished my manuscript at me. "I've got things to do."

I looked at her, nonplussed. "Is it all right

if I stay?"

"As long as you don't disturb me."

"I promise."

"All right, then. Let yourself out."

And with that, she disappeared.

I remained in my armchair, unsure what to do. I wanted to be there, just in case Rosa came barreling breathlessly out of her bedroom to tell me how wonderful it all was. I sat completely still, straining to hear any sort of reaction from upstairs. An occasional snort of laughter or a small sigh of admiration would have been enough. But she read in total silence. I tiptoed to the bottom of the staircase and listened. I did not even hear the rustle of turning pages. For all I knew she had already fallen asleep. After a couple of hours, I let myself out the front door and walked home. I did not sleep much that night.

The next morning I was shaken awake by a hand on my shoulder. I groggily turned over and saw Rosa sitting on the edge of my bed.

"Well?" I asked. "How far did you get?"

"I finished it."

I stared at her. "Really?"

She nodded. "I read through the night."

"And? What did you think?"

"Oh, James." She smiled at me. "It's just wonderful."

I grinned at her stupidly. "Wow," I said.

"Look at you," she said. "A real writer."

"You liked it," I said, elation quickly rubbing away my sleepless night.

"I *loved* it." She patted the manuscript on her lap. "And this afternoon I'm going to drive to Jefferson City and have ten copies made."

"Ten copies? Why?"

"Because we need to send this to New York."

"New York?"

She nodded. "We need to find you a publisher."

That evening Rosa and I sat down and put together ten packages, each addressed to a different publishing house. We selected the recipients by going through her library and choosing the companies that published the books we loved the best. I carefully copied the addresses from the inside pages of each novel onto the padded envelopes that Rosa had bought. The following morning we went to the post office to mail the packages. Rosa kissed each envelope for good luck.

As I walked to the diner from the post office, I became nostalgic for the little town that I would soon be leaving. I promised myself that I would not be like Frank, and just disappear. I would never forget where I had come from. Even once I was installed in my Manhattan penthouse and a literary celebrity, I would still come home. That day I listened to our customers' dreary conversation with newfound indulgence. My ticket east was all but booked.

Next to me, Joseph whistled quietly to himself as he worked. I did not dare tell him what I had done.

We sent the manuscripts off in January of 1960. Every day I came home from work and looked hopefully in the mailbox. By spring, I was becoming numb to the now familiar sensation of disappointment as I scanned each day's letters.

Rosa counseled patience, but that was easy for her to say. I didn't have time to be patient. Every day that passed was another day not spent in New York. I wrote to each publisher, politely asking them to confirm receipt of the manuscript. Those letters did not receive a reply, either.

Spring turned into summer. As the days warmed and lengthened, my despondency grew. I still hurried home each evening, but by then I was flicking through the mail with the martyred wretchedness of the unjustly wronged. Even a rejection letter would have been better than nothing at all. All those hours of hopeful toil at my typewriter, and nobody had bothered to read a word of what I'd written. By August I had reluctantly come to terms with the fact that I was going nowhere.

Poor Rosa bore the brunt of my anger. Our nightly chess games were now accompanied by a sour litany of complaint. Finally one evening my aunt reached across the chessboard and put her hand gently on mine. "James," she said, "you have to stop."

"Stop what?" I said crossly.

"You have to stop *moaning*. All you do anymore is complain."

"I have a lot to complain about," I said sullenly. "I spent years writing that book and nobody will even —"

"That may be so, but it's not helping you, and it's certainly not helping me. You're making me tired, and sad. I love you, but I don't think I can listen to you anymore." She stood up. "I'm sorry they won't read your book, because it's wonderful, really it is. But do you know what would be more useful than all this complaining?"

"What?"

"Write another one."

"Why bother?" I said huffily. "They won't read that one, either."

"You'll never know if you don't try," said

Rosa. "It's what writers do, James. They keep going. They try again." She paused. "In fact, that's what *everybody* does."

The idea of sticking a fresh sheet of paper into my typewriter and starting all over again filled me with dread. "I'll think about it," I said.

"Well, all right," said Rosa, who stood with her hands on her hips, watching me. "But while you're thinking? Find someone else to moan to."

So I did.

As often as I could bear it, I sat by Jette's bedside and told her my news. Even though she smiled at me and patted my hand, I was sure she didn't have the faintest clue who I was or what I was telling her, and so my insipid monologues took on a darker, more confessional tone. All of my bitterness about the book soon began to gush forth, unchecked and bilious. From there, I moved to other areas of complaint. I began to whisper truths that had never passed my lips before. I told her all about Miriam Imhoff. I told her that I hated Teddy and Frank for leaving. A black tide of ugly resentments and long-buried secrets spilled out of me. One night I even told her what I had done with Mrs. Fitch on the evening of my senior prom. Jette heard it all and smiled back at me in stupefied benediction.

When I had finished, I would stand up, kiss her gently on the forehead, and retreat. I returned home feeling wretched. I worried that by offering up my whispered confessions and accepting Jette's silent blessing in return, I was implicating her in my sordid little secrets. Still, I kept going back, and she kept listening — not that she had any choice, of course. I was not so naïve as to think that my grandmother would have offered up a jot of forgiveness had she been able to respond, but hearing my ungallant sentiments expressed out loud was cathartic. And so I held Jette's hand and gratefully unburdened myself.

But even this would not last for long.

On November 8, 1960, the country surprised itself by electing a dashing young president who campaigned on the promises of change and hope. Jette had always had a pretty low opinion of politicians (the twins' presidential namesakes excepted), but I was sure that she would have approved of JFK, who seemed so different from the usual ranks of creaky, cautious old men who had previously occupied the White House.

One morning about a week after Kennedy had won the election, Freddy tiptoed into Jette's bedroom with a glass of milk. For months she had not been sleeping well. She was plagued by terrible, wordless dreams and tossed and moaned through the night. This morning, though, her body was quite still in the bed.

Freddy squatted down beside her. He pulled back the quilt and looked at his grandmother's face.

It was serene and beautiful.

He kissed her on the cheek and stood up.

It had been more than forty years since the sniper's bullet had cracked through the air of a deserted French village, and put out a light half a world away. Not a day had passed since then when Jette hadn't cursed her dead husband like a hound and missed him with all her heart. Now, after her solitary waltz across almost half a century, they were re-united at last. Their lovers' duet, sweet and beautiful, would ring out again.

My grandmother's life had been one long opera. There had been drama, heroes, villains, improbable plot twists, all that. But most of all there had been love, great big waves of it, crashing ceaselessly against the rocks of life, bearing us all back to grace.

FORTY-ONE

Frank had stayed at Duke during the summer vacation, but true to his word, he came home for Jette's funeral.

A small crowd gathered in our yard for the service. The sky hung low above the house and an unforgiving wind swept cheerlessly across the mourners, chilling our bones. Joseph had stubbornly ignored our pleas for a regular funeral service, insisting that Jette would never have approved. About this he may have been right, but that didn't make any of us feel better about the unorthodox ceremony he had concocted for her. In front of the assembled company Joseph scattered his mother's ashes around the base of the apple tree that she herself had planted to commemorate her husband. By then the tree had grown beautiful and strong, and every year it delivered basketfuls of delicious fruit.

Freddy looked anxious throughout, perhaps worried about his professional reputation. Teddy, of course, disapproved of the godless nature of the whole affair. He muttered under his breath about satanic rites, incanting silent prayers for his grandmother in an effort to save her soul from whatever diabolical fate Joseph's act of paganism was condemning her to.

I knew that I was going to miss Jette terribly, but it was difficult to feel too sorry that she was gone. Alone in her curious, confusing world, she hadn't suffered much in her last years, but she hadn't been having much fun, either. The day before the service Rosa had informed me that she intended to celebrate her mother's passing, rather than mourn her. Consequently she turned up wearing a bright orange coat and matching hat that she had bought especially for the occasion, a riot of brilliant color amid the sober sea of dark gray and black. My aunt had loved her mother as much as any of us, but she simply refused to be sad. I was sure that Jette would have approved.

After Joseph had raked over the dirt and said a few words, we trudged inside for cake and iced tea. As the last of the guests entered the house, I realized that I hadn't seen Darla. I went to find Teddy.

"Nice service," I said.

Teddy shuddered. "I was half-expecting

him to sacrifice a goat."

I looked around. "No Darla?"

"I didn't think she would come. She doesn't approve of this mumbo jumbo any more than I do. Although to tell you the truth, I'm kind of glad she's not here. I wouldn't have wanted to spoil the occasion."

"Spoil it?"

Teddy sighed. "We've been fighting a lot lately."

"What's the problem?"

I watched my brother conduct a brief internal debate with himself. "Promise you won't tell a soul?"

"Cross my heart," I said.

"It's about sex," he whispered.

"Uh-oh," I said. "Holding out on you, is she?"

"It's the other way around, actually," he sighed. "She wants to, but I'm not ready yet."

I looked at him. "Not *ready?*"

"It's just — well, these days I'm trying to live by God's Word. And that means that we should wait."

"Until you're *married?*"

Teddy looked uncomfortable. "That's the idea."

"Are you telling me that you're going to marry Darla?"

"Well, no, that's kind of the point." He paused. "I mean, I love her and everything. At least, I think I do. But, no, I don't think we'll ever get married."

"And so you're refusing to sleep with her," I said flatly.

"Plus there's the whole business with Mrs. Fitch," said Teddy.

"Ah," I said. My own encounter with our singing teacher had been a far less traumatic affair than Teddy's — not a suicidal dwarf in sight — and I was still recovering from it. I could see that his guilt over what had happened would give him pause for thought before he tried anything like *that* again. "But of course you can't explain that to Darla," I said.

"Exactly." Teddy pulled a face. "So I'm stuck with just blaming God. And she's less than impressed."

"But Darla's religious, too, isn't she?"

"When it comes to faith," sighed Teddy, "we all have our limits."

I patted him on the back. "You'll work it out."

Teddy looked at me sadly. "Why does it all have to be so complicated?"

I shrugged. It didn't seem very complicated to me. Darla was a pretty girl, who was willing — eager, even — to sleep with my brother. I knew what Buck Gunn would have done.

Teddy had been right. Everyone's faith has its limits. Darla's religious beliefs were not going to stop her from having sex if she felt like it, and indeed there were other sins that she was also willing to commit when the need arose. Consequently, on the afternoon of my grandmother's funeral, she stole a bottle of sweet vermouth from her parents' drinks cabinet and swallowed it down, grimly thinking about Teddy.

Mr. and Mrs. Weldfarben were out of town for the weekend, and Darla had been hoping to lose her virginity while they were gone. But it was humiliating, having to beg a boy to do that stuff. Teddy had told her again and again that he *wanted* to sleep with her, of course he did, but that he was just trying to be good. It had been sweet at first, but as time had gone on Darla had begun to lose patience. Either you want to, or you don't, she'd say bitterly. Well, it's difficult, Teddy would reply, avoiding her gaze.

Darla had decided not to go to Jette's memorial service, as fond as she'd been of the old lady. She wanted Teddy to understand how serious things had become. She took another swig and looked out her bedroom window. The sky had been bruised into darkness by the approaching evening. She frowned. Where was Teddy? He should have come looking for her hours ago. She sat on her bed and waited for a knock on the door.

By the time she'd finished the bottle of vermouth, Darla was steaming drunk and indignant. Teddy was supposed to have come crawling to her, contrite and ready to do her bidding, but he hadn't appeared. She stared miserably up at the ceiling as her stomach heaved and the room spun. She got unsteadily to her feet and pulled on her coat. If Teddy wouldn't come to her, then she would go to him. She let herself out of the house and stood for a moment on the doorstep, momentarily stilled by the cool night air on her face. Then she bent forward and vomited on the flower bed. She wiped her mouth on her sleeve and set off through the town toward our house.

As Darla turned the final corner, she saw my brother standing by the front gate, smoking a cigarette and staring up at the sky.

"There you are!" she cried.

Teddy looked up at her and gave her a small smile. "Here I am," he said.

"Has everyone left the party?" she asked.

"I wouldn't have called it a party, exactly," answered Teddy. "But yes, the guests have all gone. There's just family left." He waved his cigarette at her. "From whose tender affections I'm taking a much-needed break."

Darla cocked her head to one side. "Did you wonder where I was this afternoon?"

"Of course I did." He looked at her appraisingly. "So where were you?"

"I was at home."

"Home, huh. What were you doing there?"

"I've been drinking vermouth and waiting for you."

"Ah."

"Don't you remember? My folks are away for the weekend. I've got the place to myself."

Teddy looked at her, his face unreadable. "I'd forgotten," he admitted.

Darla felt the booze sloshing about inside her. She took his hand. "Come on," she said. "Let's go back."

"Really?"

She hiccuped. "It's now or never," she said.

My brother paused for a moment, caught in two minds. Darla held her breath and concentrated on remaining upright. Finally he squeezed her hand and smiled at her.

"All right, then," he said.

As I sit here and write these words, fifty years later, I cannot help but speculate how things might have turned out differently if I had stepped outside at that moment and seen the two young lovers as they turned and began to walk silently back to the Weldfarbens' empty house. I would have called out; they would have turned toward me; and the half century that has passed since that night would have looked entirely different.

But I didn't. I stayed inside, oblivious to the little drama unfolding by the front gate, and off they went. It was the calamitous finale in a carnival of missed connections. We have all been paying the price, to a greater or lesser degree, ever since.

Because it wasn't Teddy that Darla drunkenly took home on the night of my grandmother's funeral. It was Frank — angry, horny Frank.

FORTY-TWO

For all of Frank's predatory instincts, his time at Duke had been a disappointment, sexually speaking. Student life was not the cornucopia of amatory delights that he had imagined. Yes, there were legions of desirable coeds who floated like angels across the campus, but they had remained tantalizingly out of his reach. My brother watched those beauties parade by, his whole body thrumming a hymn of unbridled longing. But the girls' dorms were fortresses, barricaded by lock and key. Strictly enforced curfews limited the opportunities for illicit trysts, especially since Frank didn't have a car. Back then, the consequence of getting caught having sex was certain expulsion, and nobody (except Frank, apparently) was willing to take that risk. When Darla Weldfarben threw herself at him, then, Frank had been in a state of frustrated arousal for a year and a half.

My brother had never met Darla before. He realized at once that she had mistaken him for Teddy, but when he smelled the alcohol on her breath he decided not to correct her, curious to see what would happen next. When she took his hand and told him that her parents weren't home, he had hesitated, but only for a moment. Frank silently followed her home, hoping that Darla was drunk enough not to notice that he wasn't who she thought he was.

As it turned out, she only realized her mistake the following morning. Even through the fog of a raging hangover, she could see that the boy asleep next to her was not Teddy, even though he looked an awful lot like him. With a furious cry she launched herself across the bed and delivered a stunning left-right combination punch, one ferocious wallop to each eye. Frank tried to pull on his trousers while dodging her fists. This angry pursuit around Darla's bedroom was conducted in mournful silence. Both knew that there was nothing to be said. Finally Frank fled down the stairs and stumbled out of the Weldfarbens' house. As he made his way home, Darla sat on her bed and wept.

Frank didn't tell any of us what he had done. He refused to explain where he had spent the night, but told us that he would be leaving later that day, two days earlier than planned. By lunchtime his eyes were ringed with two dark bruises. That afternoon I drove him back to Jefferson City. He sat next to me, tight-lipped and thoughtful. We drove the whole way in silence. At the train station I handed him his bag. "Whatever it was you got up to," I said, "I hope it was worth it."

He gave me a small, crooked grin. "Bye, James," he said. Without another word, he walked away.

And so my brother escaped back to North Carolina, leaving the rest of us to deal with the mess he had made. The following morning Darla appeared at our front door and confessed everything to Teddy.

My brother listened, aware that he should have been consumed with fury, his heart darkened by thoughts of fraternal revenge, but what he actually felt was relief. Frank had presented him with the perfect opportunity to end things with Darla for good. When she finished her story, Teddy played it perfectly. He patted her hand and said that he forgave her, but that he couldn't pretend that it hadn't happened. This, he told her sadly, changed everything. He couldn't see her anymore, not after this. She gasped and wilted pathetically into his arms. He listened to her pleas and her promises, but remained resolute. It was over, he told her, scarcely able to believe his luck.

Darla, though, was not going to give up without a fight. Teddy spent the next two days hiding in our bedroom while she loitered outside our house, hoping for another chance to plead her case. When he returned to Columbia, there was already a tear-stained letter waiting for him. She began to write him every day, begging for forgiveness. Teddy read the letters quickly and then guiltily dropped them into the trash. He decided to skip a few weeks of church, hoping that God would understand the gravity of the situation and grant him a pass.

I suspect that Darla's campaign to win Teddy back might have worn him down in the end, had Mother Nature not intervened. A month or so after Jette's funeral, Darla began complaining of nausea and exhaustion in the mornings. Teddy was off the hook for good, but things were about to get a whole lot more complicated for everyone else.

Hershel Weldfarben worked ninety acres of arable land out to the west of town with his three sons. Darla was his youngest child, and his only daughter. She'd come along six years after Hershel and his wife had thought they were through with babies — a blessed, if unexpected, gift from God. The Weldfarben boys had been unceremoniously hauled through their childhoods. Hershel put his sons to work in the fields as soon as they were able to drive a tractor — which, in Caitlin County, was around the age of ten. He was a gruff, undemonstrative man, whose love for his boys, if love was the right word, was proportional to their contribution to the family business. Darla, however, was different. Hershel did not possess similar tools to calibrate his affection for his little girl, and consequently his adoration for her went off the charts. The very first time that he held that squalling little bundle of flesh in his arms, he promised her that he would protect her from all the horny little toads who would one day try to have their wicked way with her.

When he learned that Darla was pregnant, Hershel Weldfarben grimly got ready for the drive to Columbia to confront Teddy. When Darla tearfully confessed who the real father was, he changed his travel plans and went to Raleigh instead. This time he took two of his sons with him.

Frank has never told me exactly how that confrontation on campus went down. I don't know, for example, whether or not an *actual* shotgun was involved. But within a week, my brother was back in Missouri, and a married man.

Frank moved into Darla's childhood bedroom, and began work on the Weldfarben farm under the hawkeyed surveillance of his new family. When Claudine Meisenheimer was born the following August, Frank was no longer considered a flight risk, and he was allowed to stop work on the farm. He applied for a teller's position at the bank that Grandfather Martin used to run. Every day he put on a coat and tie and stood behind the counter, doing his best to smile at the never-ending line of customers.

Franklin, who had only ever wanted to escape, found himself more trapped than any of us.

Claudine was as perfect and beautiful as a baby can be. Darla had half-expected the child born of her carnal sin to have tiny horns sticking out of its head, but whenever she held her daughter in her arms, she couldn't help wondering, just for a moment, if what she had done could really have been *that* bad, if this was the end result.

After Claudine came Andrew, Frederick, Nancy, Donny, Clyde, Todd, and Beatrice, each arriving within a year of the one before. Darla, it transpired, was chronically fertile; Frank couldn't look at his wife without getting her pregnant. Every egg that came careening down her fallopian tubes seemed fated for instant fertilization. For the first seven or eight years of their marriage, she was pretty much always pregnant. I think the only reason she finally stopped having more children was that she and Frank were simply too exhausted to have any more sex.

As their family grew, Hershel built Frank and Darla a house on his farm. They invited me round for supper every so often, but I never enjoyed those visits much. The amount of noise generated by all those children chilled my soul. Neither parent seemed to notice the incessant symphony of bawling, bickering, and screaming, but every indignant yowl put my nerves on edge. Frank and Darla had shut down all but the most acute of their sensory faculties, and reacted only when a child's cry achieved a degree of shrillness that I associated with physical torture. Wherever I turned, children sprawled across furniture and left a trail of infant detritus in their wakes. Their parents traipsed numbly through the house, picking stuff up, too tired to speak.

Still, they seemed happy enough. Given

everything that had happened, Darla and Frank muddled through their marriage just fine — better, in fact, than many couples who had chosen each other by more orthodox means. When they had exchanged their vows beneath Hershel Weldfarben's watchful eye, they were strangers, with no hope or expectations of the other, and this had equipped them well for married life. They were immune to the quiet creep of disappointment that can sour more optimistic unions; there was no heady first blush of romance to be mourned as the years passed. From that joyless ceremony in the empty church, there was nowhere for them to go but up.

It helped that neither blamed the other for the mess they had gotten themselves into. There was nothing to be done but to forge a way out of the thicket of their abandoned dreams. A lack of viable alternatives helped, but it was the adoration they shared for their expanding family that really drew Frank and Darla together. In the chaotic crucible of their little home, filled with all that love and noise, with each passing year they crept closer toward some sort of contentment, and each other.

FORTY-THREE

Teddy did not come home for Frank and Darla's hurried nuptials. Nobody was surprised when he didn't appear at the service, although his absence was noticed by Reverend Gresham. The clergyman knew that Teddy and Darla had been dating, and he was appalled when Hershel Weldfarben asked him to officiate at his daughter's wedding — *to the wrong twin*. He had performed the ceremony, ashen-faced with fear. His gaze kept drifting out across the empty pews as he wondered where the risen Son of God was. The words of Exodus 20:5 rattled through his head: *I am a jealous God, and will visit the iniquity of the fathers on the children, on the third and the fourth generations of those who hate Me.* After the service Reverend Gresham had gone home and prayed for forgiveness, petrified that a terrible, retributive hell would soon be unleashed on the town.

There was no apocalyptic visitation, however. Life in Beatrice went on as before. And when, a few weeks after the wedding, Teddy began to appear at church again on Sunday mornings, Reverend Gresham was hugely relieved. So the Messiah had not abandoned them in fury, after all. If anything, Teddy seemed more cheerful than ever. He sat in his usual pew and smiled at his new sister-in-law as she played the piano. The minister marveled at the Lord's capacity for forgiveness.

Of course, Teddy's behavior toward Darla had nothing to do with limitless reserves of clemency. In the circumstances, he could afford to be magnanimous. It was only when he learned about Darla's pregnancy that he realized what a narrow escape he'd had. Every day he gave thanks to God for giving him the strength to resist Darla's charms. *That could have been me,* he thought as he watched Frank amble about the church in cowed defeat. Teddy realized then that God really *was* looking out for him. We probably shouldn't have been surprised when, after he'd graduated from the University of Missouri, Teddy announced that he had applied to seminary school in Kansas City. He was going to be a minister.

The prospect of his son's ordination seemed

to knock the fight out of Joseph. He no longer ranted and raved about Teddy's faith; a bemused silence settled on him instead. He knew when he was beaten.

Teddy stopped coming home every weekend; he was busy helping to officiate Sunday services at the seminary. But he never forgot First Christian Church in Beatrice.

When his training was finished, Teddy returned home, bringing several cardboard boxes full of religious textbooks with him. It was early summer; the brutal humidity that held us hostage every year had not yet descended. One night Teddy and I were sitting on the back porch, drinking beer.

"So," I said, "what's next for you?"

Teddy grinned. "Now the fun starts," he said.

"Your first posting."

Teddy nodded, and took a long drink of his beer.

"How do you decide where to go?"

"Oh, *I* don't decide. I go where I'm sent."

"Which will be . . . ?"

Teddy shrugged. "Could be anywhere. New pastors often get sent to inner-city parishes. Not a lot of fun, so I've heard. Much of the work is done on the street, rather than in church. We minister to prostitutes, drug addicts, and criminals."

"Sounds delightful," I said.

"They're God's children, too, James. Everyone deserves a shot at redemption, wouldn't you say?" Teddy looked at me, his eyes steady. He spoke softly, but his words held a new, quiet confidence.

"If you say so."

"Anyway, that's not for me." He paused. "I want to come back here."

"Back *here?* Why? You could go anywhere."

"I don't want to go anywhere," he said. "I want to come home."

I sat there, momentarily unable to speak. Five years of study and Teddy wanted to come back to Beatrice. I thought of what Rosa had told me years ago. *You'll leave. And then one day you'll come back.* Finally I managed to say something. "What about Reverend Gresham?" I asked.

"Look, James." Teddy spoke calmly. "Like I said, it's not up to me. All I can do is pray and see what happens. Although," he added thoughtfully, "it might not hurt to talk to Reverend Gresham, and let him know what I'm thinking. See if he can help."

There was a certain inevitability about the subsequent chain of events. The more spiritually inclined might deem the whole thing divinely ordained.

The following morning Teddy visited Reverend Gresham, and told him quite frankly that he wanted his job one day, and would he mind putting in a good word for him when the time came? Reverend Gresham realized at once what was happening — finally, his sinful thoughts about Margaret Fitch were coming home to roost. He had fretted about Teddy's lingering presence for years, unsure what it meant for him and his parish. Now everything became clear. He was being ousted. He meekly accepted his fate. The news almost felt like relief. The poor man's nerves had been frayed to breaking point. That afternoon the minister wrote a letter tendering his resignation and strongly urging that Teddy be appointed in his place. His testimony about my brother's virtues would have made a saint blush.

Reverend Gresham decided that he'd had enough of the ecclesiastical life. He went to live with his sister on the southern California coast — about as far away from Teddy as he could get without actually leaving the country — and began studying for his real estate license. Every morning the ex-minister gazed out toward the white-crested waves of the Pacific. He watched the surfers as they shot back and forth across the water, and remembered the sight of my brother levitating above the Missouri River. He never did discover that all he had seen that summer afternoon was Frank, sunbathing on a pole. But that vision had revealed truths that were far greater than the mundane facts of the matter — truths that would guide him through the rest of his long, if rather anxious, life.

Thanks to Reverend Gresham's letter, Teddy's interview was a formality. Within two months my brother was installed as the new minister of First Christian Church. And so the boy with the college degree — with the passport to anywhere — came home.

Once I had recovered from my initial indignation at Teddy's unfathomable decision to return to Beatrice voluntarily, I was as pleased as anyone that he was back. I began a campaign to re-form the quartet. I cajoled and nagged my brothers until they agreed — with varying degrees of enthusiasm — to sing together again. By then, of course, we all had commitments elsewhere, so we only met once a week, gathering around the piano to learn new songs, just like old times. Sometimes we performed in public, but most of the time we just sang for ourselves. We no longer needed an audience. The simple act of making music was enough. The sound of our four voices melding sweetly together was like coming home to a warm fire blazing in the hearth.

A year or so after I had given up all hope of my novel ever being published, I quietly pulled my typewriter back out from beneath my bed and began to write again. I had kept one copy of the first manuscript, and I placed that huge brick of words, its edges meticulously aligned, in sight at all times. It stood sentry over my efforts, its physical heft a reassuring reminder that I had done this once, so I could surely do it again.

I'm not sure what prompted me to start writing another book. Rosa had been right; there was certainly nothing to be gained by feeling sorry for myself. But it was more than that. I missed my nightly communion with Buck Gunn and his friends. Telling stories was still a means of escape. And so I put a fresh sheet of paper into the machine, ready to flee once again. This time I no longer thought about getting published, but just wrote for my own amusement. The journey, not the destination, became the thing, and I rediscovered the simple satisfaction of seeing my ideas materialize before me, sentence after sentence.

My second novel was a thriller that centered around a plot to assassinate the U.S. president. The hero was a humble detective who, on a hunch, was trying to piece the puzzle together before it was too late. (His adored wife, a beautiful but callous redhead, left him halfway through the book, only to be ravaged by a rare and unspecified wasting disease that sentenced her to a long and painful death with nobody by her side.)

I vacillated for weeks when it was time to write the climactic scene — I couldn't decide whether the assassination attempt should succeed or not. The president was to be shot with a single bullet, but it was up to me whether or not the marksman hit his target. It was strange, having the fate of the leader of the free world in my hands. Finally, with a heavy heart, I decided that the president should die.

I wrote the final scene in one frenzied weekend in the late summer of 1963. The plotters were a nefarious gang of malcontents and Communists, directed from behind the scenes by a sinister mastermind, who, in a stunning denouement, was revealed to be the venal and ambitious vice president. The villains killed their man during an open-air presidential motorcade in Kansas City. Once again Rosa was my first reader, but she did not like it as much as my first effort. Still, I was pleased with my work, and decided to submit the manuscript to the same publishers as last time, just in case. Once again my aunt and I collated copies and addressed envelopes together. We dropped them in the mailbox toward the end of October.

About a month later, during a busy Friday lunch, the door of the diner was flung open and Buddy Steinhoff appeared, panting and red-faced. He glanced around the room, and then ran to the jukebox and ripped the power cord out of the wall. The song came to an abrupt stop in mid-verse. Everyone turned toward Buddy, who was standing in the middle of the room, his eyes wild.

"The president's been shot!" he cried.

There was instant uproar. Men got to their feet and started shouting; some women began to cry. My father bustled into the back room and retrieved the transistor radio that he sometimes listened to. He placed it on the counter and turned the volume up high. The news from Dallas crackled through the room, and everyone fell still and silent. The horror that I saw on people's faces was nothing compared to the flat-out terror that was coursing through me. Somewhere in the mailrooms of several New York publishing houses lay fat yellow envelopes, date-stamped *one month prior* to the killing, setting out exactly how it was all going to go down. There was page after page of irrefutable evidence of my complicity in the crime.

We closed the diner early as people scattered home to watch the tragedy unfold in front of their television sets. I hurried to Rosa's school where the children had all been dismissed. My aunt sat at her desk, a haunted look on her face. She looked up when I walked in.

"You'd better lock that door behind you," she said. I did as I was told and then sat down opposite her.

"What are we going to do?" I whispered.

"Nobody's going to believe that you just made this all up," she said flatly.

"I chose Kansas City, not Dallas."

Rosa shook her head. "They won't care about that." She sighed. "All it will take is for one person to read your book. They'll notice the date the packet was mailed, and that will be that."

Suddenly those yellow envelopes had become death warrants. I swallowed. "Can we get the manuscripts back?"

"I wouldn't know how," said Rosa gloomily.

That night we hunkered down in front of the television set and watched events unfold, wondering what on earth we had gotten ourselves into. The mug shot of Lee Harvey Oswald stared out at us from the screen. I wondered what he knew. The awful thought occurred to me that perhaps I'd been right, all along, that this *was* all Lyndon Johnson's doing. If he ever got wind of what I'd written . . . it didn't bear thinking about. After all, he was in charge now. I wondered fearfully what lengths he would go to in order to silence me.

Then Oswald was murdered by Jack Ruby, and we didn't know what to think. Was Ruby paid to silence the killer, stop him from telling the world what he knew? More important, would they be coming for me next? I waited anxiously for dark-suited FBI agents to pull up in front of the house in an unmarked car. Visions of cold, subterranean rooms crowded my imagination. Interrogators would slam their fists down on the table and scream at me, demanding to know where I'd gotten my information.

For the first time I could remember, my aunt appeared genuinely rattled. Every shadow held sinister secrets, every unexplained noise promised doom. She changed the locks on her front door, and bought a small pistol that she kept in the small table by her bed. We didn't dare tell anyone else what was going on, in case they, too, were whisked away for knowing too much. I lay awake at night and listened for the telltale sounds of approaching government spooks.

I desperately began to hope that my second book would suffer the same ignominious fate as my first. There was nothing I would have liked more than for those manuscripts to rot, unopened and forgotten, at the bottom of a pile of unsolicited submissions.

Luckily for us, the publishing industry held steady in its continued indifference to my work. My manuscript remained mercifully unread. There was no late-night knock on the door, no clandestine hush-up. As the months passed, Rosa and I slowly allowed ourselves to hope that we might get out alive.

Forty-Four

In 1965 my father hung up his apron and retired from the diner. He was sixty years old, and had cooked enough eggs by then. His back ached pretty much constantly from all those days leaning over the grill, and he was ready for a break from the early mornings.

The restaurant business was changing, too. It seemed that nobody had time to sit down and eat anymore. The nation had climbed into its car, and was reluctant to get out again. Identical drive-through establishments were sprouting up at every highway intersection, a sinister proliferation along America's arteries. Mammoth corporate franchises competed for market share, coldly slashing prices until smaller restaurants were forced to close down.

Luckily for me, none of the big fast-food companies yet had their greedy eyes on our little rural paradise back then. Still, I knew that it was only a matter of time before the grinning colonel and his secret recipe came calling for my customers. One day I would wake up to see those dumb golden arches glinting nearby, ready to run me off. I couldn't see that there was much point in worrying about it unduly; what would be would be.

My father and I continued to live together in our little house, as content and domesticated as two long-term bachelors can be. Joseph decided that he needed a hobby to occupy him during the long, empty days that he was suddenly facing, and to my bemusement he signed up for a correspondence course in taxidermy. Before long he had transformed the sitting room into a macabre workshop. There were boxes of eyeballs and claws, bags of feathers and false teeth, swatches of variegated pelts. Tacked up on a large board were photographs of deer, otters, and pheasants. An eyeless fox stood in the corner of the room. I found this frozen menagerie rather unsettling, especially since many of the animals were in various stages of either composition or decomposition — I could never quite tell which.

During this time I continued to write, although after the excitement surrounding the president's assassination, I resolved to stay away from topical themes in the future. My next book was a comedy about a publishing executive from New York who, thanks to a faulty transmission in his rental car, ends up stranded in rural Missouri on his way to Colorado. The publishing executive is accompanied on his travels by his wife, a beautiful but vacuous redhead. The couple unwittingly patronizes and offends the locals, who are good, honest, unpretentious folk. They decide to teach the stuck-up out-of-towners a lesson or two, with, as they say, hilarious results. At least, *I* thought the results were hilarious. It was certainly deeply cathartic. I inflicted a succession of grotesque humiliations on my fictional nemesis, who suffered on behalf of the entire publishing industry. (Predictably, the redhead got her fair share of grief, too.) Rosa chuckled her way through it, although she would not be drawn into a discussion as to who was funnier, me or P. G. Wodehouse. We performed the now-traditional ritual of sending out the packages to New York, but this time I didn't even bother waiting for a reply before I began my fourth book, a heartrending coming-of-age tale about a young chess prodigy whose genius goes unnoticed in his small, rural hometown.

Chess was on my mind a lot back then. When I wasn't writing, I was usually over at

Rosa's house, listening to her complain about her latest ailments and doing battle over the chessboard. We spent the summer of 1972 glued to the television set, watching Bobby Fischer beat Boris Spassky in Reykjavik to become the World Chess Champion. Every day we tuned in to Shelby Lyman on PBS, set up a board, and followed along with the moves. I was hopelessly out of my depth, baffled by the brilliance of the chess and enthralled by the spectacle of it all. Spassky was reserved, chillingly unemotional — a Soviet machine, Rosa and I agreed disapprovingly. Fischer, in contrast, was a neurotic jangle of tics and twitches. He gazed at the board with alarming ferocity. We were looking at the same board, but I knew he was seeing whole universes in those sixty-four squares that I could never imagine.

While I frowned over the chess pieces, Rosa swooned and sighed over Bobby Fischer like a teenager with a first crush. She became quite besotted with him. She was charmingly daffy about it. She wrote him long, impassioned letters of support, addressed simply to "Bobby Fischer, Reykjavik, Iceland." As the weeks went by and Fischer brilliantly clawed his way back into contention after a disastrous start, Rosa became increasingly partisan in her support. Though she had lived through two world wars, it took a brooding, sociopathic chess genius for her to buy a flag and hang it outside her front door.

After the chess book, I tried my hand at an old-fashioned whodunit, a complicated saga about the murder of the beautiful heiress to a Midwestern cured-meat empire (who just happened to have red hair). On I went in this fashion, producing a new novel every three or four years, with my loyal readership of precisely one. I would have been happy not to even bother the publishers with my manuscripts, but Rosa insisted. I still have copies of each book, stacked neatly side by side on shelves in my spare bedroom. There my words sit, slowly gathering dust, silent testament to thousands of lonely evenings. Sometimes I'll pull a block of paper down at random and flick through the pages. I do this without rancor or regret. I enjoyed every moment at my typewriter, staging my nightly escapes.

But when Rosa died, I put my typewriter away.

There was nobody left to write for.

My aunt had inherited Jette's strong political convictions, and she was appalled when Ronald Reagan was elected president in 1980. She scoffed at the matinee idol in the

White House. She thought him a buffoon. America was doomed, she was fond of telling me, when it chooses movie stars to run the country.

When the president authorized the invasion of Grenada in October 1983, Rosa's simmering dislike of the man crystallized into full-fledged loathing. America, she seethed, had no right to attack another sovereign state when not a single one of its citizens was under the slightest threat of danger. This was imperialist lunacy. Reagan was just a bully, looking for a fight. Rosa was convinced that he'd approved the aggression in order to deflect attention away from his failing domestic policies. (Since our close brush with the Kennedy assassination, she'd not lost her appetite for juicy conspiracy theories.) She became so obsessed with the president's wrongdoings that she even stopped discussing her gloomy diagnoses of her latest illnesses with me, preferring instead to rant and rage about the iniquities being perpetrated in Washington.

Looking back, I can't help wondering if my aunt had some presentiment about what would happen next, whether her anger at Ronald Reagan was a deft piece of legerdemain to distract herself from impending catastrophe. The moment my aunt stopped discussing her poor health, I should have started to worry that she was getting sick.

Rosa died of a heart attack in the summer of 1984. She was seventy-seven years old.

I discovered her body on the kitchen floor. Only the shattered plate that lay close by hinted at the violence of the myocardial infarction that had ripped the life out of her. In the oven was an untended casserole. It had been charred black. The mess would have dismayed her, I knew. I swept up the broken pieces of china and scrubbed the pan clean before picking up the telephone.

After a lifetime of expecting to be struck down by rare and exotic diseases, I knew that Rosa would have been galled to be killed by something as mundane as a heart attack. But perhaps an overburdened heart was appropriate, in the end.

I'd expected a small handful of guests at the visitation, but to my astonishment, half the town was there. I stood at the door of the funeral parlor for three hours. With each sympathetic handshake came a new story about Rosa. It seemed that for every piece of chalk that she had hurled across her schoolroom, there was a quiet act of tenderness that had gone unnoticed by the

554

rest of us. At some point everyone had seen my aunt's softer side, and nobody forgot it. It didn't take much: a gentle squeeze of the shoulder, a few whispered words of encouragement, a secretly tendered piece of candy. Over the course of that evening, the threads of a thousand small kindnesses grew into a tapestry, rich with affection.

Rosa had loved every child who ambled reluctantly into her domain. She was a maestro before an unruly orchestra, carving harmony out of chaos. She dragged her charges onward by the sheer force of her will, cajoling them with a pitch-perfect blend of public threats, private encouragement, and great big dollops of love. It had been a remarkable act of selfless devotion, sustained over generations.

That night I lay in bed and wondered whether Rosa had chosen to adore her charges to make amends for her own uneventful love life. It was only when I stood up to address the congregation at her memorial service the following afternoon, and surveyed the packed pews in front of me, that I realized I had it the wrong way round. My aunt had simply never needed to seek out the uncertain delights of traditional romantic entanglements. Her heart was already full.

■ ■ ■ ■

To my astonishment, Rosa left me her house in her will.

I won't pretend that I was sorry to be moving out of my father's home. After all, I was forty-seven years old and was still sleeping in my childhood bedroom. What was more, Joseph's gruesome zoo was starting to take over the house. He was getting old by then, and forgetful, and often abandoned projects halfway through. Featherless birds were left to jostle for space with three-legged bobcats and the dismembered head of an elk or two. I had lost count of the number of times I had inadvertently impaled myself on some forgotten antlers. So it was with some relief that I carried my meager belongings down the street and installed myself in Rosa's house. I had spent so many evenings there over the years that it already felt like home.

My typewriter lay silent in the spare room, surrounded by the forest of words that only Rosa had ever read. I often sat on the sofa and paged through her beloved encyclopedia of infectious diseases, wondering which illness she would have chosen next. The place was dreadfully lonely without her there. I bought two kittens for company. Rosa always hated pets, but I thought she would at least approve of their names — I called them Jeeves and Wooster. They quickly came to treat the place as their own. I left the chess set where it had always sat, its pieces arranged for just one more game.

In the late summer of 1986, I arrived home one afternoon to discover a small package resting against the back door of the house. Rosa's name was printed on the label in small, no-nonsense capitals. There was a New York postmark. I frowned. Rosa had never mentioned knowing anybody on the East Coast. I picked the box up and carried it inside.

I had no compunction about opening the thing. Rosa had been gone for two years by then, and I had gotten quite used to reading her mail and responding when necessary. I sliced open the tape and peered inside. On top of a stack of papers there was a black velvet bag and a small white envelope, with Rosa's name written in the same neat handwriting. I opened the letter.

Dear Ms. Meisenheimer:
It is with deep sadness that I write to inform you that my father Stefan recently passed away, after a mercifully brief fight with cancer. After his death I discovered these items in a locked box that he kept in

a drawer of his bureau.

I confess that my father has never mentioned your name to me. He was a man of many gifts, and I suppose many secrets. However, I am sure that he would have wanted these things to be returned to you. I hope that they will bring you a measure of comfort.

Sincerely,
David Kliever

I sat down and read the letter again. Over the years Joseph had occasionally mentioned Stefan Kliever as we worked side by side at the grill, so I knew about his desertion all those years before. I opened the velvet bag. The medal that the Kaiser had pressed onto my great-great-grandfather's chest fell into my hand. It had been almost fifty years since it had been stolen. I held it up to the light and inspected it, wondering what its return meant. Then I reached into the box and took out the remaining papers.

There were letters, scores of them, all beginning in the same way: *Dear Stefan.* The elegant flamboyance of my aunt's penmanship was unmistakable. Tucked in between the pages were hundreds of photographs.

Of me.

FORTY-FIVE

I flicked through the pictures, watching the years accelerate beneath my fingertips as I morphed from cherubic infant to lankily awkward youth.

Ever since I was a baby, Rosa had regularly written to this man I did not know and delivered news about me. My progress through childhood was faithfully charted. Mostly Rosa kept to the facts, but occasionally she would allow herself some editorial comment. Her opinions betrayed her fondness for me, but also her inability to pass judgment without some measure of criticism.

He seems so very shy.
That's James — always eager to please.
At least he tries his best.

Unable to turn away, I read on through the years, watching my childhood unfurl through the sharp prism of Rosa's waspish commentary. The letters ended soon after I had settled into my job at the diner.

He's grilling burgers now, she wrote in her final letter. *Standing where you used to stand.*

I sat at the kitchen table, staring into space, as the truth steamrollered over me.

Joseph was not my father. Cora was not my mother. Rosa was not my aunt. A lifetime of warm, carefree assumptions lay in tatters.

Finally, all of the special treatment that Rosa had lavished on me over the years began to make sense. Her fondness for me had nothing to do with the plight of being the second born. I thought back to the countless games of chess, our shared love of P. G. Wodehouse, all those long evenings together. Our intimacy had been real enough, but it was based on a lie. My family had closed ranks and sought to make me someone that I was not. Everybody was guilty: Joseph, Cora — and Rosa most of all. I believed that I'd known her better than I knew anyone, but she had gone to her grave with her secret. My lingering sadness over her death was suddenly laced with anger and a fresh sense of loss. Now I had been cheated out of not one mother, but two.

Even Jette, I saw miserably, had not been innocent. She must have known as much as anyone. At least, I thought bitterly, *she* was

560

still my grandmother. I remembered the unreadable look in Jette's eye when Rosa had brought me home for my first chess lesson. She hadn't been worried about me, as I'd always imagined. She'd been worried about Rosa, wondering if her daughter would be able to maintain my family's long conspiracy of silence.

I sat back in my chair. I had always assumed that Joseph and Cora had named me after Lomax, but now a new theory presented itself. What if Rosa had been allowed that privilege, before she gave me up? I remembered her stories of Mr. Jim, the raccoon she had adored so fiercely when she was young. I stared at the ceiling, and wondered if in fact I had been named in tribute to her beloved childhood pet — the animal that my father had shot.

I knew nothing.

That night I lay in bed and surveyed the unfamiliar landscape. We cannot exist without our histories; they are what define us. But my history was a lie. All of a sudden I was rootless, cut adrift from everything that I thought I knew, an immigrant in a land where I did not belong.

At two o'clock I climbed out of bed, unable to sleep. After Rosa's death I had put her old correspondence into cardboard boxes and stored them in the spare room along with my manuscripts. I carried the boxes to the kitchen table and began to work my way through the mountains of paper that accumulate around a life. I was hoping to find Stefan Kliever's replies to Rosa's letters. Surely he would have had questions about me, some words of encouragement or advice he wanted to pass on. But there was nothing, not even a postcard. Rosa had covered her tracks well.

I had reached a dead end. I stared out the window into the night. All I could see was my own dark reflection in the glass. I looked at the stranger gazing silently back at me. I no longer knew who I was. All I knew about my father was a handful of anecdotes, half a century old. It wasn't enough. I needed to know who Stefan Kliever was.

Joseph was the sole surviving perpetrator of this elaborate hoax. I knew this wasn't all his fault, but by then there was nobody else left for me to blame. I didn't have the stomach to confront him. Besides, he was an old man by then. I did not want to resurrect old, painful ghosts for him. I would have to look elsewhere for answers.

Then I remembered that there had been a return address on the package that had been waiting for me by the back door. I rummaged through the trash can, and two minutes later I was looking at an address in Eastport, New York. I went to find Rosa's road atlas.

Every map in her tattered Rand McNally bore evidence of intense scrutiny. There were doodles in the margins, smudged fingerprints, rings from the bottom of coffee cups. I turned its dog-eared pages, perplexed. It looked as if Rosa had run her finger along every highway in the lower 48. I wondered if she, too, had been planning her escape.

Eastport was on the south coast of Long Island, one of a string of villages in the Hamptons. I looked at the map for an age, wondering what on earth to do next.

After two days I realized that I could no more forget about the address in Long Island than I could cut off my own arm. It was an itch that would have to be scratched, sooner or later. I decided that there was no point delaying the inevitable. I began to pack.

One of the advantages of Frank and Darla's astounding fecundity was that their family provided a steady supply of manpower to work at the diner over school holidays and weekends. Clyde and Todd were my principal helpers that summer. They were industrious and competent, and I knew I could trust them to run the place in my absence. I called Freddy at the funeral parlor and asked him to check in on Joseph while I was gone. I didn't even tell Joseph that I was going away. I didn't trust myself to talk to him. His betrayal gnawed away at me, scraping me hollow.

I decided to drive. The journey by road would take me two days, and I needed the time to think. I pointed my car east and drove all day, marking my progress by the fading in and out of radio stations. When a song died I would twirl the dial until I found something new. I listened to country, jazz, and rock and roll, but mainly I listened to pop. All those vapid synths and drum machines didn't sound much like music to me, but it filled the car with noise, and kept me company as I slowly edged back toward my past.

By early evening I was exhausted. I stopped at a shabby motel on Interstate 70, outside Hebron, Ohio. Dinner was a dried-out turkey sandwich that I had bought at a service station earlier that day, washed down with a warm can of soda from the vending machine outside my door. There was no ice. I lay on the bed and watched *Cagney & Lacey* as I ate.

I was still unsure exactly what I was hoping to achieve with my pilgrimage. My day of solitude behind the wheel had not clarified much. I wanted answers, but I still didn't know what the questions might be. Perhaps I just wanted to get a glimpse of Stefan Kliever's second act away from Beatrice, to see what might have been. I was pretty sure that no good could come of it, but that no longer mattered. There was no turning back, not now. I did not sleep well.

The next morning I climbed back into the car and continued my journey east. Pennsylvania went on forever. Finally Interstate 78 escaped into New Jersey. As the roads became busier, traffic began to move faster, jigging and jagging between lanes. At Newark I turned north onto the New Jersey Turnpike, humming Paul Simon. Vehicles screamed past me on both sides. To my right, New York City shimmered in the afternoon sunlight. It was all I could do not to pull over and stare. I took 95 across the Hudson and through the Bronx, before turning south and hitting the Long Island Expressway. I had been driving all day, but didn't feel tired. I was electrified by the city's skyline. It was delicious, to be so tantalizingly close to the place I'd dreamed of for so many years. I decided that once I'd finished my business in the Hamptons, I would treat myself to a day or two among the skyscrapers. It had been a long time coming.

I drove east along 495, watching Manhattan retreat in my rearview mirror. Finally I turned south off the highway and arrived in Eastport. I had assumed that I would find somewhere to stay in the town, but it was the height of the summer holiday season, and everywhere was full. I finally found a bed-and-breakfast in Westhampton, a few miles down the road. The landlady was very nice. She saw my Missouri license plates and asked me what I was doing such a long way from home. Visiting family, I told her. She smiled approvingly.

The following morning I drove back into Eastport. On the way I noticed a sign for Remsenburg. The name struck me as familiar, but I couldn't remember why. Eastport was a tiny place, but I still managed to get lost as I drove up and down quaint tree-lined lanes that all looked identical. After twenty minutes I finally found the address I had copied down from the package. I pulled over, and left the engine running — either for the air-conditioning or so I could make a quick getaway, I was not sure which. The house was an Italianate villa, set well back from the road. A wide drive swept elegantly up to a grand, double-fronted entryway. There was a well-maintained garden populated by mature trees and perfectly trimmed topiary. A man in blue overalls was laboring in the shade of a lushly foliated elm. A pair of sprinklers hissed at each other, sending parabolas of water dancing through the still air. I switched off the ignition and walked up the driveway. I waved at the gardener. He did not return my salute. I rang the doorbell.

After a minute or two the door opened. A man about my height stood in front of me. His hair was shot through with gray, and his eyes creased into small deltas of wrinkles as he squinted at me in the morning sunlight.

"Can I help you?" he said.

"David Kliever?"

"Yes? Who are you?"

"My name is James Meisenheimer."

He looked at me steadily for a moment. "You're the boy in the photographs," he said. I nodded. He looked down at his shoes and sighed. "My wife said this would happen. She told me not to send those letters back."

"Is there somewhere we can talk?" I said.

"There's nothing for you here."

"You don't know what I want yet," I said. I didn't know myself.

He shook his head. "I should have listened to her. It's not as if my father would have cared. He's dead, for God's sake."

"I've driven halfway across the country to see you. At least give me a few minutes."

He sighed, and closed the front door behind him, unwilling to grant me entry to his home. "A few minutes," he said. He led me down a gravel path to a shaded patio with a wrought-iron table and two chairs. A long, perfectly manicured lawn stretched away from the house. At the far end I could see a swimming pool, shimmering blue in the morning sun. We sat down. He did not offer me anything to drink.

"Did you say you *drove* here?" he asked.

I nodded. "I needed time to think."

"Look, I've spoken to several lawyers about my father's estate. It's all in trust. Watertight wording, they tell me. You've no chance —"

"I don't give a damn about his *estate*," I interrupted. "I just want some answers."

"Answers?"

"Of course. I've just discovered that I'm not who I thought I was."

"Your mother never told you?"

"I thought she was my aunt."

"Is she still . . . ?"

I shook my head. "She took her secret to her grave."

"Dad never said a word about you, either, not even when he knew he was dying."

We contemplated the web of silence that

our parents had constructed.

"You can't prove a thing," said David after a moment.

I ignored him. "Do I have any other brothers? Or sisters?"

He looked at me as he weighed his options. "A sister," he replied finally. "Her name's Elizabeth, although everyone calls her Betty. She's an ob-gyn in Connecticut."

"Older or younger?"

"Four years younger." David paused. "We had another sister. She died when she was seventeen. Leukemia."

"What was her name?"

"Amy. She was two years younger than me."

The second child. I wondered whether Amy had suffered the same tribulations that I had. Then I realized that she wasn't the second child, not really. She was the third. I felt an acute pang of loss and longing for this sister whose existence I hadn't known about a minute before.

"Losing a sister is hell on earth," said David quietly. "It destroyed my mother. She started drinking heavily after Amy died. One night she'd spent the evening at a bar in Mastic. She came off the road on her way home. Smashed into a tree. She died on the way to the hospital."

"I'm sorry," I said.

"After that, we hardly saw my father. He just buried himself in his work."

"What did he do?"

"He had an idea, took it, and made it grow. Worked hard, got rich. The American Dream."

"What was the idea?"

"You've heard of Delish-a-Burger."

A bark of disbelief escaped me. There were two Delish-a-Burgers in Jefferson City, three in Columbia. I had eaten in all of them — clandestine expeditions to spy on the competition. Their secret signature sauce, a phosphorous orange gunk, couldn't camouflage the gristled awfulness of the pale gray meat, but there were always lines going out the door. Every time a new Delish-a-Burger opened, there was a downtick in my business. "Stefan founded *Delish-a-Burger*?" I blurted.

David Kliever nodded. "He always said that when he left Missouri, he could only do one thing well, and that was cook cheeseburgers. So he decided to carry on doing exactly that. He saved up some money, and opened his first restaurant in Newark. In ten years he had dozens of stores in New Jersey. Then he started franchising restaurants across the country. Of course, he lost control of the company years ago, when it went public, although the family retained a decent holding."

I looked again at the elegant garden and enormous house. "Wow," I said.

"You really didn't know?"

"David, a week ago I didn't know you existed."

I could see the suspicion behind his eyes. "But now that you do —"

"I told you, I don't want your money."

He leaned back in his chair, sizing me up. "So what *do* you want?"

"I want you to tell me more about him."

David pulled a face. "Well, let's see. He was an old-fashioned guy, you could say. Pretty conservative at heart."

"Must have been quite a surprise when you found those letters."

"You have no idea."

"Actually, David, after this week, I believe I do."

He gave a wry smile at that. "My father always did play his cards close to his chest," he said. "He wasn't given to huge displays of emotion. He loved us, but he was always happiest when he was working. After Mom died, he never remarried."

"What else?"

"He was a very stubborn man. Always believed he knew what was best, and not much inclined to listen to the opinions of others. There was nothing anyone could do to make him change his mind, once it was made up. I don't believe I ever heard him apologize for anything in his life."

"He never set eyes on me, not once," I said quietly. "He never tried. Not even when he knew he was going to die."

David got to his feet and turned to look down the garden. "Let me tell you one thing, James. My father was the most careful man I ever met. He never did *anything* by accident. If he left those letters in that drawer, it was because he wanted me to find them." He was silent for a moment. "That's why I sent them to Missouri, despite my wife's protests. It was what he wanted. He never could admit that he'd made a mistake, but that was the closest he ever came to expressing regret about anything."

We were silent for a long time.

"Do you have any kids?" I asked.

I knew the moment the words had left my mouth that I had made a mistake. The question was a horrible miscalculation. It reminded David of the threat that I posed to all that he held most dear. I watched sadly as he packed away his memories of his father and his expression became flat and defensive.

"Look, James, you seem like a decent guy. You tell me you're not interested in my family's money, and I suppose I've got no reason to think you're lying about that. If you are, I guess I'll find out soon enough." His mouth twitched, not quite managing a smile.

"I'm not lying."

"Here's the thing, though. This changes nothing. I don't know you. You and me, we're not about to become lifelong buddies. You have your life in Missouri, I have mine here. I'd like to keep it that way."

I was momentarily tongue-tied by his presumption. "Okay," I said.

He looked thoughtful. "You know, though, there's something I'd like you to have before you go."

I waved a hand at him, not interested in his halfhearted bribery. "No need. I'll keep my word, you'll see. I'm not going to bother you."

"Really. Dad brought it with him from Missouri. I guess it reminded him of where he'd come from. I'd like you to have it. A keepsake."

I shrugged. "If you insist."

"Be right back." He stood up and walked toward the house.

573

Alone, I stared up at the sky. I had been hoping for something more than a half brother who was frightened of losing his inheritance. The banality of it all made me want to weep. I looked up at the large house and suddenly I couldn't wait to leave.

"Here." David was back, holding a black case out in front of him. I took it from him and put it on my lap. I undid the clips and lifted the lid. "He'd take it out sometimes and blow into it. Dreadful noise he made. He used to boast that he'd never taken lessons, and I could believe it."

Inside the box, resting on a bed of dark velvet, was an old cornet.

FORTY-SIX

Later that afternoon I walked through Central Park from my hotel on the Upper West Side to the Metropolitan Museum. I wandered through the galleries, looking at famous paintings. I sat on the museum's steps and listened to a man play a squirreling bebop line on his saxophone. I ate a hot dog in the shade of the trees on Fifth Avenue. I tiptoed through St. Patrick's Cathedral. I took a crowded elevator to the top of the Empire State Building and watched the yellow taxis swarm up and down the avenues below. At the end of the island the Twin Towers majestically punctured the sky, beautiful and massive and still. Behind them the Hudson shimmered in the afternoon sunlight.

I was in New York at last, and none of it mattered a damn.

I sat in my car for some time after I had said good-bye to David Kliever, staring into space. Finally I turned on the ignition and pulled away. I drove aimlessly for a while, unable to think. I saw another signpost for Remsenburg, and then I remembered where I had heard the name before — it was the town where P. G. Wodehouse had spent the last few decades of his life. He had died ten years earlier, but I knew that he was buried nearby. I followed the sign and soon was driving through the town. I parked next to the small post office and stepped inside. Behind the counter sat an elderly lady, whose expression suggested that it was not the first time she had been asked about the great man's resting place. She gave me directions to Remsenburg Community Church, a whitewashed building with a small wooden spire a little way out of the town. Behind it was a peaceful graveyard fringed with trees. I wandered through the tombstones until I found the grave. It was rather grander than its neighbors. A stone book sat open on top of an impressive granite block. Into its pages had been carved:

JEEVES
BLANDINGS CASTLE
LEAVE IT TO PSMITH
MEET MISTER MULLINER

Poor Bertie hadn't made it onto his creator's final memorial, but his butler had. I stood in front of the grave for some time. Wodehouse, I reflected ruefully, would have approved of the plot twist my own little story had taken.

Lomax's cornet sat in the trunk of my car. Its valves were stiff with age and disuse. A constellation of green rust spots spanned the length of the horn. On the rim of the bell there was a dent — the sort of dent that might have been caused by clubbing the thing against its owner's skull.

My father had killed a man, and he'd kept the murder weapon as a trophy.

I ate dinner at a plush, darkly lit steakhouse near Times Square, then made my way north up Broadway. It was a warm night. The streets were full of people, a richly variegated slice of humanity. I walked blindly past them all. By the time I reached my hotel, I was bone-tired. I lay on my bed and listened to the sound of the city at night.

First thing the next morning I paid my bill and drove down Ninth Avenue. Without a backward glance, I turned into the Lincoln Tunnel and escaped home.

The United States of America is a large country, and — for once — I was grateful to live in the middle of it. It took every hour of that long drive back from New York for me to work out what I needed to do.

The poisonous legacy of Lomax's battered cornet savaged me as I fled home. The urge to interrogate Joseph about my mother and father diminished with every passing mile. By the time I got to Missouri, there was nothing else that I needed, or wanted, to know.

I arrived in Beatrice late the following afternoon. As I drove through the town, the sun was still hot and high in the sky. The main square was empty, the murderous humidity keeping people off the streets. I parked and got out to stretch my legs. Beatrice Eitzen maintained her grumpy vigil in front of the courthouse. I was pleased to see her familiar face, although she seemed as unimpressed as ever as she looked at me down her long nose. *What did you come back for?* she chided me silently. *You should have escaped, too, when you had the chance.*

I walked around the courthouse a couple of times, and sat on a bench in the shade. Finally I climbed back into the car and drove to Joseph's house. As I pushed open the door I heard the sound of the television. Joseph was in his usual chair, not watching the screen but squinting at the front page of the *Optimist*. He looked up as I walked in. A wide smile appeared on his face.

"James! You're back!"

I looked at this old man, this old man who loved me.

And I said, "Hi, Dad."

FORTY-SEVEN

My story is almost done.

The day after I returned from New York, I purchased a safe-deposit box at the bank, and there I hid the Kaiser's medal, the cornet, and Rosa's letters — relics from a past that could only hurt us. The key still sits somewhere in the bottom drawer of my desk, hidden beneath a pile of old papers. A quarter of a century later, I have never opened the box.

I never told Joseph that I knew his secret.

After all that he had given me, my silence was the smallest of gifts back.

Frank continued to work hard at the bank. In 1990, some thirty years after he had first stood behind the counter as a teller, he became president — Grandfather Martin's old job.

Darla and Frank passed their fertile genes on to the next generation. One by one their children left home, found a mate, and began reproducing almost immediately, and in similarly astounding quantities. Now they have sired their very own dynasty of little Meisenheimers. I am too old to keep track of all of my great-nieces and -nephews. I sometimes wonder whether Frank even knows which of his grandchildren he's talking to. He is careful never to call them by their first name as he pats them fondly on the head. Claudine's eldest, Jackie, got married last year to his high school sweetheart and now they are expecting. Soon my little brother will be a great-grandfather. I am unsure what to do with this information, save to report that he seems pleased about it.

It's funny how things turn out. Frank wanted to leave Beatrice more than any of us. Now he's one of the grand nabobs of the town, and it's impossible to imagine him anywhere else. The threads of his family's life have become interwoven with the tapestry of the place. The stories of his children and his grandchildren have played themselves out on this land, and he's tied here more firmly than by the lash of steel ropes. And he's just fine with that. The comforts of home and family will wash away every disappointment, given time.

In contrast to Darla and Frank's excessive reproductive habits, Freddy and Eleanor had just one daughter, Adeline. Throughout their long and contented marriage, they enjoyed each other with quiet delight. Their little family was a beautiful knot of love; they did not have much need for the rest of us. They kept their distance from the chaotic fray of Frank's family on the other side of town.

Freddy became Oscar Niedermeyer's lieutenant at the funeral parlor. When the old man died, he took over the business, and continued to spread his black-garbed comfort to new generations of mourners. Business was always good. Death and taxes, James, he used to say to me, death and taxes.

To Freddy's disappointment, Adeline did not have a musical bone in her body. She could not hold even the simplest of tunes. She began working in the funeral parlor the day after she graduated from high school, and she's been running the place since Freddy retired. My niece is the image of sober efficiency at work. She inherited her father's knack for greeting mourners with just the right amount of compassion and professional rectitude, but outside the funeral parlor she is the loudest, most obnoxiously cheerful person I know. She's a walking maelstrom of winks and nudges, determined to find raucous hilarity in everything. Every piece of news is greeted with a shrill bark of laughter, whether amusing or not. Her husband, a nice man who fumigates houses for a living, stands by and watches as she dominates every conversation she joins. I'm fond of Adeline, of course, but I do my best to avoid her in social situations. (I'm not too keen to meet her in her professional capacity, either.)

Freddy and Ellie were married for forty-four years, and every one of them seemed happier than the one before — even when the aggregation of mutinous cells that had been lurking in Ellie's left breast finally jumped ship and began to ravage the rest of her body. They bore the onslaught of her cancer with the bravery of two people who know they've had it good.

Eleanor Meisenheimer, the town's fabled beauty of yore, passed away in her sleep in June of 2003. The hospice had sent her home a week earlier, when there was no more to be done. Freddy was by her side, holding her hand as they both slept. He awoke to discover that death had, for the second time, stolen away a loved one during the night.

After Ellie's death, Freddy joined a choral group in Columbia. He drives over there every Monday night for rehearsals. They've performed opera, a mass or two, "Carmina Burana," and an awful lot of requiems. Almost everything is in either Latin or German. It's all terribly serious. There's not much silly, love-struck crooning going on. I go to all the concerts. Freddy stands amid a crowd of dinner-jacketed men, holding his music stiffly in front of him, never taking his eyes off the conductor's baton. There must be at least a hundred men and women in the choir, with thirty more in the orchestra. His fine voice, which has grown deeper and richer over the years, is lost among the vastness of this well-meaning crowd. He could stop singing and nobody would notice. This troubles me, but Freddy doesn't care. He just loves to sing. I watch him as he mouths all those somber foreign words, and I marvel at the fresh delight he discovers in all that beautiful music.

Adeline and her husband continued Freddy and Eleanor's modest family ways, and had just one child, a boy. Morrie has grown up tall and strong and handsome, just like his beloved namesake. He's twenty-six now, and lives in New York. Adeline worries about the next terrorist attack, of course. That, and the legion of brigands who lurk around every dark corner. She dreads the midnight phone call that never comes.

Nobody is quite sure what Morrie does. It's something complicated to do with other people's money. He lives in a tiny apartment in Chelsea, and comes back home twice a year. These visits are a cause of excitement and celebration for the rest of us, but I worry that there may not be many more of them. Last time he returned with a girl on his arm. Her name was Rita. She was a lawyer, exquisite in her chic Fifth Avenue outfits. She watched in polite bemusement as we all cavorted around her in delight, loudly admiring everything about her. She was kind, we all agreed, and funny, and obviously smart, and of course very beautiful. The one thing nobody mentioned was her gorgeous brown skin. Rita is from Puerto Rico — something that Morrie had not thought to tell us before they arrived. We all did our best to pretend that it was the most natural thing in the world to have this darkly exotic creature in our midst, but I don't think she was fooled for a minute. Not even Adeline's hysterical bonhomie could disguise her discomfort. It didn't help that our neighbors and friends stared at Rita in astonishment whenever she and Morrie set foot outside the front door.

Neither of them has returned to Beatrice since.

The last I heard, Morrie and Rita are planning a small wedding in Manhattan. We're all wondering — although nobody will dare speak the words aloud — whether we will ever see them again. Adeline has been staggering around the town looking as if she's mislaid a winning lottery ticket, as she contemplates the prospect of mixed-race grandchildren. I want to tell her that Frederick, her great-grandfather, would be pleased, because this is the American way. We are all immigrants, a glorious confection of races and beliefs, united by the rock that we live on. As the years wash over us and new generations march into the future, family histories are subsumed into this greater narrative. We become, simply, Americans. Adeline is wondering if she will be able to love babies who are not quite like her, but she's missing the point. They'll be exactly like her. They'll be Americans, too — only more so.

Once Teddy returned to Beatrice to take the helm at First Christian Church, he was never going to leave again.

Over the years, Joseph gradually made peace with his good-for-nothing, God-loving son. I often turned up at my father's house to find Teddy and Joseph arguing about abstruse theological constructs. Teddy always gave as good as he got in those encounters. He knew he would never persuade Joseph to come back to the church, but felt obliged to try.

Soon after he arrived back in Beatrice, Teddy got himself a dog, an elegant German shepherd called Maggie, and the two of them quickly became inseparable. Maggie padded up and down the aisle at church as if it were the most natural thing in the world. Whenever I saw Teddy driving through town in his pickup, she was always sitting next to him in the passenger seat. Theirs was a blissful friendship, one of uncomplicated and total devotion. Teddy loved that dog almost as much as he loved the Lord, and when she grew old and died, he was heartbroken. Joseph was desperate to stuff poor Maggie and put her on a plinth, but Teddy loved her far too much to let him do that to her. Instead he buried her in the yard and got another dog just the same. He called her Maggie, too. As I write this, Maggie is on her fourth incarnation.

At some point during the tenure of Maggie II, Teddy married Hope McClary, a girl he had unsuccessfully tried to date in his senior year of high school. Hope had married and moved away from Beatrice soon after she'd graduated. Her husband, an infantry sergeant, was killed by North Vietnamese sniper fire on Hill 875 during the battle for Dak To. After that, the pretty young widow returned to Beatrice with her son, Billy. Every Sunday morning the two of them came to church and listened attentively to Teddy's sermons. Then Hope volunteered to help Mrs. Heimstetter cook at the next church social, and that was that. Romance blossomed over the fried chicken, and she and Teddy were married six months later. Teddy and Hope never had children of their own, but that was all right. My brother adopted little Billy, and from that moment forward loved him just as if he were his own. That was typical of Teddy; he always seemed to have a little bit more love to share than the rest of us.

I am the only person who knows the strange circumstances behind Teddy's religious awakening, and we have not spoken the name of Rankin Fitch between us for many years. Perhaps when you've been the beneficiary of as many divine miracles as my brother believes himself to be, unshakable belief is easier to come by. I don't believe that Teddy has ever suffered from the kind of spiritual angst that so afflicted Reverend

Gresham during his troubled time here. A hushed, profound contentment has settled upon him as he does the Lord's work. He ministers to his flock with a quiet but forceful certainty. He believes he is doing what he was put on this earth to do. It's a beautiful thing to see.

And me?

I sold the diner to Frank's son Todd and his wife, Jeanne, a couple of years ago. They immediately closed the place down, applied for a liquor license, and reopened two weeks later as Frederico's Taqueria. Now they serve sangria and margaritas by the bucketful, and the place is packed every night. There's not a cheeseburger in sight — now it's all fajitas, burritos, and enchiladas. It doesn't seem to matter that neither Todd nor his wife has ever been south of the Arkansas state line. Authenticity isn't the point. Lots of hot salsa, sour cream, and guacamole is the point. Good luck to them, I say. Our family has fed the people of Beatrice on that spot for four generations now. Todd's dubious chile relleno is a world away from Jette's beloved sauerkraut, but that's progress for you. The restaurant will continue to evolve just as surely as we will.

I'm still on my own. It took me years to recover from my infatuation with Miriam Imhoff, but recover I did, even if nothing could ever quite measure up to that first blissful starburst of young love. There have been several flings over the years — some brief, others not so brief, but all very discreet. I always traveled for my romance. I've had affairs across the state, but never in Beatrice. I didn't want to run into my paramours in the grocery store or the post office. I especially didn't want to run into their husbands. For I have been a lover of other men's wives.

It's strange. Serial philanderer was never a role I would have imagined for myself, but the marriages from which these women were escaping were a safety net, both for them and for me. We were happy with stolen moments here and there, a pleasant hotel tryst and perhaps a light lunch afterward, that sort of thing. It was always very civilized and uncomplicated.

We all agreed that I wasn't worth risking a marriage for.

Miriam returned to Beatrice sometime during the Reagan administration, when Kevin finally retired from the army on a fat pension. They built a large house in a new subdivision on the edge of town, and have lived there in slothful indolence ever since. I hope it won't sound too ungallant to observe that half a century in the soupy mire of married life has exacted a hefty price. The beautiful red hair that I used to dream of is long gone, destroyed by gallons of toxic colorants and chemicals. It's white, thin, and brittle now, a ghost of its former glory. Miriam likes to wear sweatshirts decorated with showers of colorful sequins. She has special tops for Valentine's Day (festooned with glittering hearts), Easter (glittering eggs), July 4 (glittering flags), Thanksgiving (glittering turkeys, pumpkins, and pilgrims), and Christmas (glittering Santas, reindeer, and Christmas trees). When the calendar does not dictate more topical motifs, she wears a bright pink number with WORLD'S BEST GRANDMA emblazoned across her chest. Her voice, which I used to hear in my head each night as I fell into fitful sleep, could now freeze a rutting steer at fifty paces.

Frankly, I wished Miriam had stayed away. I would have preferred my memories of her to remain untarnished. When I see her these days, there is no rueful reexamination of the past, no awed gratitude at a lucky escape. Instead I feel just a vague sense of regret, that the youthful innocence of my dreams was no match for the bruising banality of real life.

These days I keep largely to myself. I have more time on my hands now, of course, but there's still much to keep me occupied. I like to read through my Wodehouse library at least once a year. I'm still dazzled by the same timeless wonder that first transfixed me sixty years ago, when I sat in the sun and frowned my way through *The Code of the Woosters* for the first time. Bertie is an old friend now — as affably idiotic as ever, a reassuring beacon of old-fashioned decency. He offers me ageless comfort, and I will be forever grateful to him.

For a long time after Rosa died I stopped playing chess. Recently, though, I've begun to go online and do battle with people across the globe. There's always someone out there looking for a game. We come from every continent, and speak every language known to man, but we find common ground across those sixty-four squares.

As I stare at the computer screen or turn another well-worn page, the person I loved most in the world, the person who loved me more fiercely than I ever knew, is a constant presence at my shoulder. Rosa is there, watching my games and laughing along with me. I am not alone. I am never alone.

Joseph eventually became bored of resurrecting dead animals to their former, clear-eyed glory, and instead he began to spend his days at the senior center on Philadelphia Road, looking for company and a game of dominoes. And, as it turned out, love.

At the senior center, Joseph created something of a storm with the ladies. He had two things going for him. Firstly, he still had a full, thick head of hair, even if by then it was completely white. Secondly, he was still fully ambulatory. This heady combination had the ranks of wizened octogenarians swooning in their wheelchairs. They watched him walk unassisted across the carpet to fetch another cup of coffee with the rapacious gaze of a flock of vultures.

A quiet but vigorous competition for Joseph's attention began. The air in the day room became thick with cheap perfume and bitchy comments. Armchairs close to the domino table were poached immediately after breakfast and jealously guarded thereafter. The fragrant hordes waited eagerly for Joseph's arrival, surreptitiously popping in their teeth moments before he sprang into the room with his gazelle-like grace. Most of his admirers were happy just to grin bashfully at him. But Magda Applequist wanted more.

Magda had woken up one morning a few years previously to discover her husband of forty-nine years dead in the bed beside her, stolen away by a massive stroke during the night. She did not like living alone, and so she began frequenting the senior center on the hunt for a new mate. Once Joseph had drifted unwittingly into her crosshairs, she went out and bought a new outfit and six new lipsticks, each a different shade of pink. No effort was spared to lure him into her honey trap.

Joseph was no match for these predatory wiles. He had no idea he was being hunted, like geriatric big game. Slowly, Magda Applequist reeled him in. Soon he was spending less time playing dominoes, and more time playing gin rummy (a game he'd always hated) with his new lady friend.

I was pleased for him. I thought he deserved a bit of fun, if that was what it was, after so many years alone. Then one day he announced, in a dazed voice, that he and Magda were getting married. I tried to hide my shock. I had viewed their friendship with the patronizing indulgence that the not-quite-so-old reserve for elderly romance. The two of them falling in love was a quaint idea that I couldn't take entirely seriously.

The wedding was a simple affair at the local registry office. Frank's ridiculous family filled half the room. A small convoy of cars ferried a coven of pastel-clad ladies over from Philadelphia Road for the service. I guessed from their sour, pinched expressions that these were Magda Applequist's erstwhile rivals for Joseph's attentions, and that they had been invited so that the bride could gloat in matrimonial triumph.

At eighty-three years old, Joseph closed the door on his old life, and set off into the future with Magda by his side.

The newlyweds bickered constantly, and since neither one of them was readily able to storm out of the room, their arguments tended to go on for hours. Trapped in their armchairs, they carped and grumbled endlessly at each other until neither could remember exactly what they were fighting about. It didn't really matter, because in the end they always ended up squabbling about the same thing.

Magda had been a devout Christian all her life, and she was troubled by her new husband's refusal to attend church with her. She had assumed that she would wear him down eventually, but (as I could have told her) this was one battle that Magda would never win. Every Sunday morning Joseph drove her to church and then sat in the parking lot listening to the car radio until the end of the service. Not once could she persuade him to come inside. They drove home in silence.

When Magda realized that she was never going to change Joseph's mind, she tried a different tactic. If he was not willing to be saved, she would just have to do it without him. She made plans to give him a full church funeral, in the hope that a last-ditch display of piety might do the trick. When Joseph found out what she was plotting, he became extremely agitated. He was worried enough to visit an attorney to see if his wife could do all those things against his wishes. The lawyer shrugged his shoulders and said that the only foolproof way to make sure that it didn't happen was to live longer than she did.

So that is what he set about doing. I don't know how many successful marriages have been based upon the participants' resolute determination to outlive each other, but it worked for Joseph and Magda. Joseph, haunted by the thought of prayers, hymns, and benevolent sermons (by his own son, to boot), had all the incentive he needed to eat right and stay healthy. Whenever I stopped by to visit he would surreptitiously hand me a shopping list of vitamins and supplements that he wanted, miracle pills that he'd seen advertised on the Shopping Channel.

To my surprise, the old couple flourished in this fractious, slightly morbid, atmosphere. Deep down they were very fond of each other. In the end, their marriage lasted longer than many regular unions. In 2004 they both turned one hundred, and became minor celebrities for a while. Radio and television stations from across the state reported the news. There was a huge cake, but they could only blow out a few of the candles. A week later, Oprah Winfrey and a television crew came by. I have a recording of the interview. I still watch it every now and then. Magda is guarded, distracted, perhaps a little dazed by the banks of television lights in her living room. She seems uncertain about exactly what is going on. Joseph, on the other hand, is suave and funny. I bought him a new shirt and tie for the occasion, which he wears proudly. He even flirts with Oprah a little, patting her beautiful hands and winking creakily at her. He looks directly into the camera and tells his story. At the end of the interview, Oprah softly kisses his leathery old cheek and wipes a tear from her eye.

In the end, Joseph won his race. Watching the two of them on the television, you can see that poor Magda was already fading; she died a short while later. Her decline, when it came, was swift and painless, but Joseph was swamped by his loss. Suddenly he had nobody to fight with, no reason to keep on going. He spent his days sitting in his favorite armchair, gazing sadly at the walls. After Magda's death I worried that he would allow old age to sweep him away, too, but that was never his way. He plodded resolutely on, swallowing handfuls of brightly colored vitamins, willing himself through each new day, even though he really had nothing left to live for.

CODA

Joseph Meisenheimer finally died last year, at the age of 105 — a ridiculous age, although not, apparently, to him. Two months earlier, he had renewed his driver's license for another three years.

We had been waiting for him to die for so long that when he finally did, nobody knew quite how to react. A good, long life, people agreed — and he'd been as sharp as a tack, right up until the end. *I should be so lucky,* we murmured to each other, wishing we felt a little worse about the whole thing.

Joseph had left precise instructions as to how he wished to be remembered. There was to be no fuss, no grand memorial.

All he wanted, in the end, was the four of us.

We filed into the restaurant and I locked the door behind us. Freddy carefully placed the urn holding Joseph's ashes on the counter next to a pile of colorful laminated menus adorned with Mexican flags. We stood in the middle of the floor and gazed mutely at each other, unsure how to begin.

"Shall we?" I said.

We lined up just as we had always done, and awkwardly turned to face the urn. Teddy produced a pitch pipe from his pocket and gave us our notes. Frank counted two bars, and off we went. As the music filled the room, past and future faded from view. There was nothing but the present, bright and rich with the sound of our voices. Joseph had never stopped loving the music that we made together. Neither had I. But as we bade him farewell, that sweet sound filled me with tender regret.

For I was older now, and I knew that the song would end.

Mr. Jefferson Lord, play that barbershop chord
  chord
That smooth-sounding harmony
It makes an awful awful hit with me
Play that strain just to please me again
'Cause Mister when you start that minor part
I feel your fingers slipping and a-grasping at
  my heart,
Oh Lord play that barbershop chord!

Afterward we went back to the house and scattered our father's ashes around the apple tree in the front yard.

I spent the rest of the afternoon in Joseph's house, stuffing his possessions into large black trash bags, unsure what to do with any of it. I stood on a chair and carefully took the broken terra-cotta angel's wing down from the wall, where it had watched over my family for more than a century. As I stripped the bed of its linen, I saw the corner of a cardboard box poking out from underneath the mattress. I squatted down and pulled it out. Joseph had written THINGS on one of the flaps in black felt marker. I opened it up and looked inside.

Staring up at me were Frederick and Jette and Joseph, standing in front of the courthouse on the day that they became American citizens. Beneath that photograph lay another — Joseph and Cora on their wedding day, smiling into the camera and surrounded by that chorus of unhappy ghosts. I dug a little deeper. Carefully preserved between two pieces of cardboard was an old letter. The date, barely legible, was October 13, 1918. As the afternoon sun fell through the window, I sat down on the bed and read the last words my grandfather had written to his sweetheart, more than ninety years ago.

601

Beneath everything else nestled a white envelope. Inside were court papers, tied up in faded pink ribbon. It was an adoption order, issued by the Circuit Court of Caitlin County, Missouri, in favor of Joseph and Cora Meisenheimer in June 1937. I had been less than a month old. I sat for the longest time, the yellowing paper stiff beneath my fingers.

For all but a month of my life, Joseph had been my father, after all.

I knew that nobody else would be interested in the stories that I'd found in that cardboard box. My brothers were too busy watching new generations rush headlong into the future. I was the only one who had nowhere to look but back.

As I returned to the box again and again, excavating memories, an idea slowly nudged its way into my brain. I thought of all those unpublished novels that were gathering dust in my spare bedroom, those improbable tales I'd spun out of my imagination. But as I considered the lives enshrined in that aggregation of photographs and artifacts, I realized that there was no need to invent a single thing.

This story will do.

ACKNOWLEDGMENTS

Six years is a long time to be writing a book. An awful lot of people helped out along the way.

Thanks first of all to my editor and publisher, Amy Einhorn. It's hard to know where to begin, really. There is so much to be grateful for — for rejecting the first draft of this novel with such generous candor and grace; for reading it again twelve months later; for changing her mind!; for her brilliantly insightful guidance during the extensive rewrites that followed; for being an editor who *actually edits;* for the title — and, most of all, for her faith in the story I had to tell. Thank you, Amy. Words aren't really enough, but they're all I've got.

I will be forever grateful to my agents, Bruce Hunter and Andrew Gordon in London, and Emma Sweeney in New York, for their calm stewardship, endless patience, and excellent advice throughout the publication process.

Thank you to my quartet of reading angels: Christina George, Jennifer Perlow, Elaine Johnson, and Allison Smythe. They have provided invaluable support, encouragement, and astute criticism, propping me up and urging me on when the going got tough. Every writer should be so lucky.

Other honorable mentions: thank you to Nancy Woodruff, for that party invitation; and to Chris Teeter, for naming Buck Gunn for me. Thanks, as always, to Richard Lewis and Louis Barfe. Geography has made things difficult lately, but it always helps to know that they are there, however far away. And I am grateful to my friends in Missouri who have made me feel so welcome over the past nine years, my funny accent notwithstanding.

My deepest thanks to my parents, Alison and Julian George, for their love and strength, new wells of which I keep discovering.

This book is dedicated to my darling Catherine; she and her brother Hallam are the funniest, most loving and wonderful children a father could wish for. I am grateful beyond words that they are here.

My thanks to Charlotte Ross, for the Italian translation, for the opera, and for all the music.

AUTHOR'S NOTE

When I left the country I had grown up in to begin a new life on the other side of the world, I was just following in the family tradition.

My mother was born and raised in New Zealand. In her early twenties she took a boat to England, met my father, and decided to stay. A few generations earlier, her great-grandparents had made the trip in the opposite direction, eloping from their English families, who disapproved of their union, and hoping for freedom in the wilderness of the Southern Hemisphere. I left England to live in America because that is where my wife is from. Like Jette and Frederick, the impulse that fueled all our journeys was the same: love.

Before beginning *A Good American,* I had begun, and abandoned, a couple of other ill-fated novels. Some of the most common advice given to aspiring writers is "Write what you know." It's a fine theory, but probably only if you have something worth knowing. As I was pondering this, it occurred to me that the experience of packing up my life and moving to a new country, with no expectation that I would ever return home again, might just qualify.

Finally, I had my story.

In some ways, my experience of moving to America in 2003 could not have been much more different from my ancestors' journey to New Zealand in 1864. But certain essential elements had probably not changed much: the hope for a better life, the fear of the unknown, and the paradox of wanting to adapt to your new country without forgetting where you came from. (My mother has lived in England for more than fifty years now, but she still calls New Zealand home.)

I wanted to set the story in Missouri not just because it's where I live, but also because there feels something uniquely, unflashily *American* about this strange, largely empty place; it's the quintessential "flyover" state. You don't have to spend much time here to recognize the legacy of its German settlers, so it made sense for me to have my characters depart from there, even though Frederick and Jette arrived decades after the first significant influx of German immigrants.

Writing this book was an illuminating experience. It shone a light on my own feelings about moving here. Despite the long and generally amicable relationship between England and America (if we pass discreetly over the War of Independence), people still relish the little things that divide us, like the funny way I talk. But having lived here for some time now, I prefer to consider what unites us. I practiced law for eight years in England, and when I arrived here I had to requalify as an attorney. While I was studying for the bar exam I learned that much of the American legal system was (unsurprisingly) based on the English one. But there remain important differences. Many of the rights of which Americans are so rightly proud — freedom of speech, of religion, of association — are enshrined in the amendments to the United States Constitution. England has no equivalent. We rely instead on cloudier concepts, on an unwritten constitution, shrouded by centuries of jurisprudence.

But I like the American system more. As a writer, I think that the Declaration of Independence and the U.S. Constitution are two of the most exciting and inspiring documents ever written. The principles and beliefs upon which this country was founded are unimpeachable. I am a lawyer and a novelist, and so I have a reverence for words. They are the tools of both of my trades. America's founding documents provide the guiding light by which much of the world sets its course for the future. In 1630, as he stood on the deck of the *Arabella* just before landing in New England for the first time, John Winthrop preached a sermon that talked of the new settlement as a "city on a hill." Winthrop knew that the eyes of the world would be upon them. Nothing has changed. The world still looks to America for hope, for inspiration, and for guidance. It's one reason people have always dreamed of coming here, by fair means or foul.

One of the appeals of the immigrant tale is its ubiquity. Almost every family living in the United States today has a story similar to this one somewhere in its past. Whether ten years ago or three hundred years ago, whether through due process or by way of a midnight ghosting across an unmanned border, whether by slave boat or luxury airplane, we all came here from somewhere.

A brief note for nature lovers: In general, raccoons are nocturnal animals, but some do emerge during the day. When they do, they are not — contrary to popular belief — necessarily rabid. Rosa's friendship with Mr. Jim is based on real-life experience — although not, I am willing to admit, my own. Raccoons are, of course, wild animals and do not make good pets. Jette was wise not to allow Mr. Jim into her house.

Finally, a brief word about the music. At around the same time that I was beginning to consider immigration as a theme for this novel, my former wife's great-aunt passed away. Halfway through the memorial service, four men (who, I later discovered, were brothers) stood up at the front of the church and sang a beautiful, close-harmony version of "Abide with Me." And as I listened, while I should have been thinking about our recently departed family member, all I could think was: *I must put this in a novel.* So I did. (Sorry, Ethel.)

ABOUT THE AUTHOR

Alex George is an Englishman who lives, works, and writes in Missouri. He studied law at Oxford University and worked for eight years as a corporate lawyer in London and Paris before moving to the United States in 2003.